P9-DEI-478

Madame Tussaud

Also by Michelle Moran

Nefertiti

The Heretic Queen

Cleopatra's Daughter

Madame Tussaud

A Novel *of the* French Revolution

Michelle Moran

Crown Publishers
New York

This is a work of fiction. Names, characters, places, and incidents either are the product of the author's imagination or are used fictitiously.

Published in the United States by Crown Publishers, an imprint of the Crown Publishing Group, a division of Random House, Inc., New York.
www.crownpublishing.com

CROWN and the Crown colophon are registered trademarks of Random House, Inc.

Library of Congress Cataloging-in-Publication Data

Moran, Michelle.
Madame Tussaud : a novel of the French revolution / Michelle Moran. —1st ed.
p. cm.
1. Tussaud, Marie, 1761–1850. 2. Wax modelers—France—Fiction.
3. France—History—Revolution, 1789–1799—Fiction. I. Title.
PS3613.O682M33 2011
813'.6—dc22 2010035785

ISBN 978-0-307-58865-4
eISBN 978-0-307-58867-8

Printed in the United States of America

Book design by Lauren Dong
Map by David Cain
Jacket design by Jennifer O'Connor
Jacket photography by Richard Jenkins Photography (woman);
© Rudy Sulgan/CORBIS (background); Dorling Kindersley (ring)

10 9 8 7 6 5 4 3 2 1

First Edition

For my editors

Heather Lazare, Matthew Carter, and Allison McCabe

À tout seigneur tout honneur

Time Line *for the* French Revolution

DATE	EVENT
May 5, 1789	The Estates-General meets at Versailles, bringing together all three estates: the clergy, the nobility, and the commoners
June 17, 1789	The Third Estate, made up of commoners, declares itself the National Assembly
July 14, 1789	Fall of the Bastille
August 27, 1789	Declaration of the Rights of Man and Citizen is adopted
October 5–6, 1789	Parisian women march on Versailles and force the royal family to move to Paris
October 1, 1791	Meeting of the Legislative Assembly
April 20, 1792	France declares war on Austria
August 10, 1792	After the storming of the Tuileries Palace, the royal family takes refuge with the Legislative Assembly
September 2–6, 1792	The September Massacres
September 21, 1792	The monarchy is abolished
January 21, 1793	Louis XVI is executed
February 1, 1793	France declares war on Great Britain
April 6, 1793	The Committee of Public Safety is created with the intent of rooting out all "traitors" and anyone deemed a threat to the Revolution
October 5, 1793	The Revolutionary Calendar is adopted, with Year One beginning on September 22, 1792
October 16, 1793	Queen Marie Antoinette is executed
May 7, 1794	Cult of the Supreme Being proclaimed by Robespierre
June 8, 1794	Robespierre leads the celebration of the Festival of the Supreme Being
June 10, 1794	The Law of 22 Prairial is adopted, encouraging citizens to denounce anyone who might be a counterrevolutionary

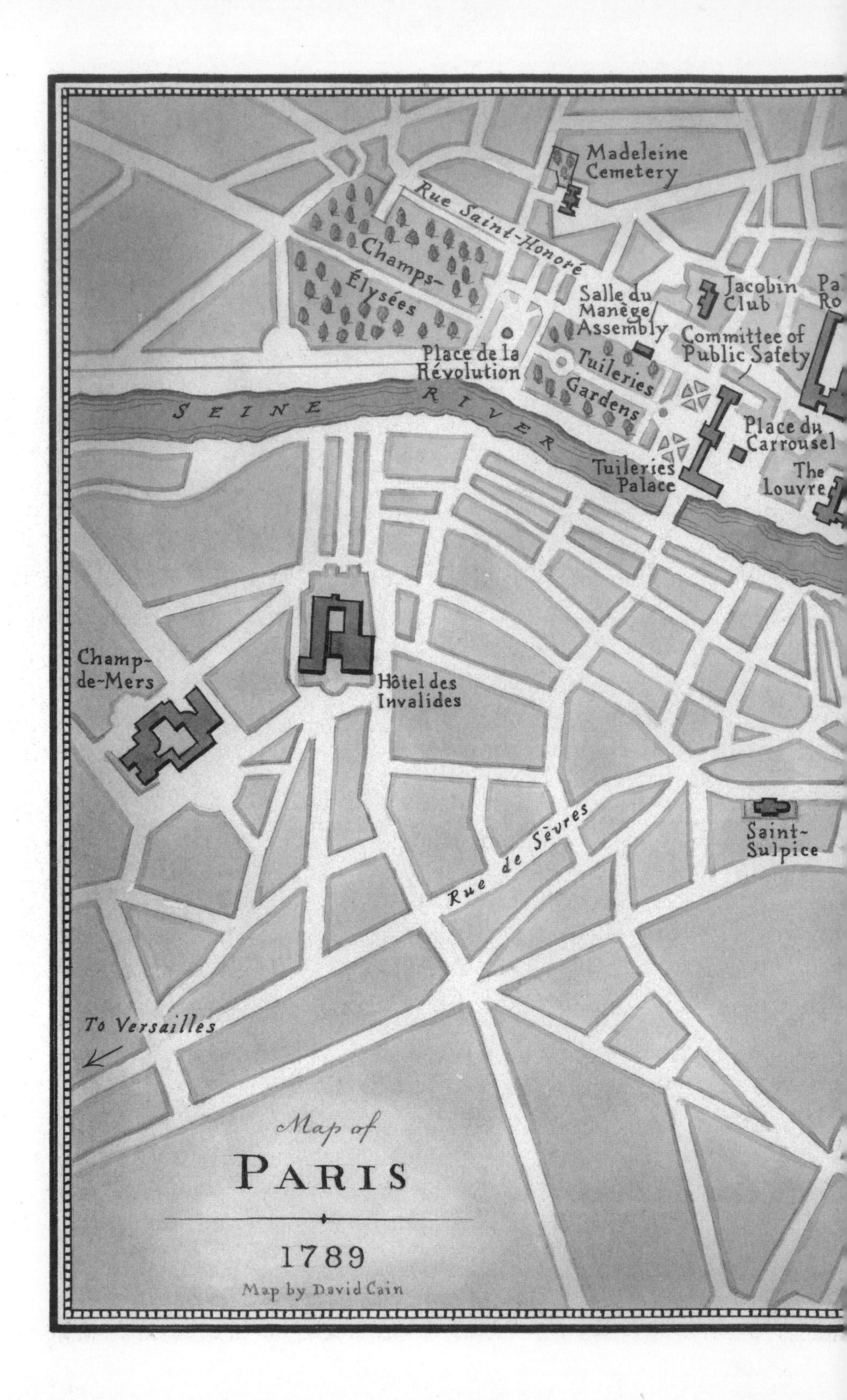
Madeleine Cemetery
Rue Saint-Honoré
Champs-Élysées
Salle du Manège/ Assembly
Jacobin Club
Committee of Public Safety
Place de la Révolution
Tuileries Gardens
SEINE RIVER
Place du Carrousel
Tuileries Palace
The Louvre
Champ-de-Mers
Hôtel des Invalides
Rue de Sèvres
Saint-Sulpice
To Versailles
Map of
PARIS
1789
Map by David Cain

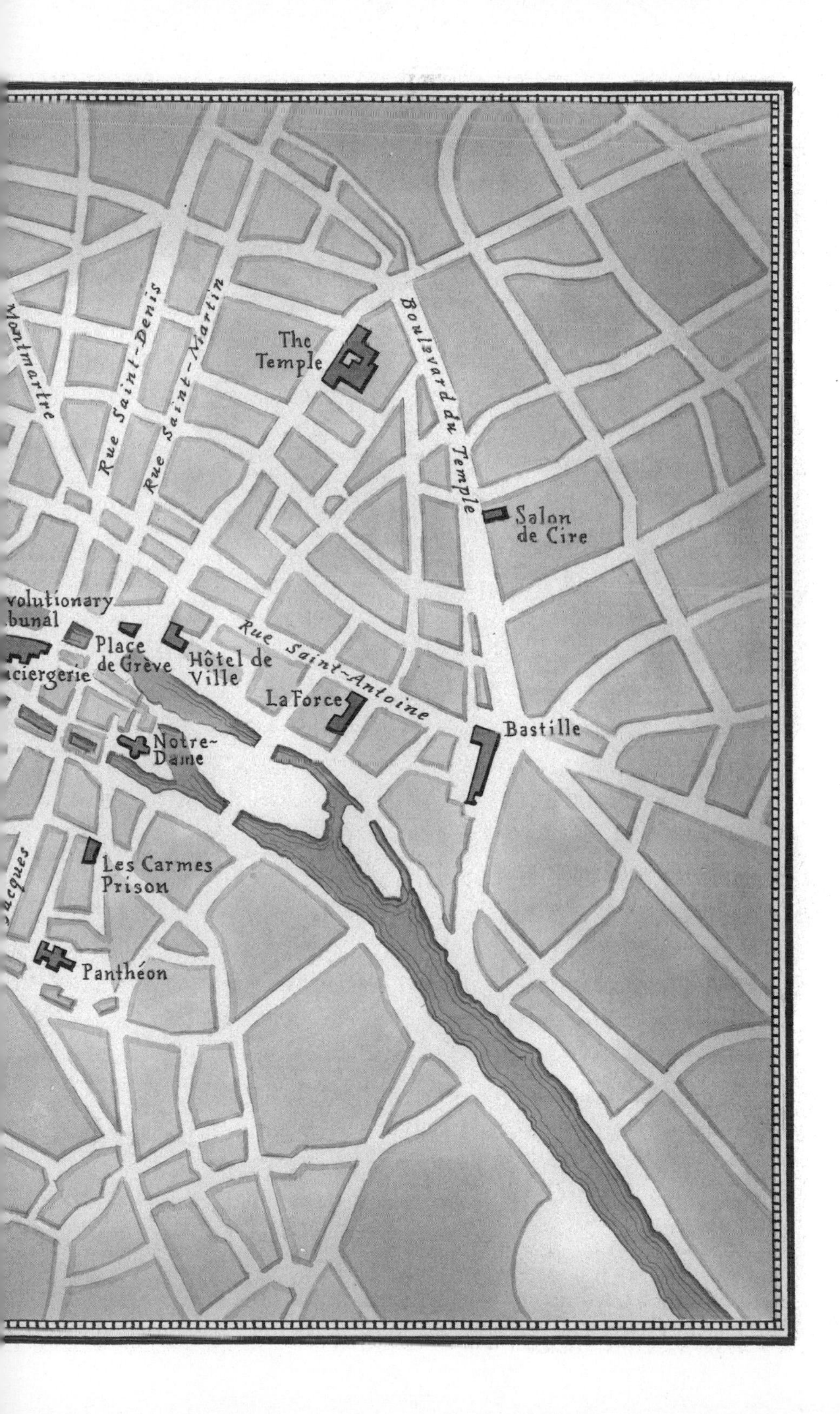

The Temple
Rue Saint-Denis
Rue Saint-Martin
Montmartre
Boulevard du Temple
Salon de Cire
Place de Grève
Hôtel de Ville
Rue Saint-Antoine
La Force
Bastille
Notre-Dame
Les Carmes Prison
Panthéon

Characters

Marie Antoinette: Queen of France

Comte d'Artois: Youngest brother of King Louis XVI

Baron de Besenval: Commander of the Swiss Guard; father of Abrielle de Besenval

Henri Charles: Inventor, balloonist, and showman

Jacques Charles: Mathematician, inventor, and balloonist

Philippe Curtius: Wax modeler and showman

Georges Danton: Revolutionary and journalist

Jacques-Louis David: Painter

Camille Desmoulins: Lawyer and revolutionary journalist

Lucile Duplessis: Young revolutionary engaged to Camille Desmoulins

Princesse Élisabeth: Sister of King Louis XVI

Anna Grosholtz: Mother of Marie Grosholtz

Edmund Grosholtz: Marie's eldest brother and captain in the Swiss Guard

Isabel Grosholtz: Wife of Johann Grosholtz and mother of Paschal

Johann Grosholtz: Marie's second-eldest brother and soldier in the Swiss Guard

Marie Grosholtz: Curtius's "niece"; wax modeler and show-woman

Wolfgang Grosholtz: Marie's youngest brother and soldier in the Swiss Guard

Thomas Jefferson: American ambassador to France

Marquis de Lafayette: French aristocrat and American Revolutionary War hero

Élisabeth Vigée-Lebrun: Popular female painter employed by the queen

Louis-Charles: The dauphin; first son of King Louis XVI and Marie Antoinette

Louis-Joseph: Second son of King Louis XVI and Marie Antoinette

Louis the XVI: King of France

Jean-Paul Marat: Swiss lawyer and journalist

Comte de Mirabeau: Revolutionary and journalist

Duc d'Orléans: Cousin of King Louis XVI who later changes his name to Philippe Égalité

Comte de Provence: Eldest brother of King Louis XVI

Maximilien Robespierre: Lawyer from Arras, revolutionary

Jean-Jacques Rousseau: Philosopher and writer

Marquis de Sade: Criminal and writer

Princesse Marie-Thérèse: Daughter of King Louis XVI and Marie Antoinette

Author's Note

The year is 1788, and Queen Marie Antoinette's popularity is on the decline. Food shortages are widespread throughout her kingdom, caused in large part by the unpredictable weather, which has destroyed most harvests, leaving the French to look to other countries for help. Now, the coldest winter in living memory has settled in, and unless food is found quickly, many thousands will perish.

The quotations at the beginning of most chapters have been excerpted from scandal sheets, newspapers, and speakers contemporary to the time, while each character in this book is based on a person who lived—and in many cases died—during France's Revolution. All of the major events in this novel took place.

Madame Tussaud

Prologue

London

1812

WHEN SHE WALKS THROUGH THE DOOR OF MY EXHIBITION, everything disappears: the sound of the rain against the windows, the wax models, the customers, even the children. This is a face I have not seen in twenty-one years, and immediately I step back, wondering whether I have conjured her from my past.

"What is it?" Henri asks. He has seen my eyes widen and follows my gaze to the figure near the door. The woman is in her sixties, but there is something about her—her clothes, her walk, perhaps her French features—that sets her apart. "Do you know her?"

"I—I'm not sure," I say. But this is a lie. Even after so many years, there is no mistaking those hands. They shaped a queen's destiny and enraged a nation. At once, my years at the court of Versailles are as near to me as though they had happened yesterday, and I am no longer standing in my London exhibition but in a great mirrored hall watching the courtiers in their fine silk *culottes* and diamond aigrettes. I can smell the jasmine from the queen's private gardens and hear the laughter in the king's marble chambers.

"Who is she?" Henri asks.

This time I whisper, "I believe it is Rose Bertin."

Henri stares. "Marie Antoinette's *dressmaker*?"

I nod at him. "Yes."

The woman crosses the room, and it is only when she is directly in front of us that I am certain about who she is. She is dressed in a pelisse fashionable among women half her age, and the feather in her hat is an extraordinary shade of blue. Outside, a young man is waiting at her coach. Passersby will suspect that he is her son, but anyone who has ever been acquainted with her will know better.

"Marie, do you remember me?" she asks.

I hesitate, letting the weight of our pasts hang between us for a moment. Then I reply, "You know I never forget a face, Rose."

"*Mon Dieu.* You haven't changed at all! Your voice, your eyes—" She glances down at my dress, cotton in plain black. "Your sense of style."

"Your unbelievable pretentiousness."

Rose gives a throaty laugh. "What? Did you think I would lose that with my looks?"

I smile, since Rose was never a beauty.

"And is this—".

"Henri Charles."

"Henri," she repeats with real affection, and perhaps she is remembering the first time they met, in the Salon de Cire. "Did Marie ever tell you how she survived our Revolution after you and I left? For twenty years, I have wanted to know that story . . ."

My breath comes quick, and there's a tightness in my chest. Who would want to remember that now? We are in London, a world away from Versailles. I look at Henri, who is honest when he says, "I doubt anyone has ever learned the half of it, Madame."

Chapter 1

PARIS

DECEMBER 12, 1788

ALTHOUGH IT IS MID-DECEMBER AND EVERYONE WITH SENSE is huddled near a fire, more than two dozen women are pressed together in Rose Bertin's shop, Le Grand Mogol. They are heating themselves by the handsome bronze lamps, but I do not go inside. These are women of powdered *poufs* and ermine cloaks, whereas I am a woman of ribbons and wool. So I wait on the street while they shop in the warmth of the queen's favorite store. I watch from outside as a girl picks out a showy pink hat. It's too pale for her skin, but her mother nods and Rose Bertin claps her hands eagerly. She will not be so eager when she notices me. I have come here every month for a year with the same request. But this time I am certain Rose will agree, for I am prepared to offer her something that only princes and murderers possess. I don't know why I didn't think of it before.

I stamp my feet on the slick cobblestones of the Rue Saint-Honoré. My breath appears as a white fog in the morning air. This is the harshest winter in memory, and it has come on the heels of a poor summer harvest. Thousands will die in Paris, some of the cold, others of starvation. The king and queen have gifted the city as much firewood as they can spare from Versailles. In thanks, the people have built an obelisk made entirely of snow; it is the only monument they can afford. I look down the street, expecting to see the fish sellers at their carts. But even the merchants have fled the cold, leaving nothing but the stink of the sea behind them.

When the last customer exits Le Grand Mogol, I hurry inside. I shake the rain from my cloak and inhale the warm scent of cinnamon from the fire. As always, I am in awe of what Rose Bertin has accomplished in such a small space. Wide, gilded mirrors give the impression that the shop is larger than it really is, and the candles flickering from the chandeliers cast a burnished glow across the oil paintings and embroidered settees. It's like entering a comtesse's salon, and this is the effect we have tried for in my uncle's museum. Intimate rooms where the nobility will not feel out of place. Although I could never afford the bonnets on these shelves—let alone the silk dresses of robin's-egg blue or apple green—I come here to see the new styles so that I can copy them later. After all, that is our exhibition's greatest attraction. Women who are too poor to travel to Versailles can see the royal family in wax, each of them wearing the latest fashions.

"Madame?" I venture, closing the door behind me.

Rose Bertin turns, and her high-pitched welcome tells me that she expects another woman in ermine. When I emerge from the shadows in wool, her voice drops. "Mademoiselle Grosholtz," she says, disappointed. "I gave you my answer last month." She crosses her arms over her chest. Everything about Rose Bertin is large. Her hips, her hair, the satin bows that cascade down the sides of her dress.

"Then perhaps you've changed your mind," I say quickly. "I know you have the ear of the queen. They say that there's no one else she trusts more."

"And you're not the only one begging favors of me," she snaps.

"But we're good patrons."

"Your uncle bought *two* dresses from me."

"We would buy more if business was better." This isn't a lie. In eighteen days I will be twenty-eight, but there is nothing of value I own in this world except the wax figures that I've created for my uncle's exhibition. I am an inexpensive niece to maintain. I don't ask for any of the embellishments in *Le Journal des Dames,* or for pricey chemise gowns trimmed in pearls. But if I had the livres, I would spend them in dressing the figures of our museum. There is no need for me to wear gemstones and lace, but our patrons come to the Salon de Cire to see the finery of kings. If I could, I would gather up every silk fan and furbelow in Rose Bertin's shop, and our Salon would rival her own. But we don't have that kind of money. We are showmen, only a little better-off than the circus performers who exhibit next door. "Think of it," I say eagerly. "I could arrange a special tableau for her visit. An image of the queen sitting in her dressing room. With *you* by her side. *The Queen and Her Minister of Fashion,"* I tell her.

Rose's lips twitch upward. Although Minister of Fashion is an insult the papers use to criticize her influence over Marie Antoinette, it's not far from the truth, and she knows this. She hesitates. It is one thing to have your name in the papers, but to be immortalized in wax . . . That is something reserved only for royals and criminals, and she is neither. "So what would you have me say?" she asks slowly.

My heart beats quickly. Even if the queen dislikes what I've done—and she won't, I *know* she won't, not when I've taken such pains to get the blue of her eyes just right—the fact that she has personally come to see her wax model will change everything. Our exhibition will be included in the finest guidebooks to Paris. We'll earn a place in every Catalog of Amusements printed in France. But most important, we'll be associated with Marie Antoinette. Even after all of the scandals that have attached themselves to her name, there is only good business to be had by entertaining Their Majesties. "Just tell her that you've been to the Salon de Cire. You have, haven't you?"

"Of course." Rose Bertin is not a woman to miss anything. Even a wax show on the Boulevard du Temple. "It was attractive." She adds belatedly, "In its way."

"So tell that to the queen. Tell her I've modeled the busts of Voltaire, Rousseau, Benjamin Franklin. Tell her there will be several of her. And you."

Rose is silent. Then finally, she says, "I'll see what I can do."

Chapter 2

December 21, 1788

What is the Third Estate? Everything.

—Abbé Sieyès, pamphleteer

When the letter comes, I am sitting upstairs in my uncle's salon. Thirty wooden steps divide the world of the wax museum on the first floor of our home from the richly paneled rooms where we live upstairs. I have seen enough houses of showmen and performers to know that we are fortunate. We live like merchants, with sturdy mahogany furniture and good china for guests. But if not for Curtius's association with the Prince de Condé when both men were young, none of this would be.

My uncle was living in Switzerland when the cousin of King Louis XV visited his shop and saw what Curtius could do with wax. Impressed, the prince brought him to Paris and commissioned an entire collection of miniatures. But these were not like any other miniatures. De Condé wanted nude replicas of the women in the hundreds of portraits he had saved; blond, brunette, and auburn conquests from all across Europe. When the prince began showing off his collection, Curtius's reputation grew. Before long, my uncle found himself hosting one of the most popular salons in Paris from his new apartment on the Rue Saint-Honoré. Of course, anyone—men, women, widowers, courtesans—may host their own salon, but who will come to enjoy the coffee and gossip depends entirely on the host's influence and importance.

Tonight, in our house on the Boulevard du Temple, all of the familiar faces are here. Robespierre, with his blue silk stockings and neatly powdered wig. Camille Desmoulins, who goes by his forename and whose slight stutter seems strange in such a handsome man. Camille's pretty fiancée, Lucile. Henri Charles, the ambitious young scientist who keeps a laboratory next door with his brother. The Duc d'Orléans, who is in constant disgrace with the king. And Jean-Paul Marat, with his feral eyes and unwashed clothes. I have repeatedly asked my uncle why he allows Marat to defile our home, and his answer is always the same. Like him, Marat is a Swiss physician, and they both share a fascination with optics and lighting. But I suspect the real reason Curtius allows him to dine with us is that they can talk about the old country together.

I have never been to Switzerland. Although my mother is Swiss, she was married to a soldier in Strasbourg. I remember nothing of him, but my brothers give out that he died from the wounds he received in the Seven Years' War. When my mother was made a widow, she came to Paris looking for work and Curtius took her in as his housekeeper. But soon she became more to him than that, and though we call him uncle, Curtius is more like a father to us. We all—my brothers, who are in the Swiss Guard, the king's elite corps of fighting men, and I—consider our family Swiss. So I am not averse to listening to Swiss tales. I simply wish they didn't have to come from the reeking mouth of Marat.

As usual, he is sitting in the farthest corner of the room, silent, waiting for my mother to bring out the sausages and cabbage. He rarely speaks when Robespierre is here. He simply comes for the cooking and listens to the debates. Tonight, they are arguing about the Estates-General. The French have divided society into three separate orders. There is the First Estate, made up of the clergy. Then there is the Second Estate, made up of the nobility. And finally, there is the

Third Estate, made up of common people like us. For the first time since 1614, the three estates are being called together to give advice to the monarchy. It is in such debt that only a miracle—or new taxes—will save them.

"And do you really think a m-meeting will change their minds?" Camille asks. His long hair is tied back in a simple leather band. He and his fiancée make an attractive pair, even if their cheeks are always hot with rage. They wish for a constitutional monarchy, like in England. Or even better, a republic like the one that has just been created in America. But I don't see how this can ever come to pass. Camille pounds his fist against the table. "It's all a charade! Those who are elected to represent our estate will be marched into a tiny room at Versailles and nothing will change! The clergy and the nobility will continue to be exempt from taxes—"

"While you will be left to pay for *L'Autrichienne*'s bonnets and *poufs,*" the Duc says. He enjoys sitting back with a glass of brandy and stirring an already heated pot. He has an unnatural hatred of Queen Marie Antoinette. Like many others, he refers to her insultingly as *The Austrian.* He smiles at Camille, knowing the fish has already been caught. "Why do you think that each estate has been given only one vote? To make sure nothing changes! The clergy and the nobility will vote together to preserve the current system, while the Third Estate will be left out in the cold."

"Despite the fact that the Third Estate makes up most of this nation!" Camille shouts.

"Ninety-five percent," the Duc puts in.

"So what can be done?" Robespierre asks levelly. He is a lawyer and has learned to control his voice. He never yells, but his timbre is arresting. The entire room listens.

The Duc makes a show of steepling his fingers in thought. "We must petition the king to allow *each* representative a vote. That is the only way the Third Estate can outvote the other two and prove that privilege is not a birthright."

"*We?*" Henri asks. Henri and I were born in the same year, both in the month of December. But whereas I am artistic, and can tell any woman which color will make her appear young and which will bring out the circles beneath her eyes, Henri's trade is science. He mistrusts the Duc's intentions. He believes the Duc sees a turning in the tide and will swim whichever way the current takes him. "Aren't you a part of that privileged estate?" he challenges.

"For now." The Duc is not an attractive man. His lips are too small, his stomach too large, his legs too thin. He has inherited the Bourbon nose, prominent and hooked, the same as his cousin the king's.

Lucile turns to me. "And you, Marie? What do you think?"

Everyone looks in my direction. What I think and what I am prepared to say are entirely different things. My uncle passes me a warning look. "I believe that I am better at judging art than politics."

"Nonsense!" Lucile exclaims. She clenches her fists, and it's a funny gesture for someone so petite. "Art *is* politics," she proclaims. "Your museum is filled with political figures. Benjamin Franklin. Rousseau. Why include them if they are not important?"

"I only know what is important to the people," I say carefully. "Our Salon reflects their desire for entertainment."

"Ah," my uncle cuts in swiftly. "The sausages and cabbage!"

My mother has appeared just in time with a tray laden with food, and when I get up to help her, I hear a knocking downstairs. I hurry to answer it and find a courtier dressed in the blue livery of the king. My God, has Rose Bertin done it? Has she convinced the queen to visit the Salon?

"Is Monsieur Curtius at home?"

"Yes," I say hurriedly. "Follow me."

I take him up the stairs, and when we reach the salon, the courtier clears his throat so that everyone can hear. "From Their Majesties, King Louis the Sixteenth and Queen Marie Antoinette." My uncle rises, and the courtier hands him the letter with an exaggerated flourish.

He passes it to me. "You should open it."

It is better paper than any I have ever seen, and the king's seal is on it. I am trembling; I can barely break open the wax. When I've finished reading the letter, I turn to my uncle. "They want to come," I say breathlessly. "In January, they wish to visit the Salon!" I look up, and the entire table has gone silent.

The Duc is the first to speak. "What? *L'Autrichienne* doesn't have enough entertainment at Versailles?"

"Thank you," I say to the courtier quickly, and my uncle is already tipping the man handsomely so that none of what has passed beneath this roof will make its way back to the palace. As soon as he is gone, everyone begins speaking at once.

"We should be here when they come!" Camille says. "We should challenge the king—"

"And let him know what his people are thinking!" Lucile adds.

"Do you wish to ruin Curtius and his Salon?" Henri demands.

Camille looks shamefacedly at my uncle. "Perhaps we could hand him a p-p-petition."

"He's had dozens of petitions," Henri says logically. "He could paper the walls of Versailles with them. You want a voice? Become a representative in the Estates-General."

The Duc snorts into his brandy as my mother serves him a large helping of cabbage. "The king will never listen until the people rise up."

"That may be," Curtius says, "but the place to rise up is not here."

The rest of our dinner is eaten in silence. Afterward, when everyone is leaving and the Duc is so drunk he requires assistance to make his way down the stairs, Henri takes my uncle and me aside. We stand together in the window embrasure, next to a sign advertising Madame du Barry. "Do you know when the royal family is coming?" he asks.

"Yes," I tell him. "After the new year."

His eyes are troubled. There's no hint of the kind smile he normally reserves for me. "It may not bring the kind of publicity you want."

"This is the *queen,*" I protest.

"Who is buried by half a dozen scandals. This is not the only salon proposing radical changes. Men like Camille and Robespierre are all across Paris."

I turn to Curtius. He has never bothered with a wig, and his hair is copper in the evening light. For a man in his fifties, he is still handsome. "It is something to consider," he says.

"But only good can come of this!" I exclaim, unable to believe I am hearing this from my uncle, the man who taught me that publicity, above all things, drives a business. I have been working toward this for a year. "Everyone will want to see what the queen has seen. Who cares about the Affair of the Diamond Necklace and whether she placed an order for two million livres of jewels or not?"

"The people might," Henri says. He measures his words, like an experiment. Five years ago, he and his brother launched the first hydrogen balloon, and since then they have been working to prove Franklin's experiments in electricity. Unlike my uncle, Henri is a scientist first and a showman second. "There is some publicity that isn't worth the risk."

But that is nonsense. "Not everyone may love the queen," I say, "but they will always respect her."

Chapter 3

January 16, 1789

[We brought the Cardinal] the famous necklace. He told us that Her Majesty the Queen was going to acquire the jewel, and he showed us that the proposals we had accepted were signed by Marie Antoinette of France.

—Memorandum to Her Majesty the Queen Concerning the Diamond Necklace Affair

I have modeled dozens of famous men and women, but no one like Rose Bertin. She sweeps into the entrance hall of the Salon de Cire, and a train of servants follows behind her, each girl carrying two baskets filled with silks and lace and gauzy bows to decorate Rose's wax figure. Curtius directs the young women to the back of the workshop while I lead Rose to the first room of the museum.

"It is crowded," she says, and I can hear the surprise in her voice.

"We do good business," I reply. "Tourists from all over Europe come here."

We begin to walk, and her eyes are drawn to the high, vaulted ceilings. The Salon de Cire takes up ten of the eleven graciously proportioned rooms on the first floor of our house. "I don't remember it being so grand," she admits. "When did this happen?"

It is as if she is asking when an ugly child suddenly grew into a pretty adult. "We have been working toward this for years," I say, a little tartly.

"Your exhibition in the Palais-Royal was not so big."

"And that is one of the reasons we moved." I explain how each room has been decorated to complement each tableau. Around the figure of Benjamin Franklin, for instance, Henri and Curtius built a mock laboratory. It is filled with images of the American's inventions: a metal stove to replace the fireplace, an odometer to track the distances traveled by carriage, and a rod to protect buildings from lightning damage. Rose nods at the descriptions as we pass. I don't know if she has understood any of this, or if only scientists like Henri and Curtius find it fascinating.

"And where is the new wax model of the queen?" she asks. We go to the tableau of Marie Antoinette in her nightdress, and Rose stands transfixed. The room has been decorated to look like the queen's bedchamber. It is based on a painting I purchased in the Palais-Royal, and the artist swore it was an exact representation. I watch Rose's face as she studies the chamber. A gilded chandelier hangs from the ceiling, and the manufacturer of the king's own wallpaper—a merchant named Réveillon—sold us the pink floral design for the walls. "This is good," she says. She circles the model of the queen like a vulture. "You've gotten the color of her eyes just right."

"Thank you," I say, but she isn't listening.

"What is this?" She points to the chair on which the queen's First Lady of the Bedchamber is sitting. "This chair should not have arms. No one except the king and queen is allowed a chair with arms. Even the king's *brother* is not allowed this privilege!" Rose looks at me, aghast. "This must be changed. I want to see the rest of the royal models," she announces.

We go from room to room, and I am forced to send for ink and paper to write down all of the ways in which we have erred. And there are many. In a tableau of the royal family at dinner, the king should be seated to the queen's right, not to her left. And apparently, Her Majesty is no longer wearing white chemise gowns or feathered *poufs*.

"She is thirty-three years old," Rose declares. "She has returned to her robes *à la française.*"

"But she hated those robes. Every woman in Paris has adopted her chemises."

"And if she dares to wear the fashion that she made popular," Rose replies, "the papers write that she is disrespecting her exalted station."

Now we will have to search through storage to find the robes *à la française* we purchased from Le Grand Mogol years ago. There are more errors Rose points out. I write in shorthand what will need to be fixed. I cannot abide inaccuracies. Although Rose's tone of superiority annoys me, I must be grateful for her knowledge. The public comes to our Salon to see royalty as they are, not as they were, and everything must be correct. Especially when Their Majesties arrive.

When we finally make our way into the workshop, I am nervous. I, who have taken the measurements of the Hapsburg emperor and chatted amiably with Benjamin Franklin, can feel a flutter in my stomach. But for once, the queen's formidable *marchande* is silent. Her ladies watch while I use my caliper to take more than a hundred measurements: from the tip of her chin to the tops of her cheekbones, from the ends of her eyebrows to her delicate ears. When I am finished, I begin the clay model of her face. It is a curious trick of the mind that I am able to look at a person and know—even without these measurements—how wide the forehead should be and how long I should extend the nose.

As the afternoon passes, Rose begins to ask questions. She wants to know how I learned to make wax models, and I tell her that I was an apprentice to my uncle from the time that I could talk.

"You and I are not so different then," she reflects. "I became apprenticed to a milliner at Trait Galant when I was young and eventually became her partner. Now I own Le Grand Mogol. No partners. Just me." She is proud of what she's done, and rightly so. For a woman to rise without a man's support is rare. Even I have had the help of my uncle. "Did you know that I was the one who suggested the Pandoras?" she asks.

She means the little dolls dressed in the ever-changing fashions of the queen and sold in every shop from here to London. "No."

Rose nods importantly. "They made her image famous. Even in America they can recognize her face."

My sitter talks enough for two people as the long hours draw on and she is forced to hold still while I sculpt. When my mother arrives with a tray of warm drinks, Rose tries to engage her in conversation, but my mother's French is poor, since our family uses German when we are together.

"How long has your mother been in France?" Rose asks.

"Almost thirty years." Then I add defensively, "She understands more than she speaks."

"The queen has been here for twenty years. Her French is flawless."

"The queen, I believe, had private tutors."

Rose smiles. "You would do well at court. The queen likes her ladies to be quick."

"And the king?"

Rose's expression is less kind. "He likes men who build. If God were just, the king would spend his life in a construction yard, not a palace."

I have heard this before and am not surprised. Then I draw her gaze to a practice bust of Franklin. "Is that why His Majesty didn't like *him*?"

Rose leans forward, and I know I am about to hear something sensational. "No," she reveals. "That was jealousy."

I stop sculpting to listen.

"Do you remember, three and a half years ago, when Franklin was here and his face was on everything?"

"Of course." Snuffboxes, necklaces, canes, buttons . . . His image was everywhere. The Countess Diana even wanted her hair *à la Franklin.*

"Well, when the king saw how Paris idolized Franklin, he grew upset, and for Christmas, he gave one of the courtiers who had praised Franklin's hat a very special present." She pauses, drawing out the suspense. "It was a chamber pot with a cameo of Franklin's face—on the bottom of the bowl!"

I gasp, caught between laughter and horror. "But there are many men who are more popular than the king."

"Men who dress in linen suits with fur caps?"

I return to the sculpture and think about this. "Was it his humble dress the king disliked, or his accomplishments?"

"Both," she replies and doesn't expound. But I imagine that Rose is fairly bursting with secrets whispered in her ear during intimate fittings. Another short silence stretches between us while she instructs her girls to unpack the baskets and lay the contents on a second table. She drums her fingers as she watches them unfold her dress. "What do you do to protect your hands from the clay?" she asks suddenly. "It must dry them out terribly."

"I have lotion for that."

"The queen has a new lotion delivered to Versailles every day. The ones she likes she keeps in her commode."

"She has a chest just for lotions?"

"There are lacquered chests for everything in the palace! Some with secret springs that pop open to reveal handfuls of gems. I have seen all the queen's best jewels."

Though I know I should not, I ask, "Yet she didn't want Boehmer's necklace?" This is the necklace that has caused so much scandal. Nearly three thousand carats' worth of diamonds fashioned by the court's jewelers Charles Boehmer and Paul Bassenge.

"That necklace," Rose says with contempt, "was meant for du Barry. The queen would never touch something intended for her father-in-law's whore. Monsieur Boehmer begged her to take it after the king died and du Barry was banished."

"And she refused?" I don't know that I could ever turn down over one million livres' worth of jewels, even for the good of France.

"Her Majesty has taste." Rose raises her chin. "No one who knows the queen could believe she would want such a thing. And it was all

Rohan's doing," she adds contemptuously. "Rohan and that prostitute of his."

She tells me the entire story. How a young woman named Jeanne de Valois tricked her former lover, the Cardinal de Rohan, into believing that she had become close to the queen. The cardinal, vulgar and greedy, had always been out of favor at Versailles. He begged Jeanne to intervene on his behalf, so Jeanne and her husband forged letters in the handwriting of Marie Antoinette pretending to forgive Rohan. The letters grew warmer and more intimate, and Jeanne then arranged an interview between the cardinal and a prostitute impersonating the queen. The impostor told the cardinal that she wished to purchase a diamond necklace without angering the commoners, and if Rohan could obtain the jewels for her, she would be forever in his debt. She told him that he should use Jeanne as an intermediary.

Immediately, the cardinal arranged to buy the necklace. He delivered it to Jeanne, who then took it to London, where the diamonds were removed one by one and sold. When Rohan failed to pay the jewelers, Boehmer approached the queen and asked for payment. Within days the entire affair was exposed, and the cardinal was arrested. But in a sensational trial, the queen's reputation was such that Rohan was acquitted. No one was willing to blame the cardinal for thinking she might secretly meet him at night or make promises to him in letters foolishly signed, "Marie Antoinette de France."

"But the queen never uses her surname!" I exclaim.

Rose gives me a knowing look from her chair. Everyone knows what happened next. The prostitute Nicole d'Oliva was set free after her testimony on behalf of the Crown, while Jeanne was taken to Salpêtrière prison, where she was whipped and branded and sentenced to life. But soon after, she escaped to England and published a book she called her *Memoirs,* detailing a love affair with Marie Antoinette.

I shake my head. "The queen has not had good fortune in France."

"No," Rose agrees. "Not when the crime of *lèse-majesté* goes unpunished and the woman responsible for the greatest con of the century is moving about London pretending to be a comtesse. Can you imagine?"

Jeanne de Valois is exactly what my uncle wants for our exhibition. Someone shocking, scandalous, a woman without morals. He would place her in the room dedicated to great thieves. Of course, I do not mention this to Rose. As I finish her sculpture, I turn the clay model around so that she may see.

"My God," she whispers. She rises from her chair and reaches out to touch the head. "The jaw. You've gotten the jaw exactly right." She peers into my face, as if she can discern the secret of my skill. "Come look," she orders, and her ladies flutter around her. I can hear that Rose is pleased. "So what happens now?"

"I will make a plaster mold from this head. When that is finished, I will pour a mixture of beeswax and a vegetable tallow into the mold and let it cool. Then I'll add tint, to make sure the skin color is just right—"

"It will be white?" she confirms.

I frown. Her coloring is far more Gallic. There is a touch of the sun in her skin. "It will look just as you do," I promise.

"And my teeth? I want everyone to know that I have good teeth."

"That is what those are for." I indicate a glass box. Several of her ladies make noises of disgust, but Rose moves toward the collection and picks it up.

"These are real," she replies, caught between horror and fascination.

"Yes. From the Palais-Royal."

"But how—"

It has clearly been a long time since Rose has had to do her own shopping. If she had been in the Palais-Royal in the past several months, she would have seen the men with their pliers in the streets. "No one can afford a dentist with a shop," I tell her. "Anyone in pain goes to a street dentist. It's fifteen sous for every extraction." Or ten, if you allow him to keep the tooth. "Then he sells the teeth to us."

Now, Rose's skin truly is pale. "I had no idea," she whispers, but I notice that none of her women look surprised. They shop for their own goods, just as I do, and they have seen these men in their bloodied aprons. "It is the same with the hair," I continue. "We can use a wig, or we can insert human hairs into the scalp one at a time. But for you, it will be a wig. We'll want to be sure we get your *pouf* just right."

"And the eyes?" I can see that she is afraid I will tell her that these, too, will be real.

"Those will be glass. The body," I add before she can ask, "will be fashioned by my uncle, using the clothes you have so kindly donated."

"And how long will all of this take?"

"Several weeks."

"But Her Majesty will be here by then! How will I know if I approve?"

"Do you like what you see in the mirror?"

She glances above my head, where the reflection of a heavy woman in pearls looks back at her. "It is acceptable."

"Then the model will be acceptable as well."

Chapter 4

January 30, 1789

I am terrified of being bored.

—Marie Antoinette to Austrian Ambassador
Comte de Mercy d'Argenteau

There are a hundred things still to do in the Salon de Cire before Their Majesties arrive in just a few hours. We must remove the figure of Benjamin Franklin and replace it with one of Necker, the king's Minister of Finance. And the recumbent model of Madame du Barry, the beautiful mistress of King Louis XV, must be hidden away. When Marie Antoinette first arrived in France, it was no great secret that she and her father-in-law's mistress had not become friends. No Hapsburg princesse could legitimize a woman of unguarded morals. If du Barry had possessed any sense, she would have seen that she was the mistress of the past while Antoinette was the princesse of the future. When Louis died, Antoinette had du Barry banished. It certainly will not do to remind the queen of her rival for her father-in-law's affections. So I hire two young boys from the street to help me carry the model into the workshop.

They look, mesmerized, at the sleeping figure of du Barry on her blue and white couch. Her back is arched and one arm is raised, suggesting complete and utter abandonment—either to sleep or to pleasure. Her golden curls tumble loosely over her pink taffeta gown, and her long neck is exposed to the viewer.

"From here to the workshop." I point to a closed door across the exhibition. "I'll give you five sous each." With a loaf of bread at fifteen sous and daily wages for the average worker at twenty, it's a fair price for a moment's work.

The boys position themselves on either side of the couch and lift the sleeping woman. I walk in front of them, guiding them past the various tableaux, then open the wooden door to the workshop and inhale the familiar scents of oil paints and clay. As they enter, their eyes go wide. It is a wonderland of gadgets and artistry. Like in the secret rooms behind the curtain of a theater, there is everything that a person might need to re-create himself. Dresses and hats, walking sticks and gloves, chairs, couches, tables, lamps, and the half-finished heads of a dozen figures. Tools and supplies are strewn across the floor where Curtius and I left them last night: calipers, chisels, bags of clay, even sacks of horsehair. I can see the boys wish to stay and explore, but I pay them ten sous, and as soon as they are gone, I cover the figure of du Barry with a sheet. I surround it with heavy bags of plaster so there is no chance that anyone will ask to see what's beneath. But as I am dragging the last bag across the room, it tears, and the plaster trails along the floor.

When my mother sees the mess, she exclaims in her native German, *"Mein Gott!"*

"I will clean it up," I promise.

"But they will be here at any moment!" she cries.

My mother goes into a frenzy of cleaning, tossing the tools into various baskets without any concern for where they belong. At this late hour, it doesn't matter, and I follow behind her, sweeping the plaster from the floor.

"Where is Curtius?" she demands. "Tell him to come in here and help us!"

"He can't," I reply in German. "He's giving instructions to Yachin."

Our barker, a young Jewish boy from Austria, is standing outside with the sign I painted for him this morning. It reads, THE SALON DE CIRE WILL BE CLOSED TODAY IN HONOR OF THEIR MAJESTIES' ARRIVAL. I have instructed him to shout it at every passerby. The boy has thought on his own to start telling the crowd that the tickets will be only twelve sous for those who wish to walk in Her Majesty's footsteps. Of course, the tickets are always twelve sous.

"We must get dressed," my mother says suddenly.

"But the king. Shouldn't we add—"

"It's too late! Do you want the queen to see you like this?"

I laugh, since it is completely unthinkable that anyone should be presented to the queen in an apron. We have spent three days searching among the shops in the Place de Grève for proper attire. It is everything that we get this right. Our Salon may deceive the eye—stucco for marble and gilt instead of gold—but there is no disguising dress. We must look as well turned out as the queen's ladies, even if it costs us a fortune.

In my mother's room, I change into a tight-waisted dress. Curtius has bought me a silk fichu for the occasion. It is trimmed in lace, and as I pin it to my bodice, I stand in front of the mirror and admire its effect across my shoulders. While most of Paris is without firewood or bread, our museum takes in three hundred sous a day. It's enough to ensure that there is always meat on our table and luxuries such as this.

"What do you think?" my mother asks. She has put on the most expensive gown she has ever owned. Although she has already passed fifty, she giggles like a girl. "Am I silly?"

"No." And I am being honest. "You are beautiful." The gown is embroidered with tiny pearls, and the bodice has been sewn with gems. It has cost my uncle nearly two hundred livres, and now I can see how du Barry could spend two thousand on a lavish court gown. "Just look at you." I turn my mother toward the mirror. The dress makes her positively youthful. "You could be forty," I tell her.

She laughs out loud. "Maybe forty-nine." She smiles at me in the mirror, then reaches out to take my hand. "I am so lucky in my children," she whispers. "Three sons in the Swiss Guard, and a beautiful daughter with her own occupation. You will never have to marry for money. You will never have to depend on anyone but yourself." This is important to my mother, whose marriage was for convenience, not love. She raises her eyes to an image of Christ above her bed. "All of Curtius's hopes are in you," she says. "You have made this happen today."

"We have all made it happen. The Salon could not continue without everyone's hard work." It takes enormous skill to coordinate and run an exhibition. I cannot imagine how Curtius ever did it alone. I have seen his record books from before I was born, and they are appalling. Tickets sold for reduced prices to friends, free tickets to various members of the nobility. It is a wonder he made any money at all. We argued last night about whether we should charge the royal family an entrance fee. He wanted to let them in free, as if the new gowns for the models had all come cheap, and I wanted to charge a fee. But my mother insisted that we be gracious subjects, and grace means allowing the royal family inside without a price. I squeeze her hand in mine.

"Sound the trumpets," she announces grandly.

Downstairs in the Salon, Rose Bertin and Henri Charles have already arrived. I notice that Rose has a wider smile for Henri than she has ever had for me. Perhaps it is because he looks particularly handsome today. His long hair has been dressed *à catogan* and tied with a blue ribbon that matches his coat. The tassels of his walking stick are also blue, like his silk *culottes,* and the long tails of his coat have been richly embroidered. It is the first I have seen him take such care with his appearance. Truly, someone as impressive and intelligent as Henri should be petitioning the king for a place at court. He could serve in the king's workshop or, better, live by the king's grants. I think of all the brilliant things he could create with enough money and time.

As soon as Henri sees me, he breaks off conversation with Rose and points to the crowds waiting outside. "Have you seen what's happening?"

"It's wonderful, isn't it? Tomorrow, the Salon will be shoulder to shoulder!"

He hesitates, and I realize that he is being critical.

"You clean up quite well," Rose remarks. "If you ever wish to make an appearance at court, you could be dazzling in my green robe *à la française.* To match your eyes."

She is as ruthless a saleswoman as I am. "If I come into an unknown inheritance," I say, "I will be sure to visit you."

There is the sound of a coach and eight outside, then of women crying, "The queen! It is His Majesty and the queen!" Despite what's been printed about her in the *libelles,* accusing her of every kind of immorality, they are excited to see her. I feel a great surge of relief. Henri is wrong. This is exactly the kind of publicity we want. I take my mother's arm, and we rush to the door.

"Curtsy," Rose reminds sharply from behind me. "Curtsy!"

I sink into my lowest curtsy, and when I come up, it is real. The King and Queen of France are before me, dressed in expensive silk and ermine cloaks. The cries of the people are shut out as members of the king's guard hurry to close the doors. None of my three brothers are among the men. Their jobs are to guard the king's chamber, not to accompany the royal family on trips to Paris. It's a pity, since we see them so rarely.

"Welcome to the Salon de Cire," my uncle says.

A servant steps forward to make the introductions. There is Madame Élisabeth, the king's youngest sister. She is twenty-four and has the cream and rose complexion of a girl in her teens. There is the royal family's eldest child, Marie-Thérèse, whom the court addresses as Madame Royale. Her dark eyes and hair are a striking contrast to her younger brothers'. I smile at the frail, sickly dauphin, who is borne on a litter by two men. Though he is seven years old—the middle child—he looks all of four or five. He shares the same fair hair and blue eyes as his four-year-old brother, Louis-Charles. The youngest boy is dressed in a little sailor's outfit: a fitted blue jacket with matching trousers.

"Papa, Maman, that's you!" Louis-Charles points across the entrance to the horseshoe table where the wax figures of the king and queen are eating. From the stools arranged for the duchesses to the high-backed chairs for the king and queen, it is as close as any tableau can come to real life.

"Very good," the queen compliments her youngest son. Then she turns to the dauphin. "Do you know what that scene is meant to be?"

The dauphin struggles to a sitting position. He looks around, not with the quick, dismissive glance of a child who has been given every luxury, but with the slow, curious gaze of a boy who is eager to learn. His eyes go first to the faux marble columns dividing the tableaux, then to the paintings hanging on the walls, which give the impression that the viewer has entered a woman's private salon. "It must be the Grand Couvert."

"Exactly!" the queen exclaims. She clearly takes pride in teaching her children.

"Can we go inside?" the dauphin asks. "Where do we pay?"

Curtius laughs. "Today, the entertainment comes free. And if Their Majesties will permit, my niece and I shall take them on a tour."

We leave the entrance hall, and I notice that the king moves with a limp. In my wax model of him, he is not nearly so short and obese. I imagine he will be pleased with what I've done. The queen, however, is more graceful than any model can convey. It is true what they say about her—that she glides instead of walks. Though there is a thickness beneath her chin and she is not as lithe as she once was, there is no mistaking the body of a dancer. Aside from her cloak, she has dressed modestly for this outing. It's a shame, since I can remember attending her Grand Couvert, the weekly ritual when the king and queen are seen to eat in public, and I know how dazzling Marie Antoinette can be. When I saw the queen at her Sunday dinner, her dress was blue velvet trimmed in white fur, and the white satin stomacher matched her plumed headdress. But today, she is dressed in a gown of puce. She has used the smallest soupçon of rouge to enliven her cheeks, and her hair has been only lightly powdered. I notice that her necklace is of pearls, not diamonds, as are the rings on her fingers.

Her sister-in-law Madame Élisabeth is dressed far more elegantly, in rich brown silk and beige taffeta. Her ermine muff has been embroidered in gold, while the same lavish trim has been used for her gown. Like his sister, King Louis has made no attempt to alter his dress to appease the populace. There are diamond buckles on his shoes, and the fashionable walking stick he is carrying is encrusted with jewels. Even so, there is very little of kingly majesty about him. In different clothes, he might be a peasant. As we enter the exhibition, he stops in front of the first painting. Because he is nearsighted, he must approach the canvas until his nose is nearly touching the paint.

"How many paintings are in your exhibition?" the king asks.

"A hundred and fifty, Your Majesty. I am somewhat of a collector," Curtius admits.

"And have you always been interested in wax, Dr. Curtius?"

"Yes. Since I first came across it in medical school."

"Ah." The king turns to his children. "And do you know what he would have used it for in school?"

The boys shake their heads. But Madame Royale, who is eleven and thinks herself too grand for this place, simply rolls her eyes.

"He would have used it for making anatomical models." The king looks at my uncle. "Am I correct?"

"Exactly so, Your Majesty." As we stop in front of the dinner tableau, expressions of delight pass through our group of royal guests. I was right. The queen is pleased with what she sees. She is smiling and asks if she may have a closer look. "Certainly, Your Majesty." My uncle opens a little gate in the wooden balustrade, and the queen passes through, followed by the rest of her family. We do not allow visitors to touch the models, but in this case, neither Curtius nor I complain.

"Exceptional," the queen breathes, caressing her wax face. "Absolutely unbelievable."

"I knew Your Majesty would approve," Rose gloats, as if I hadn't begged her for a year to invite them. She indicates the headdress made of satin and trimmed with bejeweled aigrettes. "Like the one you wore to your last masquerade."

The look on the queen's face is one of pain, but just as quickly it is gone and she has schooled her features into serenity. "Show me everything!" She claps eagerly. "Even your Cavern of Great Thieves."

We are more than happy to oblige. There are thirty full-size models in our exhibition, and a dozen busts on short marble columns. We have positioned a floor-length mirror across from each tableau to give the impression that the Salon is larger than it really is. Come evening, these mirrors will reflect the glow of the chandeliers, casting double the light over the exhibits.

The king stops before a group of figures depicting the Eastern envoys of Tippoo Sahib in their colorful costumes. "Remember this?" He turns to his wife. "They were the funniest men who ever came to Versailles." That was six months ago. The king summoned Paris's best artists to sculpt the envoys, and he was so impressed by my uncle's wax model that he had it installed in a tent outside the Grand Trianon for more than a month. Now, he holds his belly and laughs, sending his young sons into fits of giggles. The girl, I notice, never smiles.

"Those mustaches!" The queen laughs, and it's a merry sound, not high and false like those of some of the important women I have modeled.

"They smelled," Madame Royale puts in nastily.

"That was the scent of the East," her father says.

The queen's cheeks have gone pink. "And you, Mademoiselle Grosholtz. Which of these wonderful models are you responsible for?"

"This dinner scene that Her Majesty saw. And this one as well." I lead the group into the next room. It is a family portrait with all of the children. I made the decision last night to remove the princesse Sophie-Hélène Béatrix, who died a year and a half ago at eleven months old. Now I see that this was the right choice, since the queen goes at once to the model of her youngest son and caresses his cheek. I believe she is feeling sentimental, for this model was made when Louis-Charles was only three years old. I based it on a bust in the Paris Salon, and since then his face has matured.

"Look, there I am!" Madame Royale marches toward the model I have made of her and inspects it. She looks from me to the wax image and back again. "You did this?"

"Yes, Your Highness."

"And how did you know what I look like? I've never met you before."

"There are images of Her Highness in many galleries. I based this model on one of those."

The queen puts a hand on her daughter's shoulder, but the girl shrugs it off. "I wish to take this home."

"This is a museum," the queen replies, "not a shop."

"And we do not take things from museums," Madame Élisabeth says. The king's younger sister has been silent until now, and when Madame Royale hears her aunt speak, she is quieted. "Why don't you go inside the Cavern of Great Thieves?" Madame Élisabeth asks the queen. "I will stay here and watch the children."

Madame Royale stomps her foot and whines, "I want to go, too."

"When you are older," her father says. "Not now."

I lead the adults into the Cavern of Great Thieves, and immediately, the mood changes. The room is lit by only a few candles, and the walls have been constructed to look like a dungeon. I steal a look at Curtius and Henri, who both nod encouragingly at me. I am the one who gives this speech to important patrons. I lick my lips and begin. "Here are the men who have terrorized the good people of France. Thieves, forgers, and even murderers of children."

I see the king exchange a worried look with Rose. The queen, however, steps forward.

"This is Antoine François Desrues. In 1744, he was born to humble parents not far from here. After many years of hard work, Desrues purchased his own grocery. Although the business was successful, he spent far more than he could ever take in. He fancied himself part of the nobility and arranged to purchase a château from the kind and friendly Monsieur de la Motte. When Monsieur sent his wife to collect the payment, Desrues invited the pretty woman to dinner."

Curtius leads the group to the next model. She is a woman in her thirties in a beautiful gown and a fashionable hat.

"At first, the evening went well. Desrues was charming, as men like him can be. But as soon as Madame de la Motte wasn't looking, Desrues slipped poison into her wine. Within the evening, Madame de la Motte was dead!"

The queen inhales sharply.

"The next week, Madame de la Motte's sixteen-year-old son came searching for her. Enticing the boy into his home, Desrues offered the child a cup of chocolate. Like his mother, the boy was soon dead. The next week, Desrues forged a receipt and attempted to take possession of the beautiful château. But the sudden disappearance of his wife and son aroused Monsieur de la Motte's suspicion. The police were summoned, and the bodies were discovered stuffed into chests and buried inside Desrues's own cellar. In 1777, Desrues was executed by burning."

"Which is exactly what he deserved," the king says.

"His wife," I add, "is currently imprisoned in the Salpêtrière."

"But was she part of the conspiracy?" Rose Bertin asks.

I turn up my palms. "That, no one can know."

We go to the next model, and I tell them the story of the famous forger who sold works of art supposedly produced by the great Italian master Leonardo da Vinci. For twenty years he conned wealthy noblemen, delivering pieces to their homes and taking their money—two, three, sometimes four thousand livres for a single painting. Henri points out that this forger should have known better than to try to imitate one of the greatest artists—and scientists—ever to have lived.

"Then you are an admirer of his work?" the king asks.

Henri nods. "I am."

"Many years ago I saw a reproduction of *The Vitruvian Man,"* the king recalls. "It was fascinating."

"What is *The Vitruvian Man*?" the queen asks.

The king looks to Henri, allowing him to answer.

"It is a drawing of man that is perfectly proportional to a real human body. Da Vinci based it on the writings of the Roman architect Vitruvius, who discovered that the proportions of nearly every human body are similar."

"Do you have an example of this?" the queen wants to know.

Henri smiles. "Certainly, Your Majesty. Vitruvius discovered that the length of a man's ear is one-third of the length of his face, and the length of a man's foot is one-sixth of his height. As a child, I was asked to measure the distance from the tip of my head to the floor and divide it by the distance from my belly button to the ground. The number I came up with is the same number that nearly everyone will. A ratio of 1.618."

The queen turns to her husband. "Have you ever done this? And is it true? Was the number 1.618?"

"It was when I was young." The king looks down at his protruding stomach. "I'm not sure it would be now."

"I want to try it," she exclaims, "as soon as we are home!" She looks up at the wax model of the forger again. "There are so many stories," she reflects quietly.

"All of these thieves and murderers," the king says uneasily. "You modeled them?"

I nod. "But not always in person."

"They are very . . ." He searches for the right word.

"Realistic," the queen puts in.

We go from tableau to tableau, and I explain the disturbing tale behind each sculpture. There are men here whose names are synonymous with murder, and others whose faces are immediately recognizable. As we exit the Cavern of Great Thieves, Madame Royale demands, "Was it fun?"

"Yes . . ." The king shivers playfully. "But only for a few minutes."

I lead our visitors to my model of Rousseau and tell them how my mother spent many nights cooking dishes for the Swiss philosopher.

"So tell me," the king says, "was the man himself as brilliant as his writing?"

Everyone turns to me, and I can see that Henri is holding his breath. "There has never been a more remarkable man," I reply. "With the exception, of course, of Your Majesty."

The king smiles widely, and the queen steps so close to me that I catch the scent of her jasmine perfume. "Did he really dress like an Armenian?" she asks.

"In vests and caftans." I am careful not to add that he sometimes adopted the American habit of wearing a fur cap. "And he was enormously fond of my mother's *Käsespätzle.*"

"Käsespätzle," she repeats, and I wonder how long it's been since she has tasted the food of her homeland. "I would love some *Käsespätzle.*"

My mother gasps, then says in her best French, "It would be an honor to prepare some for Your Majesty."

"You understand," the king says sorrowfully, "that we cannot eat here."

But my mother is already shaking her head. "I shall make some to take home with you."

I look at Curtius, and neither of us can believe what is happening. It is one thing to feed philosophers, but to provide food for queens . . . We will have customers beating a path to our door for days. Perhaps even weeks! After the Duchesse de Polignac visited the snuff shop on the Rue Saint-Honoré, the owner had to hire extra help for a month. My mother rushes off to begin a batch of *Käsespätzle,* and I smile at Rose, who brought this all about. I take the royal family to the last tableau. It is covered with white sheets, and as Curtius unveils the final scene, Rose puts her hand to her mouth. It is always a shock for clients to see themselves as they truly are, and I have spared nothing—neither cost nor vanity. She is excessively plump, with a second chin and pudgy eyes. But her lips are beautiful, and her dress is fit for the halls of Versailles. She is part of an intimate tableau with the queen in her dressing room. The wax Antoinette stares at herself in a handsome mirror, dressed in a heavy linen shift that will be changed into a revealing gauze nightgown tomorrow. Meanwhile, the wax Rose is holding a *gazette des atours,* a heavy book filled with swatches from which the queen chooses her outfits each morning.

The queen approaches her seated figure with awe. Unlike the previous models, with their horsehair bodies, this one has been made entirely of wax, from her Hapsburg lip to her painted toes. "You are responsible for this?" the queen asks.

I can see that Henri is nervous, but there is nothing to be ashamed of. "Yes," I reply.

"And who thought of this?" the king questions.

"I did," I say, before Curtius can answer. "I wished to show Her Majesty as she truly is, full of grace and beauty even before she is dressed in her robes *à la française.*"

The queen smiles, and then her daughter speaks. "I think it is improper."

"There is nothing improper," the king overrules. "The queen is covered, and the act of dressing is a part of life."

"What about her feet?" Madame Royale sticks out her lower lip, an unattractive gesture on any child, but particularly on her. Hands on her hips, she feels obliged to add, "Madame Campan says—"

"It is quite fine," the queen says impatiently. "Dr. Curtius, Mademoiselle Grosholtz, you have an exceptional museum."

My uncle leads the royal family to the last stop on our tour. "The Curiosity Shop," he says, and both princes clap their hands in delight. Filling the shelves are miniature wax models of all the figures in our museum. There are little wax kings and tiny wax princes. There are also models of houses and theaters. On the highest shelves are the wax figures for adults. When the queen's brother Emperor Joseph II came to visit, he bought two miniatures of Venus in the nude. The princes want to see and touch everything, while Madame Royale stands back, surveying the shop from the entrance.

"You are welcome to take whatever you wish," Curtius says.

"Only one figure," the king adds. "Everything in moderation."

The princes choose wax soldiers, and Madame Royale takes an image of a sleeping cat.

My mother appears with our best china bowl, covered with a square napkin of silk. "For Her Majesty." She curtsies very low. "May she enjoy it in the best of health." She holds it out for the queen, and one of the Swiss Guards who have been following us steps forward to take it.

"I am deeply grateful, Madame Grosholtz. We shall not soon forget this trip."

Outside, the royal carriage is waiting for its charges. The sleek horses and liveried guards look like something from another world on the bleak Boulevard du Temple. We watch as the royal family is escorted into their gold and velvet coach, and when they are gone, we return to the Salon. My mother goes upstairs to our private quarters, and I'm grateful that Henri helps Curtius move the tableau of the sleeping du Barry back into its empty space. Rose, however, is standing in front of her waxen image.

"I would like to be thinner," she says critically.

"And I would like to be more buxom," I reply.

She stares at me, then breaks into laughter. "Very well, Mademoiselle Grosholtz. Very well."

Chapter 5

February 3, 1789

Man was born free and everywhere he is in shackles.

–Jean-Jacques Rousseau

It is the greatest success we have ever had. Despite the pouring rain, the line for our Salon has stretched to the Rue Saint-Honoré for nearly three days. It is as if all of Paris has heard that the king and queen have visited our waxworks, and no one wants to miss the chance to see what the royals themselves have laid eyes on. While I have rushed to complete a new model of young Louis-Charles for display, there is no need to sculpt his older brother. The dauphin's sickness has kept him small and thin; he has hardly aged at all. I hope the court physicians are watching him closely. It will destroy the queen to lose two children in such a short time.

I am about to tell our barker, Yachin, to come in from the rain when Curtius stops me at the door. "Let him shout," he says. He is smiling. All of his effort in teaching me as a child was not in vain. Someday, he can retire from the Salon knowing that his life's work will not be shoved away in some attic; that I will do whatever is required to keep our waxworks in the public eye. "Let the line grow."

"We can't possibly accommodate so many customers! There are at least three hundred people out there." I have done the calculations. "Even if we let in twenty an hour—"

"We'll give anyone who doesn't make it inside a front-of-line ticket for tomorrow."

Of course. It's brilliant. And then it occurs to me. "What about a helping of *Käsespätzle*? Three extra sous for the *Käsespätzle* eaten by the queen!"

We grin at each other. He and I could sell ice to the Empress of Russia, and in the salon that evening, while Robespierre is announcing that he and Camille have passed the first round of elections to nominate the deputies to the Estates-General, I am thinking of how tomorrow we will have Yachin shout that the queen's *Käsespätzle* is being served. I am so wrapped up in this image that I don't hear the conversation pass on to the subject of the king's recent visit. Everyone is looking in my direction. I hope I haven't spoken my thoughts out loud.

"Mademoiselle Grosholtz?" Robespierre repeats. "I asked what the king said when he came face-to-face with the bust of Rousseau."

This is an obsession of Robespierre's. A week doesn't pass without him questioning us over what Rousseau was like when he visited: how he dressed, what he ate, and where he went to play chess when he wasn't playing in our salon. "The king asked if the man was as brilliant as his writing," I tell him.

Robespierre sits back as if I have slapped him. "The king has *read* Rousseau?" His glasses have slipped down his nose. He pushes them up with his thumb. "What does he know about the *Social Contract*? Or *La Nouvelle Héloïse*? Or the *Confessions*?"

"Nothing!" the Duc exclaims. "My cousin has always been an impostor."

"And the queen?" Robespierre demands. "What did the queen have to say?"

I wish I had another answer for him, since I know how this will reflect on Her Majesty, but I don't lie. "She asked if he dressed like an Armenian."

Robespierre looks triumphantly around the room, pausing to nod meaningfully to Camille and my uncle. "What have I told you?" He has neglected his food, and while everyone else eats, he pushes back his chair. "Vanity! And while our countrymen are starving, she is decorating herself with diamond aigrettes! Did she mention," he asks rhetorically, "that his Armenian robes would bar him from attending her Grand Couvert? That he would be laughed at in her gilded halls at Versailles?" My mother and I exchange looks across the table. "Do you think she cares that we are suffering from the worst harvest in living memory? That candles are to be had only by the wealthy and flour by the even wealthier?"

"Of course not. It's a plot!" Marat interjects, speaking for the first time tonight. Because he never bothers to swallow before he speaks, we can all see his sharp teeth covered in food. Marat narrows his eyes, and now he truly looks like a feral animal. "The monarchy knows its way of life is in peril, so they plan to starve the populace into subservience!"

"You don't really believe that?" Henri asks, aghast. "The monarchy could easily deploy the army to smother any rebellious acts."

"Not in the Palais-Royal!" Marat shouts.

The Palais-Royal is owned by the Duc. Once it was a vast garden shaded by chestnut trees, but eight years ago the Duc had the trees chopped down to make way for a sprawling shopping arcade. Anything can be found in the Palais-Royal: Madeira wine, English shoes, Indian coffee, exotic women. Until last year, we rented one of the Duc's shops to house the museum, but the prostitutes who lingered outside were driving our wealthy customers away. The Palais-Royal has become a veritable den of iniquity, sheltering every type of thief and anarchist. But since the grounds belong to the Duc, the king's soldiers are forbidden from policing inside any of the hundred and eighty arcades.

"And if the king took back the Palais-Royal?" Henri asks.

"He would never do that!"

Henri fixes Marat with a practical gaze. "He is king. He may do as he wishes."

I am impressed with his rhetoric.

Everyone looks to the Duc to see if he agrees. "I have been banished twice to the Villers-Cotterêts. What is to stop my cousin from exiling me entirely and taking the Palais-Royal for himself?"

"The p-people!" Camille exclaims. "W-we—we would never allow it. The Estates-General meets at Versailles in three months," Camille reminds him. "We will s-see then how loud the voice of the people can be."

"I hope louder than their costumes," the Duc remarks. "I am told that the Third Estate is required to come entirely in black. Black three-corner hats, black coats with tails, plain black cravats, and black knee breeches. The clergy, however, will be wearing scarlet silk."

Robespierre leans forward. "And the nobility? What will the nobility be wearing?"

The Duc sighs, as if it pains him a great deal to relay this message. "Their hats will be designed in the style of Henri IV, and their vests are to be of black silk, trimmed in lace and embroidered with gold."

It is as if a powder keg has exploded. Everyone begins shouting at once, with the exception of the Duc, who sits back and watches the fire that he has ignited. When my mother and I rise to clear the plates from the table, Lucile grabs my arm.

"Do you see why Camille is so upset? They wish to humiliate us!"

"But Curtius told me yesterday that they are giving us greater representation. They are doubling the number of deputies who represent the Third Estate to a thousand."

"That's right. They can dress our deputies in sackcloth, but this meeting of the Estates-General is going to change everything. It *has* to change everything." Her dark eyes suddenly fill with tears. This is about more than representation for her. This is about whether she will be able to marry the man of her choosing. Though I have never asked, I doubt that her father knows she sneaks away with Camille. They have been coming to us for only a year, but it has been seven months since they first vowed to marry. And now that Camille has passed the first round of elections to be made a deputy of the Third Estate, perhaps it will come to pass.

"Will your father consent to the marriage if Camille can distinguish himself somehow?" I ask.

Lucile looks over her shoulder to see if he is listening, then leans closer to me. "Yes, there will certainly be a better chance. There are a hundred thousand livres waiting for the man who claims my hand. Camille is only a lawyer, and my father has already turned him away once." She blinks rapidly, to stop the tears from falling. "He is a brilliant writer. There are great thoughts in his head."

"And I am sure he will make an impression at Versailles."

This relieves her greatly. "Do you think so?"

I look across the table at her intended. He is so engaged in what he is saying that he has lost his stutter entirely. "Yes," I reply, although I don't add what sort of impression. There is no room for passion like his at court. I think of the king's recent visit, and the quiet reverence with which his family treated him. I doubt that any man has ever been allowed to grow red-faced with rage in His Majesty's presence.

"Wealthy men have asked for my hand," she says. "Men who could improve our family's standing."

"And your father has turned them down?"

"I have, and now my father has given me a year to decide. It must all happen within a year." There is panic in her voice, and for the first time, I am thankful that I am not the daughter of a wealthy man. I reach out and squeeze her hand. "What about you?" she asks. "Isn't there anyone you care for?"

"I have an exhibition to care for," I reply. "And there are options open to an unmarried woman with ambition. Look at Rose Bertin. From an ordinary seamstress to the milliner of the queen. She is the wealthiest self-made woman in France!"

"But whom does she come home to?"

I am surprised at Lucile's naïveté. A woman like Rose may come home to any man she chooses. "I am sure Rose is not lonely. Money means that there are always people around you."

After I leave to help my mother clear the table and serve the coffee, I watch Camille and Lucile from the kitchen. She is whispering something in his ear to make him blush. If Camille becomes a deputy, it will be his responsibility to take his city's *cahiers* to Versailles. I have heard that there are more than fifty thousand *cahiers* being drafted, and that these lists of grievances are long. The people are demanding that all citizens be equal before the law. They are declaring that it is not right for the First and Second Estates to be free from taxes. Some of the *cahiers* request the abolishment of censorship in journalism. But nearly all demand that the *lettres de cachet* be abolished. The people live in fear of these *lettres,* which allow anyone to be arrested, so long as the king has signed the document. For jealousy and vengeance, husbands have imprisoned their spouses, then taken up with mistresses. Parents have imprisoned unruly sons and sent away daughters who have refused good marriages. And though he has issued more than ten thousand, there is evidence that the king does not read these *lettres,* that he signs blank forms and the police fill in whichever names they wish.

I think of the Marquis de Sade, currently imprisoned in the Bastille under a *lettre de cachet* drafted by his in-laws. A thousand things conspired to send him to this place, including poisoning prostitutes in Marseille and imprisoning a young woman until she made an escape from his second-floor window. But his must certainly be the rare case of justice being served. If the Estates-General can accomplish nothing more than the banishment of these *lettres,* it will be a success.

As the coffee is finished and everyone rises to leave, Curtius asks Henri to stay behind. "I am having some trouble with the du Barry model," he says. "Since we moved her for the king's visit, the mechanical heart is no longer working." This is one of my uncle's favorite figures, not because she is scantily dressed but because he has fitted her with a beating heart that makes the model's ample chest rise and fall. Visitors always bend closer for a look, and some have sworn that they can even hear her breathing.

"Have you tried replacing the pump?" Henri asks. I follow them down to the du Barry tableau. I watch as Henri steadily tinkers with the model, his hands moving lightly over her wax breasts, and suddenly the wine from dinner has flushed my cheeks. After a few minutes

Henri declares, "It was the valve." The heart is beating again, and mine flutters under my fichu. I fan myself distractedly with my hand, but neither of the men seems to notice.

Curtius claps him heartily on the back. "Henri, I don't know what we would do without you. How is that exhibition of yours going?"

Henri smiles broadly, and I wonder how many women linger after his shows hoping he will smile like this at them. Quite a few, probably, though they are wasting their time. Like me, Henri is married to his work. But experiments with hydrogen do not pay the rent, and so Henri has taken on the task of putting on scientific shows. "I am about to install a new exhibit," he tells us. *"The Auricular Communications of the Invisible Girl.* Perhaps you would like to see it tomorrow?"

"I'm sorry," I say. "But I have—"

"We would love to," Curtius interrupts.

What's the matter with him? He knows that Madame de Sainte-Amaranthe is to bring her daughter in for a sitting. I put on my best showman's smile. "I look forward to seeing the Invisible Girl."

"Oh, you won't see her," Henri promises. "But you will hear her."

My cheeks flush again. "Of course."

"Tomorrow at seven in the morning then," he says, and he is looking at me.

After I see Henri to the door, I go upstairs to search for Curtius. I am angry with him. When does he think I will have time to prepare for a sitting if I am listening to some invisible girl? No doubt the mechanics of the show will be interesting—everything that Henri does defies logic. But there is nothing interesting about being unprepared. I stalk through the salon and stop as I'm about to enter the kitchen. Next to the unwashed pots and pans, Curtius has his arms around my mother, and they are sharing a tender moment. He is whispering something in her ear, and she is giggling. They are young again in the way they love each other. For a moment, I am tempted to interrupt. Then I turn around.

I will have to remember to be angry with him tomorrow.

Chapter 6

February 4, 1789

The contagious example of the Duc d'Orléans [is ruinous].

—Madame Campan,
first lady-in-waiting to Marie Antoinette

Although I should be laying out calipers and bowls of plaster, I am standing in Henri's workshop surrounded by the most curious instruments of science. Because I have been so busy with the Salon, I have not been here for several months—perhaps even a year, I realize with shock—and in that time much has changed. Placed haphazardly on the long wooden countertops are gadgets I have never seen before, and in between them are clear tubes filled with bubbling liquid. Everything looks new, but then that is the nature of science. Whereas wax will be the same in two hundred years, science changes daily.

Like the house that we rent, Henri's home with his brother, Jacques, has been divided into three parts. On the first floor is a vast auditorium with a sprawling workshop behind it, while upstairs are large chambers off a long hall and a kitchen. For me, the workshop is the most soothing. I imagine this is how Henri feels as well. It is probably a place where he can shut out the incessant noise of the Boulevard and concentrate on something quiet. While the crowds outside may never stop, art and science will go at your own pace. Even when an exhibition has gone poorly, I find peace in retiring to the back of my workshop to be among the tools of my trade.

At a table on the far side of the room, Jacques Charles is scribbling furiously. Above him hangs the formula for which he is known, $v_1/t_1 = v_2/t_2$. *The volume of a gas at constant pressure increases linearly with the absolute temperature of the gas.* This is how Henri initially explained it to me. His words had confounded me for days until I returned and he showed me the experiment that resulted in the equation. He took a deflated silk balloon and held it over a lighted candle. The silk envelope twitched and flickered upward from his outstretched fingers. Heat expanded air, air filled the balloon, then the balloon went up. Magic, and not magic at all.

When Jacques Charles lifts his head and greets us, I refrain from asking him what he is working on. My business is with Madame Sainte-Amaranthe and her daughter, and the fewer questions I ask, the sooner I will be able to return to the Salon. Still, I wonder when he will launch his next balloon. A model of the one launched in the Tuileries Gardens hangs next to the formula above his head. It is an exact replica, from its wicker gondola to its valve-and-ballast system. Nearly half a million people had been there to see it off, and because our family were special guests of the Charles brothers, we were granted a place in the front row across from the queen and her *ménage*. The queen had dressed her ladies in loose, flowing *lévites*, pink and yellow to coordinate with the color of the balloon. Matching scarves were tied around their waists, and their pink bonnets were identical. Only the queen herself stood out, in a *lévite* and bonnet of the purest white. I look around the workshop and realize what is missing. "The plaque from the queen," I say. "Commemorating your flight. What happened to it?"

Henri exchanges a look with his brother. Although fifteen years separate them, in some ways they are strikingly similar. I can see their kinship now in the way they both lower their eyes. "We thought it prudent to put it away," Henri explains, "in case anyone should wish to tour our laboratory."

"It could be a major draw to your exhibition!" I look at Curtius to see if he agrees, but he is silent.

"Do you know why the people were respectful during Their Majesties' visit to your Salon?" Henri asks. "Because bread and firewood were passed out in their names all along the Boulevard du Temple that morning."

So the king and queen are savvy. They know that a peaceful outing in Paris requires a donation to the local poor. "I don't see why that means you should take down her gift."

"If she had not placated the people, they would have stood at your doors shouting 'Down with *The Austrian.*' "

I don't believe it. "They've been coming in droves to see what she's seen."

"This week," he points out. "What about next week? Or the week after that?"

"She isn't popular," my uncle says quietly, and this is the first I've heard him speak against her. "We should listen carefully to what's happening. There may come a time when the Duc is more popular than the king."

"The *Duc d'Orléans*?" I exclaim. The man who stumbles into his coach too drunk to sit upright every Tuesday night? The man who has publicly humiliated his wife by installing his mistress as governess, giving her the right to educate his children despite the Duchesse d'Orléans's pleas to raise her own sons and daughters?

"He has sold art from his estate worth more than eight million livres," Jacques says. He stands next to his brother. "He is using the money to buy bread and firewood for the poor."

"And the peasants have begun calling him Father Charity," Henri adds flatly.

"So he thinks to win the crown through a popularity contest?" I demand.

Everyone around me nods. *To displace a king. It is unthinkable.*

"Come. Let's hear the Invisible Girl," Curtius says. "That is a far more cheerful subject."

But as we cross the workshop, I can't stop thinking about the Duc, imagining him on the king's throne, wearing the king's crown. And who would be his queen? His mistress, Mary Nesbitt, whose origin can be traced to a wheelbarrow according to the scandal sheets? Or perhaps it would be Grace Elliott, London's finest courtesan? And what would become of his wife, the beautiful and neglected Duchesse d'Orléans? I am so obviously disturbed by this prospect that Curtius puts his arm around my shoulder and says, "It will be fine. We didn't come here to speak politics." It is a reminder that I must look interested and enjoy the entertainment.

Henri hesitates before the door to the auditorium. "We can do this another time."

"No," I say. "I wish to see it. I don't want to be the only one in Paris who hasn't met the Invisible Girl."

Curtius smiles at me. It is important to him that we keep on good terms with the Charles brothers, and Henri in particular, who has been like another son to him, fixing our mechanics, painting our walls, helping build our tableaux. We enter the auditorium, with its hundreds of seats and darkly painted walls. At the far end of the stage, a large box has been suspended from the ceiling. A giant horn has been affixed to the box. Henri waves us toward the stage, and I put my ear to the horn.

"That is a lovely green dress you have on," someone says from the other side of the horn.

I jump back. "Where is she?" I look around. "How did she know?"

Henri laughs. "Can't you figure it out?"

I am intrigued despite myself. Curtius puts his ear to the horn, and I hear a young woman's voice tell him that his brown gloves are extremely elegant. Somehow, she can both see us and project her voice through the box. But she can't be inside the box, for it is too small to accommodate a person. "She's behind the stage," my uncle says, "and there's a peephole somewhere."

"Close, but not quite."

I listen again, and this time the girl compliments my green purse. I study the wall in front of me, then run my hands over its smooth surface. There is no hidden opening. I look up, and there, craftily disguised by a hanging lamp, is a peephole. "She's up there!" I exclaim. Henri watches me with open fascination. "She's looking down on us. And the mouthpiece of the horn . . . you have extended it all the way up to the attic."

"You are the first person to guess it."

It's incredibly ingenious. "It will make you a million livres!" I say.

"Is that all you think about?" Henri laughs, but there is earnestness in his question. "Curtius, you have raised a coldhearted entrepreneur. The only thing money is good for, Marie, is buying time. The time to do the things you like."

I often forget that exhibitions are a secondary passion for him. His first love is the laboratory, but as the more versatile brother, he has taken on the role of provider. It is only in his spare time that he is able to join Jacques among the gadgets and glass tubes. "Well, think of all the time a million livres could buy," I say. "You could construct an entire *fleet* of balloons."

"If that ever happens, I shall name one *Marie* in your honor." His dark eyes are studying mine.

Suddenly, I feel warm. "And will I get to choose the color?" I tease.

"Certainly. Which color would you like?"

I take a moment. And then it comes to me. "Gold."

~

I AM LATE for my sitting with Madame Sainte-Amaranthe's daughter. As Curtius and I rush through the door, my mother clucks her tongue disapprovingly. "They will be here in twenty minutes!"

"Then let them wait," Curtius says.

"Madame Sainte-Amaranthe?" my mother and I shriek. She is one of the most powerful women in Paris. Men would sell their children to be invited to her Thursday evening salons and give up their wives to be a part of her exclusive gambling club, Cinquante. She has been mistress to the Prince de Condé and the Vicomte de Pons, and there is loud talk that the vicomte is the father of her two children. She has her own box at the Italiens, the Opéra, the Comédie. This is not a woman accustomed to waiting.

"It will be good for her," Curtius says wryly. "A new experience."

"Or perhaps she will leave, and that will be a new experience for us," I tell him.

We enter the workshop, and I see that my mother has done her best to prepare for the sitting, anticipating our needs. "The plaster!" I ask. "Where is the plaster?"

"Right in front of you," my mother says calmly.

I am flustered. I haven't even readied the clay. And I am sure Madame Sainte-Amaranthe will not wish to have plaster applied directly to her daughter's face. That means the wax mold must be made from a sculpture. It takes a quiet mind to sculpt, not one filled with strange contraptions and horns. *The Invisible Girl!* I scowl at Curtius, who is directing my mother on how to rearrange certain items. I have barely calmed my mind when Yachin announces the Sainte-Amaranthe family, then takes it upon himself to escort them personally through the Salon and into the workshop. I see why at once. He is only two years younger than Madame's daughter, Émilie, and at fourteen she is already a stunning beauty. She has come in a dress of long white gauze threaded through with silver.

"Thank you, Yachin." But our barker cannot take his eyes from her. "You may go now," I say. I am surprised he is able to walk away without tripping over himself.

Madame Sainte-Amaranthe gives a little laugh that I hope Yachin cannot hear. "My daughter has this effect on men." She turns a dazzling smile to Curtius, and it is clear that she thinks she still has this effect as well. Many years ago, when the Prince de Condé requested a nude of his mistress, my uncle made two. One went to the prince's boudoir; the other lies scantily clad in our Salon.

"As do you, Madame. . . . You are still next to Madame du Barry," Curtius flatters her. "My two sleeping beauties."

"I thought you would have found a younger woman," Madame Sainte-Amaranthe replies, dangling her fish on the line. "I am surprised you keep it."

My uncle takes the bait. "Madame, I could search the faces of a thousand women and never find one who is your equal."

It is a credit to my mother that she is still wearing her most welcoming smile. She understands that wealthy women of a particular age, after a lifetime of bartering their beauty, do not know any other way of interacting with men. Now that Madame has assuaged her ego, she turns to her children. "Émilie, Louis, I would like you to meet Dr. Curtius." My uncle bows again. "Madame Grosholtz." My mother continues to smile. "And her daughter, Mademoiselle Grosholtz."

"Please, call me Marie," I say.

"It is a pleasure to meet you," Louis replies. He is as delicately framed and beautiful as his older sister. "Will it be possible for my mother and me to watch while you make Émilie's sculpture?" he asks graciously. She has brought them up well.

"Of course," my uncle says. "These chairs are for you." My mother has taken our best seats from upstairs and arranged them at the far end of the workshop, near the fire. "Madame Grosholtz will fetch us some drinks while Marie begins. When the head is finished, I will work on the rest of the model."

Curtius rarely sculpts faces anymore, mostly because there is too much to do entertaining guests and fashioning miniatures for our Curiosity Shop.

"Have you brought clothes?" I ask Émilie, directing her to a stool across from my worktable.

"My mother has them. Will you be putting the model in the Salon?"

"If you approve of it," I tell her and fetch my caliper.

"Oh, there is nothing I'd like more! " she says while I measure her face. "But what I *really* want is for François Elleviou to see it."

"The singer?" I ask.

"You have heard of him?" she exclaims.

Like all young people, she cannot believe that someone as old as I am might have heard of François Elleviou. "He is something of a sensation," I say wryly. "I'm certain most of Paris has heard his name."

"My mother hadn't. Not until I begged her to invite him to our salon."

I want to say that it is my job to be well informed, that people don't come to an exhibition to see figures that are of no interest. Instead, I reply, "Then she knows who he is now."

Émilie smiles, and I notice that both of her cheeks are dimpled. They are too charming not to include in the sculpture. "She certainly does. He is courting me." Before I can reply she says, "There is a man in the doorway!"

I turn, and there is Robespierre. Yachin must have sent him back. I cannot fathom what he might want. As I cross the room, I wipe my hands on my apron. "Monsieur Robespierre. What a delightful surprise."

"I do not mean to interrupt," he says quickly. "I happened to be passing and thought to deliver a message to your uncle in person."

I point to the back of the workshop, where Madame Sainte-Amaranthe is in danger of exposing her bosom. She is showing my uncle something on her feet, perhaps a new gold buckle. Robespierre makes a great performance of disapproving. "You have guests," he says with distaste.

"Allow me to introduce Madame Sainte-Amaranthe and her daughter, Émilie."

He looks at Émilie, perched on her stool like a Grecian goddess. There are few women who can live up to such hyperbole. I have seen only two: the queen's dearest friend, the Princesse de Lamballe, who was as pale and flawless as a diamond when I saw her over ten years ago at Versailles, and now Émilie.

"She is fourteen," I tell him, "and this is her first sitting."

Robespierre makes the briefest of bows, then hurries across the workshop to greet my uncle. I feel sorry for him. It's not his arrogance that keeps him from engaging with women, but a lack of self-confidence.

I return to the clay model and take up my caliper to be sure that I have the nose just right.

"Who is that?" Émilie whispers.

"Robespierre. A lawyer from Arras."

"Does he always wear green spectacles?"

"Yes. He does not see well."

"Like the king. I've heard that the corners of all his furniture are rounded in case he should run into them."

But I am stopped from replying by something else extraordinary. A courtier in the king's livery has been shown in by Yachin. The workshop falls silent as the man holds out a letter for me. "Mademoiselle Grosholtz?"

"Yes." I study the man's powdered wig, his silk stockings, his blue livery. Even the nail on his smallest left finger, grown long so that he may scratch on King Louis's doors—no one is allowed to knock but the queen—indicates his status.

"A request from Madame Élisabeth, sister to His Majesty King Louis the Sixteenth."

I gasp, and Madame Sainte-Amaranthe is already on her feet. I break the seal and begin to read. "An invitation. An invitation to instruct Madame Élisabeth in the art of wax modeling for twenty livres a day!" That is more than the Salon takes in.

Immediately, Curtius is at my side. "When?" he asks.

"Beginning the second of April!" I can hardly believe my luck. An invitation from the royal family *and* witnesses to spread the news that I shall be going to Versailles! I could not have planned it better if I had paid Yachin to shout the news in the streets. Think of all the figures I'll be able to make! A new model of the Princesse de Lamballe. And certainly one of the king's sister, who has never been done. I pass around the letter.

"We will send our answer shortly," Curtius says and tips the man handsomely, as well he should. I may see that man again in the halls of Versailles.

My mother has returned with a tray of warm drinks. When she hears the news, she lowers it onto my worktable and sinks into a chair. "Such a tremendous honor," she says in German. "But . . . what of the scandals?"

Only my uncle and I can understand, but we both look instinctively toward Robespierre.

"It is something to consider," Curtius replies, then asks Robespierre in French, "What would you do?"

"What does it matter what *he* would do?" Madame Sainte-Amaranthe exclaims. "It is an invitation from Madame Élisabeth herself, signed by the king."

Robespierre stiffens at the rebuke. "I would turn it down," he says at once.

"An offer from Versailles?" Émilie asks. "That is insane."

A flush creeps up Robespierre's neck.

"I would not be going for the queen," I say quickly. "It is the king's *sister.*"

"And Marie can tell us the mood of the palace," Curtius placates Robespierre. "When you and Camille are made deputies, you will be glad to have someone who knows Versailles."

"You are to be a deputy?" Émilie asks.

"Only if I am elected," Robespierre replies, "by a fair and undisputed vote."

"Why shouldn't it be fair?" Émilie inquires.

"Because very little is fair in this country of ours. Which is what the Third Estate has every intention of changing come the fifth of May!" He raises his hat. "I came to tell you that I am giving a speech at the

Palais-Royal at noon. But I can see that you are busy. Enjoy the rest of your morning."

When Robespierre is well gone, Émilie wrinkles her nose. "An unpleasant man."

THAT EVENING, WHEN the wax mold is cooling and I am sweeping the steps of the Salon, I see Henri leaning against a lamppost. His arms are crossed over his chest, and his dark hair has been pulled back with a leather band. He looks as though he has been waiting for me, and immediately my pulse quickens, despite the fact that I see him daily. "How long have you been standing there?" I ask.

He smiles. "Since you first began humming Gluck."

"Was it in tune?"

"Not particularly."

"I took singing lessons, you know."

"From whom? Astley and Sons?" Philip Astley runs a circus of prancing horses and performing bears. "I hear an invitation has arrived."

"This will be the making of us."

"Versailles is not . . ." Henri looks troubled. "They are ruthless there. The ladies will never permit you to get close to the queen. There are rules for everything. Sitting, standing, eating, sleeping. You are used to freedom. You are used to coming and going as you please. The women of the court won't abide this."

"Then I will adapt. But everyone in Paris will know of our exhibition. Everyone in France."

Chapter 7

March 28, 1789

It was a masterpiece of etiquette. Everything was regulated.

—Madame Campan,
first lady-in-waiting to Marie Antoinette

My brothers have come from Versailles to help me prepare. Since the news arrived nearly two months ago, it seems that all I have done is get ready. There have been fittings in a dozen different shops to be sure that I am properly attired, and lessons with a master of dance who has taught me the curtsies for court. I will be joining a palace of ten thousand people, nine hundred of them nobles, and my presence must be a good reflection on my brothers, who all guard the king.

This is the first time in nearly three months that Edmund, Johann, and Wolfgang have come home, and they are dressed in the splendid uniform of the Swiss Guard: red pantaloons, white stockings, and a hat in the style of Henry IV, with three magnificent feathers. Edmund, who never smiles, is thirty-five. Johann, who wishes to be at home with his wife and son, is thirty-three. And Wolfgang, who would sneak off with my allowance as a child to go gambling, is twenty-nine. Because we are the closest in age, I have the most affection for him. We have gathered around the table in the salon, and while my mother rushes back and forth from the kitchen, Johann, my most generous brother, is complimenting my figure of the dauphin.

"There couldn't be a better likeness," he says with an easy smile. He has the round cheeks of a painted cherub. "Did you see it, Edmund?"

My eldest brother glares across the table. "It was next to the vulgar display of the queen dressed for her boudoir."

"Then you approve," I say. I can never keep from needling him.

"The queen saw the tableau," Wolfgang reminds him. "She didn't *disapprove.*"

"Was she wearing the same shift?" Edmund demands. He knows how exhibitions work, that as soon as the queen was gone, we changed her modest gown to something with more appeal to the commoners. "This is how rumors start," he accuses.

"We've done nothing but change her shift," I argue, though I know that if we were being fair to the queen, we would not portray her so. But we have shown nothing that isn't already in a hundred different *libelles,* obscene pamphlets available in every café along the Palais-Royal. They charge her with every kind of indecency, from having an affair with the Comte d'Artois, the king's handsome brother, to lesbian orgies with the Princesse de Lamballe.

Edmund shakes his head. His face is leaner than I remember, and his arms are corded with muscle. "Every image of the queen makes a political statement, and nothing speaks as loudly as her dress. Your models are the only access commoners have to the queen. And what about those who can't read or write? This Salon is their only news. And this news is telling them that the queen prepares for her bed like some woman at the Palais-Royal. It is immodest and in poor taste. Better your exhibition take in fewer sous—"

"And shut down?" Wolfgang exclaims. "This is not the time to be taking in *less* money—there was a line outside the bakery this morning."

"There is a line every morning," I amend.

All three of my brothers look shocked.

"It has been this way for several months," Curtius tells them. "The lines begin at two in the morning, and when the baker opens the doors, only the first fifty people come away with bread. And it has doubled in price. Haven't you heard about this in Versailles?"

"The king has a country to administer," Edmund replies. "He does not make it his business to know about the bakery lines in Paris."

"It isn't just Paris," I tell him. "It's likely the whole of France."

"What about the streetlights?" Wolfgang asks. "This morning, most on the Palais-Royal and the Boulevard du Temple were out. How long has it been since they were refilled?"

Curtius and I exchange looks, trying to remember. "At least three months," I answer. The city lacks funds to buy the oil. "All of the theaters and cafés, even the Opéra, must close when the sun is set, else their patrons risk collision or robbery on the roads."

"I would not mention this in the palace," Edmund says. It is not a suggestion, but a command. "These things are not spoken of to Their Majesties."

"That goes for Madame Élisabeth as well?" I ask. People are starving, bread is scarce, and Their Majesties don't know? It is a crime, what the advisers to the king are allowing.

"To *anyone* in the royal family. If you mention it, you will bring disgrace upon us, and you will bring disgrace upon the Salon de Cire. Nothing you say remains secret in Versailles. The royal family is never left alone. There is always someone listening—*always.*"

I look across the table at Wolfgang, who does not contradict him.

"When the queen begins her toilette in the morning," Edmund continues, "there are separate attendants for her hair, her powder, her dress. When she bathes at night, it is in a long flannel gown in front of her women. When she prepares for bed during her *coucher,* the Mistress of the Robes, the *dames d'honneur,* the Superintendent of the Queen's Household—they are all present."

"How unbearable." To be surrounded by people all day. When is there time to be alone with your thoughts?

"It is her job," Johann says. "From the moment she arrived from Austria, she was trained in these rules of etiquette."

"Those are the rules of court," Edmund stresses. "That is what separates Their Majesties from everyone else."

Suddenly, I am nervous. It is one thing to model and display the royal family, but to have to live their life, that is something else. "I will be discreet," I promise.

"You must understand the queen's *lever,*" Johann says. "There are different women to help her dress. The *première femme* must hand the queen's chemise to the *dame d'honneur,* who then takes off her glove in order to hand the chemise to the queen. However, if a Princesse of the Blood should arrive in the middle, it must all be started over again so that the princesse can be the one to present the queen with her chemise."

"But that is not all," Wolfgang says quickly. "The queen is not allowed to reach for anything herself. If she wants water, it must be fetched by the *dame d'honneur.*"

"And if the *dame d'honneur* isn't present?" I ask.

"Then she goes thirsty."

Ludicrous! "And this happens every day?"

My brothers exchange looks. "Less frequently now that Her Majesty spends her time at the Trianon," Johann replies.

The king gifted Marie Antoinette with the Petit Trianon as a private residence. It is a quarter league from Versailles, and though I have never seen it, I am told that it is the most charming château in Paris, surrounded by orange trees and an English garden. The queen has turned it into her private palace, with its own special livery of silver and scarlet. "Who can blame her?" I say. "Who wouldn't want time for themselves?"

"She has a responsibility to the court," Edmund replies.

"To live like a wax model?" my mother asks, surprising everyone. None of us saw her sit down. "To be dressed and redressed like a doll?"

"She belongs to the people," Edmund says stiffly. "The king rules by God's will, and the queen reflects his glory. Whether or not she likes the rules, she must abide by them."

"But who made them?" Wolfgang challenges. "Not God. *Man.* Courtiers," he adds, "who want to know that their place in the royal hierarchy is assured. What should it matter who hands the queen her underwear so long as she's wearing some?"

My mother smiles, but Edmund has gone red in the face.

"Leave it for another time," Curtius suggests, and Johann puts a restraining hand on Edmund's shoulder. "He only says it to rile you up. Like Marie."

Wolfgang grins at me, and I suppress a laugh, since I know it will simply make Edmund more enraged and upset my mother. We see my brothers rarely enough. It would be foolish to spend what little time we have with them arguing over whether the queen deserves privacy.

There is no more talk of Versailles as we eat. My mother has prepared sauerkraut and sausages, potatoes, and warm Viennese bread. For dessert, I help her serve Bavarian crème we purchased in the Palais-Royal. There are no fruits to accompany it, since there are none to be had for any amount of money, but it is delicious. By the time the sun has set, even Edmund has relaxed.

"So when will you bring your son to see his grandmother?" my mother implores Johann.

"Next month," he promises.

My mother sighs. "And how will he know me if I see him only for Christmas and Easter?"

"I tell him stories all the time."

"Pffff." She waves her hand through the air. "It is not the same."

"We will try to come in summer."

I see that my mother is already making plans in her head: where Isabel and Paschal will stay, what she will cook, and how she will entertain her four-year-old grandson.

The church bell of Saint-Merri sounds, and Wolfgang looks out the window. "It's a shame we can't stay longer."

"But we'll see each other soon, at Versailles," I say.

Wolfgang looks uncertain. "We eat in the Grand Commune with the courtiers. Madame Élisabeth may want to you to dine in Montreuil, the little house the king gave her. It's at the entrance to Versailles. But—"

"It might as well be in another country," Johann finishes. "She is very religious, Marie. If she were not the king's sister, she would have entered a convent years ago."

"But her aunt is a Carmelite nun," I say. "Certainly she could enter a convent, if she wished."

"She does. But the king needs her," Johann says bluntly.

I look at Edmund, and when he doesn't protest, I realize what Johann is saying. "So she's given up her life for her brother."

"I wouldn't phrase it like that," Johann says, uncomfortably. "She is happy to devote her life to him. But she is very religious," he repeats.

"She dines at four and retires when the sun is set," Wolfgang clarifies. "She almost never goes to the palace. So it's unlikely we will see much of each other."

"It doesn't matter, Marie," Curtius says reassuringly. "Montreuil, Versailles, you are working for the king."

"The king's *nunlike* sister," I say with disappointment. I had imagined seeing the king riding out to the hunt and the queen in her latest coiffures. "How will this serve us?"

"She is a good woman," Edmund says sternly. "It may not serve the Salon de Cire. But you will be serving her, and that should be enough."

My brothers rise to leave, and when I embrace Wolfgang farewell he whispers in my ear, "If we don't see each other, write to me. You can trust Madame Élisabeth's lady-in-waiting, the Marquise de Bombelles, to deliver a message."

"I will," I promise. There must be some advantage to this, I think. There has to be!

I hug Johann fiercely, but I do not embrace Edmund. Instead, we stand across from each other as if oceans separate us. It has always been this way. "A safe journey," I tell him.

He nods formally. "And you." As my mother and Curtius embrace the others, Edmund speaks quietly to me. "It would do the Salon great credit if you were to clothe the queen in something modest."

"It is business, Edmund! It doesn't mean anything."

"It means *everything.* I am not mistaken. I have told Curtius many times. He doesn't care. I am hoping you have more sense."

As we watch the carriage roll away, bound for the Palace of Versailles, we hear Wolfgang's and Johann's cheerful voices carried on the night air. But I am silently arguing with my eldest brother. *There are images of the queen in every corner of Paris. What separates ours from all other images is the illusion of flesh. The tantalizing curve of the queen's neck, the softness of her hand, the painted toenails peeking out from beneath her lacy shift. The people want to see this. We are simply giving them what they want. Where is the harm in that?*

Chapter 8

April 2, 1789

The court lost no time in going à la mode. Every woman became a lesbian and a whore.

—Anonymous *libelliste*

Everyone has come to see me off, from our tailor and Yachin to the chandler down the street. As I make my farewells to all these people, I remember why this is so important. I may be spending four days of my week in Montreuil, but my absence will only reinforce to the public that our models are worthy of the royal family's notice. A freshly painted sign in the window now reads, NEW MODELS COMING SOON FROM MADEMOISELLE GROSHOLTZ, PERSONAL TUTOR AT VERSAILLES. I read it again, simply because it doesn't seem real.

"Will you bring something back for me from the palace?" Yachin asks.

I laugh. "Like what?"

"How about playing cards?"

"What? Shall I steal a deck from the queen?"

"Okay, a pair of dice."

"And how am I supposed to come across dice?" When his eagerness flags, I promise him, "I'll see what I can do."

My mother is looking increasingly worried. She thinks I won't feed myself in Versailles. While everyone is chatting pleasantly, she takes me to one side. "Please, just remember to eat. No model is so important that you should skip dinner."

"I will eat like a princesse," I swear. "Or at least, the tutor of one." But she doesn't believe me. "Look at Johann," I tell her. "Going to Versailles hasn't done him any harm."

"He is not you," she says in German. "He does not become so busy that he forgets to eat."

This is true. I doubt Johann has ever forgotten a meal. Whereas being a guard has kept Edmund fit, Johann has clearly indulged in the rich foods provided in the Grand Commune. He has the round, fat face of a German now, which pleases my mother.

"I will promise to eat," I tell her, "if you promise to watch Curtius. Don't let him give away tickets for free. If it's the Empress of Russia herself, she pays."

My mother heaves an exasperated sigh. "I will do what I can."

"Forbid him from giving anything away." I take her hands. "This is a business."

She kisses my cheek. *"Viel Glück,"* she says warmly. "Give your brothers my love."

I make the rest of my personal good-byes. I hug Curtius, then tell Henri that I will miss his rational talk of politics and science. And to Yachin I say, "I want to know if drunken theatergoers are still pissing in the urns." Our new plants have become favorite places for uncouth men to relieve themselves.

"I'll send a message," he swears. He has been given a good education at his temple. Unlike many children, he can read and write. Then he adds, "If you find perfume, I would be happy to have that as well."

"Have some manners," Henri chastens, but the boy only grins.

I make my way through the crowd to the waiting *berline.* The luggage has been tied to the roof by the driver, and Curtius helps me into the coach. Already I feel different. Like a woman of some consequence. Curtius presses his lips to my hand, and I can see in his eyes that he is proud, which is important to me. I want him to know that I shall never disappoint him.

"Remember the honors," he says, recalling the lessons I've had these two months. What he is truly saying is to mind myself at court.

"I will. If you finish the model of Émilie Sainte-Amaranthe, and make a second one for the Salon. You will, won't you?"

"There is nothing to worry about, Marie." As the carriage rolls away, he calls, *"Auf Wiedersehen!"*

I look through the window and study the faces—most happy, some resentful—crowding the steps of the Salon de Cire. Then I sit back against the cushions of the expensive *berline* and wonder how much it cost my uncle to hire. It is a coach for four, and I am the only one inside. But it is for the greater good of the Salon, I remind myself. I am like a farmer who feeds his cow the best hay for the time when it will make his own dinner. I will not disgrace my brothers at Montreuil. And however secluded Madame Élisabeth may be, I will find a way of using this position to our advantage.

I stare out the window at the lines outside every bakery. Countless shops, which once teemed with women in lace-trimmed bonnets, have gone out of business. Dirty *sans-culottes*—men who cannot afford knee-length trousers with stockings—sit on the steps of these empty shops and roll dice. Their long pants hang around their ankles, unhemmed and trailing in the dirt. My mother believes this is God's work. That last summer's driving rain and hailstones destroyed France's crops because of God's sharp disapproval. But of what? Our Austrian queen? What has she done that a dozen mistresses have not? Our king? He pursues his hobbies of lock making and building the way previous kings bought horses and bedded women. No, I cannot agree with my mother's reasoning. Nature has done this, and Nature will repair it. Already there are leaves on the trees.

By the time we reach the golden gates of Montreuil in the southeast of Versailles, I have put the hardships of Paris out of mind. I am here! It is real, and before me stretch the vast, manicured lawns of Princesse

Élisabeth's château. The king's liveried guards stand at the gates. They are dressed in blue, with white silk stockings and silver lace at their cuffs. Their hair is powdered and worn in tails tied back with silver buckles. The carriage rolls abruptly to a stop.

"She is to be driven up to the porch," I hear the guard say.

As the gates are thrown open and the *berline* passes through, I smooth the material of my blue gown with my palms. When the château comes into view, I am surprised. It is more rustic than majestic: a two-storied home nestled in the trees and painted a becoming hue of pink. The shutters have all been thrown open, and flowers spill from boxes on every window. I expected to be greeted by one of the *dames du palais,* but it is Madame Élisabeth herself who is standing beneath the colonnaded porch. She is dressed in a chestnut-colored gown of rich satin, and her thick blond hair is heavily powdered. She is twenty-five to the queen's thirty-three, and in the fresh spring light, this difference is significant. I had not noticed it at the Salon, but as I descend from the carriage and approach the steps, I am surprised by how young Madame Élisabeth looks. The plumpness in her cheeks is rather becoming, and they are red without the aid of any rouge. Immediately, I descend into the curtsy I have practiced and wait for Madame to speak.

"Welcome to Versailles, Mademoiselle Grosholtz. Was it a pleasant ride?"

"Very pleasant, Madame." Behind me, half a dozen servants are taking my baskets from the top of the *berline* and whisking them inside. "The wildflowers are bursting with color," I tell her. "The countryside looks like an artist's palette."

"Do you paint then, Mademoiselle Grosholtz?"

"Please, just Marie," I say humbly. "Yes. It is a necessary skill for wax modeling."

"Then we have something in common already." She turns and motions to a woman who has appeared in the doorway. "Marie, please meet the Marquise de Bombelles."

The marquise is extraordinarily tall, and it is unfortunate that she has chosen to wear one of the queen's fashionable *poufs.* On such a long face, it would have been better if she had simply powdered her own hair. I cannot determine how old she is. I could believe any number of ages, since she has not taken care to stay out of the sun, and wrinkles line her forehead and mouth. "A pleasure to meet you, Mademoiselle Grosholtz."

"Please, it is just Marie," I repeat and make a small curtsy.

She smiles thinly, and I wonder if I have done right. "I hear you have come to tutor our Élisabeth in wax modeling. She tells me you have an extraordinary gift."

"Then Madame Élisabeth gives me too much credit," I say. "I've simply come to teach her what little I know."

"Such humility! I have seen Marie's wax exhibition," Madame Élisabeth replies, "and I promise you, I do not give her too much credit." She links arms with the marquise; they make an odd pair: one blond and short, the other dark and tall. "Shall we show her Montreuil?"

I am given a tour of the grounds, beginning with the cheerful orangerie, painted white and gold as if to remind people of its purpose. The workers bow to us as we pass, and a gardener hurries to open the heavy white doors. "Madame," he says reverently.

Madame Élisabeth smiles. "Thank you, Antoine."

She knows his name, and I wonder if she is as familiar with everyone in Montreuil.

"Ah." There is the warm, spring scent of orange blossoms in the air, and Madame Élisabeth inhales deeply. "It will be a good harvest this year," she tells Antoine.

"Without doubt. Madame has a way with plants."

As we step inside, I can see that the orangerie is for more than growing citrus. Besides the orange trees, whose shiny leaves and white blossoms catch the light of the sun, there are roses in every color. Jasmine and wisteria climb from ceramic pots to cover the ground. It is a riot of color and fragrances.

"This is de Bombelles's favorite tree," Madame Élisabeth says. "She planted it last year, and look how it's grown."

It is tall and thin, like its owner. I am guessing from its leaves that it will produce limes. "These must take a great deal of time and care," I say.

The Marquise de Bombelles nods seriously. "We come here every morning to check on our fruits. This is a working farm." We exit the orangerie and enter the dairy. "Madame Élisabeth helps to milk the cows and plants the crops herself."

I turn to the king's sister to see if this is true. I cannot imagine a princesse of France wishing to dirty her hands with such things.

"We do it for the villagers," Madame Élisabeth explains. "They are in great want. The milk from this dairy can feed two hundred families every month. And the fruit keeps the local children healthy."

I am surprised. "And they know this generosity comes from you?"

She looks puzzled. "Yes. I distribute the food myself."

Yet the vicious *libellistes* would have the world believe that the king's family shuts itself away in velvet rooms. During all of his time in our salon, I have never once heard the Duc mention the princesse's generosity. I think of his self-satisfied grin when Robespierre and Camille rage against the monarchy, and how he sits back and swirls his brandy when Marat asks him what should be done about our king.

We step inside the sprawling château of Montreuil. Everywhere, there is religious art. Images of Christ and his virgin mother, and of the saints in their suffering. If not for the cheerful colors on the wall and the large bouquets at every table, it might be the interior of a convent.

"This is to be your room," Madame Élisabeth says, showing me a first-floor chamber that is many times the size of mine at home. It is apple green with rich furnishings, and the windows face the handsome orangerie. I am entranced, listening to the birdsong and smelling the earthy fragrance.

"It's enchanting, isn't it?" Madame Élisabeth asks. She crosses the room and opens a pair of doors on the far side. "And this shall be our workshop," she says.

We step inside, and the Marquise de Bombelles watches my expression. Windows stretch from ceiling to floor, letting in an abundance of natural light. A dozen cabinets have been arranged along the far wall, and each has been carefully labeled: paints, canvases, wax, plaster, tools, brushes. A specially designed counter in the middle of the room stands prepared for whatever takes Madame's fancy. Immediately, I am imagining ways in which we can improve our workshop at home.

"What do you think?" Madame Élisabeth asks with sincerity. "Will it do?"

It is any artist's dream. If it were Henri asking, or Curtius, I'd laugh. Instead, I school my features into an expression of great earnestness. "Yes, Madame, I think it will do nicely."

She claps her hands. "Then we will begin tomorrow. Ten o'clock." She looks at the Marquise de Bombelles. "Shall we give her the tour of Versailles?"

I am holding my breath, practically willing *yes* into the Marquise de Bombelles's head. "It is already noon," she says hesitantly, studying the clock. "If we take our dinner later than four, we will not be on time for vespers."

I feel my heart sink.

"What if it's just a quick drive?" Madame Élisabeth asks, though of course she needs no one's approval.

I can see that the Marquise de Bombelles is caught between pleasing the princesse and routine. Life in Montreuil is well scheduled, and now I have come and interrupted it all.

"Oh, let's go!" Madame Élisabeth decides. "We haven't been to the palace in days. How often am I able to show another artist the splendor of Versailles?"

I try not to look too triumphant.

THE GLASS *berline* that takes us to the palace is lined in velvet. Its rich silk cushions are embroidered with gold, and the horses are as richly dressed as the king's Swiss Guards, with white plumes that bob and sway in the breeze. I wish my mother could see me, sitting across from

Madame Élisabeth and the Marquise de Bombelles as if I had been born and bred to court. We are chatting about the royal family's paintings, and the art they have collected in Versailles since Louis XIV made this his home. I now realize how small our collection of paintings appeared to him, like visiting a rustic cottage when all you've known are châteaux.

I have not seen the palace in over a decade. I was sixteen when Curtius took me to sketch the Grand Couvert for a tableau. Although I can remember everything about the queen—down to the color of the ribbon in her hair—I recall very little about the work of the architect Louis Le Vau and the landscape architect André Le Nôtre except that it was magnificent. Now, as the carriage rounds the bend, the Palace of Versailles comes into view, and I am overwhelmed.

Perhaps I gasp, because Madame Élisabeth says, "It's like a fairy-tale palace, isn't it?"

"Yes," I breathe. At one time, when Louis XIII had determined to build his hunting lodge on this spot, the ground was marshy and unsuitable for living. But now! Now our Bourbon kings have tamed the wild, replacing the wetland with garden terraces and perfumed groves. Down Grand Avenue, bronze nymphets rise from the polished marble of a sprawling fountain. Like a giant mirror, the still waters reflect the entire length of the château. There could never be a more beautiful palace in all the world. No wonder the Duc d'Orléans covets his cousin's crown.

The Swiss Guards recognize the princesse's carriage, and we are allowed to pass directly into the Marble Courtyard. As we alight from the coach, courtiers are already crowding the upper windows of the palace, pointing and whispering behind their hands. I look down at my skirts, then at my shoes, to be certain I haven't covered them in mud. What are they staring at? I look at the Marquise de Bombelles, who says archly, "Welcome to Versailles."

"Ignore them," Madame Élisabeth suggests.

"Are they staring at me?"

"Of course. You're with us," the marquise says as we walk toward the palace. "They want to know who you are and if you're someone they should be plotting against."

"They are simply ambitious," Madame Élisabeth says with far more kindness than my brothers would have. "They all want grander and better privileges."

"Yes," the marquise adds bitterly, "such as the right to the candles."

To light them? To snuff them out?

"Every evening," she explains, "all of the candles in the palace are replaced."

"Even if they're unused?" I ask.

"That is the tradition," Madame Élisabeth says gently.

The marquise looks at me, and I know at once she disagrees with this practice. "Only a few courtiers are allowed to collect them," she says. "And the ones who do may make fifty thousand livres a year at the market."

My God. That is ten times what we collect at the Salon de Cire, even in our best years. That is more than most noble families take in anywhere in France. No wonder the men and women here are scratching at each other's eyes.

"And the clothes," the marquise says, as we approach the doors. "Nothing the queen wears may ever be worn twice. So who is to get those taffeta dresses and silk riding habits? She must have five new pairs of shoes every week. If she doesn't want them . . ."

"The *dames* order them anyway," Madame Élisabeth finishes. "There is certainly waste."

"Which is exactly how the courtiers want it!" the Marquise de Bombelles exclaims, suddenly passionate. "They are wolves, prowling around the henhouse. And when the hens are gone, they will blame the farmer that there were not enough hens and eat him, too!"

"So I should not expect a warm reception," I say, trying to make light of it.

Madame Élisabeth puts her gloved hand on my arm. "It's not anything to worry about, Marie. That is the true gift of Montreuil. We can stroll these grounds, then escape to tranquillity whenever we wish." We have reached the château, and Madame Élisabeth says proudly, "My brother's palace."

A pair of guards open the doors, bowing as we enter. I am inside the Palace of Versailles, being led through the halls by the sister of the king. I take in everything. The wide murals, the gold-framed paintings, the Savonnerie carpets and rich velvet drapes. I must memorize the magnificent features of Versailles the way I memorize a person's face. When I return to the Salon de Cire, we will re-create a different room each month!

Madame Élisabeth narrates as we walk, ignoring the bows of courtiers who stop talking as we pass to look longingly in our direction. They are like beggars, but there are no scraps to be had from her. It is not at all like I remember. I didn't realize how many people were allowed to crowd these halls. Some of them are courtiers, but many, I can tell, are hangers-on. Others wear clothes that are ill-worn, and I am certain they have not bathed in many months. Their scent lingers heavily in the air, and even the violet powder and orange blossom pomade used by the courtiers cannot disguise it. They are looking for a handout, much like everyone else. How do my brothers keep the royal family safe when anyone may enter the grounds? I am shocked to see uncivilized men relieving themselves in the vases. I see feral cats and stray dogs marking territory and making deposits. Madame Élisabeth and the marquise fan themselves for air, and I do the same.

I am shown salons dedicated to the Greek gods Hercules and Mercury. Because I am an artist, like the female painter Vigée-Lebrun, who has painted many images of the queen, I am shown inside chambers that would otherwise be closed to me. Everywhere, there is art and references to the greater days of mankind, when men built temples of marble so high they kissed the brow of heaven. I commit it all to memory, from the Salon of Apollo, which served as the throne room for the Sun King himself, to the white-and-gold baroque chapel where Louis XVI wed our queen. Then I am taken to the Hall of Mirrors, and everything that has come before is suddenly erased in the face of such beauty. I stop walking.

"It is my favorite as well," the princesse confides. She passes a triumphant look to the marquise.

The entire length of one side of the hall is lined with mirrors, seventeen mirrors so large that at night the light of the chandeliers must be reflected indefinitely. I can imagine the polished parquet floors gleaming beneath the candlelight like a lake. Like the wide sea of courtiers preening and posing in front of the mirrors, I am unable to keep from stealing a quick glance. I want to know what it looks like to be promenading through the palace with the king's sister on one side and a marquise on the other. The rich fabrics of our gowns are reflected back to us in the glass. Everyone is watching, and the sharp clicks of courtier heels suddenly fall silent as they stop to bow before the princesse. I imagine the tableau I could create of this scene: *The Princesse on Her Promenade!*

But the hall is teeming with a hundred possibilities. There is *The Courtier in White,* a man dressed entirely in one color, from his silk stockings to the plumes in his hat. And *The Man with Diamond Buckles,* whose shoes reflect dazzlingly in the glass. I want to know these men's names. I want to study their faces and re-create them in the privacy of my workshop at home. Imagine the fortune we could bring in if we could reconstruct the Hall of Mirrors inside our exhibition! But the high, frescoed ceiling alone would take a lifetime to imitate, even if we hired the best painters from the Palais-Royal. Still, it's a thought I will tuck away. If Henri can create the illusion of magic, why can't we create the illusion of a palace?

In front of everyone, Madame Élisabeth touches my arm and guides me toward a view of the gardens. The hall also possesses seventeen arched windows opposite its seventeen mirrors. Symmetry truly is the essence of beauty, not only in architecture but also in people. My most beautiful subjects have faces that are perfectly symmetrical. You can give me a group of people's measurements, and without seeing them I can predict which man is the most handsome and which woman the most attractive. I told this once to Henri. When he refused to believe me, I asked him to use my caliper to take the measurements of two friends. He was to choose one of exceptional beauty, and one that Nature had overlooked. I forbade him from telling me which was which, and when I chose correctly, Henri was forced to admit that measurements never lie. I do not have a symmetrical face.

Dozens of women are walking the garden paths outside, and Madame Élisabeth says, "Those are the queen's *dames du palais.*"

"Unfortunately," the marquise breaks in, "we don't have time to wander outside today."

I turn to Madame Élisabeth, to see if the princesse might overrule her, but this time she nods. "Yes, we would not want to be late for vespers."

I look back at the women laughing intimately behind their wide, jeweled fans. What's the point of being at Versailles if my only view will be the orangerie outside of Montreuil? Madame Élisabeth smiles at me, and immediately I feel guilty for thinking this.

"Did you enjoy your tour?" she asks.

"There could not be a more splendid palace anywhere in existence."

"Except in the kingdom of heaven." Madame Élisabeth touches the cross at her neck. "Do you ever imagine what it will be like there?"

"I'm afraid my thoughts are more of this earth," I admit.

"I imagine it always. The angels, the music, the gilded halls and crystal staircases . . ."

As we leave, each door is opened for us by a servant in blue and white silks. I wonder why the princesse would wish for heaven with all of this at her disposal. But perhaps there will be things mortals cannot imagine. Perhaps in heaven, I think rebelliously, the halls will not stink of urine.

I bring my square handkerchief to my nose again and see that Madame Élisabeth and the marquise have done the same. For all the beauty of the château, a stench has followed us throughout the halls, and here it is the worst. It is terrible, really. If I were better acquainted with Madame Élisabeth, I would ask why the king doesn't insist that his private residence be private.

We leave the palace and ride back to Montreuil, arriving in time for vespers. Because Madame Élisabeth is sister to the king, she has been granted the privilege of her own private chapel. As the bell tolls four, everyone working in the small château gathers inside. There are at least two dozen of us, but I am the only one directed to the same pew as Madame Élisabeth. It is the place of honor for the newest guest, and I do not expect I will be seated here tomorrow. But today, I am at the side of Madame, praying with the greatest woman in the land after the queen herself.

While the priest sings *Deus in adjutorium meum intende,* I think of the Cathedral of Notre-Dame. It is a few blocks from our Salon on the Boulevard du Temple, and certainly France's greatest house of God. Everyone of means attends Mass there on Sunday, and it is a place I can study the nobility for as long as I please. I have modeled duchesses based on what I've seen of them in Notre-Dame. I've had men exclaim in utter astonishment at how well I've captured them in wax and ask how it was possible for a likeness to be so close when the subject had never done a sitting with me.

Unfortunately, there is no one to be seen in here. The chapel is small, and the pews are crowded with farmworkers and servants from the château. It is of no use to the Salon. I look over to study the princesse's face while the rest of the chapel is deep in prayer and am surprised to see that she is staring at me.

"You do not attend vespers at home?" she whispers.

I flush. "No. Only Sunday's Mass."

She nods gently. "God appreciates seeing His flock whenever they come in, even if it's only once a week. Whenever I cannot steady my mind," she adds, "I think of the people of France, suffering without blankets in the bitter cold and tucking in their children at night without food. Perhaps, if you find that your mind is restless, you can pray for our people."

I bow my head, humbled by the princesse's request. There is no one in France with such a kind heart, and certainly her brother cannot be so different. The Duc d'Orléans must be a terrible man to whisper scandal about these people.

Chapter 9

April 3, 1789

Man's natural character is to imitate: that of the sensitive man is to resemble as closely as possible the person whom he loves. It is only by imitating the vices of others that I have earned my misfortunes.

—Marquis de Sade

There are molten wax and rows of calipers, plaster molds, and oil paints in small glass jars. Someone has laid out every necessity so that the princesse will not have to do it herself. It is our first day in the palace workshop, and as I watch Madame Élisabeth tie the Marquise de Bombelles's apron into a bow, it is so reminiscent of home that immediately I am at ease. Madame Élisabeth turns to me, and I see that blond curls have escaped from her bonnet. They put me in mind of Charles Perrault's story "Little Red Riding Hood."

"We will start with something simple," I tell her. The longer I stay in Montreuil, the more molds I will be able to take back to the Salon. So first it will be fruit. When she has mastered that, we shall go on to larger objects. Then, after several months, we will begin faces. I imagine she will want to model her brother and possibly her niece, Madame Royale. If I am very lucky, we shall model them live. "Fruit," I say, "is very easy to create."

"Yes," Madame Élisabeth agrees. "We have done fruit. And flowers in vases."

I am shocked. "Madame knows the basics of wax modeling?"

"Oh yes," the marquise says. "She is very good at flowers. But it is faces and bodies she wishes to do."

"Then you know about calipers and plaster molds?"

"Certainly," Madame Élisabeth replies. Then she adds, "We would not have called upon someone of such talent to waste time with fruit."

Then perhaps I will have a new figure for the Salon before the month is out! "Then we will proceed to sculpting faces in clay," I reply. "Whose face does Madame wish to begin with?" *The king*, I wish her to say; *the king*. There are hardly any angles on his face. Just round, wide planes as easy to mold as an apple.

The princesse turns to the marquise. "Angélique, what do you think?"

"Perhaps the face of our Lord Jesus Christ?"

I am sure my heart stops in my chest.

"I was thinking Saint Cecilia," the princesse admits. "But it is far more appropriate to begin with our Lord. We can do Cecilia next."

I am forced to appear jolly as a servant fetches a portrait of Christ, but this is a catastrophe. People pay to see princesses and kings, not the faces of saints! Those can be seen in any church in France. As we wait, the princesse elaborates on which saints she would like to model in the future: Saint Cyprian, who was beheaded with a sword. And Saint Sebastian, who was stoned to death. Plus a tableau of Saint Potamiaena, an Alexandrian slave boiled alive after refusing the advances of her licentious master. It is all very gruesome. Even worse, I think, than our Cavern of Great Thieves. The princesse would like to take her finished models to the Churches of Saint-Geneviève and Saint-Sulpice in Paris. If this is all we are to do, attend Mass and model saints, I must find a way to salvage my time here. Perhaps we can do a different kind of tableau, like *The Saints and Their Slaughter.* I will have to ask Curtius what he thinks.

~

When the carriage returns me to the Boulevard du Temple, I am shocked by how dull the buildings appear. Many are in desperate need of paint, and none have the cheerful look of Madame Élisabeth's golden orangerie. I have been gone for only four days, but already I have become accustomed to the grandeur of Montreuil.

As the driver stops in front of the Salon de Cire, Yachin puts down his sign. The *kippah* he is wearing is black today, the same color as his curls. When he first came to us I asked him why he wore the little hat, and he told me that it was a tradition among the Jews, a sign of respect for God. It has not been easy for Yachin's family to be foreigners in this country. Only two years ago our king overturned Louis XIV's law that forbade the exercise of any religion outside the Catholic faith. But this Edict of Tolerance has not granted Jews the right to citizenship. Perhaps the Estates-General will change this as well.

As I open the door, Yachin offers me his hand. "You're back already?" he exclaims when I step out.

"I am a tutor from Thursday to Sunday. So tell me," I say quickly, before my mother and Curtius can come outside. They will have heard the horses and carriage even from the workshop in the back of the house. "How was business?"

"There were thirty-five people yesterday. At *least*."

Thirty-five times twelve sous is four hundred and twenty. That's good. Very good. "And drunks pissing in our urns?"

"None," he promises. "So did you bring me something? Did you see the queen? What about the king? Is the château as big as it is in paintings?"

"No, no, no, and yes," I reply. My mother and Curtius come out, dressed in work clothes. My mother embraces me, then pulls back to look at my face. In four days, I am certain I have not changed, but she shakes her head. "Already you are getting thin."

"I eat every meal."

"I don't care!" She raises a finger. "I can see from your face." She points to my cheekbones, which have always been high, then to my collarbone above the lace fichu.

"Let her be." Curtius smiles. He pays the driver, then embraces me warmly. "You look the same to me."

Inside, I search the rooms for any sign of change. But everything is the same. My mother and Curtius follow me into the workshop so I can inspect a pair of headless bodies dressed in muslin gowns. Curtius has completed the two figures of Émilie Sainte-Amaranthe. One will go home with Émilie today, and the other will be placed next to her mother and our sleeping model of du Barry. I study the hands and feet, then examine the chests to be sure that the faces I began two months ago will be the same color. It is a long process to create a complete figure. It takes two weeks to perfect the clay model of any head, then another week to create the mold. Once the mold is ready, it is a week before a wax head is finished. Already then, a month has passed. By the time the hair and teeth are added and a custom body is built, two months have gone by. Today, when Émilie comes to claim her model, she will be very pleased. The head and body are a perfect match. All I need do is join the two.

"This is good," I tell Curtius. "Exceptional."

"Now let's hear about Versailles!" my mother exclaims. She hurries up the stairs, and Curtius and I follow and sit at the table. She brings us coffee and asks eagerly, "So what is it like? How does our king live? Are there hundreds of servants?"

I describe the richness of the palace to her. The marble halls, the sweeping stairs, the English gardens that extend to the horizon, though I leave out the stench of the hallways. Then I tell her about Montreuil, how the princesse keeps her own farm and the produce from her orangerie goes to the poor. "She is a kind woman. Not at all what they say in the *libelles.*"

"I knew it," my mother says passionately. "She is a woman of God."

"And your work?" Curtius asks.

"When we're not attending Mass, we're modeling the saints." I imagine I wore the same look when the princesse informed me of her intentions as my uncle wears now. "But I was thinking we could do something original. A tableau of how they died, perhaps." When I see his brows come together, I add swiftly, "We could bring in a few implements of torture. Cages, irons—"

But Curtius is shaking his head. "That is common stuff. People can see that in any church in France."

"Not a roasting pot," I say.

"It's not enough."

"Well, perhaps she will grow tired of saints," my mother offers. She seats herself next to me. "But tell us about your brothers. Did you see them?"

"No," I'm sorry to reply. "Montreuil is some distance from the palace. Madame Élisabeth only goes on special occasions."

"Perhaps you can catch a glimpse of Jacques Necker?" Curtius says. "The Minister of Finance is popular with the people, and the model we have is too old."

Necker was first to expose royal expenditures in a daring publication called *Compte Rendu au Roi.* The king's finances have always been private. Yet he is supported by the taxes of the Third Estate. Is it disloyal to wonder what we are paying for? I am not sure what to think of Necker. Or if I can convince Madame Élisabeth to go back to Versailles. "I can also sketch the Hall of Mirrors. I was thinking . . ."

"No more royal tableaux. In a year or two, perhaps, but not now."

I frown and look to my mother.

"The Duc came last night," she explains gravely.

"He is actively encouraging revolt," Curtius says. "He wants us to be a part of it."

I am shocked. "Doesn't he know that you have sons in the Guard?"

"Yes. But he wants to know if we will be ready to rise should he call upon us."

"In what way?" This is treachery. Edmund would say he should be sent to the scaffold. "What does he think to do?"

My uncle hesitates. "He thinks the revolt must begin with the people."

"Things have changed," my mother adds quietly. "Even I can see that. They've taken down the king's portrait in the Hôtel de Ville. I saw it yesterday on my way to the shops."

"They are a good family," I argue.

"It's not about good or bad," Curtius says. "It's about who has the money. And right now, that is the Duc d'Orléans. The monarchy is having to borrow money," he tells me. "They are taking out loans. It may not be prudent to keep making models of them in their silk stockings and diamond aigrettes."

And what else are they supposed to wear, I want to ask? When the queen economizes, the nobles cry out. They want the right to the candles, the silk stockings, and the clothes. They want the right to sell off whichever dresses the queen has already worn. The larger, the lacier, the more elaborate, the better. But instead, I say evenly, "I hope you did not give the Duc your assurance."

"No."

"And what was his reaction?"

Curtius takes up his pipe from a nearby table and searches for a candle. Suddenly, I realize how dark it is, despite the open windows. "Where are the candles?" we ask in unison.

"There are no more," my mother says. "I am saving the ones we have for the exhibit."

"What do you mean?" I protest. "We have the money."

My mother smiles primly. "And all the money in the world can't buy them if they're not available."

I think of the thouands of candles in Versailles and the greedy courtiers with the rights to sell them. "What about the black market?"

"I sent Yachin looking yesterday, and I will send him again tomorrow."

Yachin lives just south in the Rue Sainte-Avoye, a fifteen-minute walk. He comes to us at sunrise and leaves at sunset. I wonder how his family is faring. I must remember to ask. I know that he has sisters still too young to work and that his father makes a meager wage as a printer.

"You should see the shops," my mother continues. "Yachin stood in line for three hours. I expect we'll be buying corn on the black market soon as well."

Curtius turns up his palms, as if there's nothing to be done. "The people's deputies will make their complaints heard next month at Versailles."

"So the votes have already been counted? Did Camille—"

But my mother shakes her head. "No. He didn't win."

"So there will be no marriage after all." Poor Lucile. I think of her pretty face and trusting brown eyes. Had she given herself to a trade, there would not be this heartbreak. Money and ambition never disappoint. "And Robespierre?"

"Won easily," Curtius says.

I am not surprised. He is the kind of deputy who will represent the Third Estate well. "We should be very careful with our expenditures from this day forward," I say. "If Parisians can't afford candles, they certainly won't be able to afford wax exhibitions."

"I don't know," Curtius replies. "They are still paying to see the bust of Rousseau, who inspired so many of the Third Estate's deputies. Perhaps we should make a tableau in honor of the first meeting of the Estates-General. Or perhaps a library scene, with the busts of Rousseau and Franklin on the shelves."

Edmund wouldn't like this. "And whose library would it be?" I ask.

"How about the Duc d'Orléans?" he offers.

"The people love him," my mother remarks.

"They also love peep shows and dancing monkeys! You don't see us featuring those."

"Then the Marquis de Lafayette," my uncle says firmly. The hero of the American Revolution, the man who helped France embarrass the

British and sever their ties to their American colonies. It was Lafayette who suggested the meeting of the Estates-General. "He was elected as a deputy of the Second Estate."

"Is there a painting of Lafayette in the Académie Royale?" If so I can make a sketch, and from that a clay model, and eventually a mold.

"Even better. I shall invite him to Tuesday's salon. He is a friend of the Duc."

"And he would do this," I question, "even after you refused him help?"

"I did not refuse it. I told him that the needs of the Salon must come first."

I hold my tongue. If the Duc can persuade Lafayette to come, we can ask the marquis to a sitting. I imagine the tableau: *The Library of Lafayette.*

My mother asks, "And what of the Cavern of Great Thieves? Two men came yesterday hoping to see the Marquis de Sade."

"There is only so much that Marie can do."

My mother gives a little shrug. The kind that tells us we can do as we wish, but it will be to our detriment. "And there was another one the day before that."

My uncle looks at me. "Isn't he imprisoned in the Bastille?"

"Yes." I hesitate. It is one thing to model prisoners who are about to be hanged, another to model a madman who may someday prevail upon wealthy relatives to set him free. What would the marquis do if he should be released and see himself among the great thieves and murderers of France? "Still, I'm sure we could arrange a meeting."

"It is up to you," my mother says temptingly.

She is right. If we do not keep up with the times, we might as well exhibit old paintings.

~

"PLEASE, MAY I come?" Yachin begs. *"Please."*

It was a mistake to tell him we were going to visit the Marquis de Sade.

"Absolutely not," Curtius says firmly. "We are going to see a murderer, not a circus."

"But I can carry the bags." The offer is tempting. "I can hold the ink while you dip the quill."

My uncle laughs. "Perhaps you can carry the umbrella over my head." It is pouring, great sheets of rain that haven't let up since dawn.

"Yes!" Yachin exclaims. "I can do that."

I give him a look, and his shoulders sag. "I never get to go anywhere," he grumbles.

Curtius and I walk on, ignoring his plaintive cries from the door of the Salon. "Did you bring him back something from Versailles?" my uncle asks.

"Not yet. I'll find something this week."

"Please. Or we'll never hear the end of it."

As we pass the sign for *The Auricular Communications of the Invisible Girl,* I notice that the potted plants on either side of the steps look waterlogged and forlorn. Even the ferns disagree with this downpour. Henri emerges from the doorway, and his long frock coat with silk-faced lapels is already wet. I watch as a raindrop glides down his nose and lands on his mouth. Without noticing, he licks his lips gently and pulls his hat farther down on his head.

"We tried to hire a cabriolet," my uncle says cheerfully. "But in this weather—"

"A little rain doesn't frighten me," Henri says, though it will likely be a thirty-minute walk. "But the Marquis de Sade . . . are you sure?"

It is me he is asking, as if I am likely to be deterred by a madman in a cell. "Of course. Patrons have been asking for him."

"He's a rapist, Marie." Henri falls into step with me. "They say he paints his cell with—"

"I know." I have heard the stories. Everyone has heard them. This is why we are going. "They've warned him we are coming, and he's agreed."

"I'm sure he's agreed to many things. That doesn't make him less dangerous."

"You can admit it," I tease him. "A part of you wants to know if the rumors are true."

We are the only group outside for some distance. Even the *écailles,* who sell sugared barley water in the winter and oysters in the spring, have taken shelter beneath the eaves.

"Not everyone has the same prurient interests as you."

"It wasn't my idea! It was my mother's."

"Like mother, like daughter," Curtius tells Henri, who looks astonished.

Because my mother spends her time cooking, everyone who comes to our Tuesday salon imagines she has no interest in the world outside her kitchen. The only man who has never underestimated her is Curtius.

I look around the gloomy streets and think of Versailles, where everything is bright and cheerful. How will the deputies of the Third Estate feel when they arrive, dirty and hungry, to see the well-fed courtiers in their diamond buckles and ermine muffs? It is bound to be a disaster, and will certainly cause resentment. I recall my introduction to the palace, when the women whispered behind their bejeweled fans and courtiers watched me through the high, arched windows. Though I had been dressed by one of the finest *marchandes* in Paris and was walking with the sister of the king, it is a place where I could never belong. All the silk and taffeta in the world cannot change the fact that I am untitled.

As we near the Bastille, the rain drives harder. The streets have turned into rivers, carrying along mud and excrement. Even the boys who are normally crying *Passez, payez* have abandoned their jobs of laying down boards for passersby who pay a small fee to spare their shoes. So we are forced to cross the streets without them. I lift my hem, and we choose the least waterlogged paths. Henri's coat is all but ruined. It will take days to clean and then dry by the fire. I had thought to make an agreeable figure in my new hat and rabbit's fur muff, but I see that I shall be lucky simply to look presentable.

As we reach the Bastille, I look up at the mighty stone walls. What must it be like to be locked away in a tower so tall that only birds may reach it? The marquis has been in and out of prison for more than twenty years. First, for the brutalization of a young prostitute named Mademoiselle Testard, who was whipped nearly to death by a cat-o'-nine-tails heated in the fire. There were other atrocities committed against the woman, actions with crucifixes so vile that Madame Élisabeth would faint to hear of them. Myself, I wonder if they are true. I wonder, too, about his wife, who is supposed to have hired six young girls at his behest and taken them to the remote Château de Coste, where the women believed they were to act as servants. Instead, they were taken in chains to a dungeon, where it is said that the marquis used whips and heated irons to satisfy himself with them. If this is true, then I will see it in his face. I will know by the eyes and the set of his jaw.

We cross the drawbridge and pass beneath the portcullis. Henri reaches out to take my arm under the pretense that the ground may be slippery. But I know the truth. This is a haunted place, where men have lost their lives for nothing more than offending the king, a place where no one wants to be alone.

"Have you been here before?" I ask him.

"No. My family was kind enough not to request a *lettre de cachet* when I told them I wanted to follow in Jacques's footsteps."

I laugh, despite the solemnity of the moment. We approach a long table where a dozen guards are playing dice. The men wear the riband of the Order of Saint Louis, and none of them appear the way I would expect prison guards to be, fiendish or cruel. Their wigs are heavily powdered, and their golden military badges catch the light of the candles.

"I wish to speak with the governor of the prison," Curtius says. When one of the men asks what sort of business we have inside, my uncle replies, "We have come to visit the Marquis de Sade."

A middle-aged man separates himself from the group. The bejeweled hilt of the sword at his side is extraordinary, and his attire is more befitting the court than a prison. "I am the Marquis de Launay," he replies, "and I am the governor here." He has dark eyes and a strong, square jaw. He must have been a handsome man in his youth. He looks at our clothes and is obviously shocked that we have chosen to walk in the rain.

"There were no cabriolets to be had," Henri explains.

The marquis sighs heavily. "No. Not on days like this. I will have my men find one for your return."

After introductions are made and we pass through the prison, Henri releases his hold on my arm. Despite the forbidding entrance with its iron gate, there is almost nothing menacing about this place. Heavy tapestries have been hung along the walls to keep in the heat, and somewhere—perhaps in one of the cells—a man is playing the violin.

"Are prisoners allowed instruments?" Curtius asks.

"Of course," de Launay says. "Books as well. What else would keep them occupied?"

"But they must pay for these privileges," I guess. Why else should the king care if his prisoners are entertained unless it's to make money?

De Launay turns to my uncle. "She is quick. Yes," he says to me as we walk. "They must pay a fee to bring an instrument inside. They may also have coffee, and wine, and their own fire . . . for the right price." He winks, and I wonder what else may be had for the right price.

"It's not what I expected," Henri admits.

"No," my uncle says thoughtfully.

Perhaps there are prisoners languishing in the dungeons below our feet. But the ones shut behind these doors of heavy wood and iron do not seem to be suffering. "How many prisoners do you have?" I ask.

"Oh, not many," de Launay confides. "Only seven."

"I thought there would be hundreds of prisoners," I admit. "Thousands."

"Did you think we were imprisoning a foreign army? How would hundreds fit on the bowling green? There must be room for socializing. Imagine hundreds of prisoners at billiards."

Bowling and billiards? "And do all of the men belong in here?"

"Yes, Mademoiselle," de Launay answers me. "These are rapists and murderers. A few are vicious thieves."

"None have come unfairly?" Curtius asks. "Shut up for offending the king?"

De Launay stops. "Our king is just, Monsieur. Such things do not happen."

"What about Voltaire?" Curtius challenges. "Voltaire was sent here."

"More than sixty years ago. Those mistakes don't happen in this reign."

"So, for all of Marat's ranting," Henri says quietly in my ear, and the warmth of his breath on my skin makes my heart race, "there are only seven prisoners, all of whom belong here."

I nod, thinking about the small, enraged man. What would he say if he were walking through these richly decorated passageways and inhaling the aroma of spiced venison in stew? I wonder if the king knows that his prisons smell better than his palace. A clap of thunder echoes through the walls, and although I should be afraid, I'm not. Since my childhood, this fortress has loomed large in my nightmares as a place of interminable suffering. The reality is even more shocking. Tomorrow, I will tell Marat the truth. I will tell them all—Robespierre, Camille, even the Duc, with all of his conspiracy theories.

"You are the only people who have come to see the marquis today," de Launay says, then sighs again, since he charges all visitors a handsome fee. We stop outside an unmarked door. "Mademoiselle. About the marquis . . . I feel I must warn you. He may be old and fat—"

"So what should we be afraid of?"

De Launay looks at me as if he's never heard such an ignorant question. "His words, Mademoiselle. They are his weapons now." He takes out a key and opens the door.

I hold my breath, expecting to see a monster, a prisoner with wild hair and unwashed clothes. Instead, there is a corpulent man nearing fifty, sitting at his desk with ink and a quill. He turns slowly, and I see that it pains him to move. A lifetime of excess has stiffened his joints and ravaged his face. But his eyes. My God. They are the piercing blue of an icy winter's sky.

"Your guests," de Launay says.

The marquis rises and doffs his hat to us. "I hear you have come to make me immortal."

"We have come to sketch your likeness," my uncle replies.

The marquis looks at me. I think of a vulture, the way it studies its meal. "And is this your lovely assistant?"

"She is the artist," Henri says shortly.

"A lady artist!" His brows raise. "Well, why not? The queen's painter is a woman. Not as pretty as you, of course. And certainly not—"

"Are you going to ask us to sit?" There is a hardness in Henri's voice, but the marquis is not offended. He is interested only in me.

"Yes, sit," he says distractedly, for his eyes never leave my face. "Here are three chairs. And Mademoiselle the Artist may take my desk." He pushes his papers to one side and makes a tidy pile in the corner.

I cross the room to his leather chair, and the marquis seats himself across from me. The cell has been decorated with handsome bookshelves and an embroidered settee, a wealthy nobleman's chamber. The bed is of fine wood, and I can see that the linens are of high quality. A cheerful fire burns in the fireplace, where the marquis has hung out his stockings to dry. I cannot imagine how he has gotten them wet. On the bowling green, perhaps? On his way to billiards? Curtius hands me his leather bag, and I take out my supplies, arranging them on the marquis's table. Then I turn and study the old man's face. He is smiling—no, leering—at me, but I am not afraid. He is a shark with no teeth, a hawk without its claws, and I refuse to become unnerved. "I would like to sketch you," I say.

"Many women do."

"Then you know what I require. Sit still, do not fidget, and I will study your face."

"Only if I may study yours."

"That is enough!" Henri exclaims.

The marquis is laughing. "Would you prefer that I put on a blindfold?" He is like a child who cannot hold his tongue. "Or perhaps a blindfold and some chains?"

Curtius rises, and the marquis says quickly, "Stay!"

"Then keep civil," my uncle warns.

"If that is the price of infamy." The marquis leans forward, and I can see his strange features up close. "I hear I am to be added to the Cavern of Great Thieves."

He is a madman. That much is certain. His eyes are spaced too close together, the way they are in children who will grow up to be imbeciles. Only there is cunning reflected in them instead of ignorance.

"But tell me"—the marquis holds up his hands in protest—"what have I stolen?"

"A great deal, I hear. Lives. Innocence." I study his face while we talk. There is no symmetry in it at all. I have brought my caliper, but I have not yet decided whether I should use it. Perhaps I will ask Curtius to take the measurements.

"Ah." The marquis sits back. "Yes. A great deal of innocence."

"Which is why you are here," Henri says harshly.

The marquis stares at him. "You have never had a longing you wished to satisfy? A longing for Mademoiselle the Artist, perhaps? I noticed that you escorted her into my cell with the care that only —"

"Enough," I say sharply.

"Oh. So the feelings are not returned."

I don't dare to look at Henri. I look down at my hands, at the paper and the quill. "Curtius, will you take his measurements?" I ask.

My uncle takes the caliper while the marquis reaches beneath the waist of his *culottes*.

"What are you doing?" my uncle demands.

"Mademoiselle says you wish to take my measurements."

The marquis is so crass, so subhuman, that I burst into laughter.

"You see," the marquis says cheerfully. "Already, we have broken the tension."

"Let Curtius take his measurements," Henri says to me, "and then we will leave."

"No sketch?" the marquis exclaims.

"No," I say flatly.

I have memorized his features. With the measurements, that is all I will need.

"I will be still," the marquis promises. "As quiet as a virgin on her wedding night."

"Then begin now," Henri warns.

Curtius calls out numbers, and I write them down. As I wait for the figures, I study a large roll of paper on the desk. It is covered in writing and so thick that it must be at least ten meters in length when it's fully unrolled. The marquis sees the direction of my gaze and says quietly, "My masterpiece. I call it *The One Hundred and Twenty Days of Sodom.*"

I can see the muscles working in Henri's jaw, and Curtius is frowning over his caliper. He thinks he has taken the measurements wrong—that the marquis's eyes cannot be so close together. "A very interesting title," I say.

"For an immensely interesting story. Would you like a peek?"

I should say no. Nothing good can come of seeing the contents of a story entitled *The 120 Days of Sodom.* But I scribble the last of Curtius's measurements, then motion for Curtius and Henri to sit beside me. They pull up their chairs, and Henri whispers, "Why do you want to see this?"

"It will be offensive," my uncle warns.

But I want to see the truth of this man. I want to know what lurks behind those close-set eyes, what sort of devilry humans are capable of.

The marquis crosses the room and unfurls the manuscript across his long desk. He has drawn pictures on separate pieces of paper to accompany the story.

"What sort of perversion is this?" Curtius asks, aghast.

"Oh, every kind," the marquis says with pride.

There are images of urination, whippings, cross-dressing, and anal sex with boys who are clearly being forced into submission. Girls are chained naked to walls while the flames of lighted candles are applied to their nipples. Excrement is everywhere, as if no fantasy can be fulfilled without this.

"I've had enough," Curtius says.

"But you haven't even seen my favorite!" he exclaims and unveils an image of a girl being scalped while her attackers fondle her genitals and breasts. Beneath the picture the Marquis de Sade has written, "How delicious to corrupt, to stifle all semblances of virtue and religion in that young heart."

I put on my showman's mask, determined not to give him what he wants. "I hope you know you have not corrupted me."

"But I've surprised you."

"No. Nothing surprises me about human depravity."

"These are not just dreams. I enacted them in the Château de Coste."

Behind us, de Launay clears his throat. I had forgotten he was there.

"I run a show on the Boulevard du Temple, Monsieur. What you have created," I say, and I wave my hand, indicating the pictures and the manuscript, "is theater. No more real than my Cavern of Great Thieves."

"It happened," he says hotly.

"Perhaps. But now it's over, and the actor must return to his room and face the truth that for all of the masks, and all of the applause, there is only him. Your performance couldn't last, and now that it's done, all that's left is your own company. Do you enjoy it?"

The marquis is silent. Now I am the one who has surprised him.

~

"NO LADY SHOULD ever have to see—"

"I am not a lady. I am the daughter of a common soldier," I tell Henri from the comfort of the carriage de Launay has secured for us. "Everyone has secrets. His are simply darker. And it makes me a better artist."

Henri shakes his head. "You are a puzzle."

"It's an insight into the man," Curtius explains. "Art is not like science. It's a product of emotion. It makes the viewer feel something. Jealousy, awe—"

"Revulsion," I say. "Now that I know who he is, *what* he is, I know how to sculpt him."

We ride the rest of the way in silence, watching the rain fall slantways onto the dirty streets. I know he doesn't understand, but when Henri sees the wax model—the set of the eyes, the tension in the mouth—he will know.

When we reach the Boulevard du Temple, Curtius hurries into the warmth of the Salon while I stop with Henri beneath the awning of his shop. "I know you didn't wish to go. You went for me, and I'm incredibly grateful."

"How do these interviews not give you nightmares?" he asks. "Doesn't it make you sad to hear such stories?"

I have to think, because no one has ever asked me this before. "I don't believe in Rousseau's philosophy," I say, "if that's what you mean."

Henri laughs. "The natural goodness of man? Well, only fools like Robespierre and Marat believe that."

"And the king."

Henri smiles briefly but doesn't reply.

"I will see you tomorrow," I say. "The Duc may be bringing a guest to our salon."

"The American?" Henri asks. "Thomas Jefferson?"

Now that would be something. Thomas Jefferson wrote the

Declaration of Independence, beginning the war with England. A model of him would do very well. "No. The Marquis de Lafayette."

"I didn't realize they were friends."

I step forward, so close that I can smell rain in his hair. "Curtius says that they are. I don't know what it means for France."

"Probably that the Duc sees himself at the head of rebellion which will demand an end to the monarchy," Henri replies.

"And how would that serve him? Without the monarchy, he has lost all privilege. He will go from being the Duc D'Orléans to being simply Monsieur Philippe."

"Not if he can convince the people that he should be king instead. A new kind of king, who will grant them the same rights as the English."

"It's what he's aiming for, isn't it?" I ask. Henri has said this before, but it's hard to believe that the man who sits to dinner with us is a traitor. I have never known a traitor.

"Yes."

"So why doesn't King Louis stop it?"

"He's trying. That's why he's called the Estates-General. If he grants the French the same rights as the English, what will the Duc have to shout against?"

"But the English have a constitutional monarchy!" I exclaim.

"And that may be the compromise he will have to come to if he doesn't wish to lose the crown to his cousin."

"Then you agree with the rights the people are demanding?"

"I believe the nobility and the clergy should be taxed," Henri says cautiously, "just as we are. Do you know what you send to the king every year?"

I know exactly. "A third of our income."

"And what does he do with it? The streets of Paris are crumbling, the hospitals are in ruins. . . . The Americans are right: there should not be taxation unless the *people* consent to it. And it should be fair, which means the nobility and clergy should be taxed as well. The *dîme,* the *taille*—the nobility don't have to pay any of these—not to mention the *peage* and the *gabelle*. The Duc has found a way of riling the people. With the Third Estate's rage behind him . . ."

We look at each other in silence. "Perhaps Lafayette will help," I say finally. "He is greatly esteemed."

"He'll only be of help if he has the ear of the king. His friendship with the Duc is worrisome."

"Well, if he comes, I shall ask to make a model of him."

"All the country may fall to pieces," Henri observes archly, "but at least Lafayette will be preserved in wax."

I am shocked he would say such a thing. "I care deeply for France."

Henri smiles. "And your accounts."

I STOKE THE fire in the workshop and place my boots as near as I dare without burning them.

"You really want the table this close to the fire?" Yachin confirms.

"Yes," I tell him. "That's good." I must use these daylight hours to sculpt. Without sufficient candles, the models need to be made while the sun is up.

Yachin puts the table down, then crosses his arms over his chest. "*Now* will you tell me about the marquis?"

"He was terrible," I say. "An absolute monster."

Yachin gasps. "Really?"

I nod. "He likes to eat little boys."

"Oh, stop it! Just tell me the truth."

"The truth," I say soberly, "is that he is a very old man who did horrible things in his life."

Yachin's eyes go wide. "Like what?"

"Like taking little boys and girls by force. You understand what that means?"

He nods silently.

"He liked to kidnap innocent children, then beat them until they ran away or died."

"A feier zol im trefen," he whispers in Yiddish, then translates for me. "The marquis deserves to meet with fire. And you are going to sculpt him?"

"Yes. People are cruel at heart," I explain, "so cruelty fascinates them. Secretly, they fear that if not for their good upbringing or their religion, they might have turned out to be the marquis."

"Do you think if I stopped going to temple that would happen to me?"

"I do," I say with mock earnestness. "I think you would develop a craving for human flesh and suddenly want to eat small children!" I lunge forward, and he dashes away, shrieking.

Chapter 10

April 7, 1789

There are natural and imprescriptible rights which an entire nation has no right to violate.

—Marquis de Lafayette

The Duc has brought a guest! I rush from the window into the kitchen, where my mother is preparing our best roast with onions. "He's here!" I exclaim.

"The Marquis de Lafayette?"

"It *has* to be him. He was in the Duc's carriage. He's dressed in a blue silk waistcoat and is carrying a walking stick, exactly like his paintings."

I can hear my uncle's voice on the stairs, explaining what we do for a living. "There are over fifty figures now, and we are always adding."

My mother rushes to take off her apron and swipes at a curl that has escaped from her bonnet. I take her arm, and we appear in the salon together. The room has been lit as if there is no shortage of candles. We will have to ration harder after tonight, but it is worth the cost. Everyone has come: Marat, Robespierre, Camille, Lucile. Henri has brought Jacques. The Duc makes the introductions to his guest, and I have never seen him so charming.

"And this," he says at last, "is Mademoiselle Grosholtz."

Lafayette graces me with a smile. He has an oval face with a prominent nose and trusting eyes. He would make an easy model. "It is an honor to meet you," he says. "Your uncle tells me that you are the artist behind many of the sculptures downstairs, including the one of Benjamin Franklin."

"It is true." I guide him to a chair. I know my duty as host, and I seat him between my uncle and the Duc. "I had the fortune of meeting Monsieur Franklin several times."

"It is a very good likeness. You even managed to capture the eyes."

"I am sure Marie could make a model of you," my uncle adds swiftly. "There would be no greater honor for our exhibition."

"I am staying with the American ambassador, Thomas Jefferson, on the Champs-Élysées. Come anytime. Just send word ahead to make sure I will be there."

I bow my head gratefully. "It would be the crowning glory of our exhibition."

"And speaking of c-c-crowns . . ." Camille raises his glass. His recent loss in the elections does not seem to have changed him. His spirits are high, and his cheeks are flushed. "To America," he exclaims, "where every head is equal."

"To America!" We all raise our glasses. Lafayette tells us he believes there is a future for members of the Third Estate who wish to participate in governing France. In fact, when the Estates-General meets next month, he plans to propose a constitutional monarchy, like they have in England. Everyone at the table applauds him for this, especially Camille and Marat. I notice that Henri and his brother are not so enthusiastic.

"I—I am going to write about this," Camille vows. "I m-m-may have lost the election, but I have not lost my paper and ink!"

Once again there is wild applause, and Lucile turns to me. "He is going to be a journalist," she whispers. "Perhaps he will be the voice of the Third Estate."

"And there is money in that?" I ask her.

"Do you know how many different pamphlets were distributed yesterday at the Palais-Royal? Ninety-two. And all of them calling upon the patriots of our country to rise up and demand an end to these taxes!"

My mother looks blankly at me. *Patriots* is a word she does not understand. It is the first time I have heard the word used like this—to describe anyone in favor of replacing the king, of rendering him powerless.

"There are some businessmen," the Duc warns, "who are not on the side of the patriots." The cut of his new wig does no favors for him. It serves to accentuate the length of his nose and the sagging jowls he shares with his cousin. The Duc leans forward. "Members of the Third Estate who have forgotten their roots."

"Don't be coy," Marat says. "Who are they? We shall make them see the light."

"We cannot afford a Third Estate that is fractured," Robespierre says. "Members of our class are either with us or against us."

"I believe the manufacturer Réveillon is not a man of the people," the Duc says.

"Réveillon has been a good friend to us," Henri challenges.

His brother adds, "He allowed Montgolfier to launch the first hot-air balloon in his own garden."

"That was six years ago," Marat retorts.

"Well, six *months* ago," Jacques amends, "he gave us funds to experiment with hydrogen."

"Why do you believe that Réveillon is not a man of the people?" Lafayette asks.

"Simply look at what he makes," the Duc d'Orléans says. "Luxury wallpaper—for the king!"

"That does not make him a traitor to his class," Lafayette replies.

"He refused to sell me paper because I am not part of *His Majesty's* circle. He chooses clients based on who is loved in Versailles."

So this is the Duc's real grievance. He has been slighted.

Marat puts down his glass of wine. "Then this man is no friend to the Third Estate."

A handful of others who are not friends of the people are mentioned. I see now why my uncle has continued to invite these men to our home. They will talk in this salon or someone else's, and if it's here, we are less likely to be considered enemies. We have made a handsome living by modeling the royal family. I am teaching the king's sister at Versailles. No one should be more suspect as an enemy of the Third Estate than us.

I listen to the men argue and wonder: Will Parisians stop buying hats from milliners who are known to give steep discounts to the nobility? Will they stop frequenting the shops of women like Rose Bertin? Perhaps Curtius has been right. If we're not careful, we will find ourselves without patrons. Today, we reign over the Boulevard du Temple. But tomorrow . . . I must finish the bust of the Marquis de Sade as quickly as possible, and make a point of glimpsing Necker at Versailles so I will be able to see how our bust of him needs to be updated. Heavier jowls, perhaps. Deeper wrinkles between his brows. Certainly lighter hair.

When the evening is finished, my mother leads our guests down the stairs, but Henri and Lafayette pause at the door.

"You keep interesting friends," Lafayette tells Curtius. "These are the men who will shape the future of France. It happened for the Americans."

"They were separated from their king by an ocean," Henri replies. "We are separated from our rulers by five leagues. It's not the same."

"I am not suggesting an American-style Revolution. I would never want to see bloodshed in these streets. A constitutional monarchy would be a good compromise."

"One that cost thousands of lives when the English proposed it a hundred years ago," Henri warns.

"Yes, but they were barbarians. This is eighteenth-century France." Lafayette sees me behind my uncle and smiles. "The Champs-Élysées," he says kindly. "Anytime you wish."

I watch him leave. There is no doubt he is a great man to be admired. But in his desire for a constitutional monarchy, I believe that he is wrong.

Chapter 11

April 9, 1789

Lead, follow, or get out of the way.

—Thomas Paine

I TIE THE RIBBONS OF MY HAT BENEATH MY CHIN AND THINK TO myself, *This is how a traitor must feel.* I have no right to be the tutor of Madame Élisabeth. Not when men like the Duc d'Orléans and the Marquis de Lafayette are meeting in my home, discussing the ways in which the king's power may be carved up and shared with the people.

The carriage pulls up to the courtyard of Montreuil, and as Madame Élisabeth rushes down the stairs, I wonder if God has told her the truth. Surely He looks out for His own. And how will I explain myself then? How will I convince her that none of the men who curse the king and call the queen *L'Autrichienne* are there of my own choosing?

"Marie!"

I hold my breath, expecting the rebuke that must come. If God has not told her, then surely she has spies.

"I am so glad you are here!" she exclaims.

I step out of the carriage.

"The model of Christ is finished, and I want you to see what I've done."

At the door of Montreuil, we are greeted by the Marquise de

Bombelles and half a dozen little dogs. The moment they see me, they are jumping and barking, their long tails wagging their entire bodies.

"My puppies," the princesse says with pride. "Audrey, Amand, Camille, Claudine, Étienne, and Gaspard."

They regard me with large, dark eyes set in curiously tapered heads. I reach down and stroke the smallest one. She is smooth as silk. "Are these greyhounds, Madame?"

"Yes." She bends down and allows two of them to lick her face until the marquise claps her hands.

"Amand! Camille! That is enough." The marquise turns to a nearby servant. "If you will." As the dogs are led away, Madame Élisabeth watches them disappear like a nervous mother. "They'll be fine," the marquise promises. "Let them eat."

"I hope the cooks are feeding them well."

"They are eating better than half of Paris."

The princesse crosses herself quickly. "May God provide for them, too." She studies me as we make our way to the workshop. "The dauphin is very sick," she reveals. "The doctors say it is something with his spine. He is only seven and must wear an iron corset."

What a terrible thing for a child to endure.

"And he has fevers," she adds quietly. "Perhaps we could each make an image of him today? I would like to bring one to the Church of Saint-Sulpice."

The pious bring wax models of afflicted limbs to Saint-Sulpice in the hope that the saint will work a miracle for them. Hundreds of waxen arms and feet created by poorly skilled modelers on the Place de Grève are arranged beneath the saint's reliquary bust. I should be bitterly disappointed by this request. But instead, I am deeply touched. "I am honored to help."

"Will you come with me to the church? I want you to see what other artists have done. None are as good as you, but perhaps you will be inspired to a . . . a higher calling."

She means perhaps I will be inspired to give up my modeling of kings' mistresses and the daughters of courtesans. We may have hidden du Barry's tableau for the royal family's visit, but no doubt she has heard about what is normally displayed. "Yes," I say without commitment. "Perhaps I shall." She does not comprehend the true meaning of work. She probably imagines that if I wished, I could simply make my living by modeling the saints.

Inside the workshop, the finished image of Christ on the cross is hanging next to the door. The entire figure is the size of my forearm, large enough for me to see that she has taken pains to model each of the fingers on his hands. I step closer. The eyes and lips are good for someone who has not worked on faces before. "It is *good,*" I say honestly. The paints she has used are of superior quality, and it is clear that she is accustomed to working with oils. "*Very* good, Madame."

"Élisabeth has so much talent." The marquise is like a proud older sister. "I've told her for years that she should be working with wax." She ties an apron around her waist, and the material is so fine that it's a shame she'll have to dirty it.

We go to the counter, and once again a block of clay and all of the necessary tools have been laid out. There are three bowls of water, sponges, towels, clay needles, potters' ribs, and even loops. The long wooden spatulas have been arranged in a wide ceramic vase, and in the bright light of the workshop, I can almost believe that they are flowers reaching for the sun.

I dip my hands in the water bowl, and both the princesse and the marquise follow suit. "Be sure to keep the clay moist at all times," I remind them. "Dry clay will crack." Then we begin with three pieces. One is molded into the shape of a square, and that will be the base. The other two are rolled into medium and large balls—the first for the neck, the other for the head. When we have all joined the three, we begin the process of modeling the face.

"Most of the work can be done by the thumbs," I tell them. I show them how to apply pressure with their fingers to create indentations for the eyes and press out the nose. Extra clay must be added for the ears.

But before we can attach the ears to the heads, we must score the clay. I pick up a potter's needle and show them. "Whenever you join pieces together," I remind them, "you must score and slip." I scratch the surface of the head where I will be adding the ears, then do the same to the backsides of the ears themselves. "You see? I've scored it." I join the ears to the head. "And now I will cover the seam with a layer of slip." I dip my hands in the water and show them what this is—a paste made of water and clay.

I explain how the ears must start at the tops of the eyes and end at the bottom of the nose for symmetry. When I feel they have understood my directions, I let them work on their own. There is something soothing about modeling in contemplative silence. There are none of the distractions here that there are on the Boulevard du Temple. No pestering from Yachin, no noise from the kitchen, no customers waiting outside, laughing and calling to their friends. I score the last curl into the dauphin's head and look up to see the princesse's eyes wide with envy.

"Look how beautiful yours is! His face." She comes closer. "It's so—"

"Realistic," the marquise says.

The doors swing open, and all three of us turn. It's Madame Royale, the eleven-year-old daughter of the king, followed by two women in white chemise gowns and powdered hair.

"Marie-Thérèse!" Madame Élisabeth says. "What a wonderful surprise."

"You see?" Madame Royale turns on her two attendants. "I told you they weren't busy."

"But where is your mother?" the marquise asks.

"How should I know?" Madame Royale says. "She's never with me." She crosses the workshop, leaving her female attendants at the door. "What are you doing?"

"We are working on busts of your little brother, the dauphin," the marquise replies.

"Because he's sick?"

"Yes," Madame Élisabeth says. "On Friday, we shall take these to Saint-Sulpice in Paris."

"Why? Do you think the saint can heal him?"

"Perhaps if he recognizes these busts, he will take pity on your brother, yes."

Madame Royale studies each of the three sculptures, but it's mine she picks up. "This is yours?" she asks me. "It's better than the others."

"This is how I make my living, Madame."

"I remember," she says defensively.

"Put it back," Madame Élisabeth suggests. "They are not yet finished."

Madame Royale narrows her eyes at me, as if it's my fault that she is being chastised. As she places the model back on the counter, her finger breaks the dauphin's nose.

"You've broken it!" the marquise exclaims.

"Does this mean my brother will die?" Madame Royale asks.

"Of course not," Madame Élisabeth says, horrified. She exchanges a swift look with the marquise. "This is a godly practice, not witchcraft."

"But he won't be cured. I heard the doctors. They said there's nothing anyone can do."

"God is not *anyone,*" Madame Élisabeth says sternly.

But Madame Royale does not flinch. Instead, she squares her shoulders and replies, "I wish God would take Maman instead."

Madame Élisabeth takes her niece's hand. "It is time for you to go."

"Why? *She* gets to stay here, and she is nobody." She indicates me with her pointed chin. "May I have the model?" She is looking at my sculpture. "I want something to remind me of my brother."

Both women look at me, and I pass Madame Royale the bust. "I hope it brings you comfort," I tell her.

She smiles but doesn't say thank you.

That evening, as I am readying myself for bed, I go to the window to see the orangerie one last time before I sleep. When I open the shutters, something small and hard falls onto the ground. I lean over the windowsill and look down. The little bust of the dauphin is broken in two. Someone placed it outside my window, knowing that, as soon as I opened the shutters, it would fall.

~

IT IS FRIDAY night, and the Grand Commune is like an abandoned hive. Anyone with transportation has rushed from Versailles to spend the evening in Paris. There are a few members of the Garde du Corps, who share responsibilities with the Swiss for protecting the king, eating here tonight. And, of course, there are my brothers. But the ambassadors and courtiers have left. No one wants to be confined to a palace where the parties and masques have all stopped, a place where everyone waits for the terrible news that must come any day about the dauphin. I have received permission to come here tonight from Madame Élisabeth. Although I do not expect to be granted this privilege often, Edmund has chosen to eat with his commander, the Baron de Besenval, rather than with me.

I ask Wolfgang how long it has been since the queen last hosted one of her great fêtes.

"Years," he says and looks to Johann.

"At least two," Johann replies. "Before, every evening was a masquerade," he remembers. "One night, Norwegians and Lapps was the theme. Everyone came dressed like Scandinavians. Another night it was the court of François the First, and the men came in jerkins while the women wore Spanish farthingale skirts."

"The queen would send out lists of what her guests should wear," Wolfgang adds. "White taffeta and tulle," he says, "or sixteenth-century costumes with gabled hoods. And then there were the parties at the queen's private residence, the Petit Trianon."

"In the morning," Johann recalls, "the king would go out hunting while the queen would pick wildflowers with her ladies. Then the entire day would be spent in picnics or boating on the canal. And at night—"

"It was like nothing you've ever seen. Hundreds of multicolored lanterns illuminating the gardens. And flowers everywhere. On trellises and windows and over specially constructed archways. It was like another world." Wolfgang sighs. "It's like a tomb in here now. If the queen hosted a party, she would be accused in every *libelle* of all seven deadly sins. No matter that she is criticized just as bitterly in court circles for economizing."

I feel sorry for Wolfgang. Johann, at least, has a wife and child. But Wolfgang is young. If not for his service with the Swiss Guard, he would be sitting in a coffeehouse at the Palais-Royal. "So what do you do in the evenings?" I ask.

"The same thing you do," Wolfgang guesses. "Play cards. Talk."

"Go to vespers," I offer dryly.

"Fortunately, not that. I hear you went with the princesse to Saint-Sulpice."

"When we got there, she was surrounded by people who wanted her blessing. Some asked her to make wax images for them. She took their names and requests." I am still amazed by this. "But she was really there to pray for her nephew."

Johann shakes his head. "The dauphin is very ill. There are physicians in and out of the palace all day. I would be surprised if he lasts the month."

I cross myself quickly. I have become like Madame Élisabeth, hoping that God will intervene in human affairs. "And the queen?" I ask him.

"Overcome. It's a terrible time to be holding the Estates-General," Johann says, "but there's no way of postponing it."

"There would be riots in the streets," I say with certainty. I tell my brothers about Lafayette's visit and Camille's plan to write on next month's events. Then I tell them of the Marquis de Lafayette's intention to propose a constitutional monarchy.

Wolfgang pulls a small pamphlet from his sleeve. "Don't read it here. Put it away and look at it tonight."

"This is Thomas Paine's *Common Sense.*" I am shocked. "This is treason."

"Then all of Paris will hang."

I look at Johann. "Have you read this?"

He nods. "Everyone has."

"Not Edmund," I challenge.

"Even him, though I doubt he'd admit it."

I look from Wolfgang to Johann. "And?"

My brothers stand. "Let's talk of this outside," Wolfgang says.

I tuck the pamphlet into my sleeve, and my brothers lead me onto the Rue de la Surintendance. It is too cold to stand outside, so they take me into the château and we find an empty hall. Versailles is still shocking to me in this way—that a king's palace can be entered by anyone, even a woman carrying treason up her sleeve. The three of us stand huddled together near a tapestry of Hermes, the god of mischief and thieves.

"Not all Swiss Guards believe in this monarchy," Wolfgang whispers. "The king is weak."

"But he was chosen by God—"

"Thomas Paine proposes that all men are equal, both commoners and kings," Johann says.

I cannot believe I am hearing this. "How can you continue to be part of the Swiss Guard? Who does the king have if not you?"

My brothers put their fingers to their lips. The hall is empty, but there is no telling who may be around the corner.

"I will find some other employment," Wolfgang says.

I look at Johann. "And you?"

"I have to think of Isabel and Paschal."

"The king seems to be a good man," I protest. "His sister is all kindness."

"But they are kept in the dark about everything," Johann says. "No one is allowed to mention finances. When the queen asks for ten thousand livres, she is given twenty."

"That is the fault of the court!" I say.

"And how do you change it?" Wolfgang asks. "It's greed. The courtiers, the ministers . . ."

I think of my trip into Paris with Madame Élisabeth, and her expressions of delight over the most ordinary things, in particular the sellers peddling food in the streets. When I explained the realities of the marketplace to her—how bad meat is concealed beneath strong seasonings and the ways in which scales are tampered with—she was scandalized. Nothing good can come of blinding the royal family and then asking them to oversee a kingdom.

Wolfgang tries to lift the tension. "So, any wealthy widows come to the exhibition recently?"

I smile, despite my worry. "No, but I'm sure they would be pleased to no end with your gambling."

"Then maybe I'll become a professional cardsharp." He winks at me and holds out his arm to escort me back to the Grand Commune.

"I am going to stay here. I want to see the Hall of Mirrors again."

"There won't be anyone there," Johann warns, thinking I want to catch some member of the nobility I can model.

"I want to see it in moonlight."

My brothers don't question me. They know how inspiration can come in the reflection on a lake or in the slow, steady curl of smoke from a fire. I watch them leave, then make my way through the candlelit halls. I wish I had known Versailles when the queen hosted her masquerades and her ladies came dressed in blue velvets and white silks. I want to imagine the château as it was in happier days.

The palace isn't entirely empty. I catch giggling servant girls allowing liberties to be taken with them on the stairs, and a young man strumming a lap harp for a woman who will certainly be following him to his chambers. Without the crush of people, the heavy stench of body odor has abated. In the moonlight, the palace is beautiful. A silvery sheen falls across the floors, as though I'm walking on water. Even the cold marble statues look alive. So much care and attention have been taken to make this the most beautiful palace on earth. And really, the price has not been terribly high. Yesterday, Madame Élisabeth told me that in the most extravagant times, the court's yearly expenditures were only six percent of the national budget. And look at what that six percent has created! This is why the Americans rebelled. They never saw such majesty on their own soil. If they could have seen the rich tapestries and gilded halls that their taxes produced . . .

I reach the Hall of Mirrors, and the sight is more breathtaking at night than by day. Chandeliers illuminate the marble walls and gilded pilasters, and the entire room is like burnished amber. Only one other person has come to enjoy this vision of light and gold. She is standing in the middle of the hall, as if she is imagining, just as I am, the grand fêtes that took place beneath these painted ceilings. As I approach, she does not turn to me. Probably, she is lost in her various dreams. But as I draw closer, I realize who she must be—the curve of her neck, the width of her shoulders, the sweep of her hair. I have sculpted this person.

Immediately, I stop walking. The queen is utterly alone. I think of all the courtiers who pressed around her when her fortunes were high, and now, without the music and the masquerades, she is surrounded only by ghosts. I am embarrassed to have interrupted such an intimate moment, but as I back away, the wooden floor creaks and the queen abruptly turns. I sink into my lowest curtsy.

"Mademoiselle Grosholtz."

She has remembered me. Of all the faces she has seen, she has remembered mine. "I did not mean to intrude," I say. "Forgive me, Your Majesty. I should not have come—"

"I am the one who should not be here. Only foolish old women wish to revisit the conquests of their youth." She dabs quickly at her eyes, and I wonder if she's been weeping. "My husband tells me you took Élisabeth to Saint-Sulpice. That was very kind of you."

Not only has she remembered me, but she knows what I've been doing in Montreuil. "The entire nation is praying for the dauphin. He is the hope of France."

"Yes," she says vaguely, as if in a fog. "Yes," she says more firmly. "He is."

We stare at each other in the candlelight. She has lost weight since she came to the Boulevard du Temple. There are new angles in her face and less fullness beneath her jaw.

"It is a beautiful view out of that window." She points down the hall, and a handkerchief flutters to the ground from her sleeve. I pick up the little square of silk and see that it's embroidered with her coat of arms as well as her initials. The cloth is lighter than anything I've ever held. There is a small rip in the corner, and she sees that I have noticed it. I hold it out to her.

"Keep it." She smiles. "Let it be a reminder that nothing in this world can last."

"Even pain," I reply.

This time, the smile reaches her eyes. "Yes, that's true."

When she is gone, I walk to the place where she was standing and look down the hall. There is nothing to see but golden parquet floors, stretching on to what seems like eternity. And in the gilded mirrors, instead of noblemen dancing the minuet, there is only me.

Chapter 12

April 12, 1789

My blood boils in my veins against the so-called fathers of the country.

—Jean-Paul Marat

"The queen's handkerchief?" my mother exclaims in German. We are standing in the workshop, where Curtius has finished the body of the corpulent Marquis de Sade. Tomorrow, we will put the entire figure on display. She holds the silk square up to the afternoon light.

"We can use this," my uncle announces. "It can be *The Farewell Handkerchief*!"

I reach out and take the handkerchief back. "This isn't for exhibition."

"But everything is for exhibition," my mother says, puzzled.

"This is a present for Yachin," I reply, surprising myself.

I go outside and find our barker. We are advertising the model of Sainte-Amaranthe today. I hold out the embroidered handkerchief, and he puts down his sign and wrinkles his nose. Then he runs his small fingers over the coat of arms and looks up at me with wide eyes. "The *queen's*?"

I nod. "I met her in the Hall of Mirrors."

He wraps his arms around my waist. "Thank you, Marie. Thank

you, thank you! Wait until Maman sees this. I'll keep it with me always. This is the best gift I have ever received!"

"You can show it to your mother now if you'd like."

He is beside himself with joy. He rushes down the street so quickly that he nearly runs into the butcher.

"That was very kind of you." Henri has been sitting on the steps, washing a basket full of glass vials. He has not bothered tying his long hair back, so it hangs in his face, curling about his lapels. "Did Her Majesty really give it to you?"

"Yes. It dropped from her sleeve and she told me to keep it."

"I'm surprised you didn't want it for the Salon."

"I . . . I couldn't. We were in the Hall of Mirrors together," I confide. "She was weeping."

"The dauphin," he says quietly.

I sit next to him on the stairs. His hands are colored with dye, probably from staining the samples he places beneath his microscope. Though spring is here, the air is still crisp. "Yes." I say sadly. "His health is growing worse."

ON THE TWENTY-EIGHTH of April, just as we are opening the Salon for business, Yachin comes running.

"Not enough exercise lately?" Curtius asks. He is painting the trim outside the window while I wash the steps.

Yachin holds his chest and gasps for breath. "Monsieur Réveillon," he says, and breathes deep. "Monsieur Réveillon—they are attacking him!"

Curtius lays down his brush and I put aside the mop. "What do you mean?" my uncle asks.

"My mother heard it from the butcher that a group of men are marching toward his factory in the Porte Saint-Antoine. They intend to tear it down."

I look to my uncle. "It has to be a mistake," he says. He replaces the lid on the paint and stands. "Monsieur Réveillon is a good man. We've done business with him for fifteen years." He disappears inside and returns with his coat.

"Where are you going?" I exclaim.

"To help Réveillon."

"But what can you do?"

He doesn't answer.

This morning, little business gets done. I sit with my mother at the *caissier*'s desk in the front of the Salon, and we watch the handsome Thuret clock, a gift from my uncle's first patron. If a mob has reached Réveillon's gates, what hope does Curtius have of helping him? What can he do but put himself in danger? My mother asks every customer what he's heard. Nothing. Always nothing.

"Go to Henri," she says, at last. "He is a showman. Gossip is his job."

I go next door, but only to please her. Henri is sitting at his own *caissier*'s desk. Two women hover over him, showing him something. A snuffbox, I believe. One smells of orange blossom, the other of rose, and both are wearing hats over their towering *poufs*.

"Marie!" Henri says as soon as he sees me. "Did you hear?" He rises, and the women look disappointed.

"About Réveillon?"

"Yes. They have torn the factory apart."

I gasp. "But Curtius is there!"

"What do you mean?"

"He went to help him this morning and he hasn't come back."

Henri finds his brother and asks him to watch over the desk. Orange Blossom and Rose narrow their eyes at me. *You're not his type anyway,* I want to say. Henri is a bachelor, and if he ever decides to marry, it will not be to a woman with a fanciful hat. It will be to a woman who understands his passion for science. We hurry back to the Salon, where I tell my mother that Henri has news.

"You see?" she says to me in German. To Henri, she whispers, "What is it?"

"It's only talk," he begins, but my mother waves this away. Henri leans forward so that our patrons won't overhear. "Five thousand workers gathered outside of Réveillon's shop this morning. They were armed with shovels and clubs." My mother crosses herself. "The rioters destroyed the factory, then turned toward Réveillon's house."

The door of the Salon opens, and my uncle appears. His coat is torn. His *culottes* are splattered with mud. He sees that we have been waiting for word and holds up his hands, as if to defend himself. "I had no idea. No idea it would be so violent."

My mother rushes forward to take his coat. I tell Yachin to mind the desk, and the three of us follow Curtius up the stairs. We sit at my mother's wooden table. "It is gone. His house, his factory—as if a storm swept through and took everything," Curtius says. "There was a rumor that Réveillon planned to cut wages. Thousands of men were at the gates of the factory when I arrived, and none of them were Réveillon's workers." He tells us the Duchesse d'Orléans appeared, demanding entry. Because Réveillon had no other choice, he did as he was told and let her in. The men flooded through, destroying everything they came across. "What they didn't burn, they stole," he tells us. "Tapestries, books, lidded vases, tables—all his family's treasures either broken or carried away. They smashed the windows and cut down the trees. Destruction simply for destruction's sake."

"What of Réveillon and his family?" my mother asks.

"They escaped over the garden wall. When the Gardes Françaises arrived, the rioters climbed onto the rooftops and began to hurl tiles at the king's men. So the Gardes fired into the crowd. Five hundred are dead, at least."

Henri shakes his head, and I realize that the stains on my uncle's *culottes* are not dirt, but blood.

"When I left," Curtius says, "the mob was growing, and hundreds were making their way toward the archbishop's palace at Vincennes. A man bragged that he had stopped the carriage of the Duc de Luynes and forced him to shout, 'Long live the Third Estate!' They'll be rioting until nightfall," Curtius predicts, "unless the king sends more soldiers."

"Réveillon employed nearly four hundred people," Henri says. "He's been elected to represent his district next month. Who would start a rumor that he planned to cut wages?"

Curtius spreads his hands. "When the Gardes Françaises searched the dead, they found six-franc pieces on them."

The four of us are silent, all thinking the same thing. Finally, it is Henri who says, "So they were paid."

There is only one man with both the desire and the funds to destroy Réveillon. The Duc d'Orléans. The same man who sent his estranged wife to insist that Réveillon open the gates.

THE EVENING'S SALON is joyful. It is as if great wealth has been created rather than lost with the burning of Réveillon's house and factory. Camille brags that not only has Réveillon's manor, Titonville, been burned to the ground, but the saltpeter works belonging to Réveillon's good friend Hanriot have also been destroyed.

"It is the first step," Lucile says passionately, "in letting the elites understand that we will no longer tolerate this great division of wealth. And wait until everyone makes their way to the Estates-General tomorrow!"

I wonder what her father would think of this outburst against privilege. If not for his wealth, she would not be wearing those pretty pearls around her neck or the gold watch at her waist.

"Robespierre and I will be traveling together tomorrow morning," Camille announces. "And you, Marat?"

"If there is space in your carriage, I would be happy to come," Marat replies.

"Then w-we all go together!" Camille exclaims.

But Robespierre clenches his jaw. For as dirty and disheveled as

Marat keeps himself, Robespierre is equally fastidious. His green-tinted glasses are polished to a sheen; his silk jacket and matching waistcoat are perfectly creased. Not even Rose Bertin could find something to complain about in his attire. "I believe," he says in a slow, deliberate voice, "the space in our carriage was given to the Comte de Mirabeau." He does not wish to lower himself by riding in the same carriage as Marat.

Camille hesitates, then looks across the table to the Duc. "I thought—"

"It doesn't matter," Marat says. "I can make my own way."

There is an awkward moment before the Duc says, "I suspect that this will be the last time we shall meet in Curtius's salon until the business of the Estates-General is over." He raises his brandy, and his gold rings clink against the glass. "To Curtius and his generous family. May we all return here next month in triumph."

While everyone raises their glasses, Marat demands, "Will *you* be voting to abolish all exemptions from taxes due to privilege and rank?"

The Duc lowers his glasses, and everyone at the table holds their breath. "Yes. But this convocation must do more than ease the tax burden of the Third Estate. It must recognize the Third Estate as the driving force behind this nation. As the heart and body that gives life to the powerful beast that is France."

"Exactly!" Camille exclaims.

The diamond in the Duc's cravat catches the candlelight. "Now that the three estates have drafted their *cahiers* and presented them to the king, he must take action. The *lettres de cachet* must be abolished. Offices sold by the state to raise money must be abolished. And the *corvée* must be abolished. What gives one man the right to command another man to work for him without pay?"

"It's modern slavery!" Marat shouts. "The *corvée* must be the first to go."

The Duc smiles. "And all citizens must be equal before the law." There are eager murmurs around the table. "Even now," the Duc says quietly, so that we know this is a great secret he is about to divulge, "the Marquis de Lafayette is drafting a declaration with help from the American ambassador, Thomas Jefferson. He is calling it the Declaration of the Rights of Man and Citizen, and we shall present it to the king."

"And if the king won't agree to it?" Marat challenges.

"Then perhaps we will have to find a king who will."

When we have shown our guests down the stairs and locked the door, I turn to my uncle. "It must have been the Duc's money that destroyed Réveillon."

"He wants the crown," Curtius agrees. He takes a candle from the wall, and I follow him up the stairs. When we reach the landing, he faces me. "Look at what Thomas Jefferson managed for America. There's no telling what both he and Lafayette might do in France. We should call on him tomorrow, before he leaves for Versailles."

"What do you think the king should do?" I ask him.

"He should force the nobility to bear the tax burden, just as we do."

"That's right!" my mother yells from the kitchen, elbow-deep in dishwater.

"They will refuse," I predict.

"Then he must force them. He is king. And he must give consideration to the grievances listed in the Third Estate's *cahiers.* But I doubt he will do either. He is afraid of the nobility. When they shout, he will cower."

"Do you believe the nobles will follow the Duc's lead?"

"The Duc has no intention of being their leader. He has seen where the real power lies."

Chapter 13

April 29, 1789

The tree of liberty must be refreshed from time to time with the blood of patriots and tyrants.

—Thomas Jefferson

We have arranged an audience with the Marquis de Lafayette, and we are to meet him in Thomas Jefferson's home on the corner of Rue des Champs-Élysées! Curtius knows what Henri thinks of Jefferson, who is not only a political philosopher and ambassador but an inventor as well. As soon as the offer to come with us is made, Henri is finding his walking stick and hat.

As our carriage rolls away, I look back at the sign advertising *The Auricular Communications of the Invisible Girl.* "And you're sure you want to come with us?" I ask.

"What?" Henri puts on a look of mock offense. "Am I such bad company?"

I feel my cheeks warm. "No. But your exhibit. Who is watching it for you?"

"My apprentice. I'm training him to take over every afternoon."

"But he might let his friends in at a discount," I warn. "Or worse, for free."

Curtius laughs. "You see what I have to deal with?"

But Henri's look is endearing. "Marie is a hard businesswoman is all. You are extremely fortunate to have her."

He smiles at me, and for the first time, I am at a loss for words. They are both waiting for me to say something. "Thom-Thomas Jefferson," I say swiftly. "You said once that he's the most interesting man in America. Why?"

My uncle stares at me. He wants me to address Henri's compliment. But what did it mean? He can't be interested in me. Neither of us has ever pursued any courtship. We are married to our work. Though, when I look at him, my pulse quickens. And when I see the smile lines around his eyes, I know that his words are sincere.

"Jefferson is a great intellect," Henri replies, and I am thankful that the awkward moment has passed. "The man can speak six languages, and it's said he learned Gaelic simply so that he could read *The Poems of Ossian* in their original. He's a naturalist, and an accomplished architect as well. He designed his own estate and named it Monticello."

I laugh nervously. "Is there anything he doesn't do?"

"Fight. He's a thinker, not a soldier."

I almost say, "Like you." But instead I reply, "How funny that they should become fast friends. Lafayette, who went to war in the Americas when he was just nineteen, and Thomas Jefferson."

"They share a love of liberty," Curtius tells me. "And they've known each other for more than a decade." The carriage comes to a stop before a two-storied house that towers above its neighbors. Few homes in Paris are as tall or elegant as this. An expansive English garden in front is lush and bright, as if dampness and rain have never touched this corner of the Champs-Élysées. Topiary figures are dotted among the flowering plants, and the pretty pink heads of peonies bob and bow to us in the gentle breeze.

"Magnificent," Curtius says.

As we descend from the carriage, Henri holds out his hand to me. When I take it, his fingers close intimately over mine. I look into his face, but his eyes are fixed on Thomas Jefferson's home. A pretty girl with long hair comes out to meet us. Though her skin is porcelain, her eyes are dark and her cheekbones high. *She is an octoroon,* I think. *Seven-eighths white and one-eighth African.* The angles of her face are sharp. She has a symmetry, I realize, almost as perfect as that of Émilie Sainte-Amaranthe. She would be beautiful to sketch, and I wonder what she's doing here. She cannot possibly be a maid. Her clothes are too fine. "Welcome to the Hôtel de Langeac," she says in greeting. "Are you the wax modelers?"

Curtius lifts up the leather carrying case with my tools as evidence.

"Very good," she replies. Now that we are close, I see she is older than I first thought. Perhaps seventeen or eighteen. "The marquis and the ambassador are eager to see you."

When we have paid the coachman, we are shown inside the imposing home with its oval rooms and commanding views. "Did Jefferson design this himself?" Henri asks.

"Yes and no," the young woman says. "This house was designed by the architect Chalgrin, but the ambassador has made many changes."

We pass beneath a ceiling painted with an image of Apollo in his chariot. When the young woman sees the direction of my gaze, she says, "Jean-Simon Berthélemy."

"We have a painting of his in our exhibition," Curtius says. "Not this size, of course. This . . . this is tremendous."

"The ambassador likes his home to make an impression."

"How many rooms are in here?" I ask.

"Twenty-four," she says with pride. She takes us upstairs, and we stop at a pair of open doors leading into a salon. The oval room has been transformed into a library, with wooden bookshelves and a mahogany desk. A large bay window looks out over the manicured garden, where men in simple trousers are planting seeds. "Monsieur Lafayette," the young woman announces. "Your guests have arrived."

The men working at the desk both rise. I recognize the marquis at once, but I have never seen a portrait of Thomas Jefferson. He is very tall and slenderly built, with thick auburn hair and blue eyes. Though Lafayette is thirty-two and the ambassador is forty-six, the two men could be brothers. Their coloring, their height, their way of standing . . . Even before Jefferson moves, I can see that he carries himself well. And like Lafayette's, his clothing is immaculate. French *culottes* with an embroidered waistcoat and a white cravat.

"Ah, thank you, Sally," Jefferson says, then turns to the marquis, who makes the introductions. Curtius and Henri are presented to the ambassador as scientists and showmen, while I am introduced as a sculptress of rare talent.

"Curtius and Marie have been making wax models on the Boulevard du Temple for more than twenty years," Lafayette explains. "We are going to be a part of their exhibit on liberty."

Jefferson asks how the models will be created, and Curtius tells him that we have come prepared for every possibility. There are plaster bandages to make a live mask—which would take an hour—or paper and ink to sketch the men at their leisure. Jefferson looks at Lafayette, as if to say that it is up to him.

Lafayette hesitates, and Curtius says swiftly, "My niece, Marie, will sketch you. All we need are a few measurements."

"Shall we stand or sit?" Jefferson asks.

"If it would please the ambassador," Curtius replies, "we would like you to sit."

They return to their chairs at the mahogany desk, and Jefferson turns to Henri. "Lafayette tells me that you are the man behind the hydrogen balloon."

"He gives me too much credit," Henri replies humbly, while Curtius and I take out the caliper. "My brother and I worked with the Roberts brothers. It was a joint effort."

"But a spectacular one," Jefferson says. He recounts how Benjamin Franklin returned to America with the story of a flying balloon. "And no one would believe it when he told them it flew with hydrogen, not air."

"It took years of experimentation," Henri admits, as Curtius and I begin the measurements. "My brother and I have a laboratory on the Boulevard du Temple. Benjamin Franklin inspired him to study physics."

"They knew each other?" Jefferson asks.

"They did. Now Jacques has hopes of becoming a professor of physics at the Conservatoire des Arts et Métiers."

"And you?" Jefferson sits back and crosses his legs while I take the measurements of his jaw. He is an elegant man. I imagine that as a widower he must be very popular in Paris.

Henri smiles ruefully. "I simply hope to have enough time to finish my experiments with nitrogen. We are not independently wealthy. Our money must come from other work."

Lafayette frowns. "Not patronage from the king?"

"The king supported my brother's experiments. Then the Montgolfier brothers launched their balloon filled with air two months before ours." He shrugs. "We weren't the first."

"But it's hydrogen they're using now," Jefferson protests. "It's how Blanchard and Jeffries crossed the English Channel!"

"The king is only interested in novelty. My brother's grants stopped the moment the king heard the Montgolfiers would beat us to launch."

I have not heard this story. I look at Curtius, who seems equally surprised.

Henri continues, "Not all science can be for show. And if the king wishes to reward only the fastest performers, then that's not a show I wish to be a part of."

I had thought that pride kept Henri from asking the king for patronage. I didn't realize it was his commitment to science. Experiments, like art, cannot be rushed, even for a king who wishes to plan a great fête around the launching of the first balloon. I put down my caliper and turn to Curtius, who has finished Lafayette's measurements. Now all we have to do is make the sketches. "This won't take long," I tell the ambassador. "Half an hour," I say.

But Jefferson passes his hand through the air. "Take as long as you wish. I am quite enjoying this visit."

Curtius and I take out several sheets of paper and ink. We are sitting across from two of the finest thinkers in France, enjoying coffee and cakes. This is far more pleasant than the last time I drew a subject from life. I recall the pudgy eyes of the Marquis de Sade and shiver.

"I hope we aren't distracting you from your work." Curtius indicates a long roll of paper on Jefferson's desk.

"The Declaration is finished," Lafayette admits. "But it lacks . . ." He gestures with his hands. Unlike Jefferson, he is constantly in motion. Never still, never content. It will be difficult to draw him. "Something firm. Something about the future of this monarchy."

"It is an argument between us," Jefferson admits. "This document cannot be a declaration of independence."

"I don't see why," Lafayette disagrees. "We must assert our freedoms as men! And we must make it clear that the will of the people is more important than the will of a king. Why do we need a monarch?" he demands. "The Americans have never needed one."

"Because we were separated from our king by an entire ocean for more than two hundred years," Jefferson replies, echoing what Henri said when Lafayette was a guest at our salon. "France is not America. You must give a starving man scraps first. An entire feast will kill him."

Lafayette turns to Henri and Curtius. "We discussed this several weeks ago, but perhaps recent events have changed your mind. Are the people of France ready to govern themselves?"

Curtius considers carefully before answering. "What would happen to the king?"

"Imagine he is gone. Away. On vacation."

"If it was a choice between following the Americans and following the English, I think a constitutional monarchy would be more prudent," my uncle replies.

"I would have to agree," says Henri. "How do we know the American experiment will succeed? It cost twenty thousand lives, and four years from now, what if their President Washington refuses to relinquish his robes of office and declares himself king?"

"You can't believe that!" Lafayette is aghast. "America has ignited the torch of freedom. And that torch is now lighting up the world!"

"A republic is undoubtedly the way forth for mankind," Jefferson agrees. "But will men be willing to govern themselves, or is it more convenient to hand the reins of power to someone who promises free bread and wine?" He tilts his head, and I try to capture his elegant persuasiveness on my paper. Now I understand why the Americans chose him to be their ambassador: they wish him to persuade us to grasp at liberty just as he persuaded the colonists to sever their ties with England.

When the clock chimes three, I put away my ink. Jefferson looks at me, surprised. "Done?" he asks.

"Yes. I have made three drawings each."

"May we see?"

I hand him my papers.

"The eyes," he says. *It is always the eyes.* "And the mouth. It's like looking into a mirror." He passes the drawings to Lafayette, who is equally impressed.

"Wait until you see the actual figure," Henri promises. "It will be like looking at your double. There is no one like Marie in all of France."

"To be fair, I had a very good instructor." I smile at Curtius. "We should not keep these men any longer than we have."

But Jefferson won't hear of it. "Nonsense. You must stay and dine with us."

Curtius and I look at each other. What will my mother think when we don't come home? "My mother—" I begin, but the ambassador cuts me off.

"I will send my carriage for her and we shall all dine together."

It is the merriest time I have had in many months. The table Jefferson keeps is astounding. Soups, roasted meats, omelets, cheese, a salad of beets, and cherries in brandy for dessert. I don't know where he has come by all of these delicacies, but we are offered every kind of drink with our food as well. Jefferson is a connoisseur of wine and advises us on which vintage goes best with cheese and which should be reserved for salad and canapés.

We talk of the Estates-General and what will happen in two days' time. Will the Declaration be ready? Will the king accept it? Will he agree to have a parliament that shares his power, and if not, how will the deputies of the Third Estate react? When we return to the Boulevard du Temple and climb the stairs to our rooms, we are more nervous than tired. Tomorrow, I will go back to Versailles, but I don't see how I can pretend that everything is the same as it was last week.

Curtius stops me on the threshold of my chamber and says, "You did well tonight. Both the ambassador and the marquis were impressed."

"Thanks to you."

He grins. "Henri appeared quite impressed as well."

I am thankful it's dark and my uncle can't see the flush on my cheeks. "Yes, he is very kind."

"Perhaps he is interested in you," Curtius offers.

"Henri?" I laugh. "Of course he's interested in me. I live next door to him."

"You are twenty-eight," he reminds me gently.

Yes, twenty-eight, and what do I have to show for it? Thirty models, twenty-five busts, and a place as the princesse's tutor at a time when people are more interested in Rousseau than in the king. Until the Salon de Cire is bringing in two hundred people a day, I will never be satisfied. There are more than six hundred thousand people in Paris, and only one and a half percent of them have visited our exhibition. But this new tableau of Jefferson and Lafayette will be a magnificent draw, especially with the Estates-General so close. There is so much to do, and already I am twenty-eight.

"It's a good age for marriage," Curtius continues.

"So are you trying to get rid of me?" I ask, half-joking.

"Of course not," my uncle replies, offended. "You will always remain with the Salon."

"And how will I do that if I am taking care of a husband and children?"

"It is an option," is all he says.

But it is not an option for women like myself and Rose Bertin. Men want wives who are sweet and good with children, not women who plan and watch the accounts. What is it that Queen Elizabeth once said? "Better a beggar woman and single than married and queen." Yes, I think so. Six years ago, the queen's artist, Vigée-Lebrun, was made a member of the Académie Royale. If it can happen for her, it can happen for me.

Chapter 14

April 30, 1789

My crimson vest will be superb; I still need the trimming for the garment and for the coat. But the hat is expensive.

—Marquis de Ferrières,
letter to his wife regarding the Estates-General

Curtius reads Princesse Élisabeth's letter aloud, once for my benefit, then a second time when my mother appears.

If you should like to stay until the ninth of May, I would be an incredibly grateful host. It is only five extra days, and your presence would be a most welcome distraction.

He puts down the letter to see my mother's face. Of course, she is thrilled. She wants to know when it came, by whom, how he was dressed, and why no one thought to get her from her bath.

"He looked exactly like the man who came in February," I promise. "In fact, he might have been the same messenger."

There is no discussion of whether or not I shall stay the extra five days with Madame Élisabeth. Of course I will. It is the greatest chance I have ever been given: all of France's most important people gathered in one place! Thousands of faces, and each a possibility for the Salon.

As soon as breakfast is done, my mother is carefully folding my gowns while Curtius and I are collecting paper and ink. "Everything you see," he is telling me, "sketch. Perhaps you will be there tomorrow while the king officially greets the three estates!"

"I've been invited as a distraction," I say. "I doubt the princesse will want to hold court with her brother."

"She may have to. Be prepared." He's been reading about this daily in the *Journal de Paris.* "On Monday, there will be a procession through Versailles beginning at the Church of Notre-Dame and ending at the Church of Saint-Louis. Everyone will be there. The princesse, the queen, Lafayette, Robespierre . . ."

"I can't bring paper and ink for that!"

"Why not? You won't be part of the procession. Find a place to sit and draw. On Tuesday," Curtius continues, "is the official opening of the Estates-General. The next day, the king will address the assembly. The princesse will certainly be there for his speech. Find a place in the public galleries. By the time you return, everyone will want to know what's happening in Versailles. And where will they be going for their news?"

"To us." I am so excited my hands are shaking. We draft a list of the people I must try to find, beginning with Necker, whom I've yet to see. When the carriage arrives, we are still writing names.

"I will write to you if I think of any others," Curtius promises.

I lean out of the carriage window to wave good-bye, and my mother shouts, "The pink gown is for Tuesday! Wear the blue tomorrow." Pink is my mother's favorite color, and she wants me to look good in the public galleries. I blow them both a kiss as the carriage pulls away.

I open the leather bag I have with me and take out several sheets of paper. I must send Curtius a list of all the things that need to be done while I am gone. First, and most important, are the bodies of Jefferson and Lafayette. I am desperate to begin their models, but they will have to wait until the ninth, when I return. And then who knows what important drawings I'll have brought home with me? Still, Jefferson and Lafayette must take precedence. A new tableau must be built. *Jefferson's Desk,* I think. Or even better, *Jefferson's Study.*

The road to Versailles is choked with carriages, and all of the drivers are impatient, some using the grassy verges to cut off other riders. I close my windows against the stink of horses and excrement, and try not to imagine what it is like in the Palace of Versailles, where the heat of the day will only intensify the scent of urine and sweat in the halls. Thousands of people will want a glimpse of the palace when they arrive.

By the time I reach Montreuil, I am two hours late. Madame Élisabeth and the Marquise de Bombelles are sitting on the colonnaded porch, watching the princesse's six dogs leap and play in the grass. When my carriage appears, the little greyhounds come running. "Put them inside," I hear Madame Élisabeth tell the marquise, and when I descend from the carriage, she says, "Marie! I thought you weren't going to come."

"I am very sorry, Madame. The roads—"

"Of course. It's April nineteenth all over again."

Her brother's wedding day. "You remember that?" I'm surprised. "You were only six."

"Almost seven," she corrects. "But I can still recall all of the carriages and people. Thousands of people," her voice grows distant. "Only they were happy. Happy, and hopeful for the future and a dauphin. My sister-in-law has given France two princes, yet here we are." Her eyes darken. "It was kind of you to come. My sister-in-law's dressmaker could not manage it today. Perhaps tomorrow."

"Mademoiselle Bertin?"

She nods, and I want to ask whether she could not or would not. Imagine, being so certain of the queen's love that you refuse an offer to come to Versailles.

We enter Montreuil, and I inhale deeply. The servants have placed fresh flowers in the vases—thick bunches of roses and branches of jasmine. We spend the morning and most of the afternoon in the workshop, laughing over de Bombelles's version of a foot, which might be a very short-fingered hand. There is a visit from young Madame Royale, who has brought her little brother. Madame Élisabeth makes a great fuss over her nephew, giving him pieces of wax to play with and showing him how to fashion a ball. He is four years old, with the sweetest temperament and the roundest eyes. When Madame Royale feels that he's been too much the center of attention, she takes his hand and announces that it is time for them to go. "I wish to see all the carriages and noblemen," she tells us. "They are arriving by the hundreds, and Maman says I shall have a new dress for tomorrow, and the day after that, because everyone will be watching me."

"I believe that they will be watching your father, the king," Madame Élisabeth observes.

"But we will be sitting with the king," Madame Royale says as she leads her brother toward the door.

"Vanity can be a sin," Madame Élisabeth cautions.

"Oh, it's not vanity," Madame Royale promises. "We must all dress according to our station. That is why the Second Estate has been asked to wear white silks and gold vests, and the Third Estate black coats and breeches."

"I can tell you," Madame Élisabeth replies with certainty, "that if the queen could have her way, we would all be wearing muslin and taffeta."

Madame Royale wrinkles her nose. "Even commoners?"

It is as if I am not here. Or perhaps it is *because* I am here, occupying her aunt's time, that she is saying these things.

"Everyone," Madame Élisabeth repeats.

Madame Royale thinks on this, then pulls her little brother's hand and leaves.

"She is not like her mother," the marquise remarks.

"No," Madame Élisabeth says softly.

Chapter 15

May 1, 1789

Don't be dressed up and don't wear big hats.

—Marie Antoinette,
instructing visitors to the Petit Trianon

Madame Élisabeth is twenty-five today, and we have spent the morning collecting fruit and gathering vegetables from the gardens of Montreuil. I am wearing a soft muslin dress with a wide satin belt and an apron full of rhubarb. If Curtius only knew that, instead of joining her brother in welcoming the Three Estates, the Princesse of France would be picking red currants, he would have kept me in the Salon.

At seven this morning, a young courtier made his way through the crops to tell us the official greeting had begun. Another came a few minutes ago to let us know it had ended. We've learned that the clergy and nobility were met in the Hall of Mirrors, but the representatives of the Third Estate were received in a hall that was far less grand. It was poorly done, and I have no doubt that Camille and Marat will make much of this. If I were braver, I would tell Madame Élisabeth. But among the painted fences and the small, bright fields, I think of my brother Edmund's warning and place my red currants in a basket.

The Marquise de Bombelles has dressed for the day in dark green muslin and a wide straw hat, which complements her features. "I am done," she announces proudly. "The rhubarb is finished."

Madame Élisabeth looks up at the sky. "It's only midday. Let's collect milk from the Hameau. We have never taken Marie to see it."

The marquise frowns, but it is Madame Élisabeth's birthday, and the three of us are driven by *berline* to the Hameau. As we ride, Madame Élisabeth says, "This is the queen's little farm. It was a gift from my brother, and there is nothing anywhere in the world quite like it."

"Oh, it's more than a farm," the marquise adds. "It's an entire"—she searches for the right word—"*world.* The Prince de Condé had one built at Chantilly, but this . . ."

I cannot see how a farm can be like an entire world until the *berline* arrives. On the far edge of a pond, an entire peasants' village has been constructed, complete with a farmhouse, flourmill, cowshed, and working dairy. I am given a tour of nearly every building, from the half-timbered cottages with their newly thatched roofs to the charming water mill with its great splashing wheel. At every window, lilacs and hyacinths have been arranged in white vases, cheering up the façades of the small brick cottages. But it's the Laiterie, two sandstone pavilions nestled in the trees where the queen's well-groomed cows provide fresh milk and butter for Her Majesty at the Trianon, that is the most impressive.

We walk up the stairs and into an antechamber with a towering dome. Everything is the color of ivory: the ceiling, the walls, and the tall, rounded niches where large pieces of white Sèvres china, monogrammed in blue with the queen's initials, have been placed. Beyond this, a pair of wooden doors opens up into a grotto, where a marble sculpture of the nymph Amalthea rests among the overhanging rocks. This room is as cool and dim as the antechamber is light. Fountains chill porcelain milk pails with Roman designs, and stepping closer, I can see what the artist has done. He—or she—has taken scenes from the newly discovered city of Pompeii and used them for inspiration. There is a milk churn painted with Mercury stealing the herds of

Admetus, an amphora decorated with an image of Jupiter, and milk buckets adorned with the shepherd's god, Pan. This is life as Rousseau imagined it. Rustic, charming, peaceful . . . and expensive.

A *laiterie* this beautiful could exist only here. Where else in the world would a shepherdess name her cows Brunette and Blanchette and adorn their necks with collars of lavender? In what other dairy could you see a classical grotto with imitation wood pails made of Sèvres porcelain? I wish I had brought paper and ink with me, but memory will have to suffice.

The marquise says, "Only those who have been invited by the queen are welcome here."

I stop walking. "Were we invited?"

"Any guest of Madame Élisabeth is welcome," she replies, her face tight, and I wonder how welcome I truly am. "Tonight at seven," she continues, "the queen is hosting a fête for Madame Élisabeth. She wishes her guests to dress in red. Have you brought a dress in that color?"

There's the pink for Tuesday, and the blue for Monday. "Yes," I realize. "I have red."

"Good. If the members of the Estates-General can celebrate, then so can we."

In the privacy of my room, I laugh. A celebration for the king's sister, and I am invited! I put on the red taffeta gown. With my lace fichu and a red ribbon in my hair, I stand in front of the glass. If I saw this woman on the street, would I feel compelled to model her? She has good cheekbones and lovely dark hair. The chin is a bit strong, but with the right necklace, she might be mistaken for a comtesse. I think of Jeanne de Valois giving herself such a title and grin. No, there would be no mistaking me for a comtesse. I am too excited!

But what if I should forget the honors? There are so many. A princesse, for example, may kiss the king on both cheeks, but a noble is allowed only one. Members of the Third Estate, like myself, must simply curtsy and bow. I must remember not to cross my legs. And I must glide. Glide, like the queen herself, across the floors of Montreuil. I powder my hair and use my swan's down puff—a gift from Henri many years ago—to lighten my cheeks. My mother, as always, has thought of everything. Toothpicks, brushes, *eaux de propreté,* lavender oil, and orange blossom perfume. There are half a dozen pairs of gloves and fans to choose from, and I bless my mother's foresight as I pick out the gloves that have been perfumed *à la mode de Provence.*

When I reach the double doors to Madame's salon, an usher in the king's livery hands me a red and green mask. "For inside, Mademoiselle. The queen has decided that Madame Élisabeth must guess the identity of every guest who enters. For each one she gets right, the queen will donate fifty livres to the Church of Saint-Sulpice." I can hear the laughter from inside the salon. How many people are in there? Fifty? A hundred?

I put the mask up to my face, and the doors swing open. I am alone. Completely alone before two hundred of the queen's most favored guests. They are sitting around tables on stools and padded cushions. That is part of the honors. As Rose Bertin told me while correcting our exhibit, only the king and queen are allowed *fauteuils,* or chairs with arms. The rest of the king's family simply have chairs with elaborate backs. The duchesses have been given *tabourets,* or padded stools, but all others remain standing. I assume that, when it is time for food to be served, folding chairs will be brought out. There is an intake of breath as I step forward.

I hear someone murmur, "Certainly not any baroness."

"Look at her neck. Only a ribbon."

"The Princesse de Lamballe has only a ribbon."

I know that Madame Élisabeth will not be fooled. She sits in the middle of the room, flanked by the queen and the Marquise de Bombelles. She is wearing one of the most lavish gowns I have seen since coming to Versailles—a satin robe *à la française* in the deepest shade of carmine and trimmed with pearls. Suddenly, I realize that I am underdressed. A year's worth of savings from the Salon de Cire could not buy a gown comparable to hers. When she says, "Mademoiselle Grosholtz," I lower the mask and there is much applause. I curtsy as low as my dress will allow.

It is a sea of red. Red silks, red muslins, red taffetas, red velvets. The rich materials capture the candlelight, and I notice another woman studying the picture the fabrics create. She smiles at me, two members of the Third Estate masquerading for a night as members of Versailles.

"So your gamble worked," Rose Bertin says.

"I believe it was your gamble as well," I reply. I am glad to see her.

She offers me a seat on her little couch, and I take it. "How long has it been?" she asks.

"Three months." I take a glass of white wine that's offered to me and turn away the oysters. I must not appear greedy. "But a great deal has changed since then."

Rose places her fan between us so that no one may read our lips. "And every day it becomes more like a rats' nest. Have you been to the palace this week?"

"We rode by this morning, but we didn't go inside."

"Crawling," she says, "with men you wouldn't admit to the Salon de Cire. Men without any money at all. They blame the queen for everything. The rain, the wind, the bad harvest . . ."

I think of Robespierre, who came to Curtius to borrow a coat before he left. For all of his fine wigs and embroidered waistcoats, he could not afford a jacket with tails. I am ashamed to be speaking this way at the queen's own fête. "Perhaps she can do something to change their minds."

Rose gives me a long look. "You run a show. How do you sell a foreign queen to a people determined to believe the worst? I have tried myself. And failed. She was the ruler of style as well as France. *Now* look."

Across the salon, Marie Antoinette is attended by half a dozen women. She is wearing satin gloves and a *pouf* studded with pearls. She is flawless.

"Nothing unique. Nothing original. Every woman in Europe wanted to follow her once. I could dress her in burlap and the Duchess of Devonshire would follow. She has given up her elaborate wardrobe, and still they hate her. I am useless here."

The queen was Rose Bertin's living doll. Who else could dress herself at noon and see a hundred likenesses by noon the next day?

"And now they think they can live without a queen. There is talk," she whispers, "that the Estates-General will call for a constitutional monarchy."

I glance over my shoulder, but the other guests are all laughing and enjoying the chance to eat pâté de foie gras.

"I know that men visit your salon each Tuesday night. It's not a secret. And everyone knows that your uncle is close with Orléans."

"It's a relationship of convenience," I say. "We have no love for him."

"But what does the Duc believe?" she asks. "Will they propose a constitution?"

I owe Rose the truth. After all, it's no secret, just as she says. And it was her gamble that placed me here. "Yes," I reply, but very quietly. "And they have drafted a declaration so we can be like England."

"A country too weak even to hold on to its colonies?" We both look at Madame Élisabeth, who is reaching for her sister-in-law's hand. "They are too good," Rose says. "That is their problem. Another king would send soldiers to arrest the Duc and execute him. Anyone who dissented would follow."

Chapter 16

May 3, 1789

The hallways, the courtyards, even the buildings and corridors are all filled with urine and fecal matter.

—Jean-Louis Fargeon,
perfumer to the court of Versailles

On Sunday, after prayers, I'm allowed to visit my brothers. Wolfgang meets me at the door of the Grand Commune, under its triangular pediment and carved *cherubini.* The hall beyond us is empty, but come night, it will be filled with the hundreds of representatives who have come to Versailles.

"Where are Edmund and Johann?" I ask.

"They couldn't get away. You have no idea what it's like in the palace. Hundreds of people, and who knows what any of them are carrying. The doors are open at all hours, and cats have taken over the halls. I saw a pig yesterday—"

"In the *château*?"

"It's a zoo." We begin to walk, and I notice that his black shoes and silver buckles are new. "No more Sundays off until the Estates-General is finished."

"But then how did you get here?"

"I've become somewhat friendly with my commander, the Baron de Besenval," he confesses. "I've been making it my mission to impress him."

This isn't like Wolfgang. "Are you in debt?"

We reach a small fountain and sit on the ledge. "It's his daughter."

I study his face. "You're not serious? He's a baron! What does Edmund say?"

"Oh, Edmund doesn't know," he answers quickly. "He can't know. Not until I've convinced the baron I'm suitable for Abrielle. She is such a kind woman, Marie. And beautiful. With a face like that of the Princesse de Lamballe—only sweeter. I've been exemplary these past few weeks. And Besenval has taken notice."

"He'll want to marry her off to someone with a title," I warn. "And if she's as pretty as you say, then someone with a fortune."

His shoulders sag. "I met her last year at a celebration her father hosted. I thought I would forget about her. Then I saw her again last month in the palace. There really is no one like her, Marie. I wouldn't pursue this if she didn't want me as well. I see her at every Sunday Mass, and on Tuesdays we meet in the Château Opéra. No one uses it anymore."

Like Camille and Lucile, a pair of lovers determined to decide their own fate. "And what does she tell her father?"

"There are seven hundred rooms in the palace. You could set a dog loose and never find him again."

So he doesn't know. "And how old is she?"

"Twenty-three." He adds defensively, "She's not a child."

"But she's Besenval's child."

"Yes." He stands. "Which is why I must get back. He gave me leave to see you, but only to wish you well. I heard the queen held a masquerade in Montreuil last night," he remarks.

"Not a proper one with costumes, but there were masks."

"You were there?" he exclaims.

"I was invited by the princesse."

"I wish I could hear all about it. You will have to write to me, and I will tell you how it's progressing with Abrielle."

"Be careful," I say. "If her father discovers you—"

"Then both he and Edmund will want my head." He holds out his gloved hand, and I take it. "Don't worry." He winks. "I don't plan on being caught."

"Someone will talk."

"You are the only one who knows."

"And you don't think she's told half a dozen of her friends?"

"No. She can keep a confidence."

As we make our way toward the palace, I try to imagine my brother with a title, and giggle. "Baron Wolfgang," I whisper.

He grins. "And really, who wouldn't want me for a son?"

"It all depends," I tease him. "Do you plan on gambling away the dowry?"

Suddenly, he becomes serious. "I haven't gambled in six weeks. Honestly, Marie, I want this more than anything. Write to me. I want to know everything you hear this month. In the palace . . . on the Boulevard . . ."

I think of Rose Bertin's words, *It's no secret.* "It might not be fit for letters."

"Then we can meet at the same place on Friday nights and you can tell me."

We stop in front of the marble courtyard, where the king looks out every morning from his bedchamber down the Avenue de Paris. "Will you give my love to Edmund and Johann?"

"If you will kiss Curtius and Maman for me." He doffs his hat. "Now it's back to the menagerie."

Chapter 17

MAY 4, 1789

France revealed itself in all its splendor. And I asked myself, what muddled minds, what ambitious, vile men, for their own interests, are trying to break up this whole, so great, so respectable, and dissipate this glory?

—MARQUIS DE FERRIÈRES,
REMARKING ON THE ESTATES-GENERAL

ALL OF FRANCE HAS BEEN WAITING FOR THIS DAY. NOW THAT it's here, every person in the town of Versailles is watching. Even God, from His place in the heavens, must be looking down at this magnificent assembly of the Estates-General in Versailles's Church of Notre-Dame. It is a pageantry of silks and velvets and gold that would have gladdened the heart of the Sun King himself.

"Push to the front," Rose Bertin says. When I am too demure, she uses her parasol to make our way through the crowds. "You see?" she exclaims. "That's how it's done."

We are standing so close to the altar now that I can see the individual fleurs-de-lis embroidered into the gold and purple cloth draping the chancel. The king and queen will preside over the roll call of the *bailliages* before leading a procession through the streets of Versailles to the Church of Saint-Louis. There are so many people that it's impossible to see anything but the space in front of me. Somewhere in the crowd, Marat and Camille are watching, while Robespierre is sitting with the members of the Third Estate.

The clock strikes nine, and as the trumpets begin to sound, the entire congregation turns. But there is nothing to see. No sign of the royal family or the men who will take the velvet seats beneath them. "The dauphin was ill this morning," Rose whispers to me. "I had to dress Her Majesty while she was tending to him."

But as the time passes and the twelve hundred representatives begin to shift in their seats, I hear women say, "The queen is probably searching for another gown" and "Perhaps she forgot what day it was." When the man next to us posits, "Perhaps she is asking her lover for one last *baiser* before she goes," Rose Bertin answers him loudly, "She is with the dauphin, who is ill and may die."

This shames those around us into silence, but it is another hour before the royal couple arrive, preceded by a fanfare of trumpets and fifes. As soon as they appear, there is a collective gasp. The king and queen have come dressed as the true regents of France. From head to toe the king gleams with diamonds. In the cold light of the chancel, they shine like raindrops. Rose points to the gem in King Louis's hat. "The Regent Diamond, the largest in the world." Which means the queen must be wearing the world's second largest. It sparkles from her hair, and smaller gems catch at the light from the bodice of her gown.

"There's no necklace," I say, and Rose sniffs her response, as if to reply, *Little surprise,* given the scandal of the Diamond Necklace Affair. But the queen is still shimmering, a silver snowflake to the king's bright gold. And behind her comes Madame Élisabeth, dressed in the most exquisite gown I have ever seen her wear.

As the royal family approach, the congregation of Notre-Dame bows. First the clergy, then the nobility, then the Third Estate. Only the members of the Third Estate aren't bowing. They are standing! Over six hundred men are standing with their hats on their heads and their legs unmoving.

"They're refusing!" Rose grips my arm. "They're all refusing."

The nobility look to the clergy in confusion. Is this a sin? The king is the manifestation of God's will, the blessed leader. I can see shock register in the queen's eyes. Then the king takes his place to the right of the choir screen while the queen and her ladies take their seats to the left. The performance must go on, whether or not the dauphin is ill, whether or not the king wishes it so.

Beneath the altar, on long velvet benches, are the king's most important men: the Comte d'Artois, the Comte de Provence, the Swiss-born Minister of Finance, Jacques Necker. They are all pretending that this terrible snub has not happened. But up close, I can see that the queen is strained. She must be thinking about her son, wishing that she could be with him instead of here.

Two by two, the representatives of the First and Second Estates approach the king. They bow first to him, and then to the queen. The roll-call ceremony is long and boring, but everyone is waiting to see what will happen when the Third Estate's members are called. When the first representative's name is announced, I am sure my heart stops. But the first man bows, and then the second. The queen exhales visibly, and Rose relaxes her grip on my arm.

"Now that they stand before God's altar," someone says, "they aren't too proud to show their respect."

When it is all finished, I wonder if perhaps I haven't dreamed that first slight. The trumpeters begin to play, joined by harpists and men on fifes. Then Rose and I pour into the streets with the rest of the assembly. After two days of rain, the sun has made its way through the clouds, gilding the courtiers in their embroidered stockings and the clerics in their golden robes. The men of the Swiss Guard have lined the road from the Church of Notre-Dame to the Church of Saint-Louis, and they stand at attention like a row of toy soldiers. It is useless to look for my brothers. There are hundreds of guards, and ten times as many people.

"We can stand here for the procession," Rose says, "but as soon as it's over, we must be the first into Saint-Louis. I want to see the Princesse de Lamballe's gown. I didn't design it."

"Perhaps the court is attempting to find less expensive *marchandes*?"

"If the princesse wishes to use inferior cloth, then that is her decision. Vendors at the Palais are selling burlap sacks cheap. Perhaps she'd like to wear that." Rose will see the gown, inspect it, and tomorrow she will know the name of the *marchande* who sold it and for exactly how much. It is what I would do if I learned of a rival modeler in Paris.

The trumpeters herald the start of the procession, and the three estates begin their walk to the Church of Saint-Louis, where they will all attend Mass. I've brought paper and ink, but there's nothing of this procession I'm likely to forget. Next to the king, the queen and Madame Élisabeth look dazzling in their jewels. Behind this glittering trio, the king's brothers and their wives carry a canopy over the holy Eucharist. Following them are the members of the clergy in their long cassocks and wide, square bonnets. Then come the nobility, who have all put on their hats, plumed like those of the courtiers of Henri IV. It's like stepping back in time nearly two hundred years. The silks . . . the brocades . . .

Rose sighs. "Have you ever seen anything so beautiful?"

I wish Henri and the rest of my family could be here for this. I wish all of France could see the pomp and majesty of our monarchy. There are two hundred and ninety-one nobles, three hundred clergy, and six hundred and ten members of the Third Estate. But for every representative, there are five times as many people lining the roads. Though the applause is deafening, no one shouts, "Long live the king!"

"There is Lafayette," Rose says breathlessly. "And Duquesnoy!" She is pointing out the important nobles as they go by. Then she grabs my arm. "The Duc d'Orléans!"

"I don't see him." The nobles have already passed. Now the Third Estate has come into view, dressed in black coats and black tricorn hats.

She points wildly to a large man walking among the commoners, and for a moment, I feel sick. "He changed!" I exclaim. "That's not what he was wearing in Notre-Dame." As the crowd realizes what's happening, there is thunderous applause. The Duc d'Orléans, a cousin of the king who should be walking among the nobility, has dressed in plain black and is marching with the Third Estate.

Women begin waving their handkerchiefs in the air, and though the crowd was silent when the king passed by, someone shouts, "*Long live the Duc d'Orléans!*" The cry is taken up all along the roads, and as the cheers grow louder, the Duc bows his head, a humble subject showing his solidarity with the people.

I think of Madame Élisabeth, walking beside her brother. What must she feel—what must any of the royals feel—to hear their subjects calling for the Duc instead of the king? The Duc has turned this entire occasion into his own masquerade, a devious fraud to manipulate the people's passions.

"And look who else is marching with the Third." Rose points. "The Comte de Mirabeau!"

Everyone has heard of the hideous and pockmarked comte, who took a beautiful young heiress and forced her into marriage. After seeing her in the marketplace, he bribed one of the girl's servants into letting him visit her chamber. Then, while she was sleeping, he slipped into her bed and swore to the household that he was her lover. What could her father do? Her engagement to another man was canceled and a marriage to Mirabeau was arranged to save her honor.

"I have heard," Rose says, "that Mirabeau corresponds with the Marquis de Sade."

"It doesn't surprise me. They are both despicable men."

The cheers for the Duc d'Orléans have died down, and as the procession passes, we follow the estates into the Church of Saint-Louis. The candles flicker in the darkened sanctuary, illuminating the paintings and ancient tapestries. But it's the queen's dress, as pale and silvery as the moon, that is even more dazzling in this light.

There is a tense silence as the congregation waits for Henri de La Fare to give God's blessing on the Estates-General. As the thirty-seven-year-old bishop from Nancy reaches the pulpit, there is something in his face that makes me wary.

"Behold," he begins, "the King and Queen of Extravagance!" He points to the queen and Louis XVI, but the king has nodded off. Only those who are close to the altar can see. The bishop gives an entire sermon chastising the royal couple for their expenditures. He compares Marie Antoinette's gowns to the tattered rags belonging to the people in the streets. He condemns her for attempting to escape court life in a mock peasants' village. "Does she know what it's like to be a peasant?" he thunders. "Does she know what it is to starve and sell the milk that you are too destitute to keep?"

It is terrible. Rose closes her eyes rather than see the queen's humiliation.

"We must find ourselves a king," he sums up, "who hears his people, who feels their pain, and who controls his wife's appetite for devouring this nation!"

The entire church is silent. Even the queen's enemies are in shock. Then suddenly there is joyous applause. It rouses the king. The walls resound with whistling and cheers. God must be ashamed. If these people believe that divine displeasure has caused the rain to come and their crops to fail, what do they believe will come of this?

"Let's go," I say, and Rose follows me out.

"Shall we meet again tomorrow?" she asks quietly. It is the first official meeting of the Estates-General. Madame Élisabeth will be expected to be there.

"We can meet in the galleries," I offer.

"Yes." She is distracted. Vague. "I would bring an umbrella," she adds. "It may rain."

We part on these words. There is nothing more to say.

When I return to Montreuil, there is no mention of what has passed. But when Mass is finished, I can see that Madame Élisabeth has been weeping.

Chapter 18

May 5, 1789

On our Nation's stage, only the scenery has changed.

—Jean-Paul Marat

An entire hall has been built on the grounds of the Hôtel des Menus Plaisirs for the purpose of housing the Estates-General. It is a room so high and wide that it's impossible to believe it hasn't been here for a hundred years. On three of the four walls, public galleries have been constructed, and from any of these benches you can see the stage where the royal thrones have been placed, and the rectangular space for the speakers below.

Just as Rose predicted, it's raining. All morning the heavy torrents have fallen in thick gray sheets. The hall is lit by chandeliers, and so many candles are burning that the smell of wax overpowers even the scents of powder and musk. But perhaps it would be better if the chamber was dim. If I were the queen, fanning myself compulsively in this warm, close hall, I would not want people to read on my face just how devastating this morning has been.

Necker's opening address has gone on for nearly three hours, and he has no solution for filling the nation's empty coffers. So he speaks about the expensive American War. How supplying the Americans with frigates and troops to battle the British has nearly bankrupted the nation of France. The Minister of Finance rings his hands. If we had only saved instead of spending . . .

"There's the American ambassador," Rose whispers. She's been using the spyglass in her fan to search for Jefferson. "Look at that waistcoat."

"Did you discover who made the Princesse de Lamballe's gown?"

"Madame Éloffe. As I suspected." She continues searching the crowds. If I were wise, I would be doing the same. Curtius went to the trouble of purchasing a lorgnette fan for me, with a brass and ivory spyglass set in the center. The artist has cleverly painted the blades so that the telescope looks as if it's part of a hill where a girl is strolling along with her lover. Every woman in attendance has a similar fan, some with jealousy glasses that tilt out at a ninety-degree angle, others with lorgnettes set in the wooden pivots.

But Necker's speech is riveting to me in its failure. By now, I have memorized every line on his face and curl in his wig. No one thought of acoustics when building this hall, and the speakers must shout as if it were a barn. Only those with seats close to the floor can hear what's being said. Necker is tiring, and finally his voice is defeated. He passes his papers on to someone else to finish.

There is an audible groan from the audience, people shifting in their seats and searching their bags for something to eat. Finally, it is the king's turn to address the assembly. As slow and heavy and short as he may be, there is a majesty in his bearing today. But as he begins, his voice trembles. "There is the need for change," he says. "There is the need to economize." Yet nothing he says is far-reaching or inspiring. It is clear he is too afraid of angering the first two estates to suggest any radical reform.

When he is finished, he raises his hat and replaces it on his head. Out of tradition, only the nobles and the clergy are supposed to do the same. But the Third Estate don their hats as well! Members of the Third Estate are supposed to remain bareheaded in the presence of their monarch. For the second time in two days, they are purposely showing disrespect for the king.

There is a silence in the hall so loud it's deafening.

That evening, the papers are absolutely triumphant. EQUALS IN THE RUE DES CHANTIERS, one reads, and another writes, A NEW TRADITION IN THE HÔTEL DES MENUS. And the pictures are no better. In one image, a fat monkey wearing a crown is shown speaking to a group of chickens. "My dear creatures," he says, "I have assembled you here to deliberate on the sauce in which you will be served."

When I enter Montreuil, I hide these papers in my leather bag. It is late, but I meet the Marquise de Bombelles in the hall, and she says solemnly, "The princesse would like to see you. She is in the salon."

This summons can mean only one thing. She regrets calling me here to Montreuil when I've done nothing to distract her from her family's humiliation. A pair of ushers hold open the doors. Inside, Madame Élisabeth is on her settee, surrounded by three of her dogs. A fire warms the intimate room, crackling and popping. It is the only sound, and the princesse makes a sad and lonely picture.

"Marie." She doesn't rise. "Tell me what you thought of the Estates-General." She indicates a chair opposite her, and I look around. Are there spies hidden behind the tapestries? Are they waiting for me to divulge secrets about the Third Estate?

"It is only us," Madame Élisabeth promises. "It isn't a trap."

I can feel the blood drain from my cheeks. Is this better or worse than being dismissed? I look down at the dogs, curled like warm, sleek muffs. "They weren't kind," I say.

"No," the princesse agrees. "And I'm wondering why."

My God, where do I begin? "I believe it is to do with money."

"Yes. The money the Third Estate is being forced to pay."

I nod. At least she understands this. "It makes them bitter. They see the queen in her diamonds, and they wonder how it is that they can't afford milk."

Madame Élisabeth's cheeks burn red. It was a poor example, too close to Henri de La Fare's critique.

"It's no fault of the queen's," I assure her. "If she were to come in a simple muslin dress, they would criticize her for that as well." I open my bag and hand her the papers from today.

"They sell these on the streets? In Versailles?"

"And all over Paris, Madame."

It is terrible to see her shock. Her eyes well with tears. "They all think the Duc would make a better king. *The Duc d'Orléans!* Do they understand what they are hoping for? He's a spendthrift. A traitor! And look at the names they are calling the queen!" She is trembling, turning the pages so fast that she cannot be reading. "Is this what the Third Estate really believes?"

Her wide eyes meet mine, holding my gaze. I should lie, as Edmund would want me to. But I cannot. "Yes."

"And your family?"

"They are loyal," I say swiftly. "This comes from the malcontents in the Palais-Royal. They have been angry for years. Decades." These words are shattering to her. I can see the mask crumbling in front of me. But I owe her the truth. "They want a constitutional monarchy."

"That will never happen!" She rises, and as she does, the doors of the salon swing open. Her little dogs scatter from the settee, jumping and nipping at the heels of the king.

"Your Majesty." I stand and then sink into my lowest curtsy. Madame Élisabeth snatches up the three papers I've brought.

The king is smiling. "Please, sit," he tells me.

I take a seat on a backless stool while he occupies the embroidered chair. Even in the Salon de Cire, I was never this close to the king. He smells of alcohol but doesn't appear to be drunk. "I think it went well today."

"Your speech was excellent," Madame Élisabeth says kindly. "The people could hear you at the back of the hall. Ask Marie."

The King of France looks to me. "Were you in the audience?"

"Yes. Your Majesty's voice carried to the very farthest seats."

This makes him happy. My words—the words of a common woman—have delighted the king. "I have very high hopes for this assembly," he reveals. "Even with their little mutinies, these are sensible men. Men who want the best for us and for our kingdom."

I flinch at this astonishing ignorance. But Madame Élisabeth does nothing to correct him.

"The queen thinks I am being too kind about this hat rebellion. But the people love me. We must allow the Third Estate their small defiances."

I wait for the princesse to produce the newspapers. I wait for her to tell him about the *libelles.* But instead, she offers him bread and tea.

Chapter 19

May 8, 1789

Create citizens, and you have everything you need; without them, you will have nothing but debased slaves.

—Jean-Jacques Rousseau

The papers are calling him Rob-Pierre, Robests-Piesse, even Robertz-Peirre. In the Salle des États, where everything echoes beneath the barrel-vaulted roof and the speakers compete with chatty audiences to be heard, only his friends from our salon, Camille and Marat, have gotten it right. Their articles detail his sudden rise to prominence, stressing how this provincial lawyer from Arras has taken the Estates-General by surprise. The *Journal de Paris National,* the *Courrier de l'Europe,* even the daily *Journal de Paris,* have something to say about him. I wonder what Henri and Curtius think, reading his name from the Boulevard du Temple.

Although neither Madame Élisabeth nor I have visited the Estates-General again, it's impossible to avoid the news. It's in the halls, on the streets, and in hurried whispers during Mass. When the princesse asks me if I've heard of this man, this Robespierre, I admit that I have some acquaintance with him.

"He is bringing the entire Estates-General to a standstill," she accuses, and she's not wrong. As it is, each estate has one vote when ruling on taxes or fiscal reform. Since the clergy and nobility will vote together to preserve their privileges, Robespierre is insisting that the votes of every *deputy* be counted. The Third Estate fought to gain greater representation, but it means nothing if each estate is to have only one vote. On Friday night, when I meet Wolfgang outside the Grand Commune, it's with a packet of letters as thick as a book.

"You must be bored in Montreuil," he jokes, since he has only one letter for me. But he looks well. And again, his shoes are new. This time the buckles are gold.

"Gifts from Abrielle?" I ask.

"She is very generous."

"Is that part of her charm?"

He dismisses my question with a laugh, then takes my arm and we sit together inside the Grand Commune. Food will not be served for a few hours, and we are alone with the richly paneled walls and wooden tables. "I'm surprised you haven't found a wealthy comte, or a rich merchant in the Palais-Royal."

"Are you talking to Curtius?" I demand. "How would I have time for the Salon if I were caring for a husband and children?"

"You might find a husband who doesn't want children."

"Are there men who don't want heirs?"

My brother thinks about this. "You don't have any desire for marriage?"

"Not if it means giving up my work. And it will. Children will come, and how will I tutor, or make models, or promote? He will want me by the fireside, knitting bonnets and pouring tea."

"It's hard for a woman, isn't it?"

"Are you feeling sorry for me," I tease, "now that you're courting Abrielle and neglecting to write?"

He smiles. "A little. Here." He hands me his single letter.

"That's all your news?"

"It's long," he says, then adds swiftly, "but promise you'll burn it as soon as you're done."

"And all of mine." It goes without saying that none of them must be shared with Edmund. "Will you show these to Johann?"

"If you want me to. I think he can keep secrets. Are there things in these he shouldn't read?"

"No." I lower my voice. Though we're alone, there must be cooks in the kitchen. "It's just the news I've heard of the Estates-General. The princesse is convinced that Robespierre wishes to overthrow the king."

"If she knew that he dines with the Duc in your salon, it would be the end of our careers."

"Well, she'll never know it from me. And the Duc wouldn't say."

"Robespierre might talk."

"No. Their paths will never cross." I am sure of this. "Not unless it's in front of Rousseau's grave."

My brother finds this amusing. "He's odd, isn't he? Funny that he should be the one to stir up their passions. I suppose he quotes a great deal from his idol?"

"Every chance he gets." I repeat, "'There can be no patriotism without liberty, no liberty without virtue, no virtue without citizens; create citizens, and you have everything you need; without them, you will have nothing but debased slaves. . . .' He wants a country with citizens, not subjects."

My brother's eyes have gone wide. "He should be careful."

"Why? He has nothing to lose. He borrowed coats from Curtius before leaving Paris. He doesn't have a single livre to his name."

"He has freedom. And he must have a family."

"The king would never arrest them." I tell Wolfgang about my meeting with Louis XVI. How certain he is of the people's goodness, and how he wishes to make a speech to inspire them.

My brother shakes his head. "Then I hope he feels inspired to hear more from Robespierre."

A SMALL CROWD is waiting for me when I return to the Boulevard du Temple. Curtius must have told our neighbors that I was coming, and they have all turned up to hear the news. There are Henri and Jacques, Yachin and his father, even the butcher and his portly wife. More people appear as I descend from the carriage, and Curtius proudly leads them up the stairs to our salon. There is no time to inspect the exhibit or see the new room Henri and Curtius have built. Everyone wants to hear what's happening in Versailles. I tell them what I know without compromising Madame Élisabeth or the king.

"We've been hearing a great deal about Robespierre, that he's become an important voice in the Assembly," Henri's brother says. "He was such an unassuming man."

Everyone around Jacques Charles agrees.

"They say his voice carries across the entire hall and he holds the Third Estate in a sort of trance. Do you think that's what they're in?" the butcher asks.

"They are simply tired of shouldering the financial burden for the entire nation," I say.

The men begin to debate: Will the votes be counted by order or by head? Will the privileges of the first two estates be abolished? My mother brings out fresh rolls and pâté. It is a sign of our neighborly goodwill that we are willing to share our bread. I notice that Yachin eats enough for two. "Yachin," his father, Abraham, scolds when he notices I am watching. He explains shamefacedly, "I think he is growing."

"Let him eat." I smile. "He works hard enough."

Abraham nods, and Yachin reaches for another roll. "It was very kind of you to give him such a special token from the queen. My wife was tremendously proud. She took it to all of our neighbors in Saint-Martin." This is the quartier where most of the city's Jews are living. It is terribly poor. "My wife and I are loyal to the king, but we have great hopes for the Estates-General." He strokes his long beard. It is a habit with him. "We want citizenship. As it is, we must register in Paris and renew our *passeport* every three months. The fees for this . . . Well, most Jews cannot afford them. But where else can we go?" He shakes his head. "At least in this country, we have the freedom to pray. There is a synagogue on the Rue Brisemiche. And there are shops that follow the dietary laws of Kashrut. We have built a community," he tells me. "There is a *hebra* for the poor and the *heder* where my son can learn Hebrew. Eventually, the king must see reason. Look at what the Estates-General has accomplished: in one week, he has learned that the people have a voice. And if the deputies can speak out, then so can the Jews."

"Is that what Zalkind Hourwitz is doing?" Henri asks. I had not known he was listening to our discussion.

Abraham looks across the table in surprise. "You read the *Courrier*?"

"And the *Chronique.* I try to read as many literary journals as I can."

"Hourwitz has been sending his petitions for many months," Abraham explains. "And he's making some progress. Perhaps by this time next year . . ."

This is the kind of hope that is all over Paris. In the salons, in the streets, in the cafés that have overrun the Palais-Royal. Everyone is hoping for great things from the Estates-General.

At noon, Yachin returns to his place outside and our guests begin to leave. Only Henri stays, since he and Curtius are waiting to show me the new exhibit. We go downstairs, and when Curtius throws open the doors to the room, I gasp. It is an exact replica of Jefferson's study, from the paintings on the wall to the mahogany desk. I touch the wooden shelves, where leather-bound books have been fitted between marble busts and potted plants. "How . . . how did you do this?"

"We had Jefferson's help," Henri admits. "He allowed us to return and sketch his study."

I feel tears pricking the backs of my eyes. I don't know why I should be so affected by this. But it's the most beautiful room we have ever exhibited. The chairs, the wallpaper, the long leather couch with its clawed brass feet—it is all so *exact.* "Thank you, Henri," I say. We shall continue to repay him by sending our customers to see his Invisible

Girl, but I think of the experiments he might have had time for if not for this, and I am deeply moved. He must have spent hours here, possibly nights. I imagine his hair tied back from his face and the two lines between his brows deepening as they always do when he is hard at work. Truly, there has never been a better man than him. "You are far too kind to us."

He makes a little bow. "It was my pleasure."

"Now there is simply the matter of a few models to make," my uncle says.

"Only Jefferson and Lafayette," I reply.

"Didn't you bring drawings of anyone else? What about Mirabeau?"

I fetch my bag and take out my sketches. There are half a dozen men. The hideous Mirabeau is among them, as well as the Duc d'Orléans.

"We should do all of these," my uncle says. "Especially the Duc."

I think of the way they shouted his name in the streets, and the worry on Madame Élisabeth's pale face when I saw her. "What if we're encouraging rebellion?" I ask. "What if by making a model of him we're reinforcing the idea that he should be king? Edmund would say—"

"Forget what Edmund says," Curtius exclaims, and he walks me to the Salon's largest window. The entire Boulevard is spread before us. "*People*. And all of them are going about their business. If the Salon de Cire disappeared tomorrow, do you think that man would change his mind about polishing his boots? Or that woman would have chosen a different parasol? The events of this month are bigger than us. We are simply reporting them in the flesh."

"Or wax," Henri offers wryly.

"We aren't changing minds," Curtius says. "Think of the artist who paints a brewing storm. Is he responsible for the rain? You might say he has created a thing of beauty out of something filled with misery and danger."

He is right. The Salon de Cire exists to report events as they are happening. Mistresses, murderers, newly made queens . . .

I spend the next three days in my workshop. When it's time for me to return to Versailles, Curtius writes a letter filled with regret, stating that I will not be able to assist Madame Élisabeth again until June. I sign my name, and though I feel guilty, we are not like the princesse. We must maintain a business for a living. Madame's twenty livres a day are all well and good, but how long will the position last? The Salon must come first. There are molds and sculptures and bodies to be made. There are teeth to be found and eyes to be painted.

There must be seven new models for the Salon de Cire by the time I return to Montreuil. Jefferson, Lafayette, Robespierre, Mirabeau, Necker, Danton, and the Duc d'Orléans. I try to imagine Robespierre's face when he returns to find himself in wax. *He will be beside himself with glee,* I think. He will probably want to take the model home.

I begin by sculpting the Duc, thinking to do the unpleasant tasks first. Though in clay he's not so offensive. His lips don't sneer, and his eyes don't narrow into derisive slits. In fact, when I'm finished, he's rather pleasing to look at. Not a handsome man. But pleasant.

Mirabeau, however, is just as loathsome in clay as in the flesh. I include the pitted scars left by the smallpox, and the protrusions on his nose and lips from syphilis. The prostitutes call it the Italian disease, though I suspect it can be caught from anyone, really.

It is a far more joyous task when I begin to sculpt Jefferson. He and Lafayette have similar noses. Aquiline, strong. Though their jaws are different. One square, the other round. I close my eyes and think to myself, *I could sculpt Jefferson from memory.*

Of all the models, Georges Danton's proves the most difficult, but he has become a popular assemblyman, and there is no choice but to use the extra wax and sculpt this giant of a man. I have laid eyes on him only once, but to see him at the podium in the Hôtel des Menus is to never forget him. He has the body of a mill worker rather than a lawyer. His hands, chest, even his shoulders, are larger than any man I've ever modeled. But it's his heavy brow that distinguishes him the most, and it will probably be Danton whom our customers are most impressed with.

~

THREE WEEKS LATER, when all seven models are finished, Curtius sends Yachin to help me dress the figures. He sorts through the chests of clothes we've collected, looking for something suitable for Robespierre.

"What about this?" he holds up a pair of tattered stockings.

"I said Robespierre, not Marat." I brush Mirabeau's hair away from his face and wonder if preparing a model of Marat could truly be any worse than this.

Yachin holds up an embroidered coat and silk cravat, and I nod. We used them for a model of the Comte d'Artois several years ago. "When do you think we will have the unveiling?" he asks.

"On Friday," I tell him. That gives us three days to arrange the models and prepare the rooms. Plus, create a window display that features the Estates-General. "If you can find a pair of blue stockings in that chest, it might work."

He brings his discoveries over to me and perches on a bench to watch while I sort through his pile.

"It was a pleasure to see your father again," I say. "How is his business?"

"Well. Or better than before. Suddenly, everyone wants to use our printers. My father says most of his requests are for *libelles* attacking the monarchy. I have read what some of these papers say about the queen and her friends. They accuse her of . . ." His voice drops low. "Well, they aren't kind."

I put down the brush. The hair on Mirabeau's model is as precise as it's ever going to be. "Does your father print them?"

"He won't have it. He tells them to find someone else. That he has a family to consider. Who will take care of us if my father is arrested? I haven't even become a Bar Mitzvah. Mine will come next month, and there's to be a fine meal in my honor."

I can see that Yachin is already thinking of this meal, and I offer him some of the bread and sausage my mother left on the table.

"Don't you want it for yourself?"

"I'm not a growing young man."

"But the bread." He hesitates. "It must have been expensive."

Yes. And the newspapers are saying that the wheat we've been given from America is infested with insects. There is going to be starvation if something isn't done. The king has resorted to begging the English for flour, but their House of Commons has flatly refused, saying that this is God's justice for supporting the Americans in their war. "Don't worry." I smile. "Just eat."

While Yachin is quiet for a moment, I go to the model of Jefferson. The clothing he's chosen for the American looks exactly like something the ambassador would wear. Silk *culottes* with a waistcoat of striped velvet. I place my hand briefly on his chest. Unlike with the model of Madame du Barry, there's no gentle rise and fall. But for a moment I imagine that this strong, sculpted man is Henri, waiting for me to tie his cravat.

Chapter 20

MAY 29, 1789

This hardworking German [Philippe Curtius] produces colored wax heads of such quality that one could imagine that they are alive.

—MAYEUR DE SAINT-PAUL, EXCERPT FROM TOURIST BROCHURE

"MEET THE DEPUTIES OF THE ESTATES-GENERAL!" YACHIN cries. "Then come see the greatest thieves in France!"

"Will the queen be there?" I hear someone ask, and the people in line begin to laugh.

Commoners, noblemen, tourists from England—they are all crushed together: the rich want to walk through Jefferson's study, while the poor wish to see Robespierre in the Estates-General. This is success even greater than when the royal family came to visit, and the customers can't shove their twelve sous at us fast enough. The *Journal* can write of Robespierre, but we show him the flesh. The *Courrier* can paint a picture of the Salle des États with words, but we have brought it to life. And only the Salon de Cire can show Danton as he truly is in life—towering, immense, with a chest like a barrel and hands like heavy plates.

"We shall have to limit the time they're inside," Curtius says. "Otherwise, this line could go for days." We sit at the *caissier*'s desk from ten in the morning till ten at night. When we close the doors, there are men and women returning from the theaters who want to know when we'll be open tomorrow.

"Eight in the morning," I reply.

"And how much for entry?"

"Fifteen sous." My mother stares at me.

As they walk away, I hear one of them saying, "I'd rather see models than read the *Journal.* The papers are so tedious."

"Fifteen sous?" my mother asks when they're gone.

Forget fifteen sous. "We could charge twenty!"

My mother looks uncertain, but when eight o'clock arrives and the line stretches down the Boulevard du Temple, there is no doubt that this is a winning approach. Curtius and I decide to include posters in every room explaining the tableaux. Each day, as more news comes from Versailles, the posters will change. All of Saturday is a triumph. But as the last patrons are pushing through the door, a rider comes with the message that my brothers will be arriving tomorrow.

Curtius shakes his head. "It would be better if they didn't. Think of it, Anna," he says in German. "What will Edmund feel?"

She looks at the room that's been transformed into the Salle des États, then at the figures in *Jefferson's Study.* "He will understand that this is business," she says firmly. "He will see how we have made a great success."

"He doesn't care about success, Maman. Tell them we'll go to Versailles instead."

But she won't hear of it, and when the carriage arrives on Sunday evening, I pause on the doorstep to tell my uncle, "We've taken in three thousand sous since Friday." That's three times what we would normally make. "He will be enraged."

Curtius gives me a look. "Then try not to provoke him."

This time I won't need to.

~

MY BROTHERS LEAP from the carriage, Wolfgang first, and when he wraps me in his arms, I smell the scents of narcissus and sandalwood in his hair. He embraces my mother, and she smells the change, too. I have told her about Abrielle. But she will wait for him to say something first.

"Welcome home." She kisses both of his cheeks, then does the same for Johann and Edmund. "Come inside. We have coffee waiting."

"And something to eat?" Johann says hopefully.

"This is Maman," I reply. "The table is full." We set it this afternoon, leaving Yachin to help Curtius while my mother roasted meats and I prepared the desserts. There will be pastries and almond milk, plus Johann's favorite cheeses, Gloucester and Gruyère.

"I see the streetlights are still out," Edmund remarks. "The Estates-General hasn't changed the world."

We step into the Salon, and everyone falls silent. My mother closes the door behind us, and Wolfgang gives a low whistle. The tableau of Robespierre, Danton, and Mirabeau is the first room you see. "It looks just like the Salle des États," Wolfgang says.

"Very impressive," Johann adds. "Did Marie do this?"

Edmund's eyes are accusing. "You are no better than the *libellistes*. We *spoke* of this!"

"And while I heard your concerns, I also heard the voice of the people—"

Edmund turns on our mother. "Aren't you supposed to guide this family? Where are your principles?"

My mother inhales sharply.

"Perhaps you don't have any. After all, you live with a man you've never married. No better than a common *cocotte* really."

Curtius reaches out and grabs Edmund's throat. He is going to kill him. I can see it in his eyes.

"Don't!" Johann cries. He and Wolfgang pull them apart, and Johann shouts into his brother's face, "What's the matter with you?"

I rush to comfort my mother, who is weeping into her apron. "He didn't mean it," I say. "He isn't rational."

"I'm perfectly rational!" Edmund shouts. His face is red, and his neck is swelling. "But I'll never stay in a house of harlots and traitors." He is gone before Curtius can go after him.

We look to my mother, and for a moment there is only the sound of her weeping. Upstairs, the roasted meat and coffee are getting cold.

Wolfgang wraps his arm around her shoulders. "He says a lot of things," Johann soothes her. "You don't know him, Maman. We have to live with this. He has a temper. Everything offends him. Nothing is ever good enough."

We lead her upstairs, and my brothers and I try to be cheerful. We talk about the king, and what the queen is wearing. Then Wolfgang tells us all about Abrielle, though he swears my mother and Curtius to silence.

"I'm in love," he reveals, "and I wish to marry her."

"A baron's daughter?" Curtius is uncertain. "Wolfgang—"

"I would like to meet Abrielle," my mother says.

Dinner is spent thinking of the ways in which Abrielle can be convinced to elope.

"You could pretend to ravage her," Johann suggests, "like Mirabeau."

"Mirabeau was a comte."

"And now is not the time for buying titles," Curtius says.

"Even if I had money, I wouldn't spend it on a title. I'm not—" He almost says "Edmund," then glances at my mother. "Robespierre. I don't wish to pretend to be something I'm not."

"The baron has noticed Wolfgang's service," Johann says. "He might give his blessing."

But who can believe that this is likely? She will have to either run away or be caught in a position of dishonor. In both circumstances, Wolfgang might be arrested.

"The baron's blessing then," my mother says. "We must all pray for that."

~

AFTER I WATCH the carriage with Wolfgang and Johann drive away, I'm thankful to see Henri sitting on the steps with his barometer and a lamp. He comes out once a day to record the weather. It helps him predict when to launch the balloons. His face is set in concentration, and though I feel as if I'm interrupting a tableau of *The Handsome Scientist,* I step into the lamplight illuminating his work. "Did you see Edmund leave?" I ask quietly.

He looks up at me, then nods. "He asked if I helped to build the new room." He moves the lamp to make room for me, and I take a seat beside him. "He sounded enraged."

"Curtius and I tried to warn my mother," I say. "She wouldn't believe us. And the things he said to her . . ." My eyes fill with tears for Maman, because she loves him so much. "He threatened never to return."

"Do you think he'll keep that promise?"

"I don't know." There is very little I know about Edmund. We are seven years apart, but we might as well be twenty. "Tomorrow, my mother will be writing to him, begging for forgiveness," I predict.

"But she has two other sons. Why does she need him?"

"Because it's always that way."

He is quiet for a moment, thinking, perhaps, of whether he should go on. Then he says, "Jacques is not my only brother. I have a younger brother named Guillaume."

I didn't know. "Is he dead?"

"It's possible. He and my father used to fight about his gambling debts. My mother would come weeping to my father, begging him to pay them off and swearing that if he didn't, the debtors would kill Guillaume. Then one night, my father refused. He told Guillaume that if the debtors killed him, they would be doing us all a favor."

I cover my mouth. "He didn't mean that."

"No. But then my brother didn't come back. Not for my father's funeral, and not when my mother was dying. Bitterness does strange things to people."

"Yes." Edmund has carried the anger of not being born to a man of great lineage like a shield on his back, turning a hard shell to the world whenever it threatens him. "But your father must have been beside himself with regret."

"I don't know. Perhaps he felt relief. Every night it was Guillaume. What has Guillaume done? Whom does Guillaume owe? What brothel are we going to have to drag him from in the morning? And there were always the fights to set him free. But he was my mother's youngest child. Her *petit.* He could do no wrong in her world."

I study Henri by the light of his lamp. His full lips are turned down, and his eyes are lidded. There is no bitterness in his voice. Just sadness.

"Edmund can be very cruel," I say. "He called my mother a *cocotte.*"

"Is that what's angering Edmund? That your mother and Curtius don't marry?"

"And a thousand other things. That we aren't descended from Bourbon kings. That he isn't entirely Swiss by birth. That he doesn't have a father . . ."

"Some men are born searching. Perhaps Edmund would be that way even if he had a father." He hesitates before asking, "So why doesn't your mother marry Curtius?"

I take a deep breath. "This can never go beyond us," I warn.

"Of course not."

"She doesn't know if my father is dead. He was wounded in the Seven Years' War. When he came home, he was a different man. Before he left, he liked to sing and play billiards. And he had friends all over the village. But after the war, all he wanted to do was drink. And he was a violent drunk. Edmund was seven. He must remember how it was. No money. No food. She gathered us up one night while he was drinking, and we ran away. She had been saving money. Washing neighbors' clothes. When we came to Paris, Curtius's exhibition at the Palais-Royal was the first business she approached. He agreed to give her work when he discovered she cooked sauerkraut." I stare into the night. "A woman with four children and not a sou to her name . . . Anything might have happened. But they became partners. And now . . ." There's no need to say what she is now, or how incredibly important they are to each other. "But she can never marry Curtius. She would have to prove my father's death. And what if he's alive?"

"Does Edmund know?"

I shake my head. "And he must never find out. He would go searching for him." The bell of Saint-Merri begins to chime. It is nine o'clock. I should go, but there is something in Henri's face that compels me to stay. If I sculpted him, it would be like this. With the golden light of the lamp falling across his hair, shadowing his chiseled features.

"So do you think you will ever marry?" he asks.

I search his eyes, and my palms begin to sweat. Does he plan on proposing? I try to imagine life as Henri's wife and find it impossible. But then I think of how he told Curtius that he was fortunate to have me and I wonder. "I . . . I don't know." Now I sound like Camille. "Until the Salon is successful—"

"What is success?"

"A place in the Académie Royale," I say quickly. "And two hundred patrons a day."

"I should think you had that this weekend."

"Yes, but to sustain that . . . think of the work. How would I do that with children?"

"There are men who will wait to have children," he says. "And there are ways—"

I flush. "But it's not a science, is it? An accident might happen."

We watch each other in the candlelight, and the noise in the street seems to disappear. There are no carriages or horses or drunken brawls. The woman on the corner selling roses to the theatergoers melts into the background. There are only Henri and me on the steps. He smells of amber. It's a scent I gifted him last year from Fargeon's, the best perfumery in Paris. He reaches out to take my hand, and I let him. But I must remember my ambition.

"I can wait. I'm in love with you, Marie. You don't have to say it yet," he tells me. "I know you like to think things through. Make plans." He kisses my neck, and I close my eyes. It is greater bliss than anything I have known. "But plan on this," he whispers. "I want to marry you."

Chapter 21

June 4, 1789

Death of my son at one in the morning.

—King Louis XVI's journal

The dauphin has been released from his earthly pain. Though his death has been expected for many months, the royal family is deep in mourning, particularly Madame Élisabeth, who loved her eight-year-old nephew like a son. The news comes just as I arrive, and we spend the week in prayer while the rest of France forgets the little dauphin and the Estates-General continues.

On Sunday, when it's time for me to go, the princesse stands on the porch in her heavy black gown and asks if her secretary has already paid me. "Yes," I lie. I don't tell her that I refused his money. That I've done nothing this week to entertain her.

"Perhaps you will come again for two days a week in July." She dabs at her tears. "The month of June is finished for me."

From my carriage, I look back at her, a dark blot against the warm June sun. I wave, and she raises her handkerchief to me, but her movements are pained and slow.

~

While the royal family is in mourning, the nation's affairs are moving on without them. Camille returns on Tuesday nights to meet with

Lucile and tells us of what's happening in the Salle des États. The Third Estate has refused all efforts to vote by order, and Robespierre has given a speech stating that if the nobility and clergy will not join them in voting by head, they will form their own assembly and vote without them.

"The Third Estate has p-p-power," Camille exclaims, flush with excitement. "We will not vote until every voice is counted. If the nobility don't wish to join us, we'll leave them behind!"

On the seventeenth of June, this is exactly what happens. Curtius and I rush to change the signs in the Salon de Cire. Patrons crowd our windows, and the line to see the figures of Necker and Mirabeau stretches down the Boulevard. It is unbelievable. The Third Estate are now calling themselves the National Assembly. And their first act is to abolish all taxes levied by the crown! Henceforth, taxes shall be legal only if levied by the National Assembly. This is a blow that even the king cannot reinterpret in a harmless light. The newspapers report that the king plans to appear in the Salle des États to annul this new Assembly's resolutions, while Necker is suggesting compromise.

Then, on the twentieth of June, the Third Estate is locked out of the Salle des États. Perhaps it's a mistake. A miscommunication. But men like Robespierre and Danton insist that it's a plot to break up the National Assembly. So they meet on a tennis court on the Rue du Vieux-Versailles. Some members of the clergy are there, and all of them swear to God and country that they will never be separated until a constitution is written for France. The newspapers are calling it the Tennis Court Oath.

Curtius rushes to print these words on a poster above Robespierre, and Yachin begins shouting in the streets, "Come see the deputies of the Tennis Court Oath. Come see the men who have challenged the king!"

Every day it is something new. Now the Third Estate are meeting in the Church of Saint-Louis, where I met with Rose Bertin. I sketch it for Curtius, and our Salle des États becomes a church.

On Sunday, Henri, Curtius, and I join those who are crowding into every café at the Palais-Royal to hear orators make speeches about the monarchy. It is where all the best news is to be had. But every café is full.

"We can try the Café de Foy," Henri suggests.

There are only a few seats when we arrive, and it is almost impossible to place an order. But we sit and listen to what a man of nineteen or twenty has to say.

"Do you think it's right that while we suffer without bread the queen powders her towering *poufs* with flour? Tomorrow, the king and his family will parade through the city of Versailles. For what purpose?" he demands. "To what aim? To remind us of their majesty?"

The crowd inside the café jeers. "Or perhaps it's to remind us that the queen sleeps on beds of rose petals and silk while we sleep on rotten hay! And what of the king? How can he hear our demands when he is sleeping through his Minister of Finance's speech?"

There is a great deal of clapping and hollering over this. Henri asks me, "Did the king really fall asleep during Necker's speech?"

"Yes. And he snored."

My uncle laughs. "The queen didn't elbow him in the ribs?"

"All of Versailles was watching."

Henri shakes his head. "This wouldn't be happening under Louis XV."

"I would have to agree." The broad figure of a woman obscures our view.

"Mademoiselle Bertin." Henri rises.

"Oh, just Rose." She smiles widely for him, and though I know I shouldn't, I feel the sudden urge to keep her standing. But Henri gives up his chair and finds another for himself. "Thank you." She flutters her lashes at him. They look longer than usual. Certainly they're fake. "Monsieur Curtius. Marie." She seats herself and orders a coffee. "So tell me. What have I missed?" She leans forward so that her breasts nearly tumble from her dress. It's completely unnecessary. Where's her fichu? But Henri doesn't seem to notice.

"A lot of grumbling against the monarchy," he replies. "And tomorrow, the royal family goes on parade."

Rose dismisses this information with a wave of her hand. "Of course. I've already been asked to dress the queen."

"And how are her spirits?" Curtius wonders. "First the dauphin, now this . . ."

"Devastated," Rose confides. "She's said to me that she's no better than an actress, staging a performance for an audience that will hiss at her. But what can she do? She has encouraged the king to surround Paris with soldiers." Rose's eyes dart about the room, to see who might be listening, but the café is too noisy for anyone else to hear. "She thinks he must quell this rebellion with force."

"If that happens—"

"Oh, it won't," Rose says. "The king can never make a decision. Louis"—*Rose has called him by his first name!*—"can't decide between a green waistcoat and a brown." She turns to me. "I hear the Salon is turning a handsome profit these days."

"Much like your boutique. When's the last time the queen ordered so many dresses?"

Rose grins. "Perhaps the royal family should parade more often."

~

BUT THE PROCESSION is not successful. The people line the roads from Paris to Versailles and watch their monarchs pass in stoic silence. I refuse to watch a woman crippled by the loss of her elder son forced to dress in her finest silks to convince people that the nation is more important than personal grief. And it is. But when is the queen allowed to weep, to face the misery of loss?

The fishwives taunted her for not producing a child after she arrived in France. And then, when the child came, they cheered in the streets and lit fireworks in the sky. Now, it's as if Louis-Joseph, with his curious eyes and hopeful smile, never even was.

I can't imagine the sorrow of the queen when she learns that forty-seven members of the nobility have already joined the National Assembly, following the lead of the Duc d'Orléans. We rush to re-dress his wax model in a black coat with a white cravat. Though it's galling to me, the Duc's figure dressed in plebeian clothes is an astounding draw. People pay twenty sous. Then twenty-five. There are so many visiting Englishmen that we send our signs to Yachin's father to have them translated into English. As a printer, he can do these things. Although I cannot read the signs, I hang them in each room of the Salon.

It is all happening quickly now. Without daily trips into the Palais-Royal, it would be impossible to keep up with the news. On the twenty-third of June, the king visits the National Assembly against his Finance Minister's wishes, and declares that the divisions between the three estates must remain. He orders the errant members of the clergy and nobility to return to their own assemblies. As Camille describes it for us that night in our salon, Necker is so outraged that he resigns his post.

"And then Mirabeau stood on his seat and declared to the entire Assembly, 'We are here by the power of the people, and we will not leave except by the force of bayonets.' Can you imagine?" Camille is nearly crying with joy. "He challenged the k-king!"

"And Necker?" Lucile asks.

"Oh, Necker returned to his post," Camille says. "The king spent the afternoon begging."

"So what will happen?" Henri asks.

"I don't know!" Camille thrives off of this uncertainty. "I have to return to Versailles tomorrow. I have two articles I'm working on for the gazette."

"And something else," Lucile adds coyly. "Go ahead. Tell them."

Camille looks around the table. We are a smaller group tonight: Robespierre and the Duc have not been here since finding fame in the Assembly. They have not even seen themselves in wax. "I am writing my first political tract," he says.

"He calls it *La France Libre.*"

"I heard two publishers have already turned it down," Marat retorts. "Are they so frightened of angering the king?"

"P-perhaps," Camille stutters. "But I won't be discouraged. We'll find a press."

"He is writing about a republic," Lucile explains. "About throwing off this mantle of tyranny and embracing freedom." If Lucile were a man, she would be right there with Camille.

"It's radical," Camille admits. "But it's nothing the Americans haven't proposed."

"Only this is not America," Curtius points out.

"It could be. It *will* be. Give it time, and this National Assembly will rise above the king."

~

WE ARE IN the Café de Foy on the twenty-seventh of June when we hear the news. Just as the sun is about to set and the streetlamps of the Palais-Royal are being lit, a man stands at the doors to the café and shouts that the Revolution is over. The Third Estate has won, and the king has ordered both the clergy and the nobility to join the National Assembly. He has legitimized this strange, new body of government, and now every vote shall be counted! Men begin dancing in the streets, and women are waving their handkerchiefs from the windows, shouting down to their neighbors that the Third Estate has triumphed.

"We should leave," Henri says suddenly.

I look down at his coffee. It's not half finished. "With all this excitement?"

"Couldn't you hear what the men were saying behind us?" Henri asks. "Unless you consider troops converging on Paris exciting, we should find a carriage or walk." He fetches my uncle, interrupting his conversation.

Whispers are exchanged, and Curtius comes to me at once. "In a few hours, these men will all be drunk. We should get home."

But pushing through the crowds of the Palais-Royal is nearly impossible. There must be thousands, maybe tens of thousands, of people celebrating. Vendors are selling boxes of fireworks for twelve sous. Once, these bright lights were strictly reserved for celebrations in Versailles, but suddenly anyone can purchase them. The rockets and serpents screech their way through the air and light up the sky in different colors. Children are clapping at the noisy displays, and I wonder what their parents will do if soldiers surround the Palais Royal. There's no finding a horse and carriage, but it's only thirty minutes to the Boulevard by foot.

Every stranger we pass bids us good evening, and one man shouts, "It's a fine day to be a patriot!"

"Patriots, equality . . ." Henri shakes his head. "Everyone is celebrating as if there's bread in the bakeries and oil in the lamps. But what has really been accomplished?"

"Lower taxes?" I ask.

"They haven't voted. Anything might happen between now and then."

It takes an hour to reach the Boulevard du Temple. When we arrive, my mother is standing on the steps, her hands on her hips and a lantern at her side. "Where have you been?" she cries. "You left for the Palais five hours ago."

"You have no idea what it was like," Curtius says. "Thousands of people—"

"Well, did you hear the news?"

"Yes. The National Assembly can go forward."

"Not that. The king is sending soldiers! It's all over the Boulevard. He's sending the Gardes Françaises along with the Royal German Regiment."

"Foreigners," I whisper, "from Germany and Switzerland." Because the French can't keep their own soldiers from deserting, they are forced to look outside their borders. The Royal German Regiment has hired men who will have no compunction about firing on French citizens.

Curtius follows her into the house, but I remain on the steps with

Henri. I slip my hand into his, and we sit down together to watch the fireworks. "I hope it's the beginning of something better," I say.

"For the Salon?"

"For everyone. We had no bread last night. My mother couldn't find any. Yachin says his family hasn't eaten bread in months."

"We are living off meat and mushrooms in our house."

"That's what Curtius says we'll have to do. Everyone is growing mushrooms. I wonder how long there will be bread in Versailles?"

"Are you going back?"

"This Friday. But Madame Élisabeth only wants me for two days a week now."

"Lucky for me." Henri wraps his arm around my waist. "Obviously, she doesn't know what she's missing."

I lean my head against his shoulder and inhale the scent of his hair. For the rest of my life, I will associate the sweetness of almond oil with Henri. Sometimes I wonder what would happen if there were no Salon, if I were simply an heiress and had nothing to do with my days but be with him. Of course, that's unrealistic. If I were an heiress, I would be married off to an old man with a fortune in property. "I think the princesse may be more interested in news than in wax," I say. "I'm the only one who will tell her the truth."

"Not the entire truth?" Henri pulls away and searches my face.

"Certainly not. But most of it."

"Be careful."

"I know. That's what Edmund said."

"No word from him still?"

I shake my head. "I doubt there will be. Not until all of this is over." I hear murmuring on the other side of the door and wonder if my mother is listening to us. There's no disguising what we're doing out here, but neither Curtius nor my mother has mentioned it. "Do you think they're listening?" I whisper.

"If they are," he says loudly, "then they should know that I intend to marry their daughter, Marie Grosholtz."

"Shh." I giggle.

"What? There's nothing to be ashamed of. Is there?"

I lean forward and brush my lips against his. "No," I whisper. It is the first time I have kissed him this way, and his response is passionate. It is to his credit that he has never asked me to follow him inside, into his home, his chamber, his bed. Because I'm not sure I would have the willpower to say no. And if I go to his bed, then why not marry him? So instead, we remain outside, where theatergoers doing far worse things take no notice of a couple embracing on the steps.

Chapter 22

July 3, 1789

I would not exchange my leisure hours for all the wealth in the world.

—Comte de Mirabeau

A letter has arrived from Robespierre praising two men from the National Assembly and suggesting that we include them in the Salon de Cire. My uncle passes the envelope to me before my carriage arrives for Versailles. I stand in the door and read Robespierre's small, cramped handwriting in the light of the rising sun:

The Revolution is far from finished, and you should not be deceived by the fireworks at the Palais-Royal. Though the events of this week have proved far more powerful and productive than any in the history of mankind, there is more to be accomplished. The great leaders of this new world shall be men of strong principles like Georges Danton and Mirabeau, true patriots who gather around the fire of liberty and fan the flames with their brave actions and words. If you can, include them in the Salon de Cire. Then the people of France shall know that you are great patriots as well.

"*Men of strong principles like Danton and Mirabeau?*" I look up at Curtius. "A lawyer and a rapist? We should take down both their models," I say heatedly. The audacity, to suggest to us which models we should display! And the delusion. There is no man or woman alive in France who believes that Mirabeau is a man of principles.

Curtius puts his hand on my shoulder. "A letter came from Wolfgang as well. Earlier this morning. I gave it to your mother. He says thirty thousand soldiers are making their way toward Paris. Most of them mercenaries."

We look at each other in the red light of dawn. It will be warm today. The women brave enough to visit the Palais-Royal will be wearing muslin dresses and wide straw hats, the same clothing the queen once loved and was criticized for wearing.

"The king is surrounding the city," Curtius says. "See what you can discover from Madame Élisabeth. It may be that by tomorrow we'll be hiding our models of Robespierre and Mirabeau. And ask the coachman to take you by the Bastille. I heard from the butcher that the Marquis de Sade's making some kind of scene. If you can find out what's he doing . . ."

~

WHEN I TELL the coachman to take me by the Bastille, he smirks. "So you want to hear the rantings of a madman as well?"

"Why? What is he doing?"

The old man raises his brows. "Shouting down that they are killing the prisoners."

"What?"

"No need to be worried, Mademoiselle. My son is a guard there. The marquis is just angry that they won't give him his daily coffee anymore. But if it pleases you to hear him . . ."

"Yes," I say. "It will only be a minute."

He takes me to the Bastille, where a crowd is growing beneath a window. I descend from the coach and stand among the onlookers. Above us is the massive figure of the Marquis de Sade. He has taken the funnel from his urinal and is using it as a speaking trumpet. "Political prisoners who've disobeyed the king are being slaughtered like lambs!" he's shouting. "Somebody help us!"

"Liar!" I exclaim. "Those guards aren't killing anyone."

People turn to face me. "How do you know?" a young woman demands.

"I've met with the marquis. He's sick in the mind."

"That's what will happen," an old woman says, "after years of imprisonment and beatings."

When I return to the carriage, the coachman asks, "Well?"

"I told them they weren't killing prisoners, and no one would believe me."

"Of course not. They want to believe in the king's cruelty. It's better than believing that God and Nature are starving them to death."

I think about those words on the way to Versailles. Death is confined to the poorhouses and hospitals, both funded by the Church. But certainly people are starving. We don't talk about it at night, but I see the account books. I know what my mother is spending on food. Fourteen sous for one dinner's worth of milk and cream. Ten sous for salad. Six sous for vegetables that will feed only three. A daily worker's wage is twenty-five sous.

When I arrive at Montreuil, I'm greeted by a servant who tells me in hushed tones that the princesse will not see me for another hour. "She is in prayer, Mademoiselle."

"At ten in the morning?"

The courtier nods as we go inside. He's impeccably dressed in a long powdered wig and an embroidered coat. "It has been this way since the death of the dauphin. The princesse prays now three times a day."

I follow him into the workshop. It has been a month since I've been in here, and nothing has changed. The figure of Christ still hangs above the door, and the aprons look dazzlingly white in the sun. It could be the end of May if not for the heat and the blossoms outside.

"Is there anything I can get for you, Mademoiselle?"

"No. Thank you."

"The princesse wishes to make a sculpture of the new dauphin today. She asked me to relay this to you."

"I'll prepare while I wait."

The courtier shows himself out, and I take a seat on a wooden stool. The quiet is unnerving. Where is everyone? Hundreds of people must work in Montreuil, but there is no one in the halls and none of them can be seen outside. I look over the tools on the countertop. Everything is here. But we will need a recent bust or another likeness of Louis-Charles, the new dauphin, if we are to sculpt him.

I put on my apron and begin to knead three pieces of clay. When an hour has passed, a series of footsteps echo in the hall. But it's far too many to be only two people. I wash my hands and rush to smooth my apron. When the doors swing open, I drop into my lowest curtsy. Madame Élisabeth has brought not only the queen but the king and the four-year-old dauphin! "Your Majesties."

"Welcome back." Madame Élisabeth smiles kindly.

I'm shocked by the changes a month has wrought. Both she and the queen are thin. The queen's delicate collarbone protrudes above her lace fichu, and the angles in Madame Élisabeth's face are entirely different. The king, however, has grown fatter. Is that possible? Only the Marquise de Bombelles looks the same.

"I thought we could model the dauphin from life," Madame Élisabeth says. "And my brother wishes to see how a wax model is done."

Chairs with padded arms are brought and space is made in front of the countertop for the royal family. I wonder where Madame Royale might be, but I don't ask. Her absence is a blessing. The princesse puts on her apron, then helps the marquise into hers. "We begin by wetting and kneading the clay," she explains. "But since Marie has been waiting, she has done it for us."

"Can I touch?" the dauphin asks.

I look to the queen, who smiles and nods. I tear off a small piece of clay and hand it to him. Like his brother, he's a small, curious child.

"Can you roll it into a ball?" the king asks. The dauphin shapes the clay, and his father claps. "Excellent! Only four years old and he can already make shapes." The king looks at me. "It has been some time since you've been to Montreuil."

"Yes. June was not a month for light entertainments."

"It was a month to forget for many reasons," he admits. "I suppose the Boulevard is rife with political discontent. Filled with young people and entertainers. The restless sort."

"The restlessness is all over Paris," I confess.

"So tell us," the queen says lightly. But her face cannot lie. There are tension lines around her eyes and mouth. "What do the Parisians think of our troops?"

I look at the pair of Swiss Guards who stand stiffly by the door. Whatever I say will make its way back to Edmund. The queen sees the direction of my gaze and snaps her fingers. "Privacy please."

When the men remove themselves to the hall, everyone looks to me.

"The Parisians . . ." What should I say? The truth? A half-truth? If I tell them that there were fireworks over the Palais-Royal, will the Duc be arrested? And if the Duc discovers what I've said and the people make him king?

"Your words won't go beyond these walls," the queen swears.

I can't believe there is no one else to give our monarchs this news, no one else who will tell them how it is in Paris. Or perhaps I am one of many people they are questioning. "This morning there was a disturbance at the Bastille," I tell them. "The Marquis de Sade was shouting from his tower that they were killing prisoners on the orders of Your Majesty."

"That's preposterous!" the king exclaims. "There are only seven prisoners in the Bastille. I have wanted to tear it down for years." He turns to Marie Antoinette. "*You* asked me to tear it down."

"These kinds of lies are all over the city," I say.

The queen's question comes as a whisper. "So how do we stop them?"

I don't know. I am paid to spread news, not stop it. How do you convince people that what they wish to believe is a lie? "I don't see any way of stopping it," I say quietly, "except through action."

"We have done all we can," Madame Élisabeth replies. "We give charity. You've seen how we give."

Yes, but I am not the one you must convince, I want to say. I feel sorry for them. They do not know what to do, and I am not smart enough to give them good political advice. "You are incredibly generous," I agree. "The monarchy is the backbone of this nation."

"Of course it is," the king replies. "We can't let a handful of angry men tear down nine hundred years of tradition." The queen rests her hand lovingly on his knee, encouraging him, goading him onward. "Sending troops into Paris was the right thing to do, and anyone who disagrees with this policy—"

"Shall be dismissed," the queen finishes for him.

The dauphin holds up his clay ball and asks, "Have I done it right?"

Just like his father, worried about what other people will think. "It's absolutely perfect." I smile.

Chapter 23

July 11, 1789

Fortune does not change men, it unmasks them.

—Suzanne Necker,
wife of Jacques Necker, Minister of Finance

The Minister of Finance has been sent away! Necker, who is beloved by the Third Estate despite his long-winded speeches, has been taken with his wife to Switzerland. A carriage arrived at his home, and the coachman was given instructions to ride nonstop to the city of Lausanne. A man named Joseph-François Foulon, who agrees with the king's policies and wishes to abolish the National Assembly, has been named the Finance Minister in his place.

"When this gets out," Wolfgang says, "there's going to be chaos."

We withdraw into an alcove of the Grand Commune. "How do you know this?" I ask him.

"I was at the door when the king told his brother Artois. Word won't reach the city for another day. But tonight, lock the doors. There are thousands of troops encamped all across Paris."

"I saw soldiers yesterday at Saint-Denis."

"They're also at the Invalides on the Champ-de-Mars. The city is surrounded, and every rabble-rouser is going to take to the streets when they hear this news. And best stay away from the Palais-Royal for the next few nights."

It's unbelievable, the idea that Paris should succumb to violence. I don't wish to think about it. I won't. "How is Edmund?"

"He hasn't spoken to me since we visited Maman six weeks ago. Or to Johann."

"And Abrielle?"

"She wants to give it a little more time." He sounds uncertain. "She loves her father. Her mother died in childbirth . . . it's only her and him."

I take a deep breath. Now is the time to tell Wolfgang. He should know. "Henri asked me to marry him."

My brother steps back to study my face, and I'm sure I am blushing deeply. "Marie, that's wonderful news! Have you told Maman?"

"I can't tell her. Not until I'm ready to accept, and marriage would ruin my chances at the Académie Royale."

My brother is surprised. It's the first he's heard of this.

"I can't think of anything worse than raising a family on a few hundred sous a week," I tell him. "You remember how it was for us. The rags we used to wear and the food we would eat. It was meat once a month. If I am accepted into the Académie—or even if it's Curtius—our futures will be certain."

"But we all turned out well enough," Wolfgang protests. "Things got better. Curtius's business picked up, and now the Salon is doing well."

"Even so, the bakers and chandlers are dry. We have to buy our candles on the black market. It's not a time for starting a family."

"Well, don't tell that to Abrielle." He sighs. "It will only give her more incentive to wait."

Chapter 24

July 12, 1789

We must take up arms and adopt cockades by which we may know each other.

—Camille Desmoulins

Lafayette has presented his Declaration of the Rights of Man and Citizen to the National Assembly, and just as word of this revolutionary document began to spread this morning, the news arrived of Necker's dismissal. To say that Parisians are angry is to underestimate what's happening entirely. They're enraged, just as Wolfgang predicted, and though there should be a line of people stretching down the Boulevard for the Salon de Cire, we have locked our doors and Henri has come over to keep us company. He seats himself next to me at the empty *caissier*'s desk, and we watch the crowds fill the streets outside.

"I hope Curtius hasn't done anything foolish," my mother whispers. "He went this morning to the Palais-Royal."

Over five thousand people were said to be there, and we can hear the newsboys shouting updates in the streets. At midday it was ten thousand. Now it's twenty. By tonight, who knows? I wish I could relax into Henri's embrace and feel the strong comfort of his arms. But I know my mother would be immediately suspicious, and I am not prepared to answer any questions our closeness could bring. So instead, I watch my mother's hands working her needles. She's knitting something for Johann's son. It is a way to keep herself busy.

"If I were the queen," she says suddenly, "I would tell my husband to banish the Duc and take over the Palais-Royal!"

"I would banish the Duc as well," Henri admits. This morning, he was at the Palais. "It would certainly make it harder for *libellistes* to gather."

Was this what I should have told the queen? Would it have made any difference? "And the National Assembly?" I ask.

"It's already gone too far," Henri replies. "The faster the king consents to a constitutional monarchy, the less bloodshed there will be."

"*Mein Gott,* there's Curtius!" my mother exclaims. "And he's running!"

All three of us rush to the door, and when my mother opens it, my uncle shouts, "They're coming! Get inside."

"Who's coming?" my mother cries.

"The mob. They want our bust of Necker!"

"Absolutely not!" I exclaim.

"Marie." Curtius is out of breath. His cheeks are flushed and his waistcoat is askew. "There are a thousand people coming this way."

Henri touches my arm. "I think you and your mother should go upstairs."

"No," I say firmly. "We cannot show them fear."

My mother goes to fetch Curtius some water from the kitchen, and I pass him my handkerchief. He is sweating profusely. This sort of exertion can't be good for his health.

"What is happening?" I ask calmly.

"There were thousands of people. More than there were two weeks ago. And Camille—" He holds his chest and tries to catch his breath. He must have run most of the way here. "Camille was in the Café de Foy."

"He was there this morning," Henri replies, "writing frantically in a corner."

"Well, this time he was standing on a table and shouting. He was impassioned." Curtius wipes his neck. "Like I've never seen him before. He took out his pistol and encouraged every citizen in Paris to rise up. He said, 'The citizens of France requested Necker, and what does the king do? Banish Necker!' Then he compared himself to Othryades."

My mother has returned with a carafe of water. "Who is Othryades?"

"A warrior," Curtius explains, "who captured an enemy flag and wrote 'Sparta Is Free' across it in his blood."

"Camille thinks he's a Spartan warrior?" my mother exclaims.

"It's a metaphor," I say in German.

"He added that he would be willing to write 'France Is Free' in his own blood if the people would rise up and make it happen. That Necker's dismissal has sounded the tocsin for war, and if the people don't take to arms, it will be another St. Bartholomew's Day Massacre."

"He's developed a gift for rhetoric?" Henri asks.

"Yes. And drama. He pinned a leaf to his shirt, then told everyone they could recognize their fellow revolutionaries by their green cockades. The trees were stripped bare."

To think of calling a tree leaf a cockade, a circular ribbon used to symbolize a cause . . . It is brilliant. Nothing could be more humble than a small green leaf. "And his stutter?"

"Completely gone when he's speaking to a crowd. When he shouted 'Untimely death or eternal liberty,' I thought I was listening to Mirabeau. And now he's leading the people here."

We can hear them coming. As with the Roman army, the dust heralds their approach. They are chanting something, and as they make their way down the Boulevard du Temple, doors swing shut and women peek out from behind their shutters. As the mob comes closer, I can hear what they are shouting. *"Necker! Necker!"*

Curtius opens the door, and a sea of faces peer back at us. Everyone in the crowd is wearing green. Camille steps forward, and I see that Lucile is behind him.

"Citizen Curtius," Camille greets him formally. "We have come for the head of Necker." A shout goes up, and the mob begins to cheer. "Knowing how fervently you support this Revolution, would you be willing to part with your exhibition's most honored bust?"

"The Salon de Cire," my uncle replies, "is honored to serve the people's cause."

The mob cheers again, and someone shouts, "Give us the bust of Orléans."

"Yes, give us the Duc d'Orléans!" a woman cries.

"Would you be willing to part with Orléans as well? He has been threatened with b-b-banishment." Camille gestures dramatically. "But we shall show the king that the people support those who believe in liberty!"

My uncle hesitates. "If that is what the people wish . . ." He bows. "Come inside."

Camille takes Lucile's hand, and they separate themselves from the crowd. The mob looks more excited than angry, eager to see what Camille will produce. I go with my mother and Curtius into the Room of Notables. For the many times Camille has been to our Salon, I don't believe he's ever seen these figures. "My God," he says, like every observer. "They're so realistic." He reaches out to touch the Duc's face while Lucile caresses the head of Necker. In her muslin cap and long white dress, she is the picture of gallant youth. "I don't suppose there's any chance of taking the king . . ."

"That's an entire figure," Curtius says. "If you carry it, the model will break."

"And we would appreciate them all coming back in one piece," I reply. "Each figure takes weeks of work." Not to mention money. Fifteen livres for a wig, forty sous for real hair, and eighty sous for a full set of teeth.

"Nothing will happen to them," Camille promises.

"And you? What if something should happen to you?" I ask.

"The time of sacrifice is upon us," Lucile says. "We are willing to take that risk."

When they emerge from the Salon, the cheer that goes up must be heard in Versailles. The members of the crowd have taken off their hats, and someone has found black crêpe to drape around the busts.

"Where are you going?" Curtius shouts.

Camille takes off his hat. It's a solemn procession he plans to lead. A funeral march for the exile of Necker and the threat of exile to the Duc d'Orléans. "To the Place Vendôme!"

BECAUSE IT'S TOO dangerous for Yachin to go home, a bed is made for him in the workshop. I open the windows to let in a breeze, and our barker says nervously, "Perhaps we should close them."

I hesitate. All evening, friends have been coming in to give us news. Philip Astley, who runs the circus, said the theaters have been shut down all across Paris. A mob of three thousand stormed the Opéra, demanding that Grétry's *Aspasie* be canceled out of respect for Necker. They are treating his dismissal as though the king has ordered his execution. In the Place Vendôme, the tocsins were sounded, and when the mob spilled into the adjacent Tuileries Gardens, the king's troops were ordered to clear the space. But Camille's mob refused to move, and shots were fired. The man carrying the wax bust of the Duc d'Orléans was killed. According to Astley, the soldiers tied his body behind a horse and dragged it through the Tuileries as a warning to others. "And the bust?" I exclaimed.

My mother gasped. "A man was killed!"

"But they didn't murder the bust. So where is it?"

No one knows. The last we've heard is that the Gardes Françaises are fighting alongside the people. They are supposed to be one of the king's fighting regiments, but they have turned against their brothers, and because they far outnumber the royal troops, the king's soldiers are actually in retreat! It's an unbelievable turn of events. It means the

Third Estate has its own army, and they are defeating the Royal German Regiment. But does the fighting mean we're prisoners inside our own homes? I look outside. The streets are dark. I shut the windows, just in case.

Yachin looks pitiful. "Do you think I will see my family tomorrow?" he asks. His knees are tucked up under his chin, and his small arms are wrapped around his legs.

"The fighting can't last forever," I tell him.

"But I thought the Revolution was over. There were fireworks at the Palais-Royal."

"Yes, but now these men want more. Some think they can establish a republic, like they have in America."

"If there's no more monarchy, my father can print whatever comes into his shop."

"I should think there will always be censorship," I tell him, "of one kind or another."

"Are they allowed to print whatever they wish in America?"

I don't know. "Perhaps we should ask Curtius," I say. "I see you're not going to get any sleep."

We join the others at the *caissier*'s desk. It will be a long night, and only God knows if the Salon will be able to reopen tomorrow. Henri's brother, Jacques, has just come from the Place Vendôme. I take a seat on an empty stool and listen while he recounts what's happening.

"It's chaos. The mob has grown to at least twenty thousand. It could double, even triple by tomorrow. The man carrying your bust of Necker was killed by a bayonet to the stomach."

I feel the blood drain from my face.

"Astley told us the man carrying the Duc's model was killed as well," my uncle says.

"They are breaking into the armories now. It's anarchy in the Palais-Royal. Every shop selling swords and guns has been ransacked. They'll need gunpowder next."

There's a knock on our door, and Curtius rises. "It must be Astley," he says, and he lets in our neighbor, who searches the gloom for any sign of danger. I have never seen Astley nervous. He's tall and broad with limber hands, but when he approaches our table, he's shaking. My mother fetches a stool, and Curtius presses a glass of wine into his hand.

"They've burned the barriers to the city, and thousands of peasants are flooding in from the provinces. It's absolute lawlessness," Astley tells us. "They've attacked more than forty customs posts and burned the tax records. Now they're searching for food. The monastery of Saint-Lazare has been overcome. Everything inside was taken."

My mother crosses herself.

"Grain," Henri says. "It was a storehouse for grain."

"I am finished with Paris," Astley says. "I'm returning to London. They've already had their civil war."

"Which ended with a Constitution," Jacques reminds him. "Perhaps this is the time for new birth."

Astley takes a long sip of his wine. "The king has been a loyal patron to me. I don't wish to see him disgraced." He looks from Jacques to Henri. "I have no desire to see the Duc d'Orléans on the throne. Or any other man in the National Assembly."

"Lafayette was elected its vice president—he might make a good leader," Curtius says.

"Can you imagine the bloody coup that will come before installing him as king? He will have to fight every other man who wants it: Orléans, Mirabeau, Camille—"

"Not Camille!" I exclaim.

"Did you hear his speech in the Café de Foy? He's a man with intentions. Just wait," Astley promises. "If the king doesn't crush this rebellion and send Camille to prison, you will see him in the National Assembly."

There is another knock on the door, and the seven of us freeze. Whoever it is, they will have heard us talking. There's no point in pretending we aren't here. "Who is it?" Curtius calls through the door.

"Citizen Armand," the man identifies himself. "I have come with your wax head."

Curtius opens the door, and a young man holds out the head of Orléans. "For you, Monsieur."

I spring from my chair and rush to the door. "What about the bust of Necker?" I demand.

Armand shakes his head. He is a *sans-culotte,* dressed in trousers and a loose-fitting shirt. His long hair has been tied back with twine, and the bones in his face are prominent. I doubt he's eaten much in several weeks. "I'm sorry, Mademoiselle. It was lost among the crowds. It may still appear—"

"That bust means a great deal to us," I say sharply.

Armand steps back. He is seventeen, or eighteen, perhaps.

"Yes," Curtius cuts in. "For there is no greater patriot than Necker."

The young man smiles. "Of course. I will see what I can do." He looks over our shoulders and can see the meats on our table.

"Would you like to come in?" Curtius offers. "There is food. And perhaps you can give us some news."

Armand accepts, and I lock the door behind him. Yachin has already found a stool from the workshop where I laid his bed. He offers it to our guest, and the seven of us watch him eat. He is starving, chewing with his mouth open because he has stuffed too much inside. When he finally swallows, he sees that we are waiting. "What is the last you've heard?" he asks.

"That the monastery of Saint-Lazare was ransacked," Jacques says.

Armand reaches for a sausage. "And all of the monks have been turned out. They can live off the fat of their bellies now."

"That is a sin," my mother says.

Armand sees he has offended her and puts down his sausage. "Perhaps it is. But we are starving, Madame. It is all well and good for the National Assembly to proclaim this law and that. But where is the food? Can they force the king to give us food?"

"He doesn't have enough food to feed a nation," I reply.

"Then we shall find a government that knows how to conduct trade for grain. The members of the National Assembly are meeting at the Hôtel de Ville," he says. "If you hear cannon shots tomorrow, it might be battle, or it might be the National Assembly summoning its deputies to a meeting. They are looking to create their own militia. It will be every patriot's duty to provide this new militia with whatever weapons they have."

"Including the shops that have been broken into?" Henri asks.

"Yes," Armand says earnestly.

"Isn't that thievery?" Jacques wants to know.

"Not if it's for the greater good. We found a barge at the Port Saint-Nicholas carrying forty casks of powder. That powder would have gone to the king's army if we hadn't taken it. Where is it better used?" Armand asks. "By tomorrow, the king will be facing a formidable army," he promises. "A citizens' militia."

Chapter 25

July 13, 1789

When the government violates the people's rights, insurrection is . . . the most indispensable of duties.

—Marquis de Lafayette

Only Curtius and I are awake when the cannon fire begins. Perhaps it has gone on all night and only now can it be heard on the Boulevard du Temple. But the sound seems to shake our house on its foundations. We look across the table at each other, and my uncle puts down his coffee.

"Battle, or a meeting of the National Assembly?" I ask fearfully.

"It will be the meeting in the Hôtel de Ville. Can't you hear the tocsin?"

If I strain, I can just make out the ringing of the bells above the cannons. "What if the king's troops defeat them? What if they throw Lafayette and Robespierre into prison?"

"That's why we straddle both worlds until it's clear which side will be the victor. In three days, you'll go back to Versailles. Meanwhile, whatever good patriots are doing, we'll do. They want green cockades? We'll wear them. They need arms for the citizens' militia? We'll donate. And as soon as it's safe to reopen the Salon, the exhibits will change weekly. Daily even, if that's what events call for." He stands from his chair and begins to pace. "We'll want to change our signs from

"Monsieur" and "Madame" to "Citizen" and "Citizeness." That's what all the papers are using. We don't want to be behind."

"Then we should change the Room of Notables to the Room of Great Patriots as well."

"Yes. And whatever happens—" Curtius stops pacing to look at me. Even at six in the morning, he is wearing a waistcoat and an embroidered vest, just in case the king or the Duc should come calling. "The Salon de Cire must continue. This will be your inheritance, Marie, and you will make it your children's inheritance someday."

"Why are you saying this?"

"The Glorious Revolution in England swept away many good families. We don't know how we'll be caught up in this. Already, we've provided models for Camille's procession."

"The mob could have stolen those busts," I say quickly. "Or they could have forced us to hand them over. Why should the king believe we were part of it?"

"He might not. But men have been sent away for much less. Did you hear that the commander of the Swiss Guards, the Baron de Besenval, has been placed in charge of the king's troops?"

"Abrielle's father?"

"Yes." My uncle sighs. "Of all the women to fall in love with . . . Wolfgang might have chosen anyone." He smiles at me. "At least you have some sense."

I look down at my coffee. Clearly, Henri has taken Curtius aside and made his intentions known. "You know I cannot marry now."

"Henri told me. But Marie, you will never be left homeless or poor. That much I swear."

There is the sound of a horse and carriage outside, and both of us pause. I go to the window and recognize the man with the auburn hair and mahogany walking stick. "I can't believe it."

Curtius rises. "Who is it?"

"The Marquis de Lafayette!"

"Go and wake your mother. And make some more coffee."

I rush to my mother's chamber. The curtains are drawn against the summer's light, casting the silk-paneled walls in shadow. From the embroidered settee to the cushioned armchair, everything has been done in robin's-egg blue. I push the airy bed hangings aside and see that my mother is still asleep. I should let her be, but I know she would be angry to miss Lafayette. I gently shake her shoulder. I'm surprised she doesn't hear the cannons.

"What? What's happening?"

"The Marquis de Lafayette has come," I say.

She struggles to a sitting position. "Why?"

"I don't know. Perhaps he wants to borrow a bust. Or maybe he's come about the citizens' militia."

My mother is on her feet and at her vanity at once, twisting her dark curls into a loose bun and dabbing her petite wrists with perfume. I hand her a gown, and while she ties her fichu, I fetch a lace bonnet from the wooden commode. "The one with the good trim," she says. "Not that one. The blue." She brushes her teeth and dabs *eau de lavande* onto her breasts.

"Curtius says to bring coffee," I tell her.

"Yes. And we'll want sausages. Isn't that what the marquis liked the last time he was here?"

I can't remember these things like my mother. She can recall what she served at every salon, and which foods each of our guests preferred. "I'm not sure," I admit.

"I'm certain it was sausage. But we'll bring out the ham, just in case."

When we enter the salon, the marquis and my uncle are deep in conversation. Neither looks pleased. "Ah." Curtius stands. "Coffee and sausages."

Lafayette rises, and his dress is impeccable. His green *culottes* match his long-tailed coat. It's interesting that he has chosen not to wear a wig. It will be a great deal of work for me if false hair goes out of fashion, since real hair has to be set into the wax heads strand by strand. The marquis kisses my hand. "Citizeness Grosholtz."

"Is that really how we are to greet each other?" I ask, confirming what Curtius said this morning.

"Yes. From now on I am Citizen Lafayette."

I hide my shock and step aside so that he can greet my mother. How can there be a world with no titles? What will men be? All equals? My mother and I take seats, and Curtius explains, "Lafayette has come with news."

"A National Guard has been formed," Lafayette says, "and I have had the honor of being named its Commander in Chief. We've enlisted eight hundred men to patrol every district in France, and they're to pay for their own weapons and uniforms. This way, we know they are committed to duty. But now we're searching for good men to act as captains of each district."

My mother gasps. "And you want Curtius?"

Lafayette nods. "That is my hope."

I look to my uncle, who trained as a doctor, not a soldier.

"It is a great honor," he says hesitantly.

"One I am not offering to just anyone," Lafayette adds. "A country is only as strong as its military, and only as moral as the men who serve in its ranks."

Curtius takes his pipe from the table. He fills it with tobacco, then offers the wooden box to the marquis, who passes. He lights the bowl, and the three of us wait while Curtius thinks. "You understand I'm not a military man," he says at last. "I would be useless on the field."

Lafayette is undisturbed. "This will not be a battle like any soldier has ever known. This will be fought in the city, on the streets, and in the palaces. Good sense, not experience, is what matters now."

"And it doesn't disturb you that I am old?"

"General George Washington was forty-six when the Revolution in America began. I don't think his age held him back." He leans forward. His eyes are fixed on my uncle, and I know that whatever he is about to say, it will be something complimentary. "We are in the midst of our own revolution. Make no mistake, the events of these next few days will be recorded in history, and the men making those events will be remembered as heroes. Do your patriotic duty. There will be pay, but also rewards that go far beyond money. This nation needs men of upstanding character. It needs a captain like you."

Curtius is going to say yes. I know because his eyes are wide with the promise of it all. He puts down his pipe. "How many men would I command?"

"Forty. And they'll all be wearing the blue, white, and red."

"I thought it was green."

"That is the color of the king's brother, the Comte d'Artois. I've proposed a tricolor."

"Like America?"

"Exactly. So shall I send a man to fit you for your uniform?"

The sound of cannon fire has stopped, replaced with the voices of a growing mob. There is no knowing who is in charge anymore. The king? His soldiers? The National Assembly?

"Yes. I will do it," my uncle replies.

Chapter 26

July 14, 1789

The creation of this new National Guard has encouraged the butchers to open their shops and the milliners to begin accepting customers again. If we are lucky, the Salon may reopen tomorrow. We've lost six hundred sous over the past two days.

I smile at the tailor who arrived this morning with baskets of fabric. Lafayette sent him to turn my uncle into a captain, and while he's here, he's to make a costume for our new figure of Lafayette. We'll be the first of anyone—painters, sculptors, even engravers—to display Lafayette as Commander in Chief of the National Guard.

I study the tailor. His shoes have silver buckles, and his waistcoat is embroidered. The man is ambitious. "Don't let him overcharge us," I say in German. "We'll pay thirty livres for Lafayette's uniform. Nothing more."

"I can manage the finances," Curtius replies. "Go with Henri. Take Yachin home while the city's still quiet."

Outside, in the late morning light, it's as if nothing has changed. The vendors have returned to the streets, and the Boulevard smells of coffee and flowers. Yachin is on the steps, and Henri is showing him how to read a barometer. The people passing seem calm. "Shall we?" he asks as soon as he sees me.

As we begin to walk, I notice that Henri is carrying his pistol. When we reach the Jewish quartier, the streets become narrower and the buildings less imposing. There are broken windows and boarded-up homes. A man steps from the doorway of a printing shop in a National Guard uniform and blocks our path. "What is your business here, Citizen?"

The three of us stop, and Henri steps forward. "We are taking this boy home."

The guardsman looks down his nose at Yachin. His face is dark, meaning he's spent much of his life in the sun. He might be thirty or forty. It's impossible to tell. "What's your name?" he demands.

"Homberg," Yachin replies. "Citizen Homberg."

"Tell me, Citizen Homberg. Are you a good patriot?"

"Yes. My family—they are printers. They all—we all—believe in liberty."

"Then how come you see fit to wear your Jew cap but not your colors?" The guardsman's eyes shift to Henri, then to myself. None of us are wearing the tricolor cockade.

"We have just come from the Boulevard du Temple," I say quickly. "The shops have been shut and there's nowhere to purchase—"

"Do you think I bought this?" The guardsman points to his red and blue ribbon. "A true patriot finds a way."

"Her uncle has been made captain of his district," Henri says. "He's being fitted now for his uniform. We are friends of Citizen Lafayette."

The guardsman looks me over, and I wonder if he has the power to stop us. "I suggest," he says strongly, "that when you return this boy to his parents, you find yourselves some cockades. Patriots wish to recognize other patriots in the streets."

"Thank you," says Henri. "We will take your advice."

We walk quickly, in case the guardsman should think of something else. I whisper, "Could he have made problems for us?"

"He could have tried," Henri says.

We stop in front of a white building with broken green shutters. "Would you like to come inside?" Yachin hesitates. "My mother would be happy—"

"I don't think that's a good idea," Henri says gently. He's been so kind to Yachin. Someday, he will make a wonderful father. "Go upstairs, and tell your parents about the cockades."

"And return only when your family says it's safe," I add. "That could be a day, a week, even a month. They will know."

As soon as he is gone, Henri takes my arm. What would it be like to walk these streets without him? "The guardsman is right," he says as we hurry back to the Boulevard du Temple. "We should be wearing the tricolor."

"In support of Revolution? On Thursday, I have to return to Versailles—"

"As a tutor?" Henri stops walking. "Marie, the king has lost half of his army. A king without an army is a king in name only. What good will it do the Salon for you to be known as a royal tutor?"

"We . . . we don't know what the future holds for the National Assembly. The queen might call on her brother in Austria for help, and all of this will turn to dust." I continue walking, and Henri follows. "Remaining with the royal family is prudent," I say. "They still love the king in the provinces. Robespierre wrote to Curtius last week; his letter arrived after Lafayette visited. It's his greatest concern."

"That the king is popular?"

"That the peasants won't understand the cause for liberty. It could all go either way," I tell him.

"Agreed. And until we know which way it's going, we should wear the cockade."

When we reach the Boulevard, there are half a dozen carriages outside the Salon, and none of them belong to men we know. The horses have been decorated with tricolor sashes. Even the coachmen are wearing multiple cockades. "Guardsmen?" I ask.

"Or members of the National Assembly."

I open the door to the Salon, and two dozen men turn around to stare. Only one has a familiar face, and he's the only one not dressed in a blue coat with white lapels and leggings.

"Marie! Henri!" Camille moves through the crowd. I search the room for Lucile, but she's not here. "Where have you been?" he exclaims. "You almost missed everything. They s-s-stormed the Invalides this morning. Eighty thousand of them!"

"Eighty *thousand*?" Henri is sure he's heard wrong, but Camille is nodding in triumph. Does he understand what this kind of anarchy means? Without a king, the only ones left to govern us are men who wish to take the king's place. What happens if the National Guard should fail?

"They've captured thirty thousand muskets," Camille is saying. "And more than a dozen cannons. Now they need gunpowder, and we know where that is kept."

"The Bastille," Henri guesses.

"There's no point in going to Versailles anymore. The Revolution is happening here!"

My uncle emerges from the crowd of men, and now—like them—he is dressed as a member of the National Guard. "Some of the crowd are making their way to the Bastille. The National Guard has to be there." He looks to Henri. "Will you stay with Marie?"

"Of course," Henri replies, taking my hand.

"And Maman?" I ask.

"Upstairs," Curtius says. He turns and faces the two dozen guardsmen. It's like watching an actor onstage. It isn't real. It can't be real. If I touch his face, it will be wax and all of this just a moving tableau. But as the men file past, I smell the powder on their skin and the leather of their shoes and know that it's happening.

Curtius stops at the door to embrace me. "Tell your mother I'll be back for tonight's salon," he says in German.

Camille has moved to join the men, armed with a quill and a notebook. Henri and I watch them disappear down the Boulevard du Temple, and when he closes the door, I am speechless.

When Camille returns, he is trying to catch his breath. No one shows up on our doorstep without panting anymore. "The B-B-Bastille," he gasps, and I usher him inside. "The Bastille—"

"What about the Bastille?" Henri snaps irritably. It is three in the afternoon, and we've been waiting all day for word. My mother's food has gone cold, and the three of us have been sitting downstairs by the window, watching every passerby.

"They've stormed the Bastille!" Camille cries.

I hurry to shut the door, and Maman fetches Camille a chair and a drink. He makes a great show of taking both, keeping us in suspense. Then he tells us how a mob of a thousand men approached the gates, demanding that the Marquis de Launay surrender the fortress's thirty thousand pounds of gunpowder. But de Launay refused, saying he would have to write to Versailles and wait for instructions from the king. As the crowd grew, a carriage-maker climbed to the top of perfume shop next to the gates and cut the chains to the massive drawbridge.

"And as the bridge came thundering down, the crowd rushed into the inner courtyard. They thought the guards were letting them inside, and the guards thought the mobs were storming the fortress. So the king's soldiers opened fire!"

"And Curtius?" my mother cries.

"Curtius was calling back the mobs, but no one could hear him. Not over the shouts and the cannon fire."

"Mein Gott," she whispers, and I take her hand. Why did he agree to this terrible job? What if something should happen to him?

"Where did the cannons come from?" Henri asks.

"One was a silver-plated gift to Louis the Fourteenth. It was taken from his armory at the Invalides. The irony!" He laughs. "The end of the Bourbons, brought about by the riches of their ancestors! And as soon as the cannons were lit . . ." Camille pauses. He wants to be sure his audience is listening. "*Surrender.* De Launay surrendered with his white handkerchief."

"How many people were killed?" I ask.

"At least a hundred. But those men will be remembered. *I* will remember them. And every man who was there and survived the battle will be hailed as a Vanquisher of the Bastille, including your uncle."

"What about the Swiss Guard?"

Camille sobers. He knows my mother has three sons in the Guard. "The ones who could be found were taken into custody."

"They're the king's guards!" I exclaim. "Who has that power?"

"The National Assembly. And more important, the Paris Commune, acting on behalf of the National Assembly from the Hôtel de Ville."

"The Paris Commune?" I repeat. "Who are they?"

"Men who've been elected to do the Assembly's wishes. And their wishes are to arrest the enemies of the people."

"Those men were simply following de Launay's orders," I say heatedly. "The *king's* orders."

"They fired on good citizens."

"Citizens who were trying to overrun the Bastille!"

"Well, some of them escaped," he says tonelessly. "They took off their coats and were mistaken for prisoners."

"And the *actual* prisoners in the Bastille?" Henri asks.

"Freed. Released from decades of unfair imprisonment."

"Even the Marquis de Sade?"

"He was transferred to the insane asylum at Charenton several days ago. But all the others were set free."

"There were only seven prisoners," I say. "We toured the Bastille in April."

"Seven or seven hundred," Camille replies. "Those men were put there by *lettres de cachet* and they are symbols of tyranny. And the mob today showed the *ancien régime* how tyrants are dealt with!" He tells us of a Swiss Guardsman named Béquard who kept de Launay from detonating the gunpowder and blowing the entire fortress to pieces. As he opened the gates to let in the people, the mobs severed his hand. "The hand of a tyrant," Camille says, "and it was still gripping the key!"

"Enough." Henri stands. "What are you thinking, telling stories like this in front of two women?"

"Henri." I put my hand on his arm, but he shrugs it off.

"No." He points accusingly at Camille. "He gets pleasure from this."

"And if you were a good patriot, you would find pleasure in it, too."

Henri and Camille glare at each other from across the table. Henri has never pushed me away, and though I know he is only trying to protect me, I am hurt. What's happening, that friends are suddenly turned into enemies?

"Have some coffee," my mother says hurriedly, moving the pot toward Camille. He pours himself a cup, but his cheeks are still inflamed, and his long hair has come loose from its ribbon.

"I will be starting my own newspaper," Camille tells us. *"Révolutions de France et de Brabant.* The tyranny of the press is at an end. If the royal family could have seen the face of de Launay in his surrender, they would understand that the monarchy is finished as well."

"I assume de Launay has been arrested," Henri says. "Where are they taking him?"

"To Citizen Bailly at the Hôtel de Ville. Bailly has been named the Mayor of Paris, and he will decide what to do with such traitors." Camille puts down his cup and looks at me. "Are you coming?"

"To the Hôtel de Ville?" my mother exclaims.

"Of course." He is excited. "That is where the news is."

"He's right, Maman. As soon as it's safe to reopen the Salon," I say, "the exhibits need to reflect what's happening. What does Bailly look like? What is he wearing? Perhaps one of the rooms should be changed to reflect the Hôtel de Ville."

"I'll go with you," Henri says, and Camille doesn't object.

I bring a leather case to hold my paper and ink, and the three of us hurry south down the Rue de Saintonge. Hundreds of people are leaving their houses, making their way toward the Hôtel de Ville. They all want to see de Launay and the *Vainqueurs* of the Bastille for themselves. When we reach the hôtel, the crowd is so large that it's impossible to see anything. "Murderer!" some of the people are crying. "Murderer!"

Members of the National Guard are bringing the prisoners through. I assume that one of them is the Marquis de Launay.

"That's Jacob Elie." Camille points. "And that man over there is Pierre-Augustin Hulin. You'll want both of their faces for your exhibition. They led the storming of the Bastille."

"God in heaven," I whisper, "look what they've done to de Launay." The governor of the Bastille has been badly beaten. There is blood on his face and down his white cravat. His captors can't move him three steps without having to push away the crowds, who believe the marquis plotted to massacre the invading mobs.

"How should we kill him?" someone shouts.

Another man answers, "Let's draw and quarter him."

"Get away from me!" de Launay screams. "Just let me die. Let me die!" He lashes out with his foot, and this is all the reason the people need. He disappears beneath a flurry of bayonets and knives. I shriek, and the crowd begins to cheer. The man who was kicked is given the honor of sawing off de Launay's head, and when they hoist it onto a wooden pike, I am certain I am going to be ill. "I want to go home," I say. Even Camille has lost his color. "Are you coming?"

We walk back in silence, but the sound of the crowd seems to be following us. As we reach the Boulevard du Temple, the cries grow louder, and as I open the door to the Salon Camille cries, "The mob! My God, they're following us."

"Inside!" Henri shouts. "Get inside!" But before anyone can make it through the door, we are surrounded. Henri grips my hand and positions himself in front of me. There must be a thousand, no, two thousand of them. What are they doing here? What do they want?

A man steps forward and identifies himself as Pierre-Augustin Hulin, Vanquisher of the Bastille. "Citizeness Grosholtz. The patriots of France have come to your doorstep to make a request. We carry the heads of two tyrants, and it is our wish to preserve these heads for eternity, not only as examples of what happens to the enemies of the people but as reminders to the *ancien régime* that their time has come!"

The crowd cheers, raising their weapons in the air. Most of them are men in long trousers and tricolor cockades. But there are women as well, in muslin caps and linen skirts. Their faces look fierce. They are watching, waiting for me to make a mistake. I am about to refuse when another man separates himself from the crowd.

"Curtius!" I gasp.

"Marie." He takes me by the shoulders, and while the crowd waits, he says to me in German, "Tell them yes."

"What do you mean?" I back away from him. "You—you want me to touch a severed head?" I want to scream, to vomit, to run away, but there is something in his gaze that steadies me.

"These men are the future leaders of France."

I stare at the sea of grubby faces. These are our leaders? This murderous mob?

"If you can't, I will. But one of us has to."

"Well?" Hulin demands.

I look at the bayonets, their metal tips glinting in the sun. If we refuse, it will be the end of the Salon de Cire. It may also be the end of us. "I will do it," I say.

A deafening cheer goes up in the crowd.

"Go inside and find plaster," Curtius says.

I turn to Henri, who takes my hand. "You can do this," he whispers and kisses my neck. I feel the strength of his conviction in his voice. I can do this. I *will* do this. For us.

My mother, who has been listening at the window, helps me collect the materials. Plaster, water, a basket of cloths. I will not bring corpses into the workshop. I will sit on the steps, and the mob can watch me at their gruesome handiwork. I fetch a white apron and try not to think how it will look in an hour. The men on my father's side, generation upon generation, were executioners. It is my Grosholtz heritage. My mother and I don't speak. We take the materials onto the porch, where the mob is waiting.

Everyone stays, even Camille. Hulin passes the first head to me, and I fight against the urge to vomit. It is de Launay without his wig. Twenty minutes ago, this head was attached to a forty-nine-year-old body. The skin, the hair—it was all taken care of by a man who woke up this morning and could never have imagined that I would be holding his head in my hands. His eyes are shut, but even so, I feel certain that he is looking at me.

I cradle the back of his head so I don't have to touch the bloody stump of his neck. As I place it between my knees, it stains my apron. *God, give me strength.* My mother passes me the plaster. I work without looking up. I don't want to see the faces of these murderers. I don't want to remember any more of this than I have to. I expect the crowd to be silent, but they chat among themselves as if this were an open-air show.

"Look at her hands," someone says.

"She works so quickly!"

Without the need to sculpt a clay head first, the entire process is swift. Unlike with living models, who refuse to have anything applied to their skin, it takes only a few minutes for the plaster to set against de Launay's face and for a mold to be made. Then my mother disappears and returns with a pot of melted beeswax. While we wait for the wax to set, Hulin passes me the second head. This man is older, and his eyes are open.

"Jacques de Flesselles. A traitor," Hulin spits.

God forgive me, I think as I position the head between my knees and feel the steady presence of Henri and Curtius at my side. I don't ask why this man was killed or what he did. I just repeat to myself, *One more mold, and all of this is done.* I close the old man's eyes, then press the plaster bandages to de Flesselles's face. He is—was—a man in his sixties. Was he a father? A grandfather? Certainly he had some family that's missing him right now. What would they say if they knew what I was doing? I remove the plaster and pour beeswax into the hardened mold.

There is talking and laughing as the molds dry and I paint the faces. Someone suggests I give de Launay a woman's wig, since he enjoyed his foppery. I use the cheapest men's wig in my mother's basket and skip the glass eyes. When I am finished, I pass Hulin his wax models. With a theatrical flourish, he impales the heads on the ends of separate bayonets and lifts them above the crowd. Once again, there are wild cheers. A man hands him a leather purse, and he holds it out to me. It looks heavy. "For your service to the people."

A hundred livres, maybe more? But though we have used at least fifty livres' worth of materials, I shall not be paid to decorate death. "No."

Hulin is surprised. He turns back to the crowds. "She has refused payment for her work!" he shouts, and the mobs cheer again. He takes the severed heads and gives them to another man. He bows to me, and the throng begins to clear.

"I have to go with them," Curtius says quietly.

As soon as they are gone, I untie my apron and let it fall to the ground. My hands smell of death. My mother and Henri follow me inside, where I stand motionless. "I will draw you a bath," my mother says quickly. She kisses my brow and says to me in German, "Your grandfather was the executioner of Strasbourg. He saw death every day and then had to go home and greet his children. It is in your blood to be strong. You didn't kill those men. You simply made them immortal."

She goes upstairs, and I remain standing. Henri takes me in his arms, and it's only when I'm there, safe against his chest, that I let myself weep. "Shh." He strokes my hair, but the tears won't stop coming. "Shh . . ."

"To hold their heads. Men who were alive . . ." I choke on my tears, and Henri tightens his embrace. "What will their families think? What will they say . . ."

"No one will blame you. There was no other choice." He brushes away my hair with the back of his hand, then says softly, "Marry me. We'll go away. We'll sail to England, and we'll combine our two exhibitions as one."

I look into his eyes. They are dark and earnest. Full of expectation. What sort of fool would turn down marriage to this man? "And what would my family do?" I ask him, taking his hand. "How would they live?"

"They could come with us."

"That . . . that isn't practical. Curtius would never leave, and neither would Maman. France is their home. We've made a name for ourselves here."

"Which is why the mob came to you, Marie. What happens when they arrive with the next demand? And the next? A corpse lasts for a few days. But they can parade a wax model for as long as they please."

I put my hand to my head. Why can't I think?

"Marie, they are going to come again. Marry me, and we can stay in England until all of this is *over.*"

It's the sensible thing to do. Philip Astley is leaving, and there's talk on the Boulevard that Rose Bertin may be going as well. "When Curtius is no longer a guardsman," I say. "As soon as he's able to run the Salon, we'll marry. And if things aren't better for France, we'll take our exhibitions to England."

Chapter 27

July 15, 1789

Nobility, wealth, rank, office—all that makes you very proud!
What have you done to deserve these blessings?

—Lorenzo da Ponte, *The Marriage of Figaro*

"So what are you going to do?" my mother asks.

I look down at the plaster molds of de Launay and de Flesselles. Last night at our salon, Jefferson came with Lafayette, congratulating me for "serving the people's cause" and completing a tremendously gruesome task "to frighten the *ancien régime* into compliance." That's what they're calling the king and his nobles now. The *ancien régime,* the Old Order. A way of life that's no longer acceptable. "If the Americans can cast it off," Lafayette said, "then so can we!" He lifted the heavy key to the Bastille and promised to send it across the ocean to George Washington. Everyone cheered, and it was like old times, with the Duc, Camille, Lucile, even Marat. Only Robespierre was missing, though a letter came saying that he'd be visiting the Bastille today. Everyone wants a piece of it. They're selling large stones for seven sous, and you can pay fifteen to tour the dungeons. "It was a symbol of tyranny," Jefferson said.

I thought it had been a symbol of transgression.

I lift the plaster mold of de Launay and hold it up to the light. It's a very good likeness. However repulsive these times may be, if the Salon is to survive, our tableaux must change. This morning the *Journal de Paris* described yesterday's events in gruesome detail. Parisians will find their news in their papers or in our halls. It's up to us.

"So what are you going to do?" my mother repeats.

"We're going to remove one of our exhibits," I decide, "and replace it with *The Conquest of the Bastille.*"

My mother nods encouragingly. This is what she likes to see. Movement. Progress.

"I'll need to make our own busts of de Launay and de Flesselles. Also the men I saw yesterday: Elie, Hulin, the mayor, Bailly. We'll need clothes for them. Trousers and cockades . . ."

"What about the shop?"

"For the Curiosity Shop we'll go with miniature Bastilles. Do you think Curtius will have time for that? The entire model can be made from wax except the white handkerchief they used to surrender. That can be cotton. Or linen. Whatever's cheapest."

"And we can reopen the Salon on Saturday," my mother says eagerly.

"Perhaps Yachin can help Curtius with the miniature Bastilles. If it's calm, I'll visit Rose. She'll know what our models should be wearing." Then we will find a tailor who can make them cheaper.

It's a short walk to Le Grand Mogol, but I take the longer route so I can see the city. There's a strange euphoria in the air, as if everyone believes that the destruction of the Bastille has set the country free. Houses have opened their shutters to the world, and those who can afford it have decorated their homes in blue, white, and red. Even the poor are wearing tricolor cockades, and they greet each other in the streets with "Good morning, Citizeness," and "Welcome, Citizen." Men are sporting trousers instead of *culottes,* even the wealthy who can afford knee breeches and stockings. And powdered wigs have almost completely vanished, as if every shop in Paris has suddenly stopped selling them.

I reach Rose Bertin's shop and stand in front of the window. She's showing a long chemise gown with a black and white cockade pinned to the white ribbon at its waist. My God, does she want to be driven out of business? Black is the queen's color, the color of the Hapsburgs, and white is the color of the Bourbons! I open the door and step inside. A group of well-dressed women are at the counter purchasing similar black and white cockades. None of them are wearing powder in their hair. But their gowns are fine, and their gloves are of good leather. So this is how the nobility will show its discontent.

I wait until the crowd has cleared before saying, "An interesting window display."

"That's what my customers want," Rose replies. She's wearing a yellow gown with a black cockade on her breast. The queen would be proud.

"So does this mean you're on the side of the nobility?"

"It means I'm on the side that pays the bills. And right now, aristocrats are the only ones with any money. But I'm not a fool." She leads me into her workshop, where two dozen women are sitting at separate desks. Their heads bob up and down in greeting, but they don't stop sewing. "Show Citizeness Grosholtz what you're doing, Annette."

A young woman holds up a white muslin cap edged with a beautiful tricolor ribbon. "A bonnet *à la Nation,*" she says.

We go on to the next desk, and Rose gestures for the second woman to show us what she's doing.

"A necklace." The girl holds up a long golden chain. From the end of it dangles a smooth gray stone with the word *Liberté* written in diamonds.

"That's a rock from the Bastille," Rose explains. "So you see? I am ready for anything."

We return to the shop, where the summery scents of sandalwood and jasmine fill the light space and she is still selling gloves *à la mode de Provence.* I pick up a pair and inhale. The leather has been perfumed with orange blossom. Three hundred sous. I place them back in the basket. "So what should our models be wearing?"

"That all depends. Which models are we talking about?"

"Madame du Barry."

"I would take off the wig and show her natural hair."

I groan. That will take forever. Perhaps we can find a long blond wig instead.

"Get rid of *panniers*," she continues. "Wide dresses are finished."

"They are?"

"Done."

"But last week—"

"Was last week! The Bastille has fallen. And the king has visited the National Assembly without a single minister by his side to say that he'll be withdrawing his soldiers. He arrived in the Hôtel des Menus completely unannounced. And he went on *foot.*"

My God. It's all but an abdication.

"Only his brothers were with him. Artois and Provence. The three of them stood in the National Assembly and agreed to call back the royal troops. They're bringing the king to the Hôtel de Ville to address the Assembly there. It isn't by choice."

"It's the end of the Bourbons," I say. My gaze falls on her black cockade.

But Rose isn't disturbed. "So long as the queen has her family to call on, it's never the end. Her brother is the Holy Roman Emperor."

"So you think he'll come to her aid?"

"He's been fighting his own war with the Turks. But there's talk of it in the palace. It's all they have left to hope for," she admits. "Until then, I would dress du Barry in a light chemise gown with a lace fichu. And your male models will want black felt hats with tricolor cockades."

"I thought you were promoting the black and white cockade?"

"To *my* customers. Your customers are a different sort." Rose Bertin would dress the Devil if there was money in it for her.

But then am I so different?

The rest of the morning is spent in modeling the faces of Elie and Hulin. This Revolution has cost us several thousand sous. Although I've heard that actors have it worse. They're being told which performances they're allowed to put on, and Pierre Beaumarchais's play *The Marriage of Figaro* is the Assembly's favorite. Up and down the Boulevard du Temple and at the Palais-Royal, this same comedy is playing. And when Figaro takes the stage and declares, "Nobility, wealth, rank, office—all of that makes you very proud! But what have you done to deserve these blessings?" the entire crowd cheers. Even the Opéra Royal, which was nearly burned down, has been allowed to reopen so it can play Mozart's operatic rendition of *The Marriage of Figaro.* I find it ironic that it was the queen's brother Emperor Joseph II who commissioned the play to be turned into an opera.

At four in the afternoon, a carriage arrives outside. "Robespierre!" I hear my uncle exclaim.

The rest of Paris is discarding the fashions of the *ancien régime,* but Robespierre is dressed in blue silk *culottes* and a powdered wig. From his embroidered waistcoat to his striped nankeen jacket, he is the very picture of what newspapers are calling a *muscadin,* or scented fop. And because he stands only a little over five feet tall, some clever shoemaker has convinced him to add higher heels to shoes that already have platforms. He greets my uncle with a dignified nod. A smile is too casual for Assemblyman Robespierre. "Citizen Curtius," he says with exaggerated politeness. "I hear you have performed this country a mighty service."

I leave the wax bust of Hulin and stand next to my uncle, who says, "It was my pleasure to help in any way I could."

"There will be recognition of your service," Robespierre assures him. "The National Assembly is drawing up certificates for all nine hundred Vanquishers of the Bastille. We don't want the citizens of France to forget the sacrifice you made, or the significance of that day. There are enemies lurking around every corner," he says. "Men—even women—who wish to strangle these feats of liberty in their cradles and return this country to its recent days of tyranny." He sounds like Camille, only paranoid. "I have just come from the Hôtel de Ville," he says, "where the king told the crowds that he is proud of what the

National Assembly has accomplished. But when he returns tonight to his palace, what do you think he is going to do?"

"Write to his brother-in-law for help," Curtius guesses.

"Exactly!" Robespierre pushes his glasses back with his thumb. "That's exactly what I told the National Assembly. We are in danger." His voice drops low. "So long as the king is wearing his crown, this country is only one army away from returning to despotism. Rousseau believed in equality. And there can never be equality so long as there are nobles." He looks around, seeing the heads of de Launay and de Flesselles for the first time. "Is this for a new tableau?"

"The Conquest of the Bastille," Curtius replies.

"I hear you've become quite popular." He is obviously waiting for an invitation. He wants to see the model we've made of him. He wants to stand in front of our most popular tableau and enjoy the fact that he, a poor lawyer from Arras, is now a major speaker in the National Assembly.

"Would you like to look around?" my uncle offers. "There's one tableau in particular I think you'll enjoy."

Robespierre lets us take him from room to room, and for each tableau he gives us his commentary. *Jefferson's Study*? "Would be much improved if you removed the bust of Lafayette. Any man who commands other men to kill cannot be trusted." *Sleeping Beauty*? "A disgrace to this nation! Madame du Barry," he adds with disgust, though I notice his eyes rest on her chest, "should be sent from this country and never allowed to return." *The Grand Couvert. The Queen's Chamber. Parisian Beauties. The Foreign Envoys.* All of these have something Robespierre would change. It's unbearable, really. How do the other assemblymen stand him?

"And now, our most popular room," Curtius says, and I wonder if Robespierre will have improvements for this. We step into a re-creation of the National Assembly holding a meeting in the Hôtel des Menus. There are models of the Duc d'Orléans, Mirabeau, and Danton, who took part in yesterday's assault on the Bastille. And, of course, there is Robespierre.

Suddenly, our guest is silent. He crosses the room and stands in front of himself. What must it feel like to see your double in wax? He studies the wide feline face, the green spectacles, the short powdered wig. For a moment, I think he's going to offer a critique. Then he turns and says, "I am honored."

Curtius smiles at me, as if to say, *There. He is not such a barbarian after all.*

"To stand here," Robespierre says, "and see my likeness among so many of the good and great . . ." He puts his hand over his heart. "It is almost more than I can take. In his *Discourse,* Rousseau wrote that the arts and sciences have never served mankind, born as they are of vanity and pride. But this . . ." He casts his gaze around the room, from the walls painted to look like public galleries to the bench where the Duc d'Orléans is seated. "This is *inspiring.* Work like this will remind the citizens of France what we are fighting for, what we are struggling to achieve. Congratulations, Curtius and Marie." My uncle humors him with a little bow. "I am impressed."

We return to the workshop and my uncle's miniature Bastilles. "If you would like to take one with you back to Versailles," he offers, "I can have it wrapped."

"That would be very generous," Robespierre says. "I see you are modeling Jacob Elie and Pierre-Augustin Hulin. Have you considered including the former Comte de Lorges?"

I look at Curtius to see if he's heard of him, but his face is blank.

"There is no man in France who better symbolizes the cruelties of the Bastille," Robespierre tells us. "He was thrown into prison on a *lettre de cachet* and remained there for thirty years. When they stormed the fortress, he hobbled through the gates with the only thing in the world left to him—his cane."

"How do you know this?" Curtius asks. "I was there. I didn't see an old man."

"He was last to be freed. I met with him this afternoon, and his zeal for life is undiminished. I have already spoken with Camille. By tomorrow, there won't be citizen in Paris who doesn't know his story. I can send Citizen Lorges here this evening and you can model him."

My uncle looks to me. "Can a model be done by Saturday?"

There are already five models to finish. De Flesselles and de Launay will both need to be painted, while Elie, Hulin, and the mayor, Bailly, are all in want of hair. We shall simply use wigs; hair can come later. "I can sculpt him if you finish it while I'm gone."

Curtius turns back to Robespierre. "Send him here tonight."

"It would be an honor," my uncle replies.

Robespierre smiles. "I am going to see where this unfortunate man was kept. Would you like to accompany me to the Bastille?"

But before we can go, Robespierre stands in front of the mirror adjusting his wig, straightening his cravat, cleaning his spectacles, and polishing his shoes. When we finally leave the Salon, everyone recognizes him on the streets. They greet him the way they should be greeting the king, stopping in their tracks, even bowing.

When we reach the Bastille, Robespierre stands back. Even after the battle, it's an impressive sight. Eight towers block out the summer's sky, each seventy feet high and five feet wide. Constructed during the Hundred Years' War, it's been a prison for more than three centuries. Now, I suppose, it will become a shrine.

The three of us cross the moat into the fortress's interior, and half a dozen men rush toward us to offer their services. Robespierre nods in the youngest man's direction. "Can you show us around this bastion of horror?"

"It would be an honor, Citizen Robespierre. My name is Victor."

Robespierre smiles at the aptness of this. "A pleasure to meet you."

Victor, who can be only sixteen or seventeen, tells us his brother has been here, imprisoned on a *lettre de cachet* for writing a pamphlet encouraging rebellion.

"You come from a family of patriots, then?"

Victor shrugs. "He wished to better his reputation."

Robespierre frowns, and Victor explains. "Every writer knows that the way to lasting fame is to be sent to the Bastille. My brother did it; the Abbé Morellet did it."

"Are you saying they purposely angered the monarchy," Curtius asks, "just so they could be imprisoned here?"

"Of course! A few months in the Bastille," Victor says cheerfully, "and that's all the credibility you'll ever need. You haven't read the Abbé Morellet? 'I saw literary glory illuminate the walls of my prison,'" he quotes. " 'Once persecuted I would be much better known and my time in the Bastille would make my fortune.' "

"For someone who is clearly educated," Robespierre says, "I'm surprised you're giving tours of the Bastille." I can see from the tightness along his jaw that he means this as an insult. But with so many hangers-on walking behind us in the shadow of a famous assemblyman, he doesn't dare say anything overtly rude.

"What can you do in times like these?" Victor replies. "Even my brother has trouble keeping his family in food. It would have been better if he had stayed here. He ate boiled chicken and roasted beef," Victor remembers. "With Crassane pears and grapes for dessert. But it was the coffee . . ." He shakes his head at the memory. "My brother gave me a cup of the Moka coffee—you couldn't get better at the Palais-Royal."

"Shall we begin the tour?" Robespierre asks sharply.

Victor stops walking. "We can start with this." He points to the ground, where a mass of rubble is being cleared by a team of workers. "This was the gatekeeper's lodge," he says, "where anyone who wished to visit the prisoners had to stop and check in. Sometimes, the men would be playing cards. Over there, that's de Launay's vegetable garden. He planted it so the cooks could make soups."

Curtius looks at me, and I steady myself on his arm. It was only yesterday that de Launay was alive. His friends, his family, the men who depended on him—could they have imagined it would end this way? That his vegetable garden would be trampled underfoot by men who would paint him as a tyrant?

We enter the fortress, and Robespierre's dark mood deepens. I remember the shock of coming here for the first time myself. Where were the chains, the torture racks, the wheel? We pass through several prisoners' rooms. In each chamber is a bed with long green curtains, pillows for resting, and a large black stove. In some of the cells there are bowls on the floor, obviously meant for cats or dogs. "The prisoners were allowed to keep pets?" Robespierre asks.

"Certainly. My brother had his dog, and a friend of his kept two male cats."

"Where are the *cachots*?" Robespierre demands. "I want to see the dungeons." He wants desperate men confined in the dark with rats and vermin, scratching their names into dank walls with their fingernails.

Victor looks to Curtius and me, as if we can explain the reality of the Bastille to him. Instead, we descend into the dungeons, and here, Robespierre finds what he's looking for. A printing press becomes a rack for torture, metal armor becomes a terrible iron corset. There is no convincing Robespierre otherwise. It's a trait in him I've never seen before, and Victor is stunned.

"Did you want to see the billiards room?" he asks.

Robespierre straightens his cravat. "No. I think we have seen enough horror for one day."

As we climb the stairs, we reach a section that is covered in moss. My foot slips, and Robespierre grabs my arm. "Thank you." I gasp, then look down. "My God, I could have killed myself."

"And we wouldn't want to lose a beautiful patriot like you." His eyes lock on mine, and immediately, Curtius is there to say, "That would certainly be a tragedy. And Henri would be exceptionally disappointed."

Robespierre is surprised. "You are engaged to him?"

"Yes."

"But not married?"

"No. The needs of the Salon must come first."

Immediately, I realize I shouldn't have said this. Robespierre's eyes grow wide and full of approval. He clasps my hand and when we return to the daylight, he sees that he has an audience and declares, "Man was born free, and he is everywhere in chains. One man thinks himself the master of others but remains more of a slave than they."

The people begin to clap, and one man says, "Rousseau."

Robespierre nods. "Every man and woman here today would do well to read the philosopher's works."

"Which do you think is more important?" someone asks. "Rousseau's novel *Émile* or *The Social Contract*?"

"That's like asking to choose between the daffodil and the rose. Both are beautiful creations."

The people around us begin to laugh. There is nothing Robespierre can say that would disappoint them. "And what do you think should happen to the Bastille?"

"I believe that a monument to tyranny, such as this," he exclaims, "must be utterly destroyed!"

Chapter 28

JULY 16, 1789

My brother, the Comte, is the most enlightened of advisers. His judgment on men and things is seldom mistaken.

—MEMOIRS OF MADAME ÉLISABETH

AS THE CARRIAGE PULLS UP TO MADAME ÉLISABETH'S CHÂteau, I look at the brightly painted shutters, the rolling hills, and the sculpted trees in their pale marble urns. The air has a light, wild smell that belongs only to Montreuil and Versailles. The hills don't care that there is no bread in Paris. The flowers still bloom whether the Bastille stands or falls. I can see now why the queen built her expensive Hameau. There, nothing else exists. The cows will welcome her whether or not she's beloved in France. The water mill will keep churning even if the people have forgotten about their dauphin. All of the world's troubles cease to exist in Nature. The bees, the flowers, the trickling stream, they simply carry on.

I step from the carriage, and the Marquise de Bombelles comes out to greet me. I search behind her for the pack of greyhounds and the golden figure of Madame Élisabeth.

"The princesse is at Versailles," she tells me. She is even thinner, gaunt. These weeks have changed her. "She would like us to begin in the workshop without her." As we enter the workshop and put on our aprons, she confides in me, "It is a disaster. Two nights ago the king asked the Duc de Liancourt if Paris was in revolt. Liancourt told him it is no revolt. It is a Revolution." She studies me from across the work-table. "We listen to the servants whispering in the halls and beg the guards for information. Is it really a Revolution?" she asks me.

"Yes," I say quietly. "The National Assembly is pushing for a constitutional monarchy." I think of Lafayette and Robespierre. "Some would like to do away with the monarchy altogether and replace it with a Constitution, like they have in America."

Her hands begin to tremble. "All he's ever wanted is the best for his people. And Madame Élisabeth . . ." She shakes her head. "She will be beside herself."

The door to the workshop opens, and Madame Élisabeth appears in a long muslin *gaulle* belted with a sash of rose-colored gauze. Immediately, I curtsy. She takes a seat on the nearest stool, and tears roll down her cheeks. The marquise hurries to her friend and wraps the princesse in a tight embrace.

"They are leaving," she says. "My brother and his wife, the Comtesse d'Artois, are leaving for Turin. They are to stay with our uncle, the King of Sardinia. And the Polignacs are leaving for Switzerland tonight." She looks up at me. "The queen is to lose her dearest friend. Gabrielle de Polignac has been at Versailles for fourteen years. She is Governess to the Royal Children. What if we never see them again?"

The marquise looks nervously at me. "Why should that be? The king is here. You are here. What about the Comte de Provence?"

"He is staying."

"You see? You have two brothers in France, and one of them still wears the crown. Your family will overcome this. And when they do, Artois and the Polignacs will return."

Madame Élisabeth is wearing a black and white cockade, one of Rose Bertin's creations. Her eyes are full of pain, and I wonder if she knows that we are all fair-weather friends. That we smile and bow and then return to Paris to sketch tricolor bonnets and finish exhibits called *The Conquest of the Bastille.* "Will my family overcome this?" she asks me.

Suddenly, everything feels close and hot. The truthful answer is, *It all depends on your brother's resolve. Is he willing to tell what troops remain with him to fire on the rebels? Can he call up favors from other nations and ask for soldiers and weaponry? And when those troops arrive, can he turn away when they spill French blood? If so, he may keep his crown. If not, he is at the mercy of the National Assembly.* "It seems that much will depend on His Majesty's actions."

"Yes." She blinks away her tears. "That is what I told him. The queen and I, we're in favor of fleeing. The minister Breteuil has suggested Metz in eastern France," she reveals.

"*Madame,*" the marquise says warningly.

But the princesse waves away her concern. "Marie is a *royalist.*"

I wonder if my cheeks are burning with shame. I lower my head, in case they are.

"We could wait on the border of Germany and the Netherlands for troops there, in the strongest fortress in Europe. But my brother, the Comte de Provence, thinks we should all remain here. He has told the king that to leave Versailles is to leave the crown, and that if he plans to do that, he cannot blame anyone who might come along and reach for it themselves."

The marquise's eyes go wide. "Such as whom?"

"The Duc d'Orléans. Or the Comte de Provence himself. My brothers"—she addresses me—"are not as close as they might be."

She should not be telling me this. I am a tutor. A wax modeler.

"The queen was packing her belongings this morning, and this afternoon, the king told her that he was staying. She believes her duty is to remain at my brother's side. And of course that is where my duty lies as well."

The three of us are silent. So the royal family will remain in Versailles. Has the king considered what should happen if the National

Assembly decides against a constitutional monarchy and adopts a Constitution? Then he would be a rallying point for men who wished to see a return of the monarchy—making him popular with rebels and dangerous to the Assembly. "Given these precarious times," I say, "I understand if you wish to discontinue wax modeling."

"I can do all things through Christ who strengthens me," Madame Élisabeth quotes. "Not only do I wish to continue," she replies, "but I wish to model the patron saint of every cathedral in France. When each model is finished, it will be my gift to that cathedral."

I look to the marquise, whose face tells me that she has already heard of this plan. "Do you know how many cathedrals there are in France, Madame?"

"Nearly a hundred." She rises from her stool and gathers her apron, tying it neatly around her waist. "Shall we begin?"

~

WOLFGANG CAN'T MEET me outside the Grand Commune until eleven at night. When he appears, I see that he has brought Johann with him, and before we speak I follow my brothers inside to the back of the crowded hall. *How many men have eaten well here at the expense of the king?* Wolfgang picks out a table in the farthest corner of the room, a place where we can watch instead of being watched.

"Tell us about the fourteenth," Johann says. He looks tired, as if there hasn't been much sleep to be had in Versailles in the past two weeks. Even Wolfgang looks drawn in his white silk shirt and velvet doublet.

I tell them everything, from Lafayette and the National Guard to the mobs who stormed the Boulevard du Temple. When I come to the part about de Launay and de Flesselles, my brothers are silent. Johann reaches across the table to take my hand. "I wish we had been there," he says.

"It's better you weren't. They were desperate for a confrontation."

"These are going to be tense weeks," Wolfgang says. "Until the king decides whether to stay or flee—"

"He has already decided. He is staying." I tell them what the princesse said, and how she wept to think she might never see the Polignacs again. Suddenly, Wolfgang and Johann are fully awake.

"He's a fool," Wolfgang replies. "After what he saw today, there shouldn't be any question. The king went to the Hôtel de Ville."

"Again?"

"He wanted to greet the people and tell them that he's recalled Necker from Switzerland. He made his will before he left. There was much wailing from the women—they thought the Parisian crowds would kill him. He promised to broker peace with 'his good people.' "

"And what happened?"

"He went and riled the crowds. They shouted *'Vive le roi,'* and everyone loved him. When he returned here a few hours ago, he was wearing a tricolor cockade in his hat. The *king*! And do you know what the queen told him? She said, 'I thought I married the King of France, not a commoner.' "

My God. What did the king think? That he could return to Versailles with a tricolor cockade floating from his hat and his guards would love him for it?

"I think Curtius was wise to join the National Guard," Johann says. "We're foreigners to this country, whether or not we think of it as our own. And with the three of us in the Swiss Guard, not to mention your position with Madame Élisabeth, it may become dangerous . . ."

"That's what Curtius says. He's gone every day. And some nights, too."

"And the Salon?" Wolfgang asks.

The Salon has never been better, I think. Chaos is good for those who sell news. "I am working all the time. New tableaux. New signs. We reopen tomorrow."

Chapter 29

July 18, 1789

Curtius does not miss an opportunity to add something new to his show.

—Mayeur de Saint-Paul, excerpt from tourist brochure

I don't know how Curtius has managed it in two nights, but *The Conquest of the Bastille* is one of our best exhibits. I walk through the Salon with paper and ink, ready to write down whatever needs to be fixed, but there is almost nothing: a minor adjustment to de Launay's wig and a quick dusting of Jefferson's desk.

"Take these notes to Dr. Curtius," I tell Yachin. "And be ready for a ten o'clock opening. I'll be next door."

Yachin grins. "Are you going to see Henri?" he asks. "He likes you, doesn't he?"

"I certainly hope so." I pause in front of the mirror. "He's my neighbor, after all."

"But he likes you more than that," Yachin persists. "He wants you for his wife."

I adjust my fichu and turn around. "Now why would you say that?"

"Because he's over here so much." He notices everything, Yachin. He would make a fine wax modeler, although his future will certainly be in printing. "And at night," he continues, "before the Salon is closed, you sit on his steps."

"I never leave before the Salon is closed," I correct him.

"You did once. And I saw you. You were sitting together."

"Perhaps we were discussing the weather."

Yachin gives me a long look. "I'm right, aren't I?" he asks eagerly.

I smile. "We'll see."

"Will you tell him I made my own barometer using a bottle, a stopper, and a straw?"

I pause at the door. "He taught you to do that?"

"Four days ago. Remember?"

"No." But it's because I've been selfish. When we meet, it's always about my models, my work, my family, my tutoring. When is the last time I asked Henri about his experiments and what he's been doing in his lab with Jacques? I look down at Yachin's face and see the same hope in his eyes that I've seen in Henri's. These experiments mean so much to them, yet it's been five months since I've been inside Henri's lab, and the last time I was there I was hoping his tour of the *Invisible Girl* would be brief so I could return to my workshop and model Émilie Sainte-Amaranthe. "I will tell him," I say. "And I know he'll be proud."

I walk next door, and before I even raise my hand to knock, the door swings open. "Henri." I smile, and suddenly I'm nervous.

"I thought you forgot." Henri steps back to let me inside. The hall smells of coffee and something else—warm bread?

"When have you ever known me to forget something? Besides," I tease, "I want to know what a pair of bachelors eat for breakfast."

He takes me into the parlor, and I was right, he's found bread. It's laid out on a silver tray with an array of jellies and cheeses. Nothing has ever smelled more delightful. I inhale. No one can imitate the bread in Paris. Not even the best bakers in Montreuil.

"I told the baker I was hosting a lovely woman for breakfast, so he took extra care in finding me some flour."

I laugh. "So when is this lovely woman coming?"

He takes me in his arms. "I believe she's already here."

He kisses my neck, and I close my eyes. It can't continue like this. I can't keep dreaming about him at night and resisting him in the day. We move to the couch, and suddenly I don't care about marriage or children or what happens with the Salon. "What about Jacques?" I whisper.

"He's sleeping upstairs. He won't be awake for another three hours."

I watch him undress and think that even if I had all the time in the world, I couldn't sculpt the perfection of Henri's body. His arms, his chest . . . the lean muscle in his thighs. I take off my cap, and when my hair tumbles down my back, he sighs.

It is painful at first, as I knew it would be. But there is also pleasure, and he is careful not to spill into me. I have experienced tremendous joy in seeing wonderful places and sculpting beautiful things, but this is a different kind of bliss. A fleeting, private, exquisite kind of bliss I have never known until right now. We lie together on the couch, and I feel the warmth of him against my back. The bread must be cold, but it doesn't matter. Henri kisses my shoulder, and I think, *It could be like this always. We could wake together to the smell of coffee and sleep at night in each other's arms.* "Are you happy?" Henri asks.

"Very, very happy," I tell him.

He stands and offers me his hand. I take it, and he turns me toward the mirror. He traces my long neck with his fingers and cups my breasts in his hands. The paleness of my skin is a stark contrast to the darkness of my hair. Together, we make a pretty picture.

"What am I going to do with you, my passionate, creative, ambitious Marie?"

I turn to face him. "Help me dress, and then take me on a tour of your lab?"

He smiles. "I was thinking more like marriage."

"You know—"

He puts a finger to my lips. "Yes."

"What we've done is dangerous," I warn.

He watches me dress, and the longing in his eyes is unbearable to see.

"Curtius won't be a guardsman for long," I promise. "We've already discussed other ways to show our patriotism."

"And how is that?"

"We might do away with all our royal tableaux. Or perhaps he'll join the Jacobin Club."

"Those radicals?" Henri asks. He begins to dress, and I am sorry to see him back in his clothes. "I would try to deter him from that idea."

"It was Robespierre's suggestion when he visited the Salon to see himself in wax."

"Ah yes. Robespierre can be very persuasive."

"What is wrong with the Jacobins?"

Henri buttons his coat. "They have a habit of preaching dangerous things. I would be careful."

"Well, Curtius believes in hedging his bets, and many of the men in the National Assembly are part of the Club. If they succeed in this constitutional monarchy, Curtius will have very influential friends."

"You already have influential friends. That's why you're still going to Montreuil."

"Yes, but then we'd have important friends in *and* out of the palace. Although perhaps I should make friends with your baker," I tease.

We eat, and Henri takes me into his lab, where he tells me about the experiments they've been doing. He wants to launch another balloon, only this time it won't be for show. "There are so many possibilities," he says. "Think of all the uses for flight." He takes down a book and flips through the pages. The mahogany bookshelves stretch to the ceiling, some filled with leather tomes, others packed with glass bottles and mysterious jars. There are ladders to reach the topmost shelves, and I long to climb one.

"Listen," Henri says, and he reads a passage from David Bourgeois's book *Des Expériences de la Machine Aérostatique.* " 'Someday, man will cross burning deserts, inaccessible mountains, impenetrable forests, and raging torrents. And all of this will be done by balloon.' " He looks up at me. "Bourgeois predicted it five years ago, and I plan to see it come to pass."

I feel humbled to hear him speak. "So you're going to fly away?" I ask.

"Not me. But someone will. Imagine the uncharted territories these explorers will find. My brother was the first man in the world to see the sun set twice. What else can be accomplished? What else can we do?"

I'm in the presence of genius, yet the world is more concerned about tricolor cockades. Henri takes me to his desk, where his notes on the weather are carefully laid out. "With enough balloons, we could observe the weather from here to London and make predictions."

"As in when it's going to rain?"

"Or snow or hail . . ."

"But how?"

"By sending up a mercury barometer," he says, "or by having someone record the movements of the wind and clouds. And imagine what you could do with a telescope! Think of how close an astronomer could get to the stars. My brother ascended nearly fifteen thousand feet. With the proper gear, perhaps you could go higher. There are scientific uses, commercial uses, even *military* uses for these balloons. King George the Third is already sponsoring experiments in England."

We watch each other in the bright morning light. There is so much to hope for between us. I wrap my arms around his neck and kiss him. "Come tonight," I say. "My mother is cooking ham from Bayonne."

~

THE REOPENING OF the Salon passes by in a haze. Curtius has excused himself from his duties in the National Guard this weekend, and in front of a crowd of nearly a thousand people, he makes a great show of taking our wax model of the king and placing him outside, then pinning a tricolor cockade to his hat. They must hear the exclamations of joy in the Palais-Royal.

"What's the matter?" my mother asks. "That's the second person you've forgotten to record."

I look down at the record book and suppress a smile. It's true.

Already, Henri is detrimental to my profession. I write down, "Female, seventeen sous," then listen to the exclamations of horror as the woman comes face-to-face with de Launay and de Flesselles. But the most popular model is the one of the decrepit Comte de Lorges. Curtius has given him his very own room, painting the walls to look like a dungeon and cluttering the nearby tables with mementos taken from the Bastille. Knowing how valuable these items will become, he's purchased inkwells and armor, green curtains, and even a set of iron firedogs. A pair of men stop by my table and point to the Comte de Lorges's tableau. "So is that who you would have us believe came tottering out of the Bastille?" the younger man demands.

I frown. "What do you mean?"

"That's the beggar from Notre-Dame," the older man says. "I should know. I pass him every day."

"No. That's the Comte de Lorges. He was a prisoner."

The old man exchanges a look with his son.

"Did he have a mark on his cheek?" the younger man asks. "And a red spot beneath his eye?"

I think back three days ago to the night the Comte de Lorges allowed me to sculpt him. "Yes."

"Then he's the beggar from Notre-Dame."

"But the Comte de Lorges—"

"Is probably a myth, Mademoiselle. Why? Did someone pass that man off as a comte?"

"Yes." I think of Robespierre. "But all the newspapers . . . they're printing his story."

"Well, you know how it is," the older man says angrily. "Anything for a sale."

I am beside myself with rage. I want to take the model of de Lorges and utterly destroy it. I find Curtius outside with the wax model of the king, and I tell him the story.

"And they were *sure* he was a beggar at Notre-Dame?" he asks.

I nod. "What do we do?"

"Obviously, we have to keep him. These people believe he existed, and they'll want to know what happened to him if he suddenly disappears."

"Well, perhaps he had a tragic accident," I say angrily in German. And then it occurs to me. "Do you think Robespierre lied to us on purpose?"

"I think Robespierre believes what he wishes to believe."

Chapter 30

July 22, 1789

Tremble, tyrants, your reign must end!

—Anonymous threat to Marie Antoinette

It's happening again. Just as Henri predicted, just as I have dreamed over and over again in my nightmares. Camille comes running into the Salon, pushing past patrons so he can make his way to the *caissier*'s desk. Before he can say it, I know what's happening. "It's a mob!" he exclaims. Lucile is behind him in a muslin gown and a wide straw hat. Her dark curls are askew, and her cheeks are pink.

"They're coming from the Hôtel de Ville," she says swiftly. "They are making their way to the Boulevard to find Mesdames Foulon and Berthier."

Immediately, the people in line begin to talk. Where is the mob? Are they in danger? Should they leave?

"It is nothing to worry about," Curtius announces. "No reason to abandon your entertainment." To Yachin, he says, "Mind the *caissier*'s desk."

The rest of us follow him into the workshop. He closes the door, and Camille explains.

It began with a rumor that Joseph-François Foulon, the king's new Minister of Finance, told the starving people of France to eat hay. "And you believe that?" my uncle questions, but Camille shrugs. Either way, he says, the people believed it. And as soon as Foulon heard the rumor, he understood the danger he was in and escaped to the country. But a thousand citizens marched into the village where Foulon was hiding and dragged him back to Paris. The eighty-year-old man was hitched to a cart and told to pull the wagon to the Hôtel de Ville. Someone tied a bale of hay onto his back and crowned his head and neck with thistles. "How do you like hay now?" they shouted.

Tears are rolling down my mother's cheeks, and she wipes them away with the back of her hand. Foulon lives only a few blocks away, in the house his father built. As the king's Finance Minister, he might have bought a château. But he has never forgotten his roots on the Boulevard, and there has never been a kindlier, more considerate man. When my mother was sick with fever seven years ago, he found the court doctor, and within a week she was better. Without the care of that good physician, who knows?

"When Foulon finally reached the Hôtel de Ville," Camille says, "the mob hung him from a lamppost."

My mother cries out. She can't hear any more of this.

"Go," Curtius says gently. "Sit with Yachin."

We watch her leave, and Camille continues, "When he was dead, the mobs decapitated him. Then they went for his son-in-law, Berthier de Sauvigny. They wanted him because he's the Intendant of Paris." That's right. An administrator for the king. "So they marched to Compiègne and dragged him from his bed. They made him kiss Foulon's severed head, then dragged him through the streets and beat him as he went. When he could no longer stand, they hung him from the nearest lamppost as well."

I look at Curtius, whose jaw is clenched. "What about the National Guard?" he demands.

"Members of the National Guard were there."

"They were part of it?" he exclaims. This is anarchy. When the men who are supposed to protect French citizens are killing them instead, how can there be peace?

"Yes," Camille confirms. "And now they are bringing Berthier's head to his wife."

"No!" Curtius shouts, and Camille steps backward.

"It's already done," Lucile says nervously. "They were on their way while we were running to you."

"So why did you come? Why didn't you go for Lafayette, or a closer captain of the National Guard?"

"Because now they're coming here," Lucile replies, "and they want a wax model."

I am going to faint.

"Marie." Lucile rushes to my side and lowers me onto a stool.

"I won't do it," I swear. "They can't make me do it!"

"*I* will do it," Curtius says calmly.

"Why?" I scream. "Why should any of us have to?"

"Because the mob is looking for blood," Curtius replies. "What did Berthier do except serve the king? What did his wife do except marry an honorable man who was willing to provide? If we refuse their request—"

"Then you could be next," Lucile says fearfully.

The four of us are silent. This is a nightmare. No, it is worse than my nightmares, because we know Foulon and Berthier. We have eaten with them. We have watched Berthier's children.

"I will make sure the country hears of your service," Camille says quietly. "In tomorrow's paper—"

Curtius and I glare at him.

When the mob comes, they are carrying torches and pikes. We close the Salon, and Curtius goes to work. I will not stay to watch.

Instead, I go with my mother to the home of Madame Berthier, where a crowd has already gathered. The night is warm, and the women who are huddled on her doorstep wear light muslin gowns and simple hats. "Madame Berthier has passed to God," someone says, and the women make the sign of the cross.

"Did they kill her?" my mother asks.

"In a manner of speaking," the same woman replies. I recognize her face: the thinness of her lips and her close-set eyes. She is someone's wife. The baker's? The tailor's? "When she saw the cruel fate they dealt to her husband, her heart gave out. There was nothing they could do to wake her. She has joined him in heaven."

We cross the threshold into the parlor, where a priest is intoning the last words of a psalm. The room smells of lavender powder and sage. The body of Madame Berthier is laid on a couch, and candles illuminate her youthful face. A pink cushion rests beneath her head—a perfect match for her gown and the ribbon in her hair. Did she know when she was dressing that this would be the last gown she'd ever wear? Would she have chosen something different if she had known? My mother says a prayer at the foot of the couch, and I kneel beside her, but my lips won't move. Yesterday, Madame Berthier was alive. Laughing. Breathing. Choosing between hats. I want to stop these morbid thoughts from coming, but my mind won't be silent. She was only thirty-three years old.

When we return to the Salon, the mobs are gone. Upstairs, Curtius is with Henri and Jacques, and the three of them are drinking. They stand as soon as they see us, and Curtius takes my mother in his arms. She is weeping, telling him about Madame Berthier. How young she was. How kind. How unfortunate. Henri takes me to his chest, but the tears won't come. Instead, there is fear. What happens next time if Curtius isn't here and there is only me?

The next morning, Lafayette resigns his command of the National Guard. But without Lafayette, there will be men roaming the streets and murdering, looting, raping with impunity. Even the king will not be safe. For all the Third Estate's dreams of casting off the monarchy, it was the monarchy and its order that kept us safe. Camille writes about the day when not a single soldier can be seen in the streets. If that day comes, it will arrive with murder and rape at its back. Even the National Assembly can see this, and they beg Lafayette to return.

Reluctantly, Lafayette agrees. Perhaps they showed him Loustalot's article in today's *Révolutions de Paris*. A lawyer, like Camille and Robespierre, Loustalot has found his calling with this Revolution. Curtius hid the paper from me, but when he wasn't looking I read the account of Foulon's death. How they stuffed his mouth with hay and dragged his body over the cobblestones. But worse was Loustalot's account of Berthier's end: "Already Berthier is no more; his head is nothing more than a mutilated stump separated from his body. A man, O gods, a man, a barbarian tears out his heart from his palpitating viscera. How can I say this? He is avenging himself on a monster . . ." This is what freedom from the monarchy has brought us. The freedom to kill without consequence. I continue reading

> His hands dripping with blood, he goes to offer the heart, still steaming, under the eyes of the men of peace assembled in this august tribunal of humanity. What a horrible scene! Tyrants, cast your eyes on this terrible and revolting spectacle. Shudder and see how you and yours will be treated. This body, so delicate and so refined, bathed in perfumes, is horribly dragged in the mud and over the cobblestones. Despots and ministers, what terrible lessons! Would you have believed the French could have such energy! No, no, your reign is over. . . . Frenchmen, exterminate your tyrants! Your hatred is revolting, frightful . . . but you will, at last, be free.

Chapter 31

September 7, 1789

I believe in the cutting off of heads.

—Jean-Paul Marat

Every man with a lack of income and a talent for words now believes himself to be a journalist. In Loustalot's *Révolutions de Paris,* we have been reading about the August Decrees, in which the National Assembly has abolished feudalism. There are to be no more special privileges for the aristocracy. All citizens, from whatever class or birth, are now eligible for any civil or military office, and tithes have been done away with. How the Church will continue without its source of revenue is anyone's guess. Perhaps the French will find it in their hearts to be generous, since it's the churches that run the hospitals and the poorhouses. In Camille's weekly paper, *Histoire des Révolutions,* he has been writing about the adoption of Lafayette's Declaration of the Rights of Man and Citizen. And now, Marat is writing as well.

He bursts into the Salon on Monday afternoon, frightening our patrons with his wild eyes and unwashed clothes. They step away from the *caissier*'s desk as he holds up a paper.

"L'Ami du Peuple," I read the title aloud. *Friend of the People.*

"It's going to be a daily," he says. "I want you to include it in your exhibition. You can place it in your tableau of the National Assembly, or hang it on the wall, or even arrange it in front of Robespierre."

"I'm not sure it would go in any of those places," I say tersely. "We have enough accessories as it is."

He looks behind me. "Where is Curtius?"

"*I'm* the one who determines what goes in each tableau."

He lowers the paper, and his eyes meet mine. "No one writes like I do. Camille, Loustalot, Audouin, Fréron . . . They coat the truth with sugary words in their fear of offending. But I don't care whom I offend! This paper is the voice of the people. *I* am the voice of the people!" he shouts. I am about to ask him to leave when he adds, "And you are their eyes. To be a part of your Salon will legitimize me. Everyone in Paris comes to your exhibition. *Please.* Just help me this once."

I take the paper and look over its contents. Part reporting, but mostly encouragement for the Third Estate to stand strong.

"Please," he repeats. "I have found my calling."

"I'll put it in the tableau with Robespierre."

Marat's eyes go wide. "I won't forget your kindness," he says swiftly. "The people will know that you are a true patriot!" He is about to leave when something occurs to him. "Will you be going to Versailles tonight?"

This morning, Marguerite David came to the Salon. We are not friends, or even acquaintances, but her husband is the painter Jacques-Louis David, and Curtius has purchased art from him. She wanted to know if I would join an extraordinary delegation. Eleven women, mostly artists' wives, are going to appear before the National Assembly to present their jewels. "It will be celebrated in every newspaper in France," she said. "Women giving up their jewels for the good of the *patrie.*"

I told her that a family like ours collected wax, not sapphires.

"Then it would mean a great deal if you could be in the audience. You have made a name for yourself. The Assembly would be surprised not to see you among so many important female artists." When she saw me hesitating, she added frankly, "These are the men who make decisions now. No one cares that you were visited once by the king."

I clenched my jaw, and when my mother saw that I was going to refuse, she agreed on my behalf.

Marguerite David smiled. "That's wonderful news. We would like you to dress entirely in white. We are going as Roman wives. Muslin gowns and light fichus. We want to remind the country of a time in Europe's history when men created a republic."

I almost replied, *And that republic died when Julius Caesar made himself emperor. When people are desperate, their republics don't last. They vote themselves a king.* But instead my mother said, "We will see you in Versailles."

Now I look into Marat's eager face and want to ask if this performance will bring back Foulon and Madame Berthier. Will it put bread in the bakeries? Flour in the mills?

"Yes, we are going," my mother says. "We would never miss such a patriotic gathering."

Even my mother has learned the right words.

~

"You have become hard," my mother says as we are dressing. "God has a plan." She turns from the mirror to look at me. "Do you question it?"

I think of Madame Élisabeth with her one hundred saints. Certainly, she doesn't question God's plan.

"When God wishes me to be with His angels," she says, "He will summon me as well. And you. And Curtius. We are all going to die. It's what you do before that call that makes the difference."

"And do you think God would be pleased with what we're doing tonight?"

My mother makes a dismissive noise. "God cares for people, not kingdoms. So we are sitting in the audience of the National Assembly.

Do you think He cares about such petty things? You have a talent, Marie. A talent given to you by God —"

"And Curtius."

"But first God. Look at how you have served Him with it. A hundred saints. A *hundred*!"

"We have only completed three."

She gives me a long look. "There is no shame in what we do."

We meet Henri and Curtius in the carriage downstairs, and as the coach drives away, I sit back and look at them in the sunset. They're exquisite, really. In silk *culottes* and large tricolor cockades, they might belong to the halls of Versailles or the chambers of the National Assembly. Henri has decorated his walking stick with red ribbon—a color the women are now crassly calling *sang de Foulon,* or Foulon's blood—and the buckles on his shoes gleam in the low light.

"That gown suits you well," he compliments me.

I look down at my white dress and pearl necklace. "Gifts from Curtius," I say.

"Well, your uncle has very fine taste." He smiles at my mother, who blushes.

"So when do you become part of our family?" my mother asks.

Everyone looks to me. She's done this on purpose, I think, because there's no escaping from a moving carriage and I will have to answer. "We would like to wait for Curtius to leave the National Guard," I reply.

"You are twenty-eight," my mother says archly. "And who knows when he may leave the Guard?"

"It won't be long," Curtius promises. He pats my mother's knee. "This is the price you pay for having a talented daughter."

She wants grandchildren, I know. It's not enough that Johann has Paschal. They are too many hours away. But still, I feel irritation at her intrusion.

We arrive behind a small delegation of women carrying chests weighted with gold and purses filled with jewels. A buzz of excitement fills the hall of the National Assembly. As directed, the women are dressed entirely in white, and the men have come with shoe buckles that read, LONG LIVE THE NATION and LIBERTY. Because we've painted this hall inside the Salon, it has become as familiar to me as the Palais-Royal. The president's podium, the bright chandeliers, the heavy tapestries. But in truth, it's been four months since I was here with Rose.

I search among the women for her distinctive figure, but she hasn't come. Not surprising, really. While she's made concessions to the Third Estate and its Revolution, she is betting that the queen will triumph. My uncle, however, has brought a purse filled with five hundred livres. Even Henri has come with a bribe. Of course, none of us are calling it that. Instead, we are to call it a charitable donation. We are taken to the front of the hall, where the families of other artists are seated on long benches. Curtius recognizes Jacques-Louis David and makes a point of sitting with him.

"Old friends?" Henri asks.

"David was made a member of the Académie Royale eight years ago," I whisper. "He has a great deal of influence."

"I thought the Académie would be made up of royalists," Henri says, surprised.

"Even the world of art is changing."

"Is this bench available, Citizeness?"

It is Lafayette. He is dressed as Commander in Chief of the National Guard, with white gloves and a dark blue coat. He has brought his wife and children with him. "Adrienne, I would like you to meet the sculptress Marie Grosholtz, and the scientist Henri Charles. On the other side of Henri are Marie's mother and the artist Philippe Curtius."

"The wax modeler?" Adrienne is clearly impressed.

"Yes. But it was Marie who sculpted my model."

"I would like to see your Salon someday," she says to me.

"You are welcome at any time."

"This is my son, George Washington," Lafayette continues, "and my daughters, Anastasie and Virginie."

All three children have the same red hair as their father. They greet us politely, even the youngest, who cannot be more than six or seven. What a beautiful family. And two of them have been named for Lafayette's time in America. I remember the story of Lafayette's youth, how he left his wife while she was pregnant with their second child to help the Americans fight against the British. And now he's Commander in Chief of the National Guard, with the dual responsibility of keeping the peace in France and keeping the royal family safe.

Lafayette takes his seat next to me, and we listen as the Assembly's president calls forth the eleven women who have come with their jewels. It is a carefully orchestrated masque and will be reported in every paper tomorrow as reminiscent of Rome's glorious republic, a time when women eschewed fashion for simplicity and jewels for honor.

Madame David leads the way to the wooden podium, then tells the Assembly that she has come to offer the trappings of her previous life to a country in desperate need. "We no longer wish to own adornments," she proclaims, "that are reminders of a time when citizens were slaves to the monarchy and to fashion. Let virtue be our crowning jewel," she declares, "and liberty our most glorious ornament."

The hall erupts into cheers. Each woman in turn presents her jewels. Then deputies from all across the hall are rushing toward the podium to offer their diamond buckles and silver walking sticks. Curtius and Henri make a great show of handing over their purses, and with each person who approaches the podium, there is a new surge of cheering and applause. Women who have come simply to watch the proceedings find themselves caught up in the moment and are offering their rings, bracelets, lockets.

I turn to Lafayette. "You must be very proud."

"The path to a constitutional monarchy is never easy, but we are fortunate to be on this journey with many courageous citizens."

"I didn't realize you were in favor of a constitutional monarchy," I say. When I sketched him in Jefferson's study, Lafayette had wanted to be rid of the king altogether.

"I have come to see things differently," he admits. "There is tradition here. A court that goes back to the Treaty of Verdun. Are we going to throw it all away and risk anarchy?" He is thinking of Foulon. He couldn't stop his own men from committing murder. "The Americans never had a king on their soil. They'd been ruling themselves for several hundred years. Jefferson is right. Our nation is different."

For the first time in months, I am filled with optimism. Like Lafayette, I have never seen the purpose of trampling on so many hundreds of years of tradition. But perhaps there *can* be a compromise. Something that could benefit both Madame Élisabeth *and* Camille, the Second Estate *and* the Third.

Chapter 32

October 10, 1789

The people of Paris, always criticizing, but always imitating the customs of the court.

—Madame Campan,
first lady-in-waiting to Marie Antoinette

On Thursday, when I return to Montreuil, I feel guilty for my joy. Madame Élisabeth makes no mention of my presence before the National Assembly, but I see what she has gathered on her workshop table and I am sorry. The Assembly has passed a law granting the freedom of the press, and since then, the papers have been filled with the vilest things. Images of the queen lifting her chemise before the Princesse de Lamballe, cartoons mocking her as a ferocious beast with a human face ready to devour its prey, and descriptions of her love affairs with men whom prostitutes would be ashamed to sleep with. In a pamphlet called *The Royal Dildo,* the queen is shown with the Princesse de Lamballe engaging in the most humiliating acts, and other papers show her engaging in orgies, masturbation, even bestiality. I hope it isn't a *libelle* that Madame Élisabeth has managed to procure.

She passes me one of the papers. There is an image of the eleven women from Monday night presenting their jewels before the National Assembly. They are dressed in the flowing white chemise gowns for which the queen is criticized so bitterly, yet the caption beneath the image reads, "The virtuous maidens of France."

"When the queen wears such a gown, she's a wicked adulteress. When any other woman wears it, she's an honorable maiden. Why do they do this? Why do they hate her so much?"

I take a steadying breath. "Because they are focusing all of their resentments and frustrations on her."

"Look at the other articles," Madame Élisabeth whispers. She can barely bring herself to say, "The one they've titled *L'Autruche Chienne.*"

It means "The Ostrich Bitch" and is close enough to *L'Autrichienne,* or *The Austrian,* for people to believe it's clever and amusing. Even the Duc likes to use this offensive pun. Whoever wrote this wants to see the queen disgraced. Like those who attributed lies to Foulon, they credit her with telling the people of France to eat cake if they can't find any bread, and the accompanying pictures are equally offensive. "I wouldn't look at these, Madame. No good can come of it."

"The king has called up the Flanders Regiment for extra protection. When they arrive next month, there's to be a great banquet. Of course, none of my family shall be attending. Any common soldier can go, but imagine the scandal if we should attend a feast in our own palace? We're prisoners here. No one believes it, Marie, but that's what we are."

OF THE MANY buildings in Versailles, the Château Opéra must be the most beautiful. Tonight, the halls echo with the sharp clicks of women's shoes and the polished heels of smartly dressed soldiers. It's the king's desire that the men in the Royal Flanders Regiment be properly introduced to the Swiss Guard. While welcome banquets like this are usual, there has never been one in the Château Opéra. There's to be food and drinks, even an orchestra playing Grétry's *Richard Coeur-de-lion,* but no appearance by the royal family. I am here because Madame Élisabeth gave me permission to celebrate with my brothers. It is an honor a better person would have refused.

"I find it hard to believe there can be a celebration like this without the king. These are his soldiers. They're here on his behalf," I say to Wolfgang.

My brother takes my arm and guides me to the stairs. "Perhaps there will be a little surprise, then."

I gasp. "They're coming?"

Wolfgang winks. "I guess we'll just have to wait and see."

"Tell me," I beg him. We climb the stairs, and I'm thankful to have chosen a gown with a bustle that is trimmed and pleated at the back. Anyone climbing stairs should be wearing a *polonaise* gown.

"It's supposed to be a surprise. The king and the queen will be here with their children," he reveals. "But not the entire time."

I look down at the handsome men as they arrive, and at the women in their glittering array of dresses, and think, *The queen will be happy to see this.* "So where is Abrielle?"

"Down there." He points to the stage, where long wooden tables have been set up for the soldiers. The china sparkles in the candlelight, and the men are taking their seats. Each of the king's bodyguards has been seated next to a soldier from the Royal Flanders Regiment. Sitting beside the commander of the Swiss Guards is a milk-and-honey beauty like Madame du Barry, with thick blond hair and porcelain skin. But she is smaller than du Barry. So petite, in fact, that she might be mistaken for a little girl.

Something her father said has made her laugh, and I catch the sound all the way up here. She is dressed in a russet gown trimmed with pearls, and there are pearls around her neck at least three strands thick. *Her father's little girl,* I think. *He will not give her away so easily.*

"She's very beautiful," I say. "Exactly the kind of girl I imagined you with."

"Really?" My brother searches my face.

"Yes."

"I laugh more with her than I have with anyone," he admits.

"Have you spoken with the baron?"

"What is there to say? I have no money. No means of getting any money. The Swiss Guard is my life, and what advancement is there in this?"

I look down at the Baron de Besenval. Edmund is sitting next to him, serious and sober. Although everyone at the table is laughing, his eyes are searching the hall, as if he's preparing himself for trouble. The glass in front of him is clear, which means he's drinking water. But the baron is intent on enjoying himself, and he raises a glass of wine for a toast. He has a cheerful face and an easy smile. "He might take pity," I say. "What sort of man is he?"

"The sort that will want the best for his daughter. If we're honest, we both know there's no way I can provide it."

"That all depends on what *best* means. Thick strands of pearls, or happiness and love?" We go to the theater box where I'll be dining, and my brother looks down at the golden figure of Abrielle. I shouldn't have mentioned the baron. This is supposed to be a happy night for him. "Go and enjoy yourself," I say. "Just don't drink too much."

"I cut my wine with water now."

I raise my brows. "Sacrifices like these can't go unnoticed. Not if there's truly a God in heaven."

He laughs. "I'll come back up when dinner's over."

"Do you know whom I'm sitting with?" The box is set for two.

"Someone you know," he says mysteriously.

I take my seat, and when Wolfgang disappears, a familiar figure takes his place.

"Marie Grosholtz." Rose smiles. She is dressed in a gown of violet silk de chine with painted bouquets of lilacs across the petticoat. Small purple gems decorate her bodice, and I wonder if they're crystal or real amethysts. "It seems the court doesn't know what to do with either of us, and so we meet again." She arranges herself on the velvet seat. "I saw all three of your brothers. Quite a handsome trio."

"Are you surprised?"

"Not really. But Wolfgang . . ." She snaps her fan closed and reaches for the wine. "Now *there* is a handsome man. I suppose that he's taken?"

My God. She's forty-two years old. Does she really invite such young men to her bed? "Yes," I say at once. "Very much taken."

"What a shame. Although, if I had to guess, she is someone who is quite out of his reach."

I stare at her. How does she know this?

"He was making eyes at the Baron de Besenval's daughter, and I very much doubt she's resisted his charms."

"That is not for public knowledge," I say.

"I was young once, Marie. And though it's hard to believe, there was a man I loved whose father believed he was too good for me. Today, that family is buried in debt. I'll bet they wish they'd considered me now." Rose takes a long sip of her wine. "He died seven years ago on a ship to England. Would I want him if he were still alive?" She takes a moment to consider. "Yes. But that's how the heart is. Stubborn and foolish." She draws my eyes to the pretty figure of Abrielle. "Will she really leave her father and all that comes with him just for love?"

"Perhaps Besenval can be convinced . . ."

Rose gives me a hard look. "If you love your brother, tell him to let her go. That, or get her with child—"

I inhale sharply. "He would never do that."

"Such accidents happen," she says lightly. "And then the baron will really have to choose. His grandchildren or his pride . . ."

There is a great fanfare of trumpets, and everyone turns.

"Is it the king?" I lean over the box to see.

"And the queen," Rose says. "Her mourning has come to an end, and tonight she's making a statement. Look what I've created."

The queen is a vision of blue and white. From the feathers in her hair to the stunning turquoise at her neck, there is nothing on her person that suggests she supports the revolutionary cause. Neither the little dauphin nor Madame Royale wears any red. They are a handsome family, and as soon as they appear, a cheer goes up inside the Château Opéra.

"Vive le roi!" someone shouts, and the cry is echoed through the room.

The orchestra strikes up the stirring aria *"O Richard, O Mon Roi,"* about a minstrel who is loyal to his king, and suddenly women are passing out black and white cockades. I see the queen raise a handkerchief to her eyes, and even the king is deeply moved. I wish that Madame Élisabeth was here to see this.

~

THE FOLLOWING MORNING the curtains of my bed are pushed aside, and the bright light startles me. When my eyes adjust, the worried face of the Marquise de Bombelles comes into focus. "The princesse needs you."

I push away my covers. "I'm not late for modeling?"

"No. It has nothing to do with that." She watches me get undressed, then calls for a woman to help me with my hair and hurry me into my gown.

"So what's wrong?" The princesse normally rises at eight, and the clock reads seven.

The marquise begins worrying the lace ends of her fichu. "Every morning for the past two weeks, a servant has been collecting newspapers for the princesse. This morning . . ." Her eyes fill with tears. "Well, this morning . . . It's terrible, Marie. Come into the salon and see."

We hurry through the halls, and a solemn pair of guards open the doors with gloved hands. Madame Élisabeth has half a dozen newspapers spread across the table in front of her. I recognize Marat's title among the six. As we cross the room, the sleepy greyhounds curled around the princesse's feet lift their heads from their paws. When they see that it's us, they return to their dreams. Wordlessly, Madame Élisabeth hands me a paper.

It's Camille's *Révolutions de France.* He's turned an innocent banquet into a dangerous plot to bring down the National Assembly.

Camille claims the banquet carried on until dawn as soldiers swore to defeat the Assembly's revolutionaries and hang them from lampposts. He talks about the wine and the women's powdered *poufs,* and says the tricolor cockade was tossed on the floor and trampled underfoot. "Just as the king plans to do to our new liberties."

"He wasn't even there!" I say. I pick up Marat's *L'Ami du Peuple.* The same lies. Only in his, the queen tramples the tricolor herself. And then, on the bottom of the first page, Marat has drawn up a list of names, royalists who should be punished with death for betraying the cause of the common people. That a journalist is able to publish an article encouraging murder means that whatever the illusion the National Assembly has portrayed, however many guardsmen it has recruited for Lafayette, this is anarchy. I inhale slowly. What Madame Élisabeth needs to see is calm. "Have you shown these to the king's ministers?" I ask evenly.

"I'm sure they're poring over the papers as we speak. I can't eat, I can't think . . ." She stands, and the dogs scamper from their comfortable positions. "Marie, you should go."

"Madame—"

"I'm not a fool," she says firmly. "Every hour you spend with me here is an hour you aren't working at your Salon." She reaches out and takes my hands. "Thank you for coming this week. I have already called a carriage for you."

I look at the marquise. Then I look back at the papers assembled on the table. "Is there anything I can do?"

I'm surprised when Madame Élisabeth says, "Yes. If you know of these men, if you ever see them in Paris, will you tell them the truth?"

I feel my cheeks grow hot with shame. "Yes. I will do that," I say.

Chapter 33

October 5, 1789

Hang the aristocrats from on high!
Oh, it'll be okay, be okay, be okay.
The aristocrats, we'll hang 'em all.

—Excerpt from the revolutionary song "Ça Ira"

But before I can confront either Marat or Camille, all of Paris loses its mind. On the fifth of October, as my mother is putting the morning coffee to boil, the tocsin in the Church of Saint-Merri begins to ring. When the sound grows louder and more persistent, we hurry down the stairs. Outside, the neighbors are emerging from their houses despite the pouring rain. Henri is already on the steps with Jacques. He kisses my cheek briefly, then whispers, "Stay calm."

"What's the news?" my uncle asks them.

"A mob of women, more than five thousand strong, are coming from the Rue Saint-Bernard," Jacques says.

I glance at Henri. "My God, not here?"

"No," Jacques tells us. "They're making for Versailles."

We stand on our steps and listen as the tocsin of Notre-Dame-des-Blancs-Manteaux begins to ring. Henri takes my hand, and we stand together as the women approach. Nearly all are carrying pikes and knives. Some have muskets, and they raise the polished guns above their heads each time someone shouts, *"When will there be bread?"* I can see from their ragged dresses that these women are *poissardes.* Market women. They have come from the quay where they've been selling fish. They are hungry looking and were probably easy to rile.

"What do they think they're going to do?" I whisper.

"Stand at the gates and harass the guards," Henri guesses.

Already my brothers and the Royal Flanders Regiment are going to be tested. Curtius steps into the crowd and speaks with a man who seems to be leading the women. The conversation is brief.

When Curtius returns, his face is grave. "That man was one of the *Vainqueurs* of the Bastille. He says the women have been growing more violent each day that Lafayette has been gone."

"Where did he go?" Jacques shields his eyes from the rain with his hand.

"To the port of Le Havre to bid Jefferson farewell. Now that he's returned, he's gathering twenty thousand Guardsmen to march with the women and keep them from violence.

"Are you going to answer the call?" Henri asks. The tocsin of Saint-Merri is still ringing.

"I don't have a choice."

~

IT IS TEN the next morning before Curtius returns. Henri and Jacques arrived at seven. We closed the Salon and have been listening to the newsboys shout the latest events. If their sources are correct, it's a catastrophe for the king. My uncle's clothes are stiff with mud, and his hair is soaked. Henri takes his jacket while I remove his boots. He is too tired to speak, so we follow him up the stairs and watch while he eats.

Curtius cradles a cup of coffee in his large hands. There are circles beneath his eyes so deep they look black. "Yesterday morning," he recounts, "the National Guardsmen marched without Lafayette's approval. Twenty-five thousand people descended on Versailles, and

Lafayette might as well have been their prisoner. He sent a messenger ahead to warn the royal family so that when the mob arrived, the guards would be ready. I didn't see Wolfgang or Johann, but Edmund was there. There were thousands of soldiers. Every man in the Swiss Guard and the Flanders Regiment. When the *poissardes* realized there would be no getting into the palace, they went to the Salle des Menus Plaisirs and pleaded their case with the National Assembly. They believe the monarchy wants to rid France of commoners by killing them with hunger."

"That's *ridiculous.*" Jacques is indignant. "Without the Third Estate, there are no taxes to maintain a palace, no revenue to run a kingdom!"

"These are simple people," Curtius explains. "The women have been reading Marat's *L'Ami du Peuple* and listening to the revolutionaries in the Palais-Royal."

"They should have those revolutionaries arrested for inciting rebellion," Henri says, and Jacques agrees.

"The king has already given orders," Curtius says, "for the Duc d'Orléans to be sent to England. But this is bigger than the Duc. Bigger than any one person." The curtains in the room breathe in and out. The storm hasn't passed, and the rain is still falling in heavy sheets. "I should think that whatever the king does now," Curtius continues, "it's simply too late."

He tells us how the mob was calmed with the offer of food and drink. But as soon as the sun set and cold replaced hunger, drunken revolutionaries made their way to the palace. By then, they were at least forty thousand strong. They approached the queen's window and demanded that she appear. When she stepped onto the balcony with her daughter and the dauphin, the men began shouting, *"Without your children!"* For a moment she hesitated. Then the children were sent inside and she was left alone to face the revolutionaries. There were cries of "Shoot!" and "Kill her!" from the crowd. But the queen summoned her courage, and she curtsied to the mob.

"Then suddenly they began to cry *'Long live the queen!'*" Curtius says. He shakes his head. "Remember, these are *poissardes.*"

"And guardsmen," Henri says incredulously. "One minute they're calling for her death, the next they're hailing her as queen. Do they understand what's happening in the Assembly?"

"I don't think they care," Curtius replies. "They want bread and circuses."

Like the Romans, I realize, and think of Madame David. I always thought the purpose of time was to move forward, not backward. Curtius describes how the queen bowed her head and curtsied not once but twice. I can imagine her fear, the way she would have held her chin high despite the trembling in her legs and the nervousness in her stomach. As the crowds shouted *"Vive la reine,"* Lafayette appeared on the balcony and kissed the queen's hand. This show of camaraderie calmed them. But when the pretty doll disappeared back inside, the mob grew angry and resentful, and began to demand that the king replace his soldiers with men from the National Guard.

"Lafayette acted as the go-between," Curtius says. "It was very tense. But after several hours, the king agreed. He is sending the Royal Flanders Regiment home."

"And the Swiss?" my mother and I ask in unison.

"Are allowed to remain."

But the worst is yet to come. Despite the king's agreement, the mob outside the palace refused to leave. "At dawn," Curtius says, "they broke into the palace." A fight ensued, and two of the king's bodyguards were killed—Durepaire and Miomandre de Sainte-Marie.

Soldiers who'd taken my brothers under their wing when they were new to Versailles.

"When they realized the mob was making for the queen's chamber, they shouted for her to escape. They died saving her life," he says. "The mob would have killed her. When the people saw that she'd fled, they looted her gowns and destroyed her paintings. The men were singing songs about killing and"—Curtius looks at me uneasily—"rape. Before they could find her in the Salon de l'Oeil-de-Boeuf, the National Guard stepped in."

My mother crosses herself. The only sounds in the room are the crackling of firewood and the beat of the rain on the windows. I imagine what sort of tableau such a terrible scene would make. *The Hunted,* it would be called, with the royal children huddled next to the queen and their foolish father, whose chance to escape must now be lost. I hope that Madame Élisabeth is safe in her château. I hope the children can forget this frightening night, especially Madame Royale, whose life in Versailles has already fashioned her into a bitter child.

"If they were threatening to kill the queen," my mother says, "they must have threatened her bodyguards as well."

"Yes," Curtius admits. "But Lafayette came to their aid, even when they threatened to kill him."

This is serious. To be threatened by your own men means that all authority has been lost. But then who is leading the National Guard? I squeeze my mother's hand, since I know she is thinking about my brothers.

"And the royal family?" Henri questions.

"The mob demanded that they leave Versailles and come to Paris."

"They didn't agree?" I gasp.

Curtius nods at my question. "There was no other choice."

So the king stood on the balcony overlooking the Marble Courtyard and announced to his subjects that the royal family would depart at once. Pleased with their triumph, the crowd began to shout, *"Long live the queen!"* Ten minutes before, they had sung about her death. Now, they wished for her health again.

"But where will they live?" I exclaim.

"I assume they're to be taken to the Tuileries."

I think about the beautiful Hall of Mirrors, the cheerful Laiterie, and the blossoming gardens around the Hameau. What will Madame Élisabeth do without her little chapel in Montreuil? And who will watch over the Palace of Versailles? I wonder what happens to an abandoned château. Do they board up its windows and lock its gates? What about the hundreds of secret passageways and little doors? Do they close them, too?

Curtius stands. He looks terrible. "I'm sorry to come with such news." To me he says, "Unfortunately, Marie, the time has come to remove the royal tableaux from the Salon. The royal family came within minutes of their lives. Maybe seconds. And if they had been murdered, your brothers would not have been far behind."

That evening, it's Henri and Yachin who help me remove the royal tableaux. There have always been three rooms filled with royal models in the Salon de Cire, and I can still remember the morning, eight months ago, when the queen smiled with pleasure to see her likeness in wax. The dinner table, the dresses, the figure of Rose—all of it must go. When everything is finished and the rooms are cleared, I stand in the workshop and fight back tears.

"It's not so bad." Yachin pats my hand tenderly. "You'll find other people to model. If you'd like, you can even model me."

I laugh. "Thank you, Yachin. I don't think I'm at any loss to find subjects just yet."

"Then why are you crying?"

"I'm not crying," I say sternly.

"She's upset that time is passing," Henri explains as he comes into the workshop. He clears a space and lowers a box onto the floor. It's filled with the silver bowls and pretty china that once brightened the table in the Grand Couvert. "Things change, and not always for the better."

"You mean because of what happened this morning, and how the people were singing?"

"What do you mean?" I ask him.

"They were singing when they brought the king to Paris. I heard they surrounded his coach and were shouting that they'd brought the baker, the baker's wife, and the baker's son. My father says the revolutionaries had barrels of flour and soldiers had bread loaves on pikes. Is that true? Is there really so much bread in Versailles? Will the bakeries be filled now?"

"That's a lot of nonsense," Henri replies. "The king had enough to feed the ten thousand people who lived in Versailles, and that's it. That flour won't feed an entire city. It won't even last the week."

Yachin looks disappointed.

"Why don't you help my mother?" I say. "I think she might have a few cakes."

Yachin is gone before I can tell him to be careful on the stairs. Henri shuts the door behind him. "*Cakes* is the magic word."

"We feed him whenever he comes. And my mother gives him food to take home."

"That's very kind of her." Henri encircles my waist with his arms. "That must be where you get it from."

"*Kindness?*" I laugh.

"You wouldn't be upset about the royal tableaux if you weren't concerned about the real people."

"Perhaps I'm upset that I'll have to find new models for those rooms," I offer.

"I don't believe that for a second. I can see through that hard mask of yours, you know."

"Really?" I ask teasingly. "And what do you see?"

"A woman who wants to make sure that the door is locked . . ."

I giggle. I've discovered that there are ways to give and receive pleasure without risking pregnancy. They are a *coquine*'s ways, but that doesn't bother me. I lock the door and blow out the lamps.

Chapter 34

October 7, 1789

We have left the cradle of our childhood—what am I saying? Left! We were torn from it.

—Memoirs of Madame Élisabeth

When I look up from the *caissier*'s desk, the first thing I notice is her tricolor cockade. Rose has never come to the Salon without a reason. She hands me an envelope without speaking, and while I read the letter, she looks around.

You will have heard something by now of what has befallen my family. I do not need to tell you how devastated I am to have left behind my beloved Montreuil and the palace that has been my home since birth. Upon our flight to Paris, we took nothing with us. The queen's milliner, Rose, and her hairdresser, Léonard, have been like guardian angels, offering to retrieve our most important things from Versailles, where our lives, our possessions, even our history, have all been left behind. I understand that it is a great imposition—and I hope you know that I would never ask except under the most dire of circumstances—but I was wondering if you might go with Léonard and Rose to salvage whatever is left in Montreuil. I'm afraid my circumstances will not allow me to return to the home that has given me such joy. If you think you might be able to honor this request, please find enclosed a small list of items that are beloved by me and that I am loath to live without.

The letter is signed by Madame Élisabeth. I look at the enclosed list, expecting to find precious jewelry and gowns, but instead there are more personal items: books and portraits, papers and mementos, even her wax figure of Christ.

"Will you come?" Rose asks quietly.

With so many things to do? There are three empty rooms that need to be filled, seven new models to be made, and who knows how many signs for the new tableaux. "When are you going?"

"Now. Lafayette is outside with guardsmen. Léonard is in the coach with empty baskets and chests. We're to find whatever is on these lists and keep the items in our homes until further notice." She raises her brows. "I had no idea you were so well regarded in Montreuil."

I fold the letter and put it back in its envelope. "Neither did I."

I go upstairs to find my mother and tell her what's happening. She will need to mind the *caissier*'s desk with Yachin. Outside, Lafayette lifts his hat to me, and when he calls me by my first name, I know that Rose is impressed.

"A pleasure to see you, Marie," he says. "I didn't know you were on such close terms with the princesse." There's no accusation in his voice. After all, we are in similar positions. While we both believe that France is in need of its monarchs—that too much freedom, too fast, would be dangerous—our jobs are to serve the people.

"I was her wax-modeling tutor. But as you know from my uncle's service," I add cautiously, "there are no better patriots."

"I have no doubt." He helps me into the carriage, then holds out a gloved hand for Rose.

"Thank you," she breathes, and her fingers remain on his hand longer than they need to. She is fooling herself if she thinks she'll make a friend of Lafayette. There's nothing he despises more than the vanity of the *ancien régime,* and with her powdered hair and wide silk dress, she is the opposite of Madame de Lafayette in every way. She seats herself next to a young man who has been watching me closely. When the door is shut and the horses pull away, he introduces himself as Léonard.

"Her Majesty's hairdresser," I reply. He's a handsome man, with a shock of dark hair and exceptional skin. His *culottes* are the best quality silk, and the diamond buckles on his shoes are larger than any I've seen the king wear. He is obviously well loved by the queen, who has never cared what station of life people come from if they have talent.

"And you are the wax modeler," he says. "I thought you'd be different. I imagined you older. Uglier," he admits. Rose gives him a sharp look. "What? She's quite pretty. Most tutors in the palace are ancient," he confides. "The music tutor would make Methuselah look spritely."

I don't know what to say, so I keep my silence. Methuselah lived to see his nine hundred and sixty-ninth birthday.

"You are not a woman of many words," Léonard decides.

"She's a woman of plentiful words and firm opinions," Rose says. I've never seen her so dejected. She had always imagined that the royal family would triumph. Now they are all but held captive in the Tuileries Palace.

"Then what do you think of this?" Léonard asks. "Of all the people in Versailles, we're the ones they're trusting to retrieve their possessions. A dressmaker, a hairdresser, and a sculptress. And none of us nobility."

"It's a sign of desperation," I say. "They don't know whom to trust. And if France can carry on without Versailles," I add, "who's to say there will ever be a court again?" It's a heavy thought, and the three of us ride the rest of the way in silence.

When we reach Versailles, I hear Lafayette giving instructions to the National Guardsmen on patrol. They're to unlock the doors of the king's palace, then follow us to Montreuil, where I will collect Madame Élisabeth's belongings. Suddenly, I'm nervous. Rose opens her fan and snaps it shut again. None of us want to be in a palace empty of everything but memories.

The carriages roll up the Avenue de Paris, and when they pass through the main gate, with its golden coat of arms depicting the crown and the horn of plenty, both Léonard and Rose inhale.

"Only princes of the blood pass through this gate," Léonard whispers. "Even the nobility are forbidden."

But the carriages stop in the royal courtyard. The three of us sit motionless; then our coach door is opened and we are instructed to get out. I am conscious of the feeling that, with every step, we are trampling on tradition. Only those with the Honors of the Louvre have walked across these stones. From the time of Louis XIV, everyone else has driven into the court of the ministers, where you can hire a sedan chair to take you to the palace if you're unfit to walk.

"This isn't right," Rose says quietly.

We wait while a guardsman unlocks the door to the palace. I have never seen such a massive building abandoned. Hundreds of men are working on boarding up the windows. Tomorrow, the Palace of Versailles will be cast into darkness.

"After you," Lafayette says when the doors have been opened. Men with empty chests stand ready behind us. We step inside, and I am struck at once by the silence. A hundred years of courtiers hurrying down these halls, and all that's left are the scuffs on the marble floors where they ran to escape. For all of its laws and august traditions, it took only a mob to demolish nine hundred years of kingship.

"What we need is in the queen's apartments," Rose announces, her voice unsteady. We follow behind her and regard the damage done by the rampaging crowds. There are mirrors broken on every wall, tapestries torn as if their heavy threads were made of paper and not wool, and vases shattered into a thousand pieces, their fragments showered across the floors. Who will clean this? And what will become of all these possessions? Surely the National Assembly will want them, but they belong to the king. These are his lamps, his chairs, his commodes, all bought with the money he inherited from his grandfather, who inherited it from his father, Louis XIV.

We pass the grand staircase, and Lafayette stops to run his fingers over the pockmarked walls. I realize with shock that bullet holes have chipped the marble and scarred the paneling. Lafayette exhales angrily, and the guardsmen behind him shift uneasily on their feet. "I want this cleaned," Lafayette says. "*All* of it, before the palace is boarded up."

When we reach the queen's apartments, even Lafayette hesitates before the door. No one has ever entered without permission. But there is no one to give us permission. No ushers, or guards, or even ladies-in-waiting. He pushes open the heavy wooden doors, and Léonard goes first.

"My God! Look at what they've done," he exclaims.

The gilded walls have been torn apart, as if someone dragged a pitchfork across the paneling. The silk hangings, the mirrors, the chandeliers—everything is damaged or destroyed.

Léonard bends down to collect the broken pieces of a box and wipes a tear from his eye. "Why would they do this to her?"

Yet the bed is exactly as she left it. Rose draws back the curtains to reveal the queen's robe and her forgotten slippers. She must have run barefoot to the king's apartments in nothing but her nightgown.

"How did she escape?" I ask.

Rose walks to the corner of the room and reveals a hidden door to the left of the alcove. "If it weren't for this," she says somberly, "we'd be arranging her funeral."

We are all silent. If I hold my breath, I am sure I can catch the faint laughter of women and the sharp wit of the courtiers who filled this chamber. I see Rose square her shoulders and set her jaw. "Find her jewelry box," she commands. "Take anything that looks irreplaceable."

But it all looks irreplaceable to me. The bust of soft paste porcelain, the commode veneered with tortoiseshell and horn, the pair of brass firedogs with elaborate designs. What do you choose when everything has its own history?

I gaze up at the paintings by Boucher and wonder if he could have ever imagined a time when his *Four Virtues* would be looking down on commoners rummaging through Her Majesty's chamber.

THE GUARDSMEN HAVE left the chests of Madame Élisabeth's things in the corner of our workshop, and since their arrival, half the neighborhood has been to see what's inside. The tailor is fond of the princesse's shoes, which I packed for their beauty, despite the fact that they were not on the list. Letters, journals, a leather box for paintbrushes—everything is here when Lafayette comes for the second time in three days. The royal family has settled into the Tuileries, and Rose and I have been summoned to deliver the possessions we've salvaged. He waits at the door of the Salon while I give Curtius my last-minute instructions.

"I think we turn the first room into a tableau of Great Patriots. The second room, perhaps something with the Jacobin Club." That's all they're talking about in the Palais-Royal. Robespierre has joined, as well as Louis-Philippe, the teenage son of the Duc d'Orléans, who is now living abroad. "I don't have any ideas for the third."

"Something with the National Guard," Curtius says.

I kiss my mother good-bye, and she makes me promise to return with details about everything—the king, the queen, and the condition of the Tuileries, which hasn't been used since Louis XIV built his Palace of Versailles. Lafayette helps me into a carriage where Rose is already waiting. When he shuts the door and the horses take off, she exhales deeply. "They are barbarians. All of them!" She flicks opens her fan and begins to wave it compulsively.

For an October morning, it's oppressively hot.

"She's done her best! At all times, she's only given her best." Sweat has broken out on her upper lip, and she fans it away with sharp flicks. "She ruled the world of fashion. And there will never be anyone like her. Remember when fire burned through the Opéra? We named her red dress *incendie de l'Opéra,* and every woman from Paris to London had to have it. Even the Duchess of Devonshire! That will never happen again."

I'm not sure whom Rose feels sorriest for. Herself, because her creations will never be showcased on the world's stage again, or the queen, who has lost the power to do so.

"There has always been power in fashion," she continues. "Even *this*"—she indicates the cockade on her breast—"is power." She passes me a cockade from Le Grand Mogol. "Take it," she says. "You will need it to get into the palace. No one's allowed inside without the tricolor."

I pin it to my fichu. "Thank you," I say, and Rose looks out the window. We're approaching the Tuileries on the right bank of the Seine, and it's difficult to imagine the royal family living in this abandoned place. It was built more than two hundred years ago by Catherine de' Medici when her husband, King Henry II, died. "So what will you do now?" I ask.

"Cater to other women with fashion sense. And if they all leave Paris, then I shall close Le Grand Mogol and follow them to London. The queen has been the making of me, and I will never forget that. But if she's too foolish to plan her escape, I am not."

I think of Henri's plea that we leave. Philip Astley is already gone, and many of the actors on the Boulevard du Temple have packed their chests and sailed across the Channel.

"Madame Élisabeth tells me it's not her but the king."

"Then she should have left without him," Rose declares pitilessly. "She's too loyal, and that's what has brought us here."

The carriages stop before the Tuileries Palace. Lafayette brings us to the entrance, and after a few words with the guards, we are taken inside. I had expected cobwebs and stone, yet fresh morning light falls through the windows and illuminates an exquisite scene. "Look at the floors and the paintings," I say.

Rose makes a face. "It's not Versailles."

We are taken to the second floor, where there are courtiers hurrying about their business and workers moving heavy pieces of furniture. Somewhere in these halls my brothers are on patrol with the National Guard. "How many people are here?" Rose asks.

"About five hundred," Lafayette replies.

It's a drastic reduction in courtiers and staff, but perhaps now the people will see that the royal family is not spending their money dressing up their servants and attending soirees.

We reach Madame Élisabeth's new salon, and a pair of ushers open the doors for me. "Mademoiselle Grosholtz," one of the men announces, and it's astounding to see how the customs of Versailles have been adapted for this place. The doors swing shut behind me, and Madame Élisabeth exclaims, "Marie!"

"Madame." I sink into my lowest curtsy, but she takes my arms and pulls me up.

"You've come," she says, and when I search her eyes, they are full of surprise. "I can't believe you've come." Six groomed greyhounds dance about her feet.

"Of course, Madame. And all of the items on your list were packed."

"Thank you, Marie. You have no . . . you have no idea what it means." She looks down at my basket, and her eyes fill with tears.

"Plus a few things that weren't on the list," I say.

She pulls back the silk covering and sees it is everything she'll need to continue her modeling—wax, clay, plaster, glass eyes, a bag full of hair, and all the tools of the trade. When the guards at the entrance saw this, their brows shot up on their foreheads, but Lafayette explained who I was and what purpose this would serve. Yet it's not the wax tools that she reaches for. It's the mask I kept as a memento from her birthday, when she guessed who I was in my red gown and simple ribbon. She holds it up to the light—a reminder of better, happier times—and now the tears come fresh.

"I didn't mean to make you cry, Madame. It's supposed to be a reminder," I say. "Things may change. You may see me in a tricolor cockade, or you may have had to leave Montreuil for Paris, but that doesn't alter who we are. This"—I look around the room, which may not be Montreuil but is still very beautiful—"it's only a mask."

She puts down the basket and takes my hand. "God has blessed me with your friendship," she whispers. She tells me how the queen has been forced to wear tricolor dresses made by Madame Eloffe. "If we go outside in the gardens, the people shout insults. So we stay inside and entertain ourselves with music and needlework. But God works in mysterious ways. I have never seen Marie-Thérèse so happy. It's only been two days, but there's already a change."

It's hard for me to imagine Madame Royale wearing anything but a scowl, but perhaps now that her mother is a prisoner, there is nothing else for the queen to do but lavish attention on her children. Perhaps this is what an eleven-year-old child needs. "And the court?" I ask.

"Some friends have abandoned us." Madame Élisabeth twists the ends of her fichu in her hands. "I suppose that's to be expected. But the Princesse de Lamballe will remain as Superintendent of the Household. And my brother, the Comte de Provence, has been dining with us every night."

"The one who suggested you remain in Versailles?"

Madame Élisabeth hears the criticism in my voice. "He could never have imagined this . . ."

"And you will stay in the Tuileries?"

"Until my brother decides otherwise." She lowers her voice. "He still calls the French his *good little people,*" she confides, and I can see how this distresses her. "He doesn't see that we're at the beck and call of the National Assembly. These rooms, these furnishings, they could be taken away tomorrow. The queen's dear friend Axel von Fersen has been very good to us. He's sold his house in order to buy something closer to the Tuileries, and if anyone can, it will be Fersen who convinces the king to plan our escape."

"His Majesty trusts him that much?"

"The three of them are very close," she replies. "But my brother . . . he has a difficult time making decisions. . . . I know it's a great deal to ask, Marie, but perhaps we can work together on Fridays? There isn't a workshop yet. But I can have one set up. And I can still pay you. They haven't taken away our inheritance." She adds in a whisper, "Yet."

Chapter 35

October 20, 1789

In the arts the way in which an idea is rendered, and the manner in which it is expressed, is much more important than the idea itself.

—Jacques-Louis David

Now that the royal family is in Paris, the National Assembly has moved from the Hôtel des Menus in Versailles to the archbishop's palace on the Île Saint-Louis. Hundreds of deputies have flooded the city looking for residences close to the Seine, and only Robespierre has chosen some dingy third-floor apartment in the Rue de Saintonge.

"He's had eighteen livres a day since he was made deputy," I say. "I should think he could afford a place on the first floor."

"That's Robespierre. He'll live on soup and water if it means saving two sous," my uncle says. He hands me a coat for the new figure of Lafayette. *The National Guard* and *Great Patriots of France* are now complete. All that remains to be done are the figures for *The Jacobin Club.* "It will be a busy salon tonight. If Robespierre is here, everyone will want to come and hear the news."

He's right. That evening, friends arrive whom we haven't seen in months. Even the artist Jacques-Louis David makes an appearance so that he can bask in Robespierre's presence. His wife, Marguerite, is dressed in a red bonnet that does nothing for her complexion and a white chemise gown that billows around her legs like a loose curtain. "Marie!" she exclaims and embraces me as if we're the closest of friends. "Did you know that the National Assembly was talking about what we did for weeks? We could be as famous as Rousseau someday. Did you see the articles in the newspaper?"

"No," I lie. "I'm afraid I didn't."

She opens her purse and takes out a clipping. "There we are," she says eagerly. "Well, not you. But that one there"—she points to a picture of a beautiful woman in Roman dress—"that's supposed to be me."

I raise my brows. "How can you tell?"

"Well, obviously . . . It looks like me." She puts the clipping away, then takes a seat between her husband and Lucile. Good. Let them listen to her chatter.

"Robespierre!" A tremendous shout echoes in the salon the moment he arrives. He's come dressed in a striped nankeen coat of olive green, a matching waistcoat, and a yellow cravat. He must be the last person in Paris still wearing a wig. Camille bounds from his chair and puts his arm around his former schoolmate.

"The voice of the Revolution!" Camille declares. "Three cheers for Robespierre!" Camille steers him to the place of honor at our table, and we listen, riveted, while Robespierre recounts his battles in the National Assembly. And there are many battles to be waged. Who are the true citizens of France? Can they be Austrians who've lived here for twenty years? What about Germans? Or better yet, Jews? And who will be given the right to vote?

"I warned the Assembly," Robespierre says, "that equality is to liberty as the sun is to life. But will they listen? No. They have given the right to vote to active citizens"—he pauses for dramatic effect—"and that is it."

"So women are to be excluded?" Lucile exclaims.

"As well as any male citizen who doesn't pay enough taxes under the new laws. An annual sum equal to three days of labor."

"But that must be half the male population!" Camille shouts angrily.

"Tell that to the Assembly."

"And the National Guard?" Camille demands. "Have they changed the qualifications?"

"Why do the qualifications need to be changed?" Curtius asks.

Robespierre levels him with his strange green eyes. "Because limiting eligibility to active citizens does not promote equality."

"So you want equality at any cost?" Henri challenges. "How does that work, allowing noncitizens to join your army?"

"That's a dangerous proposition," Curtius warns. "Right now, National Guardsmen have no incentive to pillage or loot. They have money of their own and they earn a small salary. What happens when poor, uneducated men have weapons and authority? You have chaos."

"Or equality," Robespierre replies. "Isn't that what we're here for?" He looks around the room. "Isn't that what this Revolution is all about?"

A cheer goes up inside our salon.

"Wait. W-w-where is Marat?" Camille searches the room. "He never misses a Tuesday."

I look to Curtius, since it's better that he explain, and everyone follows suit.

"He was arrested on the eighth," my uncle says, "and sentenced to a month."

"For what?" Camille cries.

"Inciting rebellion."

"His paper is no more incendiary than mine!"

There is a tense silence in the room. Then Robespierre says, "We must be careful. These are dangerous times to be a patriot. Who are our friends?" His voice drops low. "But more important, who are our enemies? There are royalists waiting around every corner to slit our throats, men who want to trample our freedoms and raise the king back to his position of supreme authority!"

Is Robespierre kidding? The king is at the mercy of the National Assembly.

"Even our friends at the Jacobin Club are not entirely to be trusted," Robespierre reveals. "There are hypocrites and corrupted hearts among them. But there is a meeting tonight of great importance. Everyone in this room should come."

He rises, and Curtius is the first to stand with him.

"We need every good man we can find," Robespierre says. He looks down at Lucile. "And we also need honorable women in this war. It's not over. Not until freedom and equality are words engraved into every citizen's heart!"

More than twenty of us follow him out the door into the evening air. We begin the twenty-minute walk to the former convent of Saint-Jacques, where the Jacobin Club holds its meetings.

"Robespierre!" a woman cries. She lifts her skirts and runs across the street.

Robespierre shrinks away as if she's a viper. "What are you doing here?"

"You haven't been to see me. I've been writing you letters every day. Every day," she repeats, and her voice rises. "Why don't you come to me anymore?"

Even in the dim light of sunset, I can see the color rising in Robespierre's face. "We are finished," he says briskly.

"But why?"

He turns his back on her, and our group keeps walking. It's terrible to see, and the woman can't accept this. "I'll do anything," she cries. "Maximilien, you love me!" She has called him by his first name. "You told me you loved me!"

"Keep walking," Robespierre says through clenched teeth.

"Don't leave!" she screams and falls on her knees. Such public humiliation is too much to bear. I turn my face away, and when we round the corner, her voice is drowned out by the sounds of the carriages. I look at Robespierre, who is flushed with embarrassment. I had no idea that Rousseau's most avid believer and disciple kept a woman in Paris. She must be a terrible inconvenience to him now that he preaches about hypocrisy and corruption.

We reach the Rue Saint-Honoré and enter the old monastery. We pass through the damp, candlelit rooms into the great hall, where the monks once dined.

"The Jacobins are our next exhibit," I whisper to Henri.

He looks at me askance. Hundreds of candles are burning in tall candelabra, casting a golden light across the old walls and wooden floors. In the public galleries, where there are just as many women as men, all are proudly wearing tricolor cockades. Only Club members, like Camille and Robespierre, are allowed to sit in the center of the hall. I motion for Curtius to sit next to me so that we can discuss which members would make the best models, and he points to a figure in the center of the hall. "Anne-Joseph Théroigne."

She's dressed in the uniform of the National Guard, with pants and a vest and a jaunty black hat that rests on top of a head of full, dark hair. She's my age, perhaps a little younger, and her eyes dart about the room, as if eager for someone to challenge her right to sit among the men.

"She asked to join the Club when it was meeting in Versailles, and they honored her request to become a member after hearing what she did on the fifth," Curtius tells me. I learn she rode bareback alongside the *poissardes,* spurring them onward in their march toward Versailles. When they arrived, she took a pistol and fired it in the air, encouraging the men to join their female counterparts in beating down the gates. "She was part Amazon," he admits, "part Helen of Troy in her beauty."

I look across the hall at her again. The speaker has taken his place at the podium, and she sits forward in her seat. She's certainly one we'll want to model. But before I can take out a quill to sketch, I'm distracted by the words of the speaker.

"For as long as anyone in this room can remember, what institution has grown richer while the poor have grown poorer?"

"The monarchy!" someone shouts.

"We all know about the monarchy. But what else?" When no one answers he thunders, "The Church! We must deliver the Church the same fatal blow we will deliver to the aristocrats who bleed this nation. Not next year, not next week, but today!"

The Club members rise to their feet in applause, and most people in the galleries stand as well. But Henri and I remain seated. "Who does he think feeds the poor?" I exclaim. "Where does he think women go who are cast out because they're pregnant or unwanted? These men aren't content to just destroy the monarchy. They want to destroy God and charity as well."

"And I think I know what will take its place," Henri replies.

The National Assembly.

Chapter 36

December 25, 1789

We don't have any more nobles or priests.
Oh, it'll be okay, be okay, be okay.
Equality will reign everywhere.

—Excerpt from the revolutionary song "Ça Ira"

Despite the decrees that have stripped the Church of its property in order to use it as backing for the Assembly's assignats—a new paper currency we're all to use now instead of livres or sous—the French have not forgotten Noël. The churches are filled with rosy-cheeked worshipers willing to brave the cold in order to honor Christ's birth. I look down the pew at my brothers, and they both smile back at me. Our entire family is here except Edmund. So while we're eating Bayonne ham and drinking wine, enjoying the company of Johann's wife, Isabel, and their little son, Paschal, he'll be stalking the halls of the Tuileries, ingratiating himself with Besenval. A lonely choice.

When the sermon's finished, Paschal exclaims, "It's time to eat!"

Everyone around us laughs, even the old, humorless women who come here every day. My mother bends down to pick him up, and he rides contentedly on her hip.

"It must be nice for you to have so much of your family here," Henri says, taking my arm.

Since the king's flight from Versailles, my brothers have moved to Paris. Last month, Johann found a handsome apartment with a salon that has a sweeping view of the Seine. "Yes. My mother is very happy, too," I say. "Of course, she misses Edmund."

"Has he written?"

I shake my head. A rare dusting of snow covered the ground while we were at Mass, and now flakes have settled on the rim of Henri's hat. He's let his hair grow longer this winter, and there's a soft stubble shadowing his chin. Between the work at his exhibit and his attentions to me, he's had little time to visit the barber. I look around at the people I love most in this world, and my heart feels close to bursting. On every street, nativity scenes are nestled in shop windows, and painted *santons* hang from lampposts and doors. "This is going to be a very good year," I predict. Yesterday, Curtius spoke with Lafayette and told him of his intention to resign in twelve months.

Henri squeezes my arm meaningfully. "Yes, I think it will."

We enter the house, and the lingering scent of cooked ham fills the hall.

It's the merriest gathering we've had in many years, with food, and laughter, and wine from Bordeaux. Jacques has challenged Isabel, the daughter of a butcher, to name all the parts of a cow. I have always liked Isabel. I remember the day my brother married her, and how he never let go of her hand, not even to stand before the altar. She has plain gray eyes, but a beautiful smile. And her laugh. It is deep and throaty, full of the greatest *joie de vivre,* and it's completely infectious. She's still naming the parts when the sound of a horse and carriage echoes outside, followed by a sharp knock on the door. The conversation stops while we look at one another.

"I'll get it," Wolfgang says at once. He hurries from the table, and I look to my mother. Perhaps it is Edmund. Perhaps he's had a change of heart. But it's a woman's light footsteps on the stairs, and a moment later Wolfgang appears with the baron's daughter, Abrielle. Johann passes a meaningful look to Isabel. Did they know she'd be coming?

Wolfgang clears his throat and announces nervously, "I'd like you to meet the daughter of the Baron de Besenval, Abrielle."

Her gaze roams quickly around the room, and she looks like a small, startled deer. She is dressed in an exquisite red velvet gown with a white ermine cloak and matching muff. She belongs in the queen's rooms, not on the Boulevard du Temple, but she tries for a smile, and everyone raises their voices in welcome. My mother hurries to take her cloak, and Curtius finds her an extra chair. The room is silent while she seats herself between Wolfgang and Johann. How did she get here? Does her father know she's come, or did Wolfgang steal her away somehow?

"I suppose you're all wondering what Abrielle is doing here," Wolfgang begins.

"Not at all," my mother says cheerfully. "In fact, she's just in time for the ham."

"Yes, well . . ." He looks around the table and begins fidgeting with his napkin. I have never seen Wolfgang nervous about anything. Then finally he blurts out, "We are both here to stay."

My mother lowers her glass of wine. "You mean a little vacation?"

Wolfgang hesitates. "No." He looks at Abrielle, who nods slowly. "I mean Abrielle is pregnant, and this morning we were married."

I think my mother is going to faint. She begins fanning herself with her hand, and Wolfgang adds quickly, "It wasn't planned. It simply happened. But now we are married in the eyes of God—"

"And in the eyes of her father?" my mother exclaims.

"Yes, well that . . . That hasn't gone so well."

"He tried, Maman," Johann explains. "He went to me first, but I'm not close to Besenval. Then he went to Edmund . . ."

My mother stops fanning. "Edmund has always been a favorite with the baron. He must have done something."

Wolfgang clenches his jaw, and Abrielle is close to tears. "Yes," Wolfgang replies. "He did."

"He went straight to Besenval and told him the news," Johann says. "Wolfgang has been dismissed from his position, and Abrielle . . ."

He doesn't have to say what has become of Abrielle. This is a disaster for them both. I can only imagine the sort of scandal that was created. A heavy silence has fallen, and my mother covers her eyes to weep. Then Curtius raises his glass and says loudly, "To Wolfgang and Abrielle!"

I repeat, "To Wolfgang and Abrielle!"

Everyone follows, and there is no more talk of traitorous brothers or angry fathers. She is nine weeks pregnant, and Wolfgang is sure it will be a girl, but Paschal has decided it must be a boy. "Else who will I play with?" he exclaims. We all laugh, and Abrielle bears it as best she can.

"Soon, it will be Marie's turn," Johann says, and they all look at me. "We've heard the rumors. So when will it be?" My brother looks from me to Henri.

"When Curtius retires from the National Guard," Henri replies and takes my hand.

"Another year," I confirm.

"And then you will be bouncing a fat baby on your knee," Isabel teases.

It's what every woman wants, surely. And in another year, who knows what will be? I might be made a member of the Académie. Or perhaps Curtius will be. If that happens, there will be money enough to hire an apprentice.

As everyone leaves, Wolfgang and Abrielle linger behind. The guest room will now belong to them, and I wonder how Wolfgang must feel to know he will never serve the king with his brothers again. Johann embraces him tightly, and whispers what must be words of encouragement in his ear. When everyone is gone, my mother asks quietly, "Shall we see to your room?"

She is still upset, but as soon as the shock is over, this will be a great joy to her. She'll finally have a grandchild in her home.

Abrielle follows her down the hall, but Wolfgang remains with me. We watch each other in the low light of the candles. "It may be a blessing," I say to him.

"It's hard to see that right now."

"I know. But it wasn't your calling."

"I can't afford a family," he worries, "let alone a woman like her. Marie, she is inconsolable."

"She just lost everything. Her father, her home. Give her time."

Wolfgang nods. "Will you go to her? Maman is preparing her room, but she should have someone else—"

"Of course." She's my sister now. I must support her in any way I can. I climb the stairs and pause in front of Curtius's door. I can hear my mother speaking to him in German, something about the clothes Abrielle has brought.

"They're too fine," I hear her telling him. "How will she ever be happy here?"

I continue to the guest room, with its sweeping view of the Boulevard du Temple, and peek around the open door. She is sitting on the wide four-poster bed with her beautiful velvet gown spread out around her, watching the snow settle on the rooftops and across the windowsills. She turns when she hears me, and her eyes are filled with tears.

"Is there anything you need?" I ask softly.

She shakes her head, and I think of the chances I took with Henri and realize now how foolish we were. For a moment's pleasure, we risked altering our lives forever. "No. Thank you," she says. "Your family has already been more than generous." I see my mother has brought her heated bottles and a cup of hot chocolate, probably spiked with liqueur, to help her sleep. But she hasn't touched it. She hasn't even unpacked her chests.

"I know it must be difficult for you," I say, "being torn from your father like this. But if it's any consolation, I can tell you that Wolfgang loves you deeply, and my family is very happy to have you here."

She begins to weep, dabbing her eyes with a square of silk. "Thank you, Marie. It's more than I deserve."

"Nonsense," I say and cross the room to sit next to her on the bed. "You are married," I remind her. "And unlike most women, you've had the opportunity to marry someone you love. Wolfgang adores you. He has spoken about you for months on end."

She looks up at me, and her wide blue eyes are like pools of light. "Really?"

"Yes," I assure her. "And as soon he is able, he will find employment and take care of you. Until then, you are always welcome here."

She straightens her shoulders, and I can see that this talk has done her some good. "May I ask you a favor?" she whispers.

"Of course."

"I—I have never undressed myself," she admits, "and I don't know how. . . . I'm not sure how I should take off this gown."

The poor child! She doesn't even know how to prepare for bed. How does Wolfgang think she will survive here, on the Boulevard du Temple, with prostitutes and fish sellers shouting over one another for business in the streets? I unlace her corset and help the gown from her shoulders. Her body is as smooth and flawless as her face. She's like a porcelain doll. And this is how it must be for the queen. Every day someone to help her dress and undress. If she wants water, someone is there to fetch it. If she lacks perfume, or powder, or pomade for her hair, a dozen servants are happy to make it appear. Women like this have never known any different. I hand Abrielle a clean nightgown from her chest, and I wish her good night. "Tomorrow, I'll be in the workshop," I say. "You're welcome to come and see what we do."

"Thank you," she says with real affection, and my heart breaks for her.

~

Since the National Assembly has moved from the Salle des États to the Salle du Manège, we must change the backdrop of our tableau. This time it's Wolfgang, not Henri, who helps Curtius, and while the sawing and painting go on, Abrielle peeks around the workshop door. I'm reminded of a little mouse, and when Yachin sees her and shouts, "Come in!" she freezes in the doorway.

"It's fine," I say and rise from my stool. "This is our workshop."

She takes a tentative step inside. I can see how this place could be intimidating: on the far wall are the bodies of all the previous figures we've ever done, and on the shelf above that are a dozen wax heads we no longer need. Jars of teeth and glass eyes line shelves around the room, and baskets filled with hair clutter the ground.

"Are—are those real?" she asks. She points to the eyes.

Yachin snickers, and I give him a sharp look. "They are glass."

She steps farther inside, and now she can see the discarded tableau of the royal family at dinner. A letter came last week asking if we would loan this exhibit to Versailles. With the château sitting empty, the National Guard has hit upon a way to make money: installing our wax figures in the Petit Trianon and charging visitors ten sous to see what life used to be like. It's a terribly offensive idea, but the request is more than a simple request: it's a command. All we can do is negotiate what percentage of the ten sous will be ours.

Abrielle steps closer to *The Grand Couvert* tableau to touch the face of the queen. "Did you do this?" she asks.

"The faces, yes. Curtius makes the bodies."

She circles the table, and I catch Yachin grinning from ear to ear. He has seen this before. The disbelief, the fascination, then finally the questions about how long the models take to sculpt, what kind of wax we use to make them, and how long they will last. Abrielle asks all of these things and more. "But what will happen to this? It won't stay back here forever?"

"As soon as the backdrop for the National Assembly is finished," I tell her, "Curtius and I are taking this tableau to Versailles. They want to display it in the Petit Trianon."

Her eyes go wide. "And you're going today?"

"Yes."

She begins to tremble. "My father will be there. He's the only one with the keys to the Trianon." She sits on the nearest stool, and I go to her.

"Perhaps you should come with us," I say gently.

"No." She shakes her head, and tears roll down her cheeks. "He doesn't want to see me again. He said as much before the coach began driving away. He doesn't care what happens to me. To either of us." She looks down at her belly, and now Yachin must understand why she is here.

"He allowed you to pack your clothes," I say helpfully. "He might have given them away, or sold them."

"Because he was too angry to care. He just wanted me gone." She looks up at me through her tears. "I was his little girl. His only child," she adds, "and I betrayed him."

I'm glad that Wolfgang's not in the room. It would be too painful for him to hear this. "Do you regret the child?" I ask quietly.

She lifts her chin. For the first time since arriving, she looks like a woman. "I have no regrets over this baby, and no regrets over choosing Wolfgang. I only wish I'd had the courage to tell my father that I wanted to marry him. I should never have waited until this happened. I knew better," she admits, "but I was a coward."

That afternoon, as Curtius and I are riding to Versailles, I tell him what Abrielle said.

"Then Wolfgang is lucky," my uncle replies. "If she were full of regret, he would have to live with her resentment for the rest of his life." Curtius sucks thoughtfully on his pipe. "He'll become a private soldier," he predicts. "Or join the National Guard. I can speak with Lafayette."

This is exactly what my uncle does, and in three days, my brother is made a captain of the National Guard. I hope it enrages Edmund as much as it enrages me to think of what he did. The baron would have discovered his daughter's pregnancy on his own. But to learn about it from another soldier? It's embarrassing, and worse, it is unforgivable.

Wolfgang and his wife will be moving to their own apartment now, so Curtius and I oversee the packing of Abrielle's chests. My mother wipes away her tears, and I exclaim in German, "What's the matter with you? On Noël, you were upset that Wolfgang was here."

"That was five days ago. I've changed my mind now."

Chapter 37

1790

WE WATCH THE NEW YEAR'S FIREWORKS FROM OUR BALcony, and with every explosion, Paschal squeals with delight.

"Look at the colors!" Henri shouts.

But I can't. When Curtius said everyone was coming tonight, I assumed he meant everyone who had been with us on Noël. He didn't say that Marat, on the run from the king's authority, would be coming here to hide. So while Henri is explaining the science of fireworks to me, my eyes wander to the shadowy figure in the corner. His head is wrapped with bandages soaked in vinegar, and the stench is repulsive. His face is covered with open sores. Curtius whispered to me that he caught these from hiding in the city sewers.

This is my first clue that the year 1790 will be filled with unpalatable news.

On the thirteenth of February, the National Assembly passes a law forbidding monastic vows and dissolving every ecclesiastical order. Nuns are dragged into the streets to be whipped, and monks are given six months to marry or be killed. The Pope, without his own army, without any real power at all, sits in the Vatican while convents all across France are closed. Priests who are allowed to remain with the Church are instructed on the new order of things: before the Pope, before salvation, before even God Himself, there is the nation.

In the Church of Saint-Merri, the priests must wear the tricolor cockade over their holy vestments, and the altar has been defaced to read, "Glory be to God *and the Nation.*" At every Mass, before every prayer, the priests must ask God's blessing over the Revolution. And in Marat's newspaper *L'Ami du Peuple,* he repeats Diderot's vicious philosophy: "Men will never be free until the last king is strangled with the entrails of the last priest."

Seven days later, news comes from Austria that Joseph II, the queen's eldest brother and the Holy Roman Emperor, has died. He has been her greatest hope, and now Leopold II, a brother she's never really known, has inherited the crown. Madame Élisabeth tells me this has crushed the queen. If Leopold refuses to offer his help, where will the king turn?

It is blow after blow for the royal family. In the spring, when Marie-Thérèse is to celebrate her First Communion, there are no gifts or celebratory feasts. The ceremony is held at Saint-Germain-l'Auxerrois. The king does not dare to attend, and the queen is forced to watch from behind a curtain. Madame Élisabeth confides that Marie-Thérèse asked her father why her friends could celebrate their First Communions, while she could not. She was told that any sort of fête would be too extravagant. In this, I feel sorry for Madame Royale. Every child across France receives gifts for this passage. When I ask if the dauphin was in attendance, Madame Élisabeth's face turns pale. "He had a fever," she says quietly. "The doctors say he is coughing up blood."

At some point, I think, God must look down and take pity on the royal family. But the terrible news doesn't stop. In April, the National Assembly votes to transfer all four hundred million livres of church property to the state. Camille and Marat applaud this new law as saving the nation. Catholics, they write, have secret royalist tendencies, and schools run by the Church teach pupils to love God and, *even worse,* the king.

But no one is thinking about who will run the hospitals and poorhouses when the anniversary of the Bastille approaches. Instead, a celebration—larger than any celebration to come before—is planned for the fourteenth of July. The National Assembly is calling it the Fête de la Fédération. On the Champ-de-Mars, a tremendous stadium has been built for the occasion. Tens of thousands of people flood into Paris to take part in the festivities. The fête begins with deputies from foreign nations parading with their flags to remind us that we are one people, one race, one human nation. The Swedes, the Turks, the Mesopotamians—they are all here to celebrate this great oneness. Then Lafayette mounts a podium to swear an oath to the Constitution, which is still in the making, and the entire stadium falls silent.

"We swear forever to be faithful to the Nation, to the Law, and to the King, to uphold with all our might the Constitution as decided by the National Assembly and accepted by the King, and to protect according to the laws the safety of people and properties, transit of grains and food within the kingdom, the public contributions under whatever forms they might exist, and to stay united with all the French with the indestructible bonds of brotherhood."

The king takes his place at the podium to swear his oath. Then the queen appears, and when everything is finished, there is cannon fire all around the Champ-de-Mars.

"Study these faces," Curtius suggests. "These are men you may never see again."

With two family members as captains in the National Guard, I am introduced to every foreign delegate. There is John Paul Jones, the Scottish fighter who has founded the American Navy. And Thomas Paine, whose pamphlet *Common Sense* inspired the Americans to rebel against England. It was over a year ago that Wolfgang gave me a copy. These men have traveled to Paris for this occasion, and both believe this is a great day for France.

"Not every action the Assembly makes will be for good," Paine tells me. "But tyranny can never be allowed to flourish."

Perhaps I should be happy. But I see the misery of Madame Élisabeth when I visit her, and I hear of the way the people treat the queen, and I have to think it cannot be this way in England. Not even King

George III, who is said to be mad and ruled by his son, is slandered in the streets and spit on in his gardens.

In all of this, there are two events that bring us real joy. Near the end of July, Abrielle is delivered of a healthy son. He is christened Michael Louis Grosholtz, and although the baron does not come to see him, no child has ever brought his family greater happiness. His bassinet may not be lined with silk, but he will never be cold and he will never go hungry.

Then, in December, Lucile brings us the news she has been waiting years for. She and Camille are finally to marry. In this new world of assemblies and liberty, Camille has become someone of great importance. When the king is forced to sign the Civil Constitution of the Clergy, commanding all priests to swear an oath of loyalty to the nation or be labeled a dissident, it's Camille's paper the people turn to for information. And when the Assembly abolishes all hereditary titles of nobility, it's Camille's paper that inspires the celebration in the streets. He has become a man of rousing metaphors, and Lucile's father has turned down proposals from men with incomes of twenty-five thousand assignats a year to give her to Camille.

The wedding is held in the fashionable Church of Saint-Sulpice, with its view of the Left Bank and its Italian colonnades. I am wearing the very best gown I own, and the pearls around my neck are a gift from Curtius.

I look around the church and see many of the faces from our new *Fête de la Fédération* tableau. There is Lafayette, sitting with his pretty wife, Adrienne. And there is Mirabeau. He looks terribly frail for such a large man. He is sitting at the front of the church with a bloodied handkerchief around his neck. When I ask Curtius what this is for, he tells me, "The leeches. He uses them for his eyes." When I recoil, he adds, "Apparently, the Salle du Manège has poor ventilation, and no one can see. The room is filled with smoke, but it's the only place they can find that is large enough to house the Assembly."

I look back at Mirabeau, who is clearly suffering. It can't just be his eyes. His cheeks are hollow, and my guess is that his syphilis is very bad. He is sitting next to the Duc d'Orléans, who returned to France several months ago with a new name, Philippe Égalité. He has proclaimed himself a man of the people and is now a member of the Jacobin Club. Nearly everyone here, including my uncle, has also become a member. Every law, every act, every possible decree, is debated endlessly before the Club, with the hope that the members who hold positions of power will return to the National Assembly with a single agenda. They are all men of dreams, but none of them speak as long or as passionately as Robespierre.

If I lean to the side, I can see him near the altar in a pale blue coat and silver cravat. He is acting as witness for Camille. I wonder if, in their schoolboy days together, they ever imagined standing in Saint-Sulpice with all the important players of the nation behind them. When the ceremony is finished, Robespierre steps back while Camille shouts triumphantly, "Lucile Desmoulins!"

The entire church erupts into applause. Then we are on our feet and moving to follow the happy couple out the door.

"Perhaps that will be us someday," Henri remarks, and I can hear the edge in his voice.

"The Austrians are at our gates," I tell him. "You know Curtius can't leave his position now. There could be war at any moment. Today, tomorrow—"

"Next month, next year . . ."

I can see the mistrust in his face. He's beginning to believe that I don't love him, that I'll postpone our marriage forever. "I hope I've never given you any cause to doubt how much I love you. Or that I want to marry you."

"Then let's do it now. Today."

"Henri—"

"How long will this continue? Last year, Curtius promised to resign his post. So when will it be? Another year? Two? I'm a patient man,

Marie, but everyone has a breaking point. You must make a choice. Do you want to be Rose Bertin or Vigée-Lebrun?"

My eyes fill with tears. Élisabeth Vigée-Lebrun was the queen's artist. She married a fellow painter named Jean-Baptiste, and the pair of them have traveled across Europe together, arranging commissions and painting portraits. They have a daughter, little Jeanne Julie Louise. Somehow, Vigée-Lebrun has balanced motherhood with art. But how am I to do that? I can't. Not yet.

Henri wipes away my tears with the back of his glove. Then he puts his arm through mine. "Think on it," is all he says.

Chapter 38

April—June 1791

War is the national industry of Prussia.

—Comte de Mirabeau

Mirabeau is dead.

I am in the workshop when I hear the news that the great voice of the Revolution has passed. A year ago, almost to this date, it was Benjamin Franklin. Now, it is the man who was only recently made president of the National Assembly. At first, there is the hope that the news is wrong. Then there is talk that perhaps he has gone to the countryside to escape from politics and live incognito. But when Mirabeau's body is displayed to the public, the wailing and beating of chests begins.

Immediately, we make the bust of Mirabeau the centerpiece of our Salon, and the people who come dressed in black to mourn his passing would fill a stadium. On the day his ashes are interred inside the Panthéon—built to reflect the great masterpiece in Rome—the Assembly requests our bust for their procession.

"The Revolution has been the making of us," Curtius says as Robespierre carries away the wax head.

I reflect on this. While good men like de Flesselles and de Launay have died, we have thrived. While the Swiss Guards are mistrusted for being the king's men, Curtius and Wolfgang are greatly respected as captains of the National Guard. Why does life carry some people on the crest of the wave while others drown beneath the water?

I look across the room to a white certificate hanging above the *caissier*'s desk. It is the Assembly's official recognition of Curtius as one of the *Vainqueurs de la Bastille.* In a splendid ceremony at Notre-Dame, he was given this document along with a sword inscribed with his name. We are good patriots. That is clear for anyone to see. And perhaps this is why Jacques-Louis David helped Curtius become a member of the Académie.

I remember the moment when the news arrived—as exciting as the night the letter came from the king to say that he'd be visiting our Salon. At last, the recognition of my uncle's talent has come. It doesn't matter that I wasn't made a member as well. What matters is that the Salon de Cire will finally be in every guidebook to Paris. We have been recognized by the Académie as worthy of being seen, and for the rest of his life, perhaps on his gravestone, my uncle will be Philippe Curtius, member of the Académie Royale.

But Austrian and Prussian troops are amassing at our border. The fear that the Revolution may be crushed drives two men to break into the Tuileries and attempt to take the queen's life. Marat, now a master of sensationalism, has written on the front page of his *Ami du Peuple:*

> Five or six hundred heads would have guaranteed your freedom and happiness, but a false humanity has restrained your arms and stopped your blows. If you don't strike now, millions of your brothers will die, your enemies will triumph, and your blood will flood the streets. They'll slit your throats without mercy and disembowel your wives. And their bloody hands will rip out your children's entrails to erase your love of liberty forever.

All of Paris is in a frenzy. Our family has cleverly played both sides, and if the queen's Austrian allies march into France, we will not have much to fear. But men who've been outspoken against the king?

They've gambled everything, and they have no choice but to press forward. It will be their lives in danger if the queen's brother Leopold II gathers his troops to restore the monarchy. So now, more than ever, the Assembly appreciates the men in the National Guard. They will be the ones to fight against any invading army hoping to prevent a Constitution from being signed. The king's aunts have both escaped to Rome, and each day is more dangerous for the royal family. When I visit Madame Élisabeth in June, she confides in me that everyone in the Tuileries is despondent.

"The National Assembly means to take my brother's power and leave him with nothing more than a veto. Why not just strip him of everything right now?" she asks. "Because, in the end, that's what they plan to do."

We are in the workshop with de Bombelles, who must no longer be referred to as the marquise. At every door, along every hall, the National Guardsmen who have been posted to the Tuileries have found a hundred ways of making life miserable for the royal family. They whisper threats under their breath as the family dines. They warn the innocent and impressionable dauphin to be careful in the gardens, because assassins might be waiting behind every bush. They leave behind crude drawings for Madame Royale to find, and they threaten anyone who mistakenly addresses them with a hereditary title.

"It's become unbearable," de Bombelles agrees, taking from me a pair of glass eyes. "And now they've forbidden the royal family to leave. Élisabeth can no longer go out to deliver her saints."

I look up in surprise. "Not even to a church?"

Madame Élisabeth shakes her head. "We are prisoners in here," she says, repeating something she told me two years ago. "I predicted this, and my brother wouldn't believe me."

"We will find someone to deliver your models," I promise. She has completed thirty-three to date. Now we are working on a figure of Saint Stephen, who was stoned to death for his visions of God. His head is crowned with thorns, and his upturned palms are filled with rocks.

"Now I know how it felt for Daniel, pacing the lions' den with no chance of escape."

"Except through God," de Bombelles adds immediately.

"Yes." Madame Élisabeth hesitates. "Except through God."

On June seventeenth, when I return to her workshop, a new mood has settled over the Tuileries. From down the hall, I can hear the king whistling. Madame Élisabeth is insistent that we finish the model of Saint Stephen today, even though there's no time to paint on his sandals.

"He'll go barefoot," she decides. "That's not so terrible, is it?"

I laugh. "No, Madame."

"So tell me," she says, and her voice is full of intrigue and hope. "The queen says that there are shops now that sell ready-made clothing at the Palais-Royal. Is it true?"

"Yes. You can walk in and purchase a dress without hiring a tailor or having to be fitted."

"Imagine!" She looks at de Bombelles. "A world without tailors."

De Bombelles wrinkles her nose. She wants to say, *A world run by commoners.*

"And what do they charge?" Madame Élisabeth asks.

"They have a list," I tell her. "Fancy chemise gowns trimmed with pearls are more expensive than plain ones, and the same goes for bonnets and fichus."

"And the men? Are there shops for ready-made men's clothing as well?"

"Yes. They can pick out wool jackets or choose *culottes* in three different sizes."

This is something de Bombelles cannot conceive of. "And if someone is gigantically fat?" she demands. "What do they do?"

"Well, if they look like the Duc d'Orléans," I whisper, "they continue to hire a tailor."

Both women laugh uproariously. There's no love between them and the Duc—or Philippe Égalité, as he wishes to be called, though I shall never think of him this way. Madame Élisabeth wipes tears from her eyes. "Things are truly changing," she says. Her face becomes serious. "Thank you, Marie, for everything you've done for us."

"It is nothing, Madame."

"It is. And I want you to know I will never forget it."

That evening, as I make my way down the hall, I recognize a woman's voice on the stairs. Rose is talking to Léonard while half a dozen women trail behind them with baskets of accessories and heavy dresses. "Rose!" I exclaim.

Everyone freezes, as if they've been caught in a shameful act. "Go." She motions for the others to continue, and when they've disappeared down the hall, she turns to me. "So you are helping them prepare as well?"

I frown. "Who?"

"The royal family," she whispers impatiently. "Did they want something I couldn't bring?" When I am silent, she realizes the mistake she has made. "Never mind," she says quickly.

"Why? What are they planning?"

"Nothing." Rose levels me with her gaze. "I never said anything."

Chapter 39

June 21, 1791

It is with regret that I pronounce the fatal truth: Louis ought to perish rather than a hundred thousand virtuous citizens; Louis must die that the country may live.

—Maximilien Robespierre

On June twenty-first, just after dawn, while most of the city is still asleep, a tocsin begins to ring. The sound starts as a single chime, then becomes a cacophony of bells as I hurry into a simple muslin dress. In the hall, my mother is covering her ears. We wait for Curtius to put on his boots, then we hurry downstairs and open the door. People are in the streets, shouting above the relentless ringing. Henri and Jacques are speaking with our grocer, and we join the three of them.

"The royal family has escaped," Henri tells us. "They made away last night without anyone suspecting."

"Everyone is gone!" The grocer is pulling at his apron. He has been a vocal supporter of this Revolution, and it will not go well for him if the tide turns. "The king, the queen, the children, and their governess. Madame Élisabeth is gone. Even the king's brother the Comte de Provence has escaped. As well as his wife."

My first feeling is of immense relief. Whatever happens now, it is in God's hands. Then I think of what may happen if the king returns with Austrian troops. Wars do not discriminate in their destruction. With certainty, the entire city will be punished. The Palais-Royal, with its cafés and salons, will be the first to be destroyed. And who's to say that foreign troops won't look to the Boulevard after that?

"Curtius!" someone shouts. A small man is trying to make his way through the crowds, and when I glimpse a pair of green spectacles, I recognize Robespierre. When he reaches us, his voice is filled with emotion. "Curtius," he says, and for a moment I wonder if he is going to embrace him. "This is the day when every patriot will be put to the test. There is no doubt about it now. Our lives are in danger. Every aristocrat in France is hoping to rise up and crush this Revolution. Tell me," he begs, and his hands are shaking. "Is the National Guard with us?"

"Of course," Curtius replies.

"Then come with me to the Manège. We must inspire the people to stand against this!"

There is no hope of taking a coach, so the six of us follow Robespierre through the streets. The bells have stopped ringing, but the roads are so crowded with panicked citizens that the forty-minute walk takes us more than two hours. When we finally reach the Salle du Manège at the edge of the Tuileries Gardens, thousands of people are crushing one another in a desperate attempt to get inside. It will be another half hour just to get through the masses.

"There's another way," Robespierre says. He leads us through a back door built for the royal equestrian academy. The hall was constructed to house horses, not people, and as we take our seats in the public gallery, I can imagine how Mirabeau must have suffered in here. The room is ten times as long as it is wide, with high vaulted windows that let in little air. Because it's impossible to hear anything from the back, Robespierre finds us seats in the balcony. As an assemblyman, however, he does not sit with us. He takes Curtius with him to the benches below, where other members are listening and shaking their heads.

The mayor of Paris has taken the podium and is attempting to create calm by telling the Assembly that the king has not fled of his own accord. "He must have been kidnapped!" Mayor Bailly cries. "Look at the men who surround him, the ministers we've allowed to give him advice. Are they as trustworthy as our king, who has only the good of his people at heart?"

There are hisses from the crowd, and several assemblymen make threatening gestures. Then a tall man with dark hair strides forward, holding a fistful of papers in the air. I recognize him as Alexandre de Beauharnais, a nobleman who once came to the Salon looking to order a model of himself and his wife. He pushes aside the mayor and takes the podium. "Proof," he shouts, "in the king's own handwriting that he will never support a Constitution!"

Alexandre begins to read the damning evidence purposefully left behind in the Tuileries on the king's desk. In the letter, the king complains about the creation of the Assembly and goes so far as to call for a counterrevolution in Paris. There is no doubt now about his intentions. Wherever the king has fled, there is going to be war. If he should reach Austria, he will summon his own troops and any the queen's brother is willing to provide. Paris has two weeks, perhaps a month at most, before an army descends.

Robespierre takes the podium, but no one can hear him above the chaos. He gives up and appears on the balcony. "Come with me to the Jacobin Club," he tells us. "There will be order there, and we can decide what to do."

But inside the Club, there is pandemonium as well. When Robespierre is finally able to command silence, his speech is scathing.

"There are those in this audience who have perfected the mask of patriotism," he says. "They wear the tricolor on their hats, yet they are royalists in their hearts. These are the enemies who are most dangerous to us. These are the men who will be your assassins as soon as the new flower of our liberty is plucked. Look around you!" he shouts. "Unless you wish to be crushed by the growing sea of tyranny about to descend, I suggest we find these false patriots and root them out!"

I look at my mother, whose face is as pale as mine must be. My brothers are in the Swiss Guard. Our first language is German.

"He trusts you," Henri whispers. "It was Curtius he went to when the news came."

"In twenty-four hours," Robespierre continues, "if the king isn't captured, we should all expect war. I have prepared myself for whatever is to come. I am willing to give my life for the liberty of my country."

"And we would give our lives to save you!" someone shouts. It's Camille, and he has brought Lucile with him. They are sitting together at the front of the room, both wearing enormous tricolor cockades. The Club members rise and swear to defend Robespierre's life with their own. "Until the end!" they cry, and the shout is echoed throughout the old monastery.

As we leave the Club, Robespierre is on the verge of tears. "They love me," he says. "They can see I serve my country even before myself." He stops in front of a young sapling and gently reaches out to touch its leaves. It's one of the many liberty trees planted by the revolutionaries in the past three months. Before the dinner to celebrate Camille's marriage to Lucile, the guests gathered in the Tuileries Gardens to plant a liberty tree in their name. It's the fashionable thing to do among patriots now.

"The National Guard will be ready to fight by this evening," Curtius swears. "I'm going now to see Lafayette."

"The king will return with more troops than you can fight," Robespierre worries.

"That may be true, but we won't be unprepared. Where are you going?"

"Home," Robespierre says quietly, "to make my will."

That evening, as Alexandre de Beauharnais assumes the leadership of France, we push through the crowds to the Boulevard du Temple, where we each make wills of our own.

"There has never been a better time to marry," Henri says. The rest of the house has gone to sleep, and we are the only ones inside the salon.

"In a time of uncertainty?"

"In a time when we don't know if we'll be alive to see the end of this month or the next."

"Tomorrow," I say. "Let's discuss this tomorrow."

But he reaches across the couch and pulls me toward him. "I am tired of tomorrow, Marie." His eyes are wide and full of conviction. "I love you now."

Chapter 40

June 22, 1791

"They have been captured! The royal family has been captured!"

As the newsboys shout, the words spread like fire throughout the city, burning from street to street until all of France is consumed. Everyone is outside gossiping with neighbors or pushing into the cafés at the Palais-Royal. Although it's ten in the morning, there is no one inside our exhibition. I look at my mother. We are alone at the *caissier*'s desk. "Let's go," she says in German. "Curtius won't be back until to-night. The only way we are getting news is if we go to the Palais."

We shut the doors and tell Yachin that he has been given the day off.

"On account of the king's capture?" he asks eagerly. "I heard they discovered him in the city of Varennes. What will they do with him?"

That is the question, isn't it? Is he a king? A prisoner? "I don't know," I say, although I can guess. "That is what we are hoping to find out."

I convince Henri and Jacques to come with us, since their exhibi-tion is empty as well, and we find a driver who is willing to brave the crowds and take us to the Palais. Jacques and Henri debate which café we should go to. Committed revolutionaries like Camille and Georges Danton will be inside the Café de Foy. To be seen there is to tell your neighbors that you support the overthrow of the king. But constitu-tional monarchists will meet inside the Café de la Régence.

"We'll go to the Régence," Henri says firmly. "We still don't how this will all unfold."

"I can tell you how it will unfold," Jacques says darkly. "The king is about to be made a prisoner in his own country. No better time to show our love of Revolution."

The brothers look to me.

"The Café de la Régence," I tell them.

"Of course you would side with Henri!" Jacques exclaims wryly.

"We might see Rose Bertin in the Régence, and no one will know more about what's happening than her."

I am right. As soon as we enter the café, I see Rose's commanding figure. She is surrounded by half a dozen women, all of them eagerly listening to her tale, but when she sees me, she excuses herself and joins us at a table in the corner. The five of us pull our chairs close together, and I ask, "Is it true? Are they captured?"

"Last night." She tells us the story. At Easter, when the royal family was forbidden to leave the Tuileries for their annual visit to Saint-Cloud, the king realized that he should have listened to the queen and escaped. "All this time," she laments, "when everyone with sense was telling him to flee, he wanted to believe in the good of the people. But at Easter, there was no denying reality," she says. "So the queen summoned Fersen's help, and they began to plan."

This is not the first time I've heard Fersen's name associated with the queen's. Madame Élisabeth called him her sister-in-law's *dear friend.* But what *dear friend* risks his life for a married woman unless there is something more between them?

"She stopped ordering cheap gowns from Madame Éloffe," Rose says, "and began buying robes *à la française* in black and lavender from me."

"And that's when you knew," I say.

"Yes." She brings a handkerchief to her nose and blows discreetly. It wouldn't do to be seen weeping openly over the royal family's capture. "The preparations went on for months," Rose admits. "She wanted so many dresses that it took a second coach to carry them."

"What vanity," Jacques says critically.

"Her wardrobe was the only thing she felt she could control," Rose offers. "I tried to convince her that there would be dressmakers in Montmédy—"

"So that's where they were going?" Henri asks. Montmédy is a city on the border of the Austrian Empire, near Flanders. "That's nearly eighty leagues away. How did they get there?"

"They didn't. But they hoped to go through Varennes. The king refused to split up the carriages, so they all went together. The queen, the children, the Marquis d'Agoult, Madame Élisabeth, three attendants, several bodyguards . . . And all of them in two enormous green-and-yellow *berlines.*"

I put my hand to my head. "And no one told them that this was disaster?"

"I did!" Rose exclaims, then lowers her voice. "They might have gone in separate, smaller carriages and traveled through Reims. That's the quickest route. But the king thought this was the first road his pursuers would take, and the queen refused to leave her wardrobe behind."

"Count Axel von Fersen is the Swedish ambassador," Jacques says. "He must have told them this was madness."

"This is the king," Rose says dryly. "Of course, he knew best."

So Fersen found the funds to build two coaches and purchased them in the name of the Baroness von Korff. He kept them at his home, and on the night before last, he arrived at the Petit Carrousel, not far from the Tuileries, dressed as a coachman. He waited in this square while each member of the royal family escaped the palace and made their way to him. The governess was disguised as the Baroness von Korff, while both the six-year-old dauphin and Madame Royale were dressed as her daughters. The king was her valet, while the queen was costumed as the children's governess.

Everything was loaded into the carriages. Bread, cheese, a dozen bottles of wine. The queen's jade manicure set rode with her, along with a chess set and a mahogany writing palette. Fersen only accompanied them for four leagues to Bondy, then made his own escape to Flanders while the royal family switched drivers. But without Fersen, everything fell apart.

"Léonard was supposed to meet the *berline* in Varennes with fresh horses and soldiers," Rose says. "But he wasn't there."

"The queen's *hairdresser*?" Henri asks. "They could have chosen a soldier, someone with experience."

"But they didn't," Rose says.

I imagine Madame Élisabeth clutching her silver rosary as the carriage was stopped sixteen leagues from their destination. She would have been praying to all the saints in heaven, but most especially to the Virgin. "How were they discovered?" I ask quietly.

"There is talk that a man recognized the king's face from a fifty-livre-assignat," Rose says, then closes her eyes. The early assignats were printed with the image of King Louis. Now they carry only symbols of the Revolution. "It could be rumor, but if I know the king, it will be true."

"But why would he show his face?" my mother asks.

Rose opens her eyes. "Because he's a fool!" she says in exasperation. "Because he wanted to stop and dine at an inn along the way. They should have kept Fersen," she says. "They should never have separated from him. Of course, the king's brother the Comte de Provence has escaped and is probably at Koblenz by now."

"With the Comte d'Artois?" I ask.

"Yes. The pair of them should enjoy that," she says bitterly. "Nothing to do but make trouble in their uncle's city while Antoinette and the king are prisoners here." She looks at me. "Curtius is close with Lafayette, and he is the one who signed the order for their arrest. So what does he say will become of them?"

I wish she spoke German. Then I could tell her what my uncle learned yesterday without worrying who might overhear. As it is, I say as softly as I can, "They will probably take them back to the Tuileries and keep them under guard. My guess is they will force the king to sign the new Constitution."

"And the queen?"

The news will not be as good for her. Especially not when the people discover that her family was making for Montmédy, so close to her brother's empire. "They are talking about sending her to a convent and finding the king a new wife."

My mother exhales. "You cannot break up a marriage sanctified by God," she says in German.

"God does not rule here anymore. It is the National Assembly," I say. I don't tell her that the Assembly has already mentioned the Duc d'Orléans's daughter as a possible replacement.

"And do you think this is likely to happen?" Rose asks.

"If it doesn't, then there is talk of trying her for adultery."

"Leopold will save her," Rose says fervently.

My mother crosses herself. "He must."

Chapter 41

September 14, 1791

The king has signed the Constitution into law this morning. France is to be a constitutional monarchy, with an assembly that will share power with the king. A hundred years from now, perhaps even five hundred, this will be a day remembered by the people of France, possibly by people across the world. The rejoicing in the streets has already begun. Henri and Jacques are to launch a balloon over the Champ-de-Mars announcing an end to the Revolution.

At sunset, we ride to the Champ-de-Mars, where people are already filling the stands. Two months ago, this was the scene of a massacre. A group of angry citizens, gathered to sign a petition to overthrow the king, became unruly. Lafayette appeared with his National Guard, and when the petitioners began throwing stones at the soldiers, shots were fired. Thirty men were killed, and Marat's *L'Ami du Peuple* called it the Champ-de-Mars Massacre. The papers turned against Lafayette. And when it emerged that the queen had slipped past him on the night the royal family escaped, men like Robespierre started to speak openly against him.

But today, the crowds are joyful. Jacques has brought the wicker basket and the balloon, and both have been arranged in the grassy center of the stadium so that thousands of people can watch it take flight. Henri asks if my mother and I would like to hang tricolor ribbons from the gondola, and while we're helping, a woman comes up to Henri and asks, "Are you one of the Charles brothers?"

"I am," he says.

She claps her hands. "Then this must be the *Charlière*!" She looks up at the giant gold balloon—a color chosen in my honor—then back at Henri. "I am a great admirer of men of science."

Henri grins. "Are you?"

"Oh yes." She is dressed in a revealing chemise gown with a fetching bonnet of blue and white.

"Well, perhaps you can express your admiration to Jacques. My brother enjoys speaking with devotees."

She looks at Jacques, with his heavy jowls and protruding belly. "I think I would prefer to speak with you."

"I'm sorry," he says kindly. "We are busy here, and my fiancée is the extremely jealous type."

"Henri!" I exclaim.

He laughs. "If you'll excuse me."

The young woman studies me with a critical eye, then turns on her heel.

"Your fame precedes you," I say.

He sighs. "Just another day for the Charles brothers."

"Or at least Henri Charles," I whisper. I wonder how many times this happens to him in his exhibition. If we were married, then I suppose I would know. "Tell me about the balloon," I say.

"What? Are you an admirer as well?"

"Very much so."

"Well, what do you want to know?"

"Explain to us the difference between using hot air and hydrogen," Wolfgang says.

"Wolfgang!" My brother has arrived with Curtius and Abrielle. "What are you doing here?"

"What—captains aren't allowed to watch the festivities?" My brother and I embrace while my mother rushes to take Michael from Abrielle. My little nephew shrieks with delight. It has been eight weeks since we've seen him. We live only twenty minutes away, but the work in the Salon never stops. He is all big cheeks and wispy blond hair. He wraps his chubby arms around his grandmother's neck, and everyone praises him for looking like his parents.

"When will he walk?" I ask Abrielle.

"Oh, not until November or December I should think."

I know nothing about children, and even less about how they learn to walk and talk.

"Don't look so worried." She laughs. "You'll learn all about children once you are pregnant. It's the only thing anyone will want to talk to you about."

Two years ago, she was sitting in the queen's rooms fending off the attention of every man in attendance. Now, she is dressed in a simple chemise gown with ribbon instead of pearls for her neck. "So does it bore you?" I ask.

"I was afraid it would be lonely." She looks at Michael, bouncing happily on my mother's hip, and adds, "But I was wrong. Motherhood is not at all what I expected."

"For the good," I say hopefully.

"Oh yes. But it never stops." She adds, "There is always something to do or to buy. He grows so quickly. Every month he needs new clothes."

It must cost a fortune. How do they afford it? Even now that we are part of every Catalog of Amusements, we barely take in enough to pay for the wax, the costumes, the wigs, the accessories, plus food for our small family and our own clothing.

"But it's simply a matter of economy," Abrielle says, as if reading my thoughts, and I am impressed at how she has grown up. At no time during these past two years has her father tried to see her. Yet she has made do with what she has.

"I wish I could learn to be more like you," I admit.

She is puzzled. "I have never met anyone better at economizing. You could convince the king to pay for his own crown."

I laugh. Then we turn to Wolfgang and Curtius, who are listening to Henri. "So there are limits to hot air," Henri is saying. "When the air cools, the balloon is forced to descend."

Curtius crooks his finger at me, and I follow him to the edge of the grass, where Jacques is tampering with his altimeter, away from all the noise and excitement. "A letter," he says, taking an envelope from his jacket. "From the American ambassador, Gouverneur Morris, to George Washington."

He hands it to me, and I can see that it is not the original. "How did you get this?"

"It was intercepted this morning and translated into French," he tells me.

It begins with a salutation and a brief note on how happy Gouverneur Morris is to be in Washington's favor. Then he continues with the important news of the day:

> The king has at length, as you will have seen, accepted the new Constitution, and been in consequence liberated from his arrest. It is a general and almost universal conviction that this Constitution is inexecutable. The makers to a man condemn it. . . .
>
> You doubtless recollect that the now expiring Assembly was convened to arrange the finances, and you will perhaps be surprised to learn that after consuming church property to the amount of one hundred million sterling, they leave this department much worse than they found it. . . . The aristocrats who are gone and going in great numbers to join the refugee princes believe sincerely in a coalition of the powers of Europe to reinstate their sovereign in his ancient authorities. . . .
>
> The Prince de Condé has requested that all French gentlemen capable of actual service will immediately repair to the standard of royalty beyond the Rhine or rather on the banks of that river. To the troops mentioned in this note are added by the counterrevolutionists here 15,000 Hessians and 16,000 French refugees, so that

exclusive of what the emperor may bring forward, they muster an army, on paper, of 100,000 men.

A panic wells up inside me that is hard to suppress. "A *hundred* thousand men?"

"This is not the end," Curtius warns. "Gouverneur Morris was one of the authors of America's Constitution. He doesn't believe our Constitution has been written to last. If that is true, and an army is being mustered by the emperor on his sister's behalf . . . We must be sure the royal family knows we are still with them. Visit Madame Élisabeth in the Tuileries soon. They are under guard, but I can arrange for a pass."

"What are we?" I ask, hopelessness in my voice. "Royalists? Revolutionaries?"

"Survivalists," he replies.

Chapter 42

November 29, 1791

How many hearts are open to fraternity and sweet equality!

—*Journal de Paris*

But it is nearly two months before Curtius can arrange for a pass. And although the guards know me, they are extremely cautious. They search my basket, with its heavy blocks of wax and clay; then they pass around my caliper, conferring with one another as to whether the tool might be used for escape.

"Do you understand what this new Constitution means?" the oldest guard asks.

"Yes."

"There's to be no bowing or scraping to the king or queen, and they are no longer to be called Your Majesty. You may now sit in their presence and keep your hat on your head. They are no different from you and me."

"I understand."

He nods for me to go on. Inside, the air is chill. Whoever has been put in charge of tending the fires has not been doing their duty. Or possibly, they were dismissed. The halls are nearly empty, and it's strange to be passing through them alone. I feel small and cold beneath the half-lit chandeliers and tapestries. It's like being on board an abandoned ship.

"Marie."

I put my hand to my chest, and Johann laughs. "Did I frighten you?"

"Where has everyone gone?" I ask him.

"Most of the courtiers have been sent away, and those who could afford it have fled to Koblenz to be with the rest of the émigrés." He lowers his voice. "All of the royal family's closest friends are gone, including Angélique de Bombelles."

"She *left* Madame?"

"The princesse instructed her to."

Johann follows me down the hall, and I notice that he is wearing a thicker cloak. "New?" I ask as we climb the stairs.

He exhales so that I can see his breath. "For every guard in the Tuileries. How is Maman? Isabel and I are thinking of coming on Saturday evening. Is there anything we should bring?"

"Paschal. That's all Maman is really interested in. She asked yesterday about Edmund, but I told her I never see him. Is he—"

"Still angry. I try not to see him either."

We reach the door to Madame Élisabeth's salon. There are no ushers, so my brother opens the door for me and announces grandly, "Mademoiselle Grosholtz."

It is a miserable scene inside. Madame Élisabeth is alone on her couch, buried beneath three blankets for warmth. Her greyhounds are huddled together, shivering visibly as they bury their noses in their paws. "Madame!" I exclaim. "It's freezing in here."

"They won't light the fires for me."

"This cannot continue. We must ask the guards for firewood," I say.

"You can ask, but they will tell you no."

I look down at the tiny, shivering dogs and reply, "We'll see about that." I go back into the hall, but Johann is gone. The first guard I find, I ask for firewood.

"And who are you?" the young soldier asks. "Madame's new servant?"

"I am the owner of the Salon de Cire," I reply, "along with my uncle, Curtius, who is a captain in your army."

A light flickers in his eyes. "You mean the wax modeler on the Boulevard du Temple?"

"Yes."

"And you are his sculptress?" The boy looks me up and down.

"I am also his niece."

"I've always wondered about those figures," he says. "How do you decide who to place inside your exhibition?"

"We look for well-known patriots and celebrated servicemen." I step closer to him. "Like yourself."

He laughs self-consciously. "Me?"

"Do you know what it is to be immortal? To have your face seen by thousands of passersby?"

His eyes go wide.

"Perhaps you would like to come to the Salon, and I shall make a model of you."

"Really?"

He cannot be more than fifteen or sixteen. What is he doing here, guarding the Tuileries? "Yes. And all I ask is a simple favor."

He backs away and scowls. "So there's a price!"

"Everything comes with a price," I say evenly. "Especially fame. All I want is some firewood for Madame Élisabeth."

"I don't know that I can get that," he says. He names the guard who is in charge of it.

"Can he be convinced?"

"If there is a good reason." He hesitates. "But how will I know if I'm to be a model?"

"Because tomorrow you'll come to the Salon de Cire and I shall make you famous."

Within the hour, there is a crackling fire. Madame Élisabeth is thanking me again and again for my kindness. "Look at them." She indicates her dogs, who have curled up as close to the flames as possible. Even by the light of the fire, wrapped in an ermine cloak, she looks pale and cold.

"The guard has promised to bring you wood every morning and evening."

"What did you say?"

"That there might be a wax model in it for him. For a great deal of timber."

We both laugh, and I feel closer to her than I ever have before.

"It was very good of you to come," she says. "Most courtiers left after . . . after we fled. And those who haven't escaped abroad are too frightened to come back. My brother has no one to attend his *coucher*. Neither does the queen. In the morning, when it's time for her to dress, she is practically alone. And at night," she confides, "I can hear her weeping."

I think on the tragic irony of this. For years, the queen tried to avoid the rigid ceremonies of the court, and now she desperately needs them back. She has discovered that without them, there is nothing to separate her from us.

"It's too cold for wax modeling today," I tell her, "but I am happy to continue coming here."

"It would have to be on Wednesdays. The guards have forbidden us any entertainments on Fridays. That is the day the queen used to see her friends."

Wednesdays are busy days for the Salon. But I think of all of her unfinished saints and the loneliness she must feel her with only her dogs to keep her company, and I nod. "Certainly. I am sorry for all of this," I begin.

She sighs heavily. "I hear the National Assembly has renamed itself the Legislative Assembly. And that Robespierre has been made president of the Jacobin Club. I heard his portrait is hanging in the Paris Salon."

Citizens are suffering, there is no bread, and now coffee and sugar are scarce. But Robespierre's portrait is displayed next to Curtius's wax model of the dauphin. "He's not a member of the Legislative Assembly," I assure her. "His only power is as the president of the Jacobin Club."

"But the members of the Legislative Assembly will listen to him. Most of them are Jacobins as well, and their Club is hungry for war."

"Robespierre will never vote for that. If France were to be defeated, he knows it would return to a monarchy. Whatever gains might be had in winning, Robespierre would never put the Constitution at risk. He considers himself to be a man of great principles."

"Is that why they are calling him *The Incorruptible?*"

No, I think. They are calling him *The Incorruptible* because that is what people wish to believe, and the people's imagination has proven stronger than reality these past three years.

Chapter 43

April 20, 1792

Men of limited intelligence lack the imagination to be touched by inner suffering.

—Élisabeth Vigée-Lebrun, royal portrait artist

It is Robespierre who brings us the news. The queen's brother Leopold II has also died, and the Jacobin Club has now voted for war on the emperor's successor, Francis II.

"Against the Holy Roman Emperor!" Robespierre is beside himself with grief. We offer him a place at our table, and he seats himself between Henri and Jacques. He holds his head in hands. "No one would listen to me," he says. "No one would listen!"

"Then we must hope the Legislative Assembly will vote differently," Henri offers.

"It's too late!" Robespierre is distraught. "They have already voted."

"Does Curtius know this?" my mother asks. He is on duty and will not be home until midnight, perhaps later.

"If he doesn't, he will," Robespierre says darkly. "All of France will know it when the emperor comes storming to Paris, to crush everything we have achieved! Now there will be enemies within as well as without. Foreign war as well as civil war."

"And where will the soldiers come from," Henri asks, "to fight off an enemy a hundred thousand strong?"

"Is it to be a conscripted army?" Jacques questions.

"I don't know," Robespierre admits.

I think of Edmund and Johann in the king's service. Certainly, they will not be asked to fight. But what about men like Wolfgang and Curtius? This will be a war of brother against brother. And these foolish men of the Jacobin Club are betting everything on the peasants of the Holy Roman Empire rising up and joining forces with our revolutionaries. If they don't rise, what then? We will be a leaderless nation with a misfit army taking on the greatest power in Europe.

For days, this is all anyone talks about. Lafayette has been convinced to turn our army into a respectable fighting force the way he did with the Americans. It's to be expected that there will be many prisoners of war, and the question of how to humanely dispatch them has been taken up by the Legislative Assembly.

"A guillotine," Robespierre informs us at our Tuesday salon.

Lucile frowns. "And what exactly is a *guillotine*?" she asks.

"I . . ." Robespierre hesitates. "Perhaps . . ." Lucile is seven months pregnant, and obviously this is not something he hopes for her to know. But she persists, and he is forced to explain. "It is a device built by Dr. Guillotin," he says. "A wooden contraption that will make for a swift death whether the criminal is rich or poor."

Ah, so that is why the Assembly has adopted this. Whereas before, noblemen were beheaded with the ax and commoners were hanged, now there is to be equality in death as well as life.

"But how does it work?" The scientist in Jacques wants to know.

Robespierre shifts uncomfortably in his seat. "There are two high pieces of wood and a board in the middle where the criminal lies."

"Facedown?" Camille asks.

"Yes." Robespierre is not comfortable talking about death, I realize. "There is a blade at the top with a rope attached. When the executioner lets go of the rope, the blade comes down and the criminal is executed."

"Decapitation?" my mother cries.

"Apparently so," Jacques says.

"Tomorrow," Robespierre continues, "the guillotine will be erected outside the Hôtel de Ville at the Place de Grève. We are executing a criminal, and that is something every patriot should be concerned about. I hope you will all be there."

"At an execution?" I ask.

"It is a matter of the nation's security," Robespierre replies.

THE NEXT MORNING, Henri and Jacques join our family in hiring a coach bound for the Place de Grève. "I have never been to an execution," I admit.

"Never?" Jacques asks. "But they're everywhere—"

"Yes. And I've tried to avoid them."

"When the blade is about to fall," Curtius promises, "you can look away."

"Who is the criminal?" my mother wants to know.

"A killer named Pelletier," Curtius replies. "He will be either very lucky or very unfortunate today."

I had not thought of this. What if this guillotine should fail? What if dying by the blade is slower and more painful than dying by the ax? This is a show staged to convince the populace that the war will be won and vengeance will be swift. But I do not want to see it. I don't care how it may vouch for our patriotism or how many Jacobins will see us and know that we are friends. When the coach stops before the Place de Grève, my palms are damp.

"Don't worry," Henri says. "There will be so many people, it will be impossible to see anything anyway."

But when Robespierre notices we have come, we are given places in front of the scaffold.

"Have you ever seen so many tricolor cockades?" he asks eagerly. He is not expecting an answer, and I don't give him one. Thousands of people have come to witness this first execution by guillotine. Some in the crowd are carrying children on their shoulders, and women are selling roses like they do outside of theaters. Every guardsman in Paris must be here today. I search for Wolfgang among the phalanx of soldiers dressed in blue and red.

"Do you see him?" my mother asks.

"No. But then he could be anywhere," I tell her.

The drums begin to roll, and an expectant hush falls over the square. The sound of hooves echoes over the cobblestones, and the guards clear the way for a pair of horses carrying a man in an open wagon. He is perhaps twenty-four, with a dirty face and a dark red shirt provided to him by the executioner. I wonder whether he killed out of self-defense or something more sinister.

Someone in the crowd shouts, "There is the murderer!" and abuse assails him from every side. A woman throws a heavy stone at his head, and it misses by only the breadth of a hand. The guards around the scaffold begin to laugh. Tomorrow, many of them will be leaving for war, so today they'll get their entertainment where they can.

"I don't want to see this." I shake my head. Henri puts his arm around my shoulders. When Robespierre looks in our direction, I see the line along his jaw tighten.

The victim is led onto the wooden scaffold. I can see he is surprised that the machine has been painted red. He looks up at the heavy blade, and if his hands were not bound behind his back, he would probably shield his eyes from the sun on the metal. The executioner leads him to the board, and Pelletier doesn't fight as he's instructed to lie down. He is facing the wicker basket that will receive his head, and his neck is held in place by a wooden lunette. After a few moments, he will never have another thought. Whatever hopes and dreams he once had will be finished. Although this is when I should be closing my eyes, I can't look away as the drumroll intensifies and the executioner releases the rope.

It is over in a second. The moment the blade falls, Pelletier's head is separated from his body, and the spray of blood is disguised by the color of the guillotine. The executioner bends down to retrieve Pelletier's severed head from the basket, but as he holds it by the hair for the crowds to see, there are angry cries.

"Is that it?"

"Bring back the wheel!" someone shouts.

The executioner has done his job too well, and the audience isn't satisfied. The gallows at least provided twitching and slow death by strangulation.

"The people want what is good, but they do not always see it," Robespierre says. It is a phrase of Rousseau's. "They wish to see criminals punished," he adds, excusing their behavior.

Or they are simply barbarians, I think.

The next day, it is guillotine madness. Customers flood into the Salon asking whether the guillotine Curtius has built for the window is available in miniature for purchase.

"You would like to buy a miniature guillotine?" I repeat.

A tall woman in a lavender gown giggles. Her curls hang in clusters on either side of her head, and her necklace is made up of a large Bastille rock with the word *Liberté* engraved in diamonds. "I would like it for my table," she admits.

Her companion adds, "Think how surprised guests would be if we brought it out to slice the cucumbers!"

"Or better yet, the bread, now that the harvest is coming!"

The pair of them laugh.

"It would be at least thirty livres-assignats," I warn them.

Lavender dismisses my concern with a wave. "It would be worth it to see their faces!" she gushes.

When he returns home, I ask Curtius what he thinks.

"If our customers want guillotines, then that's what they'll get. I can take this week off and teach Yachin how to assemble them."

The next morning, the pair of them are out in the courtyard, sanding toy guillotines to amuse the rich.

Chapter 44

June 19, 1792

The rest of the world lives on in vain
And roars, calling us to fight.

—EXCERPT FROM THE SONG *"LA MARSEILLAISE"*

ALL ACROSS EUROPE, WORD IS SPREADING THAT TWO-THIRDS of France's officers have fled rather than take their chances against the Holy Roman Empire. In the city of Lille, soldiers murdered their own general for losing a battle against the Austrians. But Jacques Brissot, the new president of the Legislative Assembly, has a plan to spread liberty throughout Europe at whatever the cost, however many men must die.

"Liberty cannot come without a price!" Camille exclaims at our Tuesday salon.

Robespierre rises from his seat. "Last week you were against the war, but now that Georges Danton is shouting about freeing oppressed people abroad, suddenly you're ready to risk everything we've worked for?"

Lucile puts her hand on Camille's arm. "Why don't we let Wolfgang speak?"

Everyone turns to my brother in his captain's uniform and red cravat. Neither he nor Curtius has been sent abroad, but that may change.

"So what do the guardsmen think?" Robespierre asks. "Not what you want us to *believe* they think, but what they're actually *saying.*"

"That there is hope," Wolfgang replies cautiously, "but only because three heroes of the American War have been made generals and sent off to fight." Lafayette has gone to Reims, while Rochambeau is in Belgium and Luckner is in Alsace. "I'm not sure how many men believe this war is winnable."

Curtius agrees. "With the Prussians sending Austria their troops, it will be only a matter of time before they invade. The king has vetoed a proposal that would post twenty thousand guardsmen all around Paris. Why do you think this is?"

"To clear the way for the Austrians," Camille exclaims, "as they come marching in!"

"We should send the queen to a convent and try the king for treachery," Robespierre suggests. The Duc d'Orléans, who has only recently rejoined our salon, gives the loudest cheer.

The next morning, when I reach the Tuileries, I am shocked to find the king and queen whispering with Madame Élisabeth in her workshop. Immediately, I turn away to give them privacy, but as I reach for the door the queen exclaims, "Please, stay." She is dressed in black for the death of her second brother, Emperor Leopold, and I admire her nerve to wear mourning clothes despite the express orders of the Assembly.

Although it is not permitted anymore, I curtsy. There are no guards to see me.

"We are talking about the commotion outside," Madame Élisabeth says, stepping away from the windows where, clearly, something is happening below.

"I didn't see any commotion," I tell her, and the three of them exchange looks.

"Nothing?" the king questions. "No men making for the palace?"

"Or groups of women in red caps?" the queen worries. This is the new fashion in Paris. Red Phrygian caps like the hats worn in ancient Rome as a sign of liberty. True patriots are now sporting everything Roman. Men's hair is straight and unpowdered, like that of Brutus, who was the killer of a tyrant. And women wear long chemise dresses in white like the Vestal Virgins, the keepers of Rome's flame. In the Jacobin Club, there are as many busts of Romans as there are of Frenchmen.

"No," I tell them. "Nothing like that. The streets have been calm."

But there is clearly a storm brewing below. The queen looks nervously over her shoulder at the shuttered windows, and the king explains, "They want to plant a liberty tree in the middle of the royal gardens."

I don't understand. "Who does, Your Majesty?"

"A group of agitated citizens—"

"A *mob*!" the queen exclaims. Her color is high, and even though she is using a fan to conceal it, she is clearly sweating. "They are enraged at being denied the chance to plant their tree in the last garden of France where monarchy still grows."

"You saw nothing on your way to the Tuileries?" the princesse confirms.

"Madame, if there is anyone coming—" But my words are cut off by the sound of a gate crashing against its post and someone crying, "God save the king! They're storming the Tuileries!"

The four of us rush to the windows, and Madame Élisabeth opens the shutters. Across the courtyard, thousands of angry men armed with sabers and pikes are making for the palace. Many are shouting, "Death to the royals!"

"They are going to kill us!" the queen cries.

The doors of the workshop swing open, and a dozen Swiss Guards hurry inside. Both Edmund and the Baron de Besenval are among them, but Edmund does his best not to look at me. Even as a child, my oldest brother was unyielding. He will not change now. "Your Majesties!" the baron cries, breaking the ban on using honorifics. "Hide yourselves at once."

"In separate rooms," adds Edmund. "If His Majesty will agree, we will take him now to the Salon de l'Oeil-de-Boeuf."

The king has tears in his eyes. "It is better this way," he tells his wife and sister. They embrace him, and their parting is swift. The mobs are so close that I can distinguish the words of *"La Marseillaise,"* a song Parisians have adopted as their war cry.

"What about my son?" the queen asks. "He is all alone—"

"We have already made arrangements for him," the baron says.

"And my daughter?"

"She is in the salon."

The room is cleared, and I am left alone with the baron. He watches me, and I wonder if I am to be punished for my brother's transgressions. All it would take is a brief comment to the mobs, a whisper that I am a royalist or an aristocratic sympathizer. "You are Curtius's daughter," he says.

I swallow quickly. "Actually, his niece."

He doesn't move. There is nothing threatening in his face. If anything, there is a deep sadness in his eyes. Perhaps he has realized that if he dies today, he will never see his only grandchild. "Leave through the servants' entrance. Down the back stairs next to the kitchens," he instructs. "Go. Quickly!"

I take the stairs two at a time, and when I reach the kitchens, I am part of a long line of escaping servants. Everyone is silent, intent on the task at hand. We must get out the door and then run. Heavy footsteps echo on the stairs above our heads. The mob is inside the palace.

Twenty more people and I will be through the door. I glance around the kitchen, at the baskets of warm bread ready to be served up to the royal family. No one has decided to take it. On a center table, a pile of silk napkins has been left unfolded, and a tray of silver forks has been abandoned. There are so many forks. What does the royal family do with all of these? If members of the mob make their way here, this will all be stolen.

"Go!" Someone pushes me forward. "Go!"

My turn has come. I do as I'm instructed and run. I don't look back, and I am ashamed to say that, as I follow the other servants across the courtyard and through the gates, I don't think of Edmund or Johann. I have no idea if I am being pursued. I lose myself in the alleys of Paris and don't stop until I have reached the Boulevard du Temple.

"What's happening?" Yachin cries when he sees me. Women do not run. It is undignified.

I stop to catch my breath. "I will tell you inside."

In the Salon, crowds have gathered around my uncle's tableau of Nicolas Luckner at the guillotine, which I refused to make. The customers are shocked when they catch sight of me. When I glimpse myself in the mirror, I can see why. My bonnet is gone and my cheeks are red. My hair is hanging loosely over my shoulders, and I have lost my fichu somewhere in the city.

"Mein Gott!" my mother exclaims. "What is this?"

I tell her the news, and when I finish, there is a crowd around the *caissier*'s desk.

"What about Edmund and Johann?" Yachin worries.

My mother looks to me, but there is nothing I can offer.

It is the longest ten hours of our lives. While customers laugh over Madame du Barry and question whether my uncle's guillotine might work, we sit at the *caissier*'s desk and wait for news. When the door opens at nine and it is Johann who comes through, my mother begins to weep.

"Johann!" she cries. She searches his body for cuts or wounds, and when she sees that he is sound, she takes him to her chest.

"Are they alive?" I whisper.

Johann separates himself from my mother. "Yes." He recounts what happened after I fled, and although I'm aware of customers listening, I am too engrossed to send them away.

"There wasn't a room in the palace they didn't enter. When they found the king, they threatened him with pistols, and as God is my witness I thought they would shoot. But he was eloquent. For the first time in his life, the king knew what to say. He said he was the father of our country and a believer in liberty. That he would protect the Constitution until his dying breath and that the Austrians would never make their way into Paris. Then the mob forced a liberty cap on his head. It was shameful," he admits. "It was embarrassing."

TWO DAYS LATER, when Lafayette hears what has transpired in the Tuileries, he is beside himself with rage. He returns to Paris and calls for the destruction of the Jacobin Club, whose members participated in the storming of the Tuileries. In Tuesday's salon, that is all we hear about.

"Liberty cannot coexist with men like Lafayette," Robespierre threatens.

"So what do you propose?" the Duc wants to know.

Robespierre is thoughtful for a moment. "That death be brought to all traitors."

Chapter 45

July 6, 1792

You are young, Camille Desmoulins, candor is on your lips . . . but you are often fooled by that very candor.

—Jacques-Pierre Brissot, revolutionary leader

For the first time in more than three months, good news is delivered to our doorstep. Camille has come to tell us that Lucile has survived childbirth and a healthy son, Horace, has been delivered. We are all overjoyed for him. Despite our vast differences in politics, he is a good man at heart. And for all of Lucile's impassioned speeches, she has only wanted a better future for France.

"I know you are b-b-busy with the Salon," Camille says. He is so excited that his stutter has returned. "But I was wondering if you might come to our ap-p-partment and sketch my son. We would like to have a wax model done of him."

It is not an unusual request. If parents can afford it, many times they will want wax sculptures of their infants. Particularly if the children are stillborn.

I gather my papers while Camille goes next door to give Henri the news. When I step outside, he is trying to convince Henri to leave his *caissier*'s desk to visit Horace and Lucile. "Why not?" I encourage him. "It's a beautiful day."

"Are you suggesting I close the exhibition early and risk *profit*?"

I grin. "Of course not. Your assistant can stay here. That's what he's for."

The three of us make our way through the streets. On every lamppost is a red and blue sign encouraging young men to enlist in the army. One of the posters catches Camille's eye, and the color rises on his neck. "We are losing this war!" he says angrily. Several passersby turn to look at us. "I have a son to take care of, and the Austro-Prussian army is advancing. Every National Guardsman has been ordered to protect Paris, but with what weapons?" he asks. "With what cannon?"

"Is there any news from the fronts?" Henri asks cautiously.

It is not wise to appear too eager for word, especially if it is dire. The Assembly has ordered the closure of every theater, and our exhibits must show our patriotism in new ways: every model must wear a *bonnet rouge,* which the commoners are calling a liberty cap, and shoes that lace instead of buckle. Men's knee breeches have been replaced with long striped pants, and women's skirts must be white, red, and blue. Poor Madame du Barry, in her beautiful court dress, has been reduced to skirts *à la circassienne,* as if she's wrapped herself in a tricolor flag. Only Robespierre, who stands at the Jacobin podium and preaches against hypocrisy, is allowed to retain his silk *culottes* and powdered wig.

"The news is not good," Camille replies as we reach his apartment. "The Comte de Provence and the Comte d'Artois have joined forces with the Austrians and are commanding an army of émigrés." He stops on the stairs. "Please do not mention any of this to Lucile."

Inside of Camille's beautifully decorated salon, more than two dozen people are celebrating. There are spirits, wine, and bowls of tobacco for the men who are lighting up pipes. Lucile reclines in a chaise lounge at the center of the room, and the infant Horace is at her breast. The image is so striking that I ask Camille if he would like mother and son sculpted together.

"What do you think?" he asks Lucile. "A wax b-b-bust of mother and child?"

She looks lovingly into her little son's face. "Why not?" she asks tenderly. "Then we can keep this moment forever."

Camille finds me a chair, and while I take out my paper and ink, he introduces Henri to his friends. "Congratulations," I tell Lucile.

She beams up at me with a mother's pride. "It was all done so quickly. Everyone told me to expect labor pains for twenty-four hours, but it was over before it even began."

"You are fortunate," I say, beginning to sketch. She did not gain much weight in her pregnancy. She appears much the same, with her dark hair falling around her shoulders and her sharp eyes darting about the room.

"Well, soon it will be you." She runs her finger down her son's little nose, and her expression changes. "Do you think we have done right in naming him Horace Camille?" She searches the room. "His godfather is to be Robespierre, but he hasn't come. Perhaps he is angry?"

"It has nothing to do with the name," I promise her.

"Is it politics then?"

I look across the salon at Camille, who has his arm around Henri's shoulders and is laughing. He specifically asked us not to speak about war. This is supposed to be a happy day, a time of new life, not of loss and death. "Yes," I reply. "Politics."

"You can tell me," she says. "I'm not a delicate flower just because I've become a mother."

Now I am caught between the truth and my promise. Finally, I say, "They have a difference of opinion on the war."

Lucile leans back against the couch and groans. "It is always this way with Robespierre. You are either with him or against him, a traitor to the country or a defender of liberty. There is no in between. And he never forgets an indignity or a slight."

I nod quietly and do not say anything.

"Now that Camille can live on my dowry, he has dedicated himself to the Jacobin Club. He is no longer a journalist, and I think this makes Robespierre envious," she confides.

In place of Camille's paper, a dozen new journals have sprung up, including Robespierre's weekly *La Défenseur de la Constitution.* The bloodred cover symbolizes the bloodshed that liberty and equality require. I can imagine Robespierre being jealous now that Camille has both the money and the time to dedicate himself exclusively to politics, while he must still work for his living.

"This feud cannot continue," Lucile says. "Camille and Robespierre have known each other since they were children. Marie, will you do a favor for me?"

I put down my sketch and wait for her to go on.

"Will you deliver something to Robespierre?"

"Without your husband knowing?" I ask.

"It would only be a letter. I could write it now, and it would make peace between them."

"I have no idea where he lives," I confess.

"With Maurice Duplay. He is a cabinetmaker in the Rue Saint-Honoré. His wife and daughters take care of Robespierre." She looks at Camille while I wonder what sort of care Robespierre needs. "Please," she begs. "You can say you are leaving to find new paper or ink."

I nod, and while she puts Horace in his bassinet to write, I finish the sketch. When she is done, she folds the paper neatly in half. "It isn't far, only a few doors from the Jacobin Club." She gives me the address: 366 Rue Saint-Honoré. "Thank you, Marie."

"He doesn't want to make this peace on his own?" I ask.

"He is fire and brimstone. I fell in love with that, but sometimes it blinds him."

I cross the room full of warmongers and politicians from the Jacobin Club to whisper where I'm going into Henri's ear. "You don't have to come with me," I say. He gives me a wry look, and I have to suppress a laugh.

Outside, the sky is a brilliant blue, and women are fanning themselves in the heat. "Summer is my favorite time of year," Henri admits. "There's nothing better than sitting on the porch and counting the stars."

"You told me winter was the best time for stargazing."

He squeezes my arm. "In winter," he explains, "the sky is clear and the air is dry. But in summer, you have the benefit of not freezing to death."

We reach the Duplay house and stop in front of a small, cluttered courtyard filled with wood-making tools and a narrow saw pit. We knock on the door, and a young woman answers. She has long dark hair and striking green eyes. I would guess her age to be twenty-four or twenty-five. "My father is not at home," she says.

"We have come to see Robespierre," I tell her. She narrows her eyes as she looks at me. Is there jealousy in them?

"What are your names?" she demands.

"Marie Grosholtz, and this is Henri Charles. We have come to deliver a letter."

She holds out her hand. "I will give to him."

"If we cannot deliver this to Robespierre himself, we will try another place and time."

She is not used to being spoken to like this. She hesitates while she considers what to do. "Maximilien," she calls finally, using his first name. "You have visitors." She steps to the side. "He is up the stairs. I will take you to him, but only if you are brief."

I look at Henri and wonder if he is thinking what I am. "We can be brief," I say.

The three of us climb the stairs, and the young woman pauses before an open door. Inside, Robespierre is hunched over a desk, writing furiously. "Your visitors," she says.

Robespierre pushes his glasses back on his nose and rises. "Thank you, Éléonore." It is obvious that he is surprised to see us. "Henri. Marie. What are you doing here?" There is tension in his voice. He is worried that we have come to deliver ill news.

"From Lucile Desmoulins." I hold out the letter to him, and he takes it.

"Oh." He sounds relieved. "Please . . . come inside."

We enter the small room, with its blue and white curtains and plain wooden bed. There is nothing remarkable about the furniture. Just a pair of tattered chairs, a used mahogany desk, and a broken commode. But it's the décor that is the most interesting. I exchange a look with Henri, who is having trouble concealing his shock.

Robespierre has papered the walls with every award he has ever received and any honor he has ever been given. Letters, keys, ribbons, cockades—even a dried laurel wreath he wore on the day the Constitution was signed—it is all here. Some of the awards, I am astonished to see, date back to his childhood and are signed by the headmaster who officiated at Camille's wedding. Robespierre is thirty-four years old! What sort of troubled ego needs to see these affirmations daily?

He unfolds the letter, and we wait while he reads. When he is finished, there are tears in his eyes. "This came from Lucile herself?" he questions.

"She wrote it while I was watching," I tell him. "She would not let me out of the house without promising that I would take it to you."

He nods sagely, pushing the glasses back on his nose. "I must go to see my godson," he says. "I must go to see him right now."

Whatever Lucile has written has moved him to forgiveness. He follows us down the stairs, and when we part company in the streets, Henri stares at me.

"I know," I say.

"What sort of man turns his room into a shrine to himself?"

"The kind of man who is terribly insecure," I tell him. Then I add darkly, "And this is who the revolutionaries believe will deliver them from tyranny."

Chapter 46

July 25—August 14, 1792

Can you watch, without shuddering in horror
As crime unfurls its banners
Of Carnage and Terror?

—excerpt from the song "The Alarm of the People"

At first, it is hard to hear what the newsboys are screaming. Then Yachin dashes inside and tells us, "The Duke of Brunswick has issued an ultimatum! Either the monarchy is reinstated or the Austro-Prussian armies are going to march on Paris and treat its citizens with unforgettable vengeance."

"Unforgettable vengeance?" I stand behind the desk. "That's what he said?"

"Those were his exact words."

"I want you to go home. When the rest of the city hears about this, there will be mobs looting the Palais-Royal, breaking into every shop that carries weapons. And you are an Austrian Jew."

"Our family is made up of patriots," he argues.

"The Salon will be closed for the rest of the week. Go home," I tell him.

As I predicted, thousands of *sans-culottes* tear through the Palais searching for gunpowder and muskets. The next morning, the Assembly issues every citizen in Paris his own ten-foot pike. When the

Austrians come, we are to defend ourselves by every means necessary. Cannon, sabers, pistols, knives, even fire and oil if that is all we have.

It is a grim time. There is talk of shutting down the ports, and no one is allowed out of the city without a passport and proof that they are not fleeing to join the émigrés.

Over a Sunday dinner to which the entire family except Edmund has come, Johann confides that Lafayette has drawn up a plan to rescue the royal family. "But the queen refuses to put her life in Lafayette's hands a second time. She does not wish to be indebted to him any more than she is."

"That kind of pride will be the end of her," my mother warns.

"What about the king?" Henri asks.

"Lafayette's plan calls for four companies of Swiss Guards to take them out of Paris, whatever the cost to the Guard and to the people."

"There are no better soldiers in France," Wolfgang says. "Perhaps in all of Europe. A few companies could ride them to safety in two days."

But the king is concerned about the welfare of his people, and the queen is concerned about how it would all appear. So no action is taken.

ON THE EIGHTH of August, Robespierre nearly convinces the Legislative Assembly to arrest Lafayette as a traitor to France. The vote is taken and only narrowly defeated, and when word reaches the American war hero on the front, he flees to Liège.

On the tenth, Henri and I sit together on his steps, watching the stars at two in the morning. I never knew that the city could be so quiet. Perhaps in the Palais-Royal there are cafés open and coffee being served, but with the theaters shut down, the Boulevard du Temple is silent. A rat scurries along the cobblestones, sniffing for garbage left behind by the fish sellers, but the street has already been picked clean by hungry children.

"Lafayette was a rallying point for the soldiers. If he is fleeing to Liège, what will stop the rest of our army from following?" I ask.

"The Assembly hasn't thought of this. They are listening to Robespierre and taking advice from Camille and Danton. *Danton,*" he repeats, and I think of the model in our most popular tableau featuring the heavy-browed assemblyman. "What do these lawyers know about war? They're simply going after anyone who believes in a monarchy now."

I am about to reply when the sound of a church bell drowns out my voice. The two o'clock hour has already been rung. Why are there bells? "My God," I say, as I realize what's happening. "They are sounding the tocsin!" Have the foreign armies arrived? Are we to be invaded?

We open the door to Henri's house, and Jacques is hurrying down the stairs. By the time we enter our Salon, my mother and Curtius are already downstairs. Curtius is half-dressed in his captain's uniform, and the four of us stand in fearful silence as he slips on his boots and calls for his belt. "If I don't return, I want you to keep this door locked and the curtains closed. Find our muskets and take out every weapon."

My mother embraces him once, and then he is gone. We lock the door, and outside the only sound is the constant ringing of the bells. Jacques and Henri have found and loaded our muskets. We stand frozen for at least twenty minutes. Then there is a pounding at the door. Henri takes up a musket and shouts, "Who is it?"

"Curtius!"

My mother opens the door, and my uncle hurries back inside. He has brought Wolfgang, Michael, and Abrielle. Their faces are pale. Whatever it is, it cannot be good news. "They have stormed the Tuileries," Curtius says gravely, "and the monarchy has fallen."

Jacques, who is surprised by very little, asks, "And the Imperial army—"

"Is not here. This is chaos of a different kind," my uncle replies. "Members of the Jacobin Club gave the signal this morning at the Hôtel de Ville, and thousands answered the call. The mobs marched on the Tuileries, and the palace has fallen."

Wolfgang presses his lips together, as if he's afraid of what he is about to say. Then he tells my mother, "The Swiss Guards are waging battle as we speak."

I hurry to my mother's side and help her into the nearest chair. The ringing of the bells has not stopped, and Wolfgang's son begins to cry. His ears must be traumatized by the sound, and Abrielle bounces him on her hip. "Shhh," she coos into Michael's ear. We hear a heavy pounding on the door. This time, it is Curtius who answers it.

"Are you Captain Philippe Curtius?" a man's voice asks.

Next to me, Abrielle sucks in her breath. "Papa."

The baron sees her and steps inside. "Abrielle!" He looks down at the child in her arms, and the emotion is too much for him. He blinks rapidly. "Is this . . . is this my grandson?" he asks. His voice breaks with emotion, and Abrielle begins to cry.

"Yes. This is Michael Louis."

The baron holds out his arms to him, but Michael only cries louder in fear.

"He is afraid," Abrielle says. "The ringing of the bells—"

"Of course." The words remind the baron of why he's come. He looks around at the eight of us in the dimly lit room, and when he finds Wolfgang's face in the candlelight, he says, "You must come with me."

My mother stands. "Wolfgang is not going anywhere!"

"Madame, the mobs are massacring every Swiss Guard they find." My mother covers her mouth in shock. "Inside the palace or outside. I am offering him a chance at escape. To London. Your entire family may come." He looks to his daughter and grandson. "You are my heir," he says. "And someday, Michael Louis will be a baron as well."

"They have banished all titles," Abrielle says. Her cheeks are wet with tears.

"Not in England. There is a boat waiting for us. Those of you who wish to come will have to leave everything behind."

"I cannot leave," Curtius says. "My life is here. But Wolfgang, you must go—"

"I am a National Guardsman!"

"But you were once a Swiss Guard," the baron warns.

"What about Johann and Edmund?" Wolfgang asks.

The baron shakes his head. "I don't know. The royal family has taken shelter with the Assembly in the Manège. The king left no orders, so the Guards are defending the walls of the palace. But there are twenty thousand armed men."

Abrielle whispers, "How did you escape?"

"I was in the Manège drafting a petition." He closes his eyes briefly, and I can see how much this pains him. These are his men, and tonight he has had to choose between family and duty. "If any of our brothers make it out alive, it will be because they have dressed like *sans-culottes* and fled."

No one in the Salon says a word. Surely God will watch over Edmund and Johann. They are good men. He will not take them from us now.

"When does the boat leave?" Wolfgang asks.

"In an hour. The queen's dressmaker is to sail with us—"

"Rose Bertin?" I confirm.

The baron nods. "She has left the keys to her shop with an assistant. Many of the Jews are fleeing as well. The mobs are burning their houses."

"*Yachin.*" My mother clutches the rosary around her neck and whispers a prayer. There will be a great deal of praying tonight.

"I thought they closed the ports," Henri says.

"We are on a ship carrying arms supposedly bound for Le Havre," the baron explains.

My uncle looks at me. "Marie, go."

"And leave you?" I panic. "And leave Maman?"

"You and Henri can begin a new life."

"And when all of this is over," Henri says, "we can return."

But who knows when all of this will end? I think of the Salon. Of all of our hard work. And then I think of Maman left alone with only wax figures for company. "No . . . I . . . I cannot."

"Marie—"

"Henri, I cannot! Not without my family."

"Not without your family, or not without your models?" he asks cruelly. "Wolfgang is leaving—"

"And don't you think that is enough for one family? If you want to go . . ."

Everyone is weeping. Who knows if any of us shall ever see Wolfgang or Abrielle again? My mother is caressing Michael's hair, and I know that she is memorizing his feel, his smell. What will he look like when he is five? Seven? Even ten years old. I should have taken the time to sculpt him, I realize. I should have made a mask on one of those Sundays when he came to visit. Except I was too busy sculpting foolish men like Marat and Camille.

I cannot bear to say farewell to my brother. Of all my siblings, we have always been the closest. He takes my hand and squeezes it forcefully. "We have to," he says.

I am crying. "I know." They will come for him.

Abrielle embraces me good-bye; then the four of them slip into the darkness. When the door closes, my mother bends double with grief and cries.

THE ARTIST JACQUES-LOUIS David is the one who brings us the news. He is ashen-faced and has come to find out whether the Boulevard will now be closed, like the Opéra Royal and the theaters. We have been up all night. None of us have had any sleep. Then Jacques asks if my mother would like to leave the room. She is strong, she promises. There isn't anything she can't hear. But when we learn that nearly every member of the Swiss Guard has been killed, she faints. Curtius springs from his chair, and Jacques rushes to find alcohol. She is taken upstairs and laid on the couch, but I do not move. I cannot move. I stare at Jacques-Louis and am sure I heard wrong.

"It was the king's fault," he says, desperate to explain. "He fled the palace without leaving any orders for the Swiss. So when the mobs came, they defended the Tuileries."

"What?" Henri demands. "Without anyone inside? Without the royal family?"

"They had no other orders," Jacques-Louis says. "And they were nine hundred against twenty thousand. They tried to surrender, but the mobs wanted blood."

"Just tell us how many are dead!" I shout.

Jacques-Louis averts his eyes. "Seven hundred Swiss, and at least three hundred commoners. I am sorry, Marie."

I will not faint. I will not fall into a swoon. "Where are their bodies?" I demand.

"Marie," Jacques-Louis begins. "You do not want to—"

"Yes, I do! Where are the bodies?"

The painter looks at Henri, as if it is for him to decide.

"We must find them," Henri affirms.

"They are in the courtyard of the Tuileries. But I warn you . . . they have been mutilated. And no one who can be recognized as family must touch them. If you send Curtius, they will murder him where he stands."

I close my eyes. "Then I will go."

Henri takes his pistol from the *caissier*'s desk. "I will come with you."

Like a pair of butchers, we take a wheelbarrow and blankets. We travel through the back alleys to avoid being seen, but there is no one in the streets and the city is silent. It is the longest journey I have ever made. Henri takes the wheelbarrow from me, and I press my hand against my stomach and inhale. Breathe. All I must do is breathe. It is only midmorning, but the air is so humid that even in the shadows of the buildings I am perspiring. Perhaps we will find my brothers alive. Perhaps Jacques-Louis is exaggerating.

But when we reach the courtyard of the Tuileries, Henri puts a steadying hand on my elbow. "God have mercy," he whispers.

It is a scene from a battlefield. Corpses litter the ground from the gates to the palace, naked, mutilated, in some cases hacked into multiple pieces. Not a single body has been left with its clothes. These men, the finest soldiers in France, have been given worse deaths than any criminal in our Cavern of Great Thieves. I stop at the gates and hold on to the posts.

"Let me go," Henri says. His shoulders are squared and pulled back. He is ready to do battle, but I cannot burden him with the task of picking through the corpses alone.

"No." I must simply catch my breath. "Wait." In a moment I will be well. But the stench of the rotting bodies overwhelms me, and I bend low. Henri rushes to hold back my hair. I am sick three times, and when there is nothing left to heave, I gasp at the air.

"There is no reason you should have to come with me."

"I can do this." I stand. "I *have* to do this."

"Why are you so stubborn?"

"Because they are my brothers!" And even if I must walk among these corpses like the Grim Reaper harvesting death, I will do it.

This time, Henri does not argue with me. We enter the courtyard, and I cover my mouth and nose with my fichu. Dozens of bodies have been piled, one on top of the other, and set ablaze. The scent of burning flesh is suffocating. But the soldiers whose corpses have escaped the flames are worse to see. There are men whose genitals have been removed, and bodies that have been eviscerated with the organs left to rot in the blazing sun. There is nowhere you can turn without seeing blood. It has seeped into the ground like water, staining the cobblestones and attracting flies, which have gathered like black clouds over the corpses. Henri rolls the wheelbarrow through this field of death. There are others among us with wagons and carts. But no one speaks. The only sound in the courtyard is the screaming of the birds. We are denying them their meals, and once we are gone, they will set to work.

I am not the one who finds Johann. It is Henri. But before I can see what they have done to him, he covers my brother's body with a blanket, and he pushes my hand away when I move to pull it back. "It is nothing you want to see."

"I *have* to know."

"There are some things you must simply trust!" he says forcefully.

The other mourners in the courtyard turn to stare at us, and I nod. I am too numb to fight. Too numb to cry. We move through the Tuileries Gardens, where children used to giggle beside the marble fountains. The towering statues are splattered with blood where soldiers clambered to escape, only to be struck down with halberds and pikes. And on the pretty gravel roads, even chambermaids and cooks have been slaughtered by the mobs. I wonder if I will remember their faces when I close my eyes. Brown-eyed maids, square-jawed ushers, heavily jowled cooks . . .

It takes hours to view all the unburned corpses. One young soldier has not been stripped. He has been left to lie in his shredded Swiss uniform, a pool of blood like a halo around his head. The sun reflects from his gilded epaulets, and this is the image I carry with me when we return my brother's body to the Boulevard du Temple. Although I am conscious of my uncle's sorrow, of my mother's hysteria, and of Henri's announcement that Edmund could not be found, it all passes as if it were a dream.

THERE IS A funeral the next morning. Johann is buried quietly in the Madeleine Cemetery, and our neighbors are told that Wolfgang and Abrielle have perished with him. A cross is provided for Edmund, but since there is no body, no services can be held. Curtius tells me that Marat and the giant Danton were behind this. That if not for their influence, the massacre of the Swiss Guards would never have happened.

I storm through the Salon and rip their figures to pieces in a rage. I would burn them in the courtyard if I thought it would not attract the attention of the Assembly. At night, Henri is strong for us both. I sleep in his chamber, where there are no images to haunt me, and in the morning, I return to the Salon to comfort my mother in her weeping. Then, as though our family has not suffered enough, Curtius tells me about Yachin.

I am sitting in the workshop when my uncle appears and closes the door. He sits on a stool across from me, and my grip tightens around my cup of coffee. In the two days since the massacre, there has been no word from Yachin or his family. "Marie," he begins, and I shake my head. His eyes are filled with tears, and I will him not to say it.

"No," I whisper.

Curtius reaches out to take my hand. "I am sorry."

"No!" I cry. It is too much to bear. "How—"

He tells me how the mobs sought out foreigners, looting their homes and then burning them down. "They tried to board a ship," he tells me, "possibly the same ship that Wolfgang took. They were caught at the port and killed."

"But his siblings," I protest. "They would not have killed children."

Curtius's face is grim. "They have been buried at Petit Vances." A Jewish burial ground.

So this is anarchy. This is life without order or laws, the way our ancestors lived it before chieftains and kings. It is impossible to believe that everyone—Johann, Edmund, Yachin and his entire innocent family—is gone. Paris has become a city of ghosts, and everything I see reminds me of them. I sit at the window of the Salon and remember the France of only three years ago. Philip Astley's circus was entertaining the king, and Rose Bertin's shop sold powdered *poufs* to women draped in diamonds and ermine cloaks. I can hear Yachin telling passersby that they must come to see the queen, that there is not a better likeness anywhere in France.

I will never hear his voice again.

Three days after Johann's funeral, his widow and their seven-year-old son, Paschal, come to live with us. They will stay in the room that Wolfgang and Abrielle once occupied. When I tell this to Henri, my voice breaks. "Will you take me to your laboratory?" I ask him. "I want to be in a place where everything makes sense." Where there are rules, and it is impossible for life to defy them.

He shows me what he is working on. A great planisphere clock with five circular plates.

"What do they all do?" I ask him.

"Guess," he challenges me.

I study the four smaller plates first. "This one is for the days of the week." That is easy. "And this one is for the phases of the moon." But the other two . . .

"A tidal calendar for our northern ports," Henri says. "And the phases of Jupiter's Io."

"You can't possibly know the phases of another planet's moon."

"They're right here. But the largest plate is the most interesting."

I look at the golden disk in the center of the clock. There are so many rings and dials. "The outer ring tells the time," I say, "and the smaller ring indicates the months and the signs of the zodiac. But that is all I can make out."

He points to various abbreviations. "For telling time in cities all across the world."

There is London, Rome, Boston, and a place I have never heard of named La Californie. It is unbelievable. "*You* should be teaching at the Académie," I tell him.

He smiles. "I prefer the laboratory."

So while the *sans-culottes* are tearing down a kingdom, Henri is studying a distant moon.

Chapter 47

August 28, 1792

Five or six hundred heads cut off [would assure] your repose, freedom, and happiness.

—Jean-Paul Marat

In losing three brothers, I have gained a sister. Although Isabel has greater cause than any of us to abandon herself to despair, she is the one who washes the dishes and cooks the food when my mother is too ill with sorrow to get up. It is Isabel who marches into my mother's room and demands that she leave her bed for good—that this is what Johann would want her to do now that several weeks have passed. And it is Isabel who insists that the time has come to reopen the Salon.

She sits across from me in the workshop, sorting glass eyes by color while I finish the model of Rochambeau. From the moment she arrived, she has kept herself busy. Cooking, cleaning, sorting, arranging, playing with Paschal. I suspect this comes from not wanting time to think. "It is very kind of you to help my mother the way you do," I tell her.

She looks up at me, and every emotion registers on her face. I imagine the tableau I would create of her. *The Butcher's Daughter*, I'd call it. And people would recognize simply from the width of her mouth and the set of her eyes that she is strong, earnest, a hard worker. "It is the least I can do," she says. "Your mother and Curtius have been kind to take us in."

I put down my paintbrush. "Of course. You are family."

"Not all families are as generous," she remarks. "So when do you reopen the Salon?"

"When men like Marat and Danton are no longer in power. My brother warned me," I tell her. "Edmund said that we would be planting the seeds of anarchy."

"Marie, you cannot blame yourself."

"We were part of it!"

"Then every citizen who ever put on a tricolor cockade was part of it. This is your business. My father butchered lambs for a living. Some were our pets. But that was his work."

I think of the royal family, imprisoned now in the medieval fortress known as the Temple, and wonder if Madame Élisabeth has remained so resilient. Everyone who was found with them in the Tuileries that night was sent to La Force prison, including the beautiful Princesse de Lamballe. How do you live knowing you have caused other people's misery?

"You must reopen the Salon," Isabel says. "Johann always believed in this. He believed in you. *My little sister* was all he would talk about." I search her face for the lie. "It's true. When he wasn't talking about Paschal or the Swiss, he was talking about you. Whatever happened in that courtyard, Marie, he died a happy man."

She didn't see the corpses. She doesn't understand . . .

"I know that they were slaughtered," she whispers. "But I've seen animals die, and death is quick. What is important is the happiness that came before it."

THAT EVENING, I speak with my mother and Curtius in the kitchen. Though it's Tuesday night, there will be no salon. I doubt there will ever be gatherings in our house again. I join them at the small table where my mother would normally be preparing food for our guests. Instead, she and Curtius are entertaining Paschal.

"Marie!" my nephew exclaims. He is a lovely child, with dark curls and expressive eyes.

"What do you have here, Paschal? Hot chocolate?"

"Do you want some?" he asks.

"No, thank you," I say. "But perhaps you can go and find your mother. Tell her we will be having coffee soon." Paschal slips out the door. I turn to my mother. "Isabel believes we should reopen the Salon."

"I don't have the time for that right now. Paschal—"

"Can sit with you at the *caissier*'s desk. Maman, Johann and Edmund are dead. But two of your children are still alive, and you have two grandchildren, one of whom is here. I understand that you are still grieving. But we will always be grieving. So what do we do? Let the rest of our lives turn to dust because evil exists and has stolen something from us?" Her lower lip trembles, but I continue. "What do you wish to teach Paschal?" I ask her. "Strength or weakness? I know what you taught me, and it was always strength."

"Anna," Curtius begins, "Marie is right."

There are tears in her eyes, but there is also resolve.

Though it is not a joyful event, we reopen the Salon with new figures of the generals Luckner and Rochambeau, and Paris has not forgotten us. The lines are as long as they have always been, filled with jostling children and *sans-culottes*. My mother and Isabel sit at the *caissier*'s desk with an excited Paschal between them. I show Isabel the books and how to write a ticket. "Is it always like this?" she asks me. She is impressed. "No wonder . . ."

No wonder Johann was so proud.

I am expecting the model of Rochambeau to be the greatest draw. I hear women in line wondering aloud what he'll look like, and men guessing that he will be tall, as all generals ought to be. But it's the model of Lafayette that causes the greatest stir. It begins with one man remarking loudly that a traitor like Lafayette should not be displayed.

Then a group of *sans-culottes* begin shouting to the other patrons to come and see.

"It's true. A model of Lafayette!" I hear someone cry.

"Why would they display an enemy of the *patrie*?"

"Because they speak German, just like the queen!"

I rise from the desk and hurry into the workshop, where Curtius is modeling soldiers. "They are about to riot in the Salon," I cry, "over the model of Lafayette!"

He follows me out the door, and the crowd around Lafayette's figure has grown even larger. Women are tearing at his clothes, and a man has taken out his dagger to scratch at the waxen face. My mother and Isabel are at the door, trying to keep people from pushing inside. In a moment, it will be a stampede.

"I am responsible for this model!" Curtius shouts, but no one can hear him. He stands on the desk in *Jefferson's Study,* where the figure of Lafayette is conferring with the ambassador. "I am responsible for this model!" he shouts again, and this time the angry patrons stop to listen. "And as its creator," he lies . . .

I hold my breath. As its creator what?

"I sentence Lafayette to the guillotine!"

It is madness. Shouting, applauding, whooping madness. The men pick up the figure of Lafayette and follow Curtius to the window, where he drags his wooden replica of the guillotine onto the street. Outside, the crowds start singing *"La Marseillaise,"* and the women begin waving their cockades in the air.

Henri steps from the door of his exhibition and comes to stand at my side. "More publicity?" he asks.

"No," I whisper, sick with dread. "It was this or they would have killed us."

He studies my face to see if I am jesting. Then I take his hand and close my eyes.

Chapter 48

August 29, 1792—September 2, 1792

The vessel of the Revolution can arrive in port only on a sea reddened with torrents of blood.

—Louis Antoine de Saint-Just, revolutionary and lawyer

"Marie." Someone is shaking my shoulder. "Marie, wake up. It's already eight."

I open my eyes and see Henri's face in the fresh morning light. His long hair curls around his naked shoulders, and his chest is covered with a blanket.

I rush from the bed, and the two of us find our clothes. I watch in the mirror as Henri pulls on a pair of striped brown trousers. Every showman in Paris is now a *sans-culotte.* The only benefit that I can see is that it's easier to dress. He waits while I slip on a white chemise gown and helps to tie the blue ribbon in the back. Then he sits on the bed. "Marie," he begins, and I can hear from his voice that this will not be light conversation. "You were almost killed yesterday."

I come here to escape the world, not be reminded about it.

"We had the chance to escape. And now the chance has come again. A chemist has offered Jacques a passage to London on a ship that's supposedly bound for Rouen. He isn't going. But I am. I want you to come with me. The mobs have taken your brothers. They have taken Yachin, and they will take your family if we don't escape."

For the past two weeks we have slept together as husband and wife. "Stay," I say desperately. "I will marry you. I *want* to marry you."

But Henri is firm. "Then marry me in London."

"And risk crossing the Channel?"

"Wolfgang made it safely. You have heard from him. Marie, the Austrians are coming, and when they're at the walls, what do you think this city will be like?" He stands from the bed. "Come with me."

"And do what? Be what when we get there? Beggars?"

"Showmen."

And start all over? Without a house, without a place to exhibit? "What about your laboratory?" I ask. "What about your planisphere clock?"

"It will be here. Jacques will take care of it. And if it's all destroyed, then there will be others."

"My mother and Curtius will never leave."

"Then they will have each other. As well as Isabel and Paschal. But if they stay, death is the risk they are taking. Is it one you're willing to take? There are things I still wish to accomplish in this life. I have no intention of meeting my end here. Aren't there things you still wish to do?" he presses.

I think of Johann and Edmund, who will never have the chance to pursue their dreams. "Of course. But if the ship is leaving tonight," I tell him, "there is no time to pack. No time for anything—"

"There will never be a perfect time. You can't plan this out like a tableau. Either you love me enough to leave or you don't."

I think of my family, of the Salon. "Henri, I'm sorry . . ."

There is devastation in his eyes. "Me too."

ISABEL SITS ON my bed and holds me while I weep, deep, racking, uncontrollable sobs. She pushes the hair away from my face and whispers that my uncle doesn't know what to do for me and that my mother is beside herself with grief. A small figure stands in the doorway, hesitant to come in, but Isabel beckons him forward. Paschal climbs into my lap. He puts a tiny hand on my cheek. "Be happy, *Tatie.*" Paschal calls me by the affectionate word for *aunt,* but I am afraid I may never be happy again.

"You chose this," Isabel reminds me softly. "You could have gone."

I look at her through my tears, unsure I've heard right. "Would you leave?"

"My place is with your mother. But you have an entire life ahead of you. A man who would be your husband. You chose this," she repeats.

For the rest of the morning, I stay in my chamber with Henri's letter. "When you are ready to live in London," he wrote, "come and find me. However long it takes, I will be waiting." I read the words over and over again, and when the pages are so stained with tears that the ink begins to run, I let them dry by the window and cry myself to sleep.

I am being crushed by the heat of the afternoon when a voice wakes me. "Marie?" Isabel knocks on the door. When I don't answer, she turns the knob and lets herself in. She sets a tray on the table beside me. There's a pot of coffee, and the scent fills the room. "The Prussians have taken Longwy," she says. "All the Imperial army needs to do now is cross the Marne Valley and the road to Paris is stretched out before them."

I sit up in my bed and move to stand, but Isabel holds out her hand. "Curtius is already gone. He left this morning while you were sleeping. Eat."

I look at the dishes she has prepared for me and cannot imagine ever having an appetite again. "Henri left just in time," I realize. "Another day and it might have been too late."

"If God wills it, then you will join him in London."

"But I've missed my chance." I can hear in my own voice that I am growing hysterical. "He is in a different country and may never return!"

Isabel pours a cup of coffee and hands it to me. "Try not to think like that," she suggests.

I look into her face, so steady and earnest. "Why can't I be like you?"

"A widow with a son who will never know his father?"

My God, I am selfish. She has lost her husband, the father of her child, and she is waiting on me while I mourn the loss of a man I refused to follow. I put down the coffee and take her hands. "I'm so sorry for your loss, Isabel."

"Sometimes I can hear his laughter," she whispers, sitting on the edge of my bed. "In my sleep mostly. But also if Paschal is overjoyed. So that is my duty now. To keep Johann laughing through Paschal."

I am humbled by her goodness, and I will do my duty as she has done hers. I have stayed in Paris for my family and the Salon. I must honor them both. Although my appetite is gone, I do my best with the salad. "I don't hear any noise downstairs," I worry.

"That's because the Salon is closed. Every man in Paris has gone to the Palais to volunteer. Robespierre came this morning to ask if Curtius would help Danton recruit."

"Danton?" The same man who called for the massacre of the Swiss Guards? "And he went?"

"What could he do?" she asks. "He has set up a Revolutionary Tribunal to find royalists and arrest them. Last night, they arrested eight hundred citizens. He told us they have taken all the priests who refused to swear an oath to the Constitution and locked them in the Abbey of Saint-Germain-des-Prés. There will be more arrests today. They are searching for anyone who ever served in the king's household."

My hands go cold. "Then they will come for me."

"No," she says firmly. "Robespierre believes your uncle is a patriot. He would never have asked for his help if he thought otherwise. And if your uncle is a patriot, then so are you."

"So it's guilt or innocence by association."

She can see the absurdity in this, just as I can. "It's like they're hunting witches," she says. "Anyone wearing a black-and-white cockade or using an honorary title is suspect. This evening, they are transferring the guillotine to the Place du Carrousel next to the Tuileries Palace."

"Are they going to kill everyone who has ever worked in Versailles?"

"They killed your barker's family for less."

What is she saying? "They killed him because he was fleeing."

Her eyes go wide as she realizes that I have not been told. "Oh, Marie—"

I put down my cup. "What? I will hear it anyway," I swear. "Why did they kill him?"

"You should ask your uncle."

"He is with Danton."

"Then your mother—"

"Perhaps she has not been told either," I say angrily.

"No. She was there when Robespierre . . ."

I wait for her to say it.

"When Robespierre told us that they searched Yachin's bags and found a handkerchief with the queen's initials on it."

I cover my mouth with my hands.

"They accused his family of being royalists," she says quickly. "I'm sorry, Marie. Your mother told me it was a gift. You couldn't have known . . ."

My heart is breaking. A handkerchief! The death of an entire family for a scrap of silk. My throat is burning and my eyes blur.

Isabel wraps her arms around me. "I know," she says.

THAT EVENING, THE Revolutionary Tribunal sends soldiers to our door at eleven. There are no men in the house, so I am the one who must meet them.

"Is this the residence of Captain Philippe Curtius?" a soldier asks. He has the wrinkled face and thinning hair of a man who is a grandfather many times over. "We are here on a domiciliary visit."

Is that what they are calling them? Not organized looting or raids? My mother and Isabel stand behind me. There are fifteen of them and three of us. "Of course," I say politely. "Would you like to come in?"

They fill the Salon de Cire with their boots and exclamations of surprise. These men who were once cabinetmakers and grocers now have the right to open private cupboards and sift through chests of clothes. "What is this place?" a young soldier asks.

His friend slaps his arm. "This is the Salon de Cire. Robespierre comes here."

"Oh." Now there is a new tone of respect. They will not be taking whatever they want.

"We have come here for weapons," the older soldier explains.

"We have two muskets and my uncle's pistol," I tell them honestly.

"And is it true that Robespierre visits this place?"

"He has been many times. I should like to think he considers us good friends."

"Then there is nothing we need from you," the old soldier says. He takes a last look around, and I know if he had more time he would want to stay. But there are houses to raid and women to defile. "A good night to you, Citizeness."

As soon as they are gone, I lock the door. My hands are shaking.

WE DO NOT reopen the Salon. The mood in the city is too tense, and with every knock on our door I expect to see soldiers from the Revolutionary Tribunal coming to arrest us. Neighbors ask if we have had any news. But we've heard nothing except what Curtius told us when he returned. The men volunteering in the Palais-Royal are worried that if they are sent to war, there will be no one to guard the many thousands of prisoners, and the criminals will break free to do with Paris's women and children as they please.

"That is the concern?" Jacques Charles asks.

It is painful for me to see him, but we do not discuss Henri and he does not mention my decision to stay behind. After all, he has chosen to remain here, too, taking his chances with war rather than abandon everything he has built over a lifetime. I find him a chair, and he joins us at our empty *caissier*'s desk. "Yes. They are more afraid of their own people than of the invading army," I reply.

"I blame that on Marat and his good friend Fabre d'Églantine." Jacques pushes a copy of the *Compte Rendu au Peuple Souverain* across the desk at me, then wipes his forehead with a handkerchief. The afternoon heat is unbearable. Every day this summer it has been worse.

"Translate please," my mother says, and I read d'Églantine's words for her in German:

> Once more, citizens, to arms! May all France bristle with pikes, bayonets, cannon, and daggers so that everyone shall be a soldier; let us clear the ranks of these vile slaves of tyranny. In the towns let the blood of traitors be the first to be spilled . . . so that in advancing to meet the common enemy, we leave nothing behind to disquiet us.

Jacques hands me a placard. "Marat has stopped publishing his *L'Ami du Peuple* and has begun posting these." It is a single paper designed to look like an official proclamation. Now, he can post his hateful words on every lamppost in the city.

I read it and look up in horror. "He is encouraging citizens to go to the Abbey of Saint-Germain and run a sword through the priests." My mother crosses herself, and I do not tell her what else it says. Marat is asking citizens to kill not only men of God but the hundred and fifty Swiss officers who survived the tenth of August as well.

My mother turns over Marat's placard. On the back, he has published the names of fifty prisoners considered dangerous enemies of the *patrie.* "A death list," she whispers.

For the first time in many days, I think of Madame Élisabeth and the rest of the royal family in the Temple. What will Marat scream for the mobs to do if the Imperial army makes its way to Paris?

That evening, I wait up in the salon for Curtius to come home. I can hear his boots on the stairs, his breathing as he makes his way to the landing, then his exclamation of surprise as he sees the glow of a candle burning. "Marie?" he calls. He peers around the door, and I can see how tired he is. There are circles beneath his eyes, and his lids are heavy. He is fifty-five, an age when most men are retired and enjoying their grandchildren. He takes a seat across from me at the table, and I pour him a cup of tea. "I thought you might need this."

He takes a long sip and sighs. "Couldn't sleep?"

"I was wondering what's going to happen with the royal family," I admit.

He puts down his cup. "I know you have grown attached to Madame Élisabeth. But if the Austrians arrive, the Tribunal doesn't plan to hold them as hostages."

"So is that who is controlling this country now? The Tribunal?"

"Or the Jacobins. Or the Assembly. Or possibly Danton and the Minister of the Interior. No one knows. Antoine Santerre certainly doesn't, and he has been made the new Commander in Chief of the National Guard." Curtius makes a face. "Apparently, he's a brewer."

This is a world turned upside down. They have given the keys of the palace to its servants, and now we all look to them to make things right. "And the king? Will he have power again?"

"Not if the Assembly can help it. And certainly not if they should see what the Empress of Russia has written in response to these events." He begins to quote Catherine the Great, "Kings ought to go their own way without worrying about the cries of the people, as the moon goes on its course without being stopped by the cries of dogs."

"That's the kind of talk that began this Revolution!"

Curtius finishes his tea. "Exactly. And this dog is tired, Marie. You should find some sleep as well. Perhaps we'll reopen the Salon tomorrow."

Chapter 49

September 2, 1792

Terror is the order of the day.

—Anonymous

But there is no reopening the Salon. There are riots in the Palais-Royal demanding that more soldiers be sent to guard the prisons, and when Robespierre arrives, fidgeting with his glasses and in search of my uncle, I tell him, "He is recruiting volunteers."

"But I need him here!" Robespierre exclaims. He looks past me to the *caissier*'s desk, where Isabel is teaching Paschal how to write tickets.

"Would you like to come inside?" I ask. "My mother is making lunch."

"There's no chance I can eat," he replies. But he comes inside and begins to pace.

Isabel exchanges a look with me, and I shake my head. Robespierre is to be humored. If he wishes to pace, we must let him. "Is there something I can help you with instead?" I ask.

"It's going to be a massacre! Curtius—"

My uncle bursts through the door as if summoned by the heavens. "They are killing the priests in the Abbey of Saint-Germain-des-Prés!" He looks at Robespierre. "What are you going to do? The mobs are moving from prison to prison!"

"What are *you* going to do?" Robespierre cries. "You are the National Guard." He looks as though he may faint. "We must stop this." Now he is tearing at his cravat. "What can the National Guard do?"

"Men like Danton and Marat have called for an uprising, and now they have it." My uncle is brutally honest. "We are a group of men with muskets and pistols and no real leadership. We can do nothing to stop this!"

Isabel sends Paschal to his room, and my mother appears with sauerkraut and cold beef. But no one has the stomach to eat.

"I can't go outside," Robespierre worries. He begins to pace again. "Find out what is happening," he begs. "See if they will listen to you!"

For two hours after Curtius leaves, we watch Robespierre move back and forth. One moment he is hopeful, shouting, "We will win this war and liberty will prevail!" The next moment he is railing against the queen and her Austrian allies. Then there is a rumbling in the distance, and Robespierre stops pacing.

It is the sound of a mob moving down the Boulevard du Temple.

"Go upstairs and join Paschal," I tell Isabel. She is gone before the pounding on the door begins.

"Don't open it!" Robespierre exclaims. "They could be assassins." The pounding continues, and sweat begins to glisten on his forehead. I go to the window and open the curtain. *"In the name of liberty,"* someone shouts, *"open the door!"*

"Do it," my mother says in German, "or they will beat it down!"

"What is she saying?" Robespierre demands. He is practically gasping for air.

"That we must let them inside."

His eyes go wide, and he pats down his wig.

"You should sit," I tell him, and he takes a chair at the *caissier*'s desk. I open the door and steel myself for whatever horror they have brought for me. A young man separates himself from the mob and holds up a head for everyone to see. *Oh, God.* I stagger backward.

"I am Jean Nicholas, and I have come with the head of the Princesse de Lamballe!"

Immediately, I recoil. The queen's dearest friend, her closest confidante. When everyone else fled from the palace, the Princesse de Lamballe remained. Robespierre rushes to the door, and the crowds cheer. "Is that her?" he asks swiftly.

I don't want to look. But I must. I would know her face anywhere. The paleness of her skin, the blue of her eyes, the symmetry of her features. She was the envy of every woman at court. They have taken her head and speared it on a pike. The mobs begin to laugh as Jean lifts the pike in the air so that her curls bob up and down. Then he grabs the crown of the princesse's hair and pulls it from the pole.

"Citizeness Grosholtz." He thrusts the head at me. "Will you do us the honor of a mask?"

"Where did this come from?" Robespierre demands.

"La Force prison," Jean Nicholas says loudly. He is obviously the leader of this mob, for they grow silent to listen to him speak. "Today, we have done a great service to the *patrie* by ridding Paris of its traitorous priests and whores!"

"I cannot watch this." Robespierre flees back into the house, and I am left alone with the mob. Jean Nicholas is still holding out the head. He will kill me if I refuse it. I think of Isabel's words. I have chosen this, and now I must do my duty. I hold out my hands and can feel the presence of my mother behind me. "I will get the plaster," she whispers.

I take the head, and my stomach clenches. It smells of powder and blood. Her eyes are open, fixed on whatever horror was in front of her when she was murdered. And her neck—her long, elegant neck—has been severed as if with an ax. The guillotine's cut is swift and clean. This . . . this is a butcher's work. I sit on the steps. There is a restlessness in the crowd. My mother appears, and they watch her tie my apron. Now there is excitement. I am a performer dancing with death for their pleasure. *Here, let me entertain you.* I press the plaster against the princesse's face. I expect her to cry out and resist. But there is nothing left of her personality. I wonder what they have done with her body.

"Aren't you interested in how this came to be?" Jean asks.

I know what is best for me, and so I lie. "Of course. Did you raid each of the prisons?"

"We began at the Abbey of Saint-Germain-des-Prés," he boasts, "where three hundred priests were sent back to God." The mob laughs, and I concentrate on the princesse. The dead have fewer horrors for me now than the living. "Then we went on to La Salpêtrière and Bicêtre." Bicêtre is a prison for children and religious men. "When our work there was done, we discovered the Princesse de Lamballe in La Force."

I remove the plaster, and my mother helps me pour beeswax into the hardened mold. *I will not hear him. If I ignore him, it will all go away.*

"Her last words were 'God save the queen!' even as they were tearing off her clothes." He laughs. He is a madman.

"I am finished." I give him the head and the terrible death mask. He wants a blond wig and paint for her eyes. "I have a wig, but no more paint."

He searches my face, to see if I am another lying aristocrat. But he can watch me all day. I know how to command my features. "A wig will be fine," he says at last.

My mother fetches the hair we once used for Madame du Barry. Her model is hidden now, along with anyone who cannot be safely called a patriot. I fit the golden curls onto the princesse's wax head, and Jean Nicholas lifts his hat to me.

"To the Temple!" he shouts. And the mob echoes his cry.

When Curtius returns, we learn how the Princesse de Lamballe met her savage end. "They cut off her breasts and tore out her heart," he says quietly, and I am glad that Isabel and Paschal are upstairs. "But her death came swiftly compared with the prostitutes in La Force."

"Enough," Robespierre pleads. "Enough! I must go," he says weakly.

Curtius and I stare at him. These are his mobs, his country, his "liberty." This is the violence he summoned by encouraging the masses to rise up against their king. What did he think would happen? Did he imagine we would all be planting liberty trees and singing songs?

He pauses at the door. "And there is nothing the National Guard can do?" he asks Curtius.

"Many soldiers are part of the rampaging mobs. They have guns and powder, and there is nothing to stop them."

Their passions forge their fetters, I think. I remember this line from Edmund Burke's *Reflections on the Revolution in France,* and the night Henri read the pamphlet to me. I think of Henri now, walking the streets of London, and my heart aches. I can still feel the warmth of his skin against mine and smell the scent of almond oil from his hair. But I am thankful he isn't here to see this.

THE NEXT MORNING, the Assembly begins distributing free wine. "A bottle for each patriot!" We lock our doors, and Curtius does not report to the Palais-Royal. By the end of the weekend, fourteen thousand prisoners have been killed. Thousands of women and children are among them.

Chapter 50

September 21, 1792—January 17, 1793

The Nation has condemned the king who oppressed it.

—Maximilien Robespierre

We have a new government. This one is called the National Convention, and its members have sworn to defend the *patrie* and keep its citizens safe. Robespierre, Danton, Marat, and Camille have all been elected. And the Marquis de Sade, newly released from his asylum and calling himself Citizen Sade, has been made a member as well. These are the men who shall build a "New France," and on the twenty-first of September, their first act is to abolish the monarchy.

The proclamation is read on every major street corner in Paris. I am in the workshop preparing a *National Convention* tableau when Isabel shouts for me to come. Immediately, I join her at the door and listen.

"From this day forward," the crier shouts, "the king shall be known as Citizen Capet. Anyone who is interested in the day's executions can read the list here." The boy holds up a newspaper, and a few timid citizens creep forward to buy one.

"What does it mean?" Paschal whispers. We are a city of furtive glances now. The patrons who buy tickets for the Salon do so in silence. No one wishes to bring unwanted attention to themselves. The only place where you are allowed to speak openly and cheer is the Place du Carrousel, when the guillotine falls.

"It means the king is no longer a king," Isabel explains. She returns with Paschal to the *caissier*'s desk, and I can see he is confused. He takes a seat in a chair that is much too big for him and furrows his tiny brow.

"But why?" he asks.

"Because that is what the National Convention has declared," his mother says.

"And now the National Convention is king?"

"No one is king," I tell him. "Everyone is the same. Just like you and me."

"But if everyone is the same, what will the old king do?"

~

The answer comes on the eleventh of December. Instead of opening the Salon de Cire, I stand on the Boulevard and whistle for a carriage. When an empty coach arrives, our family of five step inside, and Curtius tells the driver, "The Salle du Manège." We ride most of the way in silence.

I think of the letter I've had from Wolfgang as the carriage draws closer to the crowded Manège. He, Michael, and Abrielle are living in grand style in London, with good food and all the comforts of home. He has seen Henri and found him an apartment. Every corner he turns, he is meeting another émigré. "When are you coming to us?" he wrote. "Convince Curtius and Maman and take the first opportunity that arises, Marie. It will only get worse."

I stare out the carriage window at the overcast skies. The worst has already come. Our army has had some success in Valmy, and the Prussians have retreated, leaving the Austrians to fight this war alone. The National Convention has declared this victory. "You see," Marat wrote on his most recent placard, "defeat is not in our destiny!" Flush with success, the National Convention has put the king on trial. In the history of France, no king has ever been tried for crimes against liberty.

"This is a circus," Curtius says critically as we enter the Salle du Manège. There are thousands of people, all pushing and talking and eager to see a king who's not a king. We find seats in the public gallery on the second floor. I search below us for any sign of Madame Élisabeth and the rest of the royal family. "They won't be here," Curtius says. "They were not allowed to come."

So every commoner in France may watch while the king argues for his life, but not his wife and children. "Do you know who the ki—who Louis Capet's lawyer will be?" I ask.

"I heard it is a man named Tronchet," my uncle says. "He was Capet's second choice."

"The first didn't want to defend him," I guess.

"Only two citizens volunteered their services. A lawyer named Malesherbes and the actress Olympe de Gouges. She wrote the *Declaration of the Rights of Woman.* She might have been one to include in the Salon de Cire," my uncle says sadly, "if she had not put her neck beneath the blade like that."

A bell begins to ring, and an expectant hush settles over the crowd; I see that Paschal has taken his mother's hand.

A deep voice announces, "Citizen Louis Capet," and the king is led through a pair of double doors into the middle of the room. The sound of rustling fabric echoes in the hall as thousands of bodies shift to get a better view. He is dressed in green, from his embroidered *culottes* to his long silk coat. There is no chair provided for him until the president of the Convention decides he may be seated. And this is how the trial unfolds. With a hundred little slights to a man who never chose his birth.

"This is all a show," my mother says. "They will find him guilty, and the only question is what his punishment will be. I will not go back." She has changed since losing Johann and Edmund. She is not as strong as she used to be.

So it is Curtius and Isabel who join me in the Salle du Manège, day after day, as the lawyers present their cases to the members of the National Convention. *Louis Capet on Trial* is our first tableau, then we add Bertrand Barère, since he is the president and is arguing the case against the king. Curtius prints an excerpt of his final speech on a sign, including the words, "The tree of liberty grows only when watered by the blood of tyrants!" I wince when I see it, but this is the news.

~

THE TRIAL IS over on the fifteenth of January, and though we try to convince my mother to come to hear the verdict, she firmly refuses. "History will remember this," she says. "I do not need to."

The crowds are overwhelming. But on this day, they are silent. The driving rain echoes on the roof, and the candles sputter each time the doors are opened. They have accused the king of tyranny, and we listen as they read out all thirty-two charges for the last time. Then the voting begins. First, they must decide whether the king is guilty. If so, they must determine what the punishment will be. Bertrand Barère stands before the Convention and announces, "As proposed by Marat, this will be an oral vote."

There is a murmuring in the audience. Now, anyone who dares to vote for the king's innocence will be exposed as a traitor. More than seven hundred deputies approach the bar, and each man announces his verdict. By the afternoon, every deputy has declared Citizen Louis Capet guilty.

"The vote on punishment will now begin." Barère takes his seat at the head of the Convention, where the king should be. Citizen Capet is not here today. He will never be seated in a place of power again, and everyone in this hall is conscious that they are witnessing history.

"They will banish him," I whisper to Isabel. "They cannot vote for death."

But deputy by deputy I am proven wrong. It is the Duc d'Orléans, the king's own cousin, who casts one of the final votes against him. The Salle du Manège is completely silent. Then the president stands and announces, "Citizen Louis Capet has been found guilty of the charges leveled against him, and for these crimes his punishment shall be death."

Chapter 51

January 20–21, 1793

You have to punish not only the traitors, but even those who are indifferent; you have to punish whoever is passive in the republic, and who does nothing for it.

—Louis Antoine de Saint-Just, revolutionary and lawyer

As I am about to lock the doors of the Salon de Cire, three men emerge from the darkness of the Boulevard. I recognize the middle figure at once. No one else wears powdered wigs or *culottes* on this street. But the other two are unfamiliar to me. "Robespierre," I say.

"Marie." He nods curtly. "These are my guards. May we come in?"

I open the door. It is dark inside, since I have snuffed out the candles. I call for my mother to bring us a lantern, and we wait in the hall's shadows until light appears.

"Thank you, Maman."

"Robespierre," she exclaims, then stares at the strangers.

"His bodyguards," I say in German. She is wise enough not to make any kind of remark. I turn to Robespierre. "Would you like to come upstairs?"

He looks nervous. His eyes are searching the shadows. "Who—who is that?" he cries. His guards withdraw their pistols, and Isabel shouts, "It's me!"

"That's my sister-in-law and her *child*," I say angrily.

Robespierre looks behind him. "There are royalists who wish to kill me, Marie. They want to see me dead for voting to condemn Capet."

"But hundreds of other men voted as well."

"And *I* am the one they'll blame!" Behind his glasses, his eyes are searching. Does he think we're hiding assassins in the hall? "There are conspiracies being hatched throughout this city. Royalist conspiracies," he snaps. He has never spoken like this to me. "I have come with a request for which the National Convention is willing to pay."

I clench my hands nervously. "And what would that be?"

"We need proof," he says, and I can see that this discomforts him. "There is no way of showing the world that Capet has died unless we have evidence." He clears his throat. "We wish for you to make a mask," he says.

A death mask. So they can see every hair on his head—brows, lashes, even a day's worth of stubble. My mother has gone pale. Isabel steps forward and says, "This is too great an honor for our Salon. Perhaps the work should go to someone more deserving."

"I can think of no family more deserving than this," Robespierre replies. "The Convention will allow you to keep a copy to display in whatever way you see fit."

"That is very kind," I say. Henri would hear the sarcasm in my voice.

"And there would be others. Other *traitors*. We must have proof for our citizens that these criminals have died. Now, is the Salon de Cire willing to help our country in this way?"

Isabel takes my hand. I look to my mother and Paschal, who are standing together like a tableau of loss and sorrow. "Maman, why don't you take Paschal upstairs?" I watch them go, then turn to Robespierre. "As always," I say quietly, "our family wishes to serve the *patrie*."

The corners of his lips turn upward. "Tomorrow, you will find Capet's head and body in the Madeleine Cemetery. He will not be buried until your arrival."

"And the other—traitors?" I ask.

"The Convention will send word the night before. The bodies will be delivered to the graveyard at nine in the evening. It would be advisable to visit before the corpses—"

"Rot?" I ask brutally.

He pushes his glasses back on his nose. "Yes."

"Models are better taken from life," I say.

"The purpose of these masks is to prove that they are *dead.* The Convention will not forget your service." He moves toward the door. "I knew we could consider you a friend," he adds gravely. "Good night."

It is only when they are gone that the tears roll down my cheeks.

"Marie!" Isabel cries and puts her arm around my shoulders. But I sit behind the *caissier*'s desk and weep. I look out at my kingdom, and it is a vast stretch of darkness. So this is what I traded for love. This is what I traded for safety.

"I will come with you," she says.

"I would never ask that—"

"I want to."

"You don't know what it's like."

"I don't care," she swears. "I will not let you go alone."

I dry my tears with the ends of my fichu. "You are too kind to me. I was not half as kind to the only man I ever loved."

To this, Isabel is silent.

"He isn't coming back," I tell her. "I made my choice, and now he isn't coming back."

"You don't know this—"

But I nod. "I do. He sent a letter."

"To this house?" She is surprised. She is the one who greets the mail carrier when he arrives.

"It came by private courtier last night. I was outside, sweeping the steps." I think now of all the times when Henri would sit outside waiting for me. "He is staying in London."

"Oh, Marie. In a year, in two years, when all of this is over—"

I give her a long look. "You heard Robespierre. One day, he will come with a request I cannot honor. And what will I do then?"

We watch each other in the red glow of the lantern.

"We can think about that tomorrow," she says.

I DO NOT sleep. I lie in my bed imagining the many terrible scenes transpiring somewhere in the Temple. By now, the king's family must know what is happening. What will he say to Marie Antoinette, who traveled from Austria as a fourteen-year-old girl to be his bride? Louis XVI is the father of her children. She will be devastated.

And how will he tell his son, the little dauphin? I think of Paschal, who is the same age as Louis-Charles, and how he still asks every few weeks when his father will be coming home. How will the prince be made to understand that his papa is to die? That tomorrow, the guillotine will be moved to the Place Louis XV—now renamed the Place de la Révolution—and he will ascend the scaffold like a common criminal and lay his head beneath the blade?

The horrors are too many to imagine. I close my eyes and picture Wolfgang and Henri strolling the streets of London together with Michael and Abrielle. I imagine the bakeries where they buy as much bread as one person can eat. And the streets, all brightly lit with lamps. Somewhere in those streets there will be beautiful women, intelligent women, but Henri will wait for me. I know he will. My eyes begin to sting, and I squeeze them tighter. I have given away life for a career among the dead. I bury my face in my pillow and wish for sleep. But it comes only after many hours.

When I wake, a heavy fog hangs over the streets. I dress in my thickest cloak to ward off the damp, but when I step outside and whistle for a carriage, I can still feel the chill through my clothes. Because Curtius is on duty in the Place de la Révolution, only Isabel and I are going. We kiss my mother and Paschal good-bye, and when a cabriolet arrives, we climb in.

"Do you want to check your bag?" Isabel asks.

My mother packed it this morning with everything I should need, but I haven't looked inside. "No. I trust her." I put it on the seat next to me. It is the same as any physician's leather case, only this will be for death.

"Do you think Robespierre will be there?" Isabel asks.

"In the Place de la Révolution or at the graveyard? My guess is neither. He faints at the sight of blood. He's not a strong man."

Though we are several blocks from the Place de la Révolution, our carriage comes to a sudden stop. The streets are filled with too many carriages to go any further. "You will have to walk the rest of the way," the driver shouts. We pay the old man in livres-assignats, and he tips his hat to us as we leave. "A historic day," he says. It's impossible to know exactly what he means, whether he is for the king's death today or against it. No one gives their opinion now.

Twenty thousand people have filled the public square, and it is a sea of red, from the brightly painted guillotine to the liberty caps that both men and women are wearing. Thousands of soldiers line the route where the king will be taken from his prison to the scaffold, and somewhere among those men is Curtius. If there are royalists who are hoping to save the king, there is no chance that their uprising will succeed.

The clouds are low and dark in the sky, and fog has obscured much of the courtyard. "Perhaps God is already in mourning," I say. We stop at the edge of the crowd. More people will be coming. It is nine, and the king will not appear until ten. "I don't think we need to go any farther."

"I'm glad your mother isn't here," Isabel tells me.

We huddle against our cloaks and listen to the people talking around us. They are commoners mostly, dressed in long trousers and ill-fitting coats. They are curious to see what the king will look like, since most of them have never laid eyes on him in person. "I heard he's enormously fat," one woman says, and her family hurries to agree. "What else would you be on a diet of cake and wine?" Another woman offers, "I bet they will sing *'La Marseillaise'* when he comes and force a liberty cap on his head."

But when the king arrives, there is silence in the Place de la Révolution. His coach is pulled through the crowds by a pair of horses made skittish by the number of people. And when the door to the carriage opens, it is no fat man in ermine who climbs the narrow steps to the scaffold. In the six weeks since I have seen him, the king has lost a great deal of weight. His simple suit and cloak hang loose on his frame, and he looks older than his thirty-eight years. His white hair has been cropped at the neck for the guillotine, and as he stands before the masses who once adored him, it is a pitiful sight.

Charles Sanson, the executioner, has allowed him to speak his last words. Although we cannot hear them, they are repeated through the crowd. He is declaring his innocence, and is using the last breaths he will ever take to pardon those who are about to shed his blood. Although it's clear he wants to say more, a captain of the National Guard orders the drumroll to begin and he is taken to the plank. His hands are tied behind his back, and his neck is held in place by a piece of wood. The drumroll quickens. Isabel looks away, and in a moment it's over. Sanson pulls the string, and the blade comes crashing down.

There is silence. Then Sanson reaches into the wicker basket and holds up the king's head. Cheers resound throughout the square, and the crowd surges forward. "What are they doing?" Isabel cries.

We are carried along by the momentum of the crowd. They are pushing from behind us, and from what I can see, they are struggling to reach the scaffold. "They want to dip their handkerchiefs in his blood!" I shout. I grab Isabel's arm so that neither of us falls in this moving tide of people. We struggle for an hour to leave the square, and when we finally escape, Sanson has already sold the king's belongings. It is an executioner's right to strip the corpse and sell its clothes. In this case, he has even sold King Louis's wig.

We begin the walk to the Madeleine Cemetery. Neither of us speaks about what we have witnessed. Nine hundred years of august tradition died on the scaffold today, yet every *sans-culotte* we pass is humming a tune and the children in the streets are waving flags. Now that the king is dead, we shall all be rich. No one will ever go hungry. There will be bread in the bakeries and cheap coffee in the shops and a respectable job for every patriot. We reach the cemetery gates, and a guardsman demands to know our business.

"We are here on the orders of Robespierre," I tell him.

"You are Citizeness Grosholtz?" He peers into my face.

"I am."

He gestures with his toothpick to Isabel. "And who is this?"

"My assistant," I lie.

He studies her, and his eyes come to rest on her tricolor cockade. "Follow me."

Isabel takes my arm as we pass through the graveyard. Thunder echoes in the distance. It will rain at any moment. A fitting tribute, I think, to regicide. We reach a small house at the edge of the cemetery, and the guard says, "The charnel house. The body is in there. I will stand here while you work." He hands Isabel a lantern, and she holds it out before us.

"Thank you for coming with me," I whisper.

"I would never have let you come alone."

We enter the room together. It is dark and cold, and immediately we are assaulted by the stench of rotting flesh. It is almost sweet and cloying, a scent that will remain in our hair and clothes until we wash. There are a dozen bodies waiting for burial, but I hardly notice them. All I see is the dismembered corpse of the king in his plain wooden coffin. Isabel has never been so close to him, and to see our monarch like this is both humbling and horrifying. She crosses herself. But someday, this is what we shall all come to. I open my leather bag.

"I'll need water," I say.

Isabel goes to the door and asks the guard for a cup.

"Thirsty work?" He laughs.

She does not laugh with him. "It is for the plaster. A bowl will do as well."

I am finished in a few minutes. I replace the king's head between his legs—there is no room for it anywhere else in the coffin—then wrap the plaster death mask in a cotton shawl.

"I thought it would take longer," the guard remarks. He takes the toothpick from his mouth and casually investigates what he's pulled from his teeth.

"I am taking the cast to my workshop," I reply. "The wax head will be created there."

"As long as it's somewhere. Those men from the Convention were eager to have it done."

"And the body?" I ask quietly. "What will happen to it?"

"Quicklime, I suppose. That way there's nothing left to dig up. We're not looking to have his bones made into relics."

"And it will be an anonymous grave?"

"Of course. He was a tyrant." The guard smiles. "That mask is the last that anyone shall see of him."

Chapter 52

January 25, 1793

I was a queen, and you took away my crown; a wife, and you killed my husband; a mother, and you deprived me of my children. My blood alone remains: take it, but do not make me suffer long.

—Marie Antoinette

The guards scrutinize my papers and ask me again what I am doing here.

"I am visiting on the orders of Robespierre. I am to report on the conditions of the royal family."

"I can read that," the younger one snaps. But he has searched my basket and discovered the wax miniature of Saint Denis, the patron saint of Paris, and become suspicious. "And what business does Robespierre have in sending a woman? Did he ask that you bring a headless saint?"

I raise my chin. "I am here on Robespierre's request," I repeat. "I brought this as a warning," I lie. Saint Denis was beheaded with a sword on Montmartre. He was the only saint I could plausibly bring. Although he is holding his head in his hands, like his image outside the Cathedral of Notre-Dame, he will give Madame Élisabeth comfort. "I am here to serve the Convention," I tell him.

"Not to convey a message, or warn her of an uprising?"

"My uncle is a captain of the National Guard."

"And Lafayette was their commander. That means nothing, Citizeness."

The guard watches me, and I return his stare. I don't know what they want from me. I have a pass with the words *Officier Municipal* written diagonally. It is obviously official. Clearly, it was a mistake to convince Robespierre that I should come. But if the guard is looking for tears, he will not find them. I have no more.

"You may go," he says at last. Then adds threateningly, "My men will be watching."

Four soldiers escort me into the Temple, and I follow them through the halls. Unlike the Tuileries, this is not a palace. It is a fortress built by the Knights Templars with cold, damp walls and rising turrets. Somewhere, far beneath my feet, the victims of the Inquisition were once imprisoned. Now this is where the royal family must live.

We reach a wooden door, and the guard pushes it open. "A guest!" he shouts, and inside the chamber a woman with white hair and a black taffeta gown rises to greet me. *My God, it is the queen.* I remind myself that I must not curtsy. She is Madame Capet now, not Queen Marie Antoinette.

"Thank you, Thomas," she says kindly, but the soldier warns her that I shall not be staying long. The door is left open, and the queen takes my hands. "Mademoiselle Grosholtz." After so many years, she still remembers me. "Or is it Madame now?"

I think of Henri and swallow my hurt. "No, still Mademoiselle."

She guides me to a chair, and it feels very much like I am walking through a dream. Her children are sitting before the fireplace, reading books from the vast library spread along the walls. They look up at me, and while the boy smiles, the girl watches me with open suspicion. There is a small dog warming itself by the fire. I think of Madame Élisabeth's little greyhounds. There is no sign of them here, and I wonder if they have been sent away.

"Marie-Thérèse, would you go and find your aunt? She will be very glad to see Mademoiselle Grosholtz."

"Just Marie," I correct her.

The princesse stands. "I don't see why Louis can't do it."

The queen smiles self-consciously at me before turning to her daughter. "Because you are the one I asked."

She doesn't argue further. She stalks through the door, and I think to myself, What an unfortunate child. How is it fair to heap such losses on a child? The moment Madame Élisabeth appears I stand, but we do not embrace, since the guards are watching. She looks me over. "Marie, how did you come here?"

Unlike the queen, who has aged into an old woman, Madame Élisabeth is still in the full bloom of youth. But her eyes tell the truth. We sit across from each other near the fire, and the queen takes a chair next to her sister-in-law. The guard is lost in conversation with his friend.

"I begged a pass from Robespierre," I say quietly. "I told him we were old friends and that if anyone could learn of an escape plan in the making, it would be me."

"A *spy*?" Madame Élisabeth whispers.

"How clever," the queen says. "And do you know, that's what these men believe. We are imprisoned in a Templar fortress and they think that hordes of men are rushing to save us. If that were the case, wouldn't someone have saved my husband?"

A deep heaviness settles over the room.

"That is what I came to tell you, Madame. Your husband met with an easy death."

Madame Élisabeth stifles a sob.

"There was no pain," I promise them. "No suffering."

Both the dauphin—who is now Louis XVII—and Madame Royale are listening intently. The queen's gaze is hollow. She is a shadow of herself. Pale and thin with sunken eyes. Around her neck, she wears her husband's wedding ring on a simple ribbon. It is likely the only jewel she has left in the world. They have taken everything from her. "Do you know what they plan for us?" she whispers in German.

I look over my shoulder. But the guard has obviously heard enough weeping in this room to no longer be concerned by it.

"Life in a convent," I mouth wordlessly. I have heard this news from Robespierre.

"And my children?"

Both of them are watching me. Louis-Charles, who looks like an angel, and Marie-Thérèse, whose future is uncertain. "I'm sorry. I don't know." I reach into my basket and take out the miniature of Saint Denis. I give it to Madame Élisabeth, and she puts a hand to her heart.

"Oh, *Marie.*"

Marie-Thérèse rises from the fireside. "Won't you get in trouble for bringing that?" she asks curiously.

I meet Madame Royale's narrowed eyes. "It is a miniature of a saint."

"No one else brings gifts." She watches me with a strange expression.

Madame Élisabeth reaches forward to take my hands. "You have no idea what this means to me. Please, will you pray for us?" she asks.

I am taken aback by the princesse's request. What good will my prayers do? My brothers are dead, just like her brother. The National Guard murdered Yachin for nothing more than a square of silk. And Henri is gone. If God is listening, it is not to me.

Chapter 53

January 31, 1793

I shall be an autocrat, that's my trade; and the good Lord will forgive me, that's His.

—Catherine the Great

Every country on earth has turned against us. England, Russia, Holland, Austria. When their monarchs hear of King Louis's murder, they unite in their horror and condemnation.

Empress Catherine the Great has declared mourning for all of Russia, and in England the prime minister, William Pitt, has called the king's death "the foulest and most atrocious deed which the history of the world" has ever seen. I can find nothing in the papers to indicate what America's President Washington believes. Perhaps he is neutral. But whatever he feels, we have made more enemies than we can fight.

On the first of February, the Convention declares war on both England and the Dutch Republic. Curtius says this is a preemptive strike, that England would declare war on us anyway. But I think it is pride. The hulking figure of Georges Danton stands before the Convention and swears that the limits of France will someday reach "the ocean, the Rhine, the Alps, and the Pyrenees." When I ask my uncle what he thinks of this, he closes his eyes and shakes his head.

I imagine Wolfgang and Henri reading this news, and I wonder what will happen to them now. What will happen to us all? Their letters have stopped. Nothing arrives in or leaves from Paris except for soldiers. At night, the patrols go from house to house, searching for weapons, powder, illegal flour. Anyone caught hoarding is sent to prison. Then on the fifth of October, to cheer the populace, we are given a new calendar. From this day forward, no one is to celebrate the Catholic festivals or use the calendar that dates from Christ's birth. "We are a nation of thinkers," Danton declares, "and as such, we shall celebrate the glorious rationalism that has brought us to such liberty."

Not a single journalist in all of Paris dares to point out that our new liberty has imprisoned us within the city. That our dead are buried the same day they die—in mass graves—because there is no longer room and even gravediggers are not allowed outside the city gates. And so we all must pretend to embrace this new calendar. Those who do not use it are branded enemies of the *patrie*.

"Repeat the names," my mother instructs, and we listen while Paschal recites the names of the months.

"Vintage, Fog, Frost, Snow, Rain . . ." He hesitates on the sixth month.

"Wind," she says helpfully. We are all sitting at the *caissier*'s desk, and it is very important he get this right.

"Wind," he repeats after her. "Seed, Blossoms, M-Mead—"

"Meadows," I say.

"Meadows, Harvesting, Heat, and Fruit."

Isabel claps. "Very good."

"And what year is this?" my mother asks.

Paschal frowns. "Seventeen ninety-three?"

"No," Isabel says forcefully. "It is Year Two."

"But I don't understand."

"The first year began on September twenty-second, seventeen ninety-two." The day France declared itself the First Republic.

"But how?" He doesn't see how he could have been alive before time began.

"That is the decree of the Convention," she explains.

"But it doesn't make sense." He is frustrated.

"It doesn't have to," I tell him. "You must simply learn the rules and obey."

"Is that what liberty means?" he asks earnestly.

The three of us are silent.

"No," I say. "That is what tyranny means," but I don't explain.

Paschal repeats the names of the months again, but we do not ask him to memorize the fruits, animals, and minerals associated with each day. Now that the Convention has declared the Church an enemy of the *patrie,* no day shall ever be associated with a saint again. Instead, on the twenty-second of September, we are to all praise the grape. On the fifteenth of March we must remember the tuna. The twenty-second of April is reserved for the fern, and we shall not forget the onion on the twenty-first of June. In a similar fashion, all Christian holidays have now been abolished. Despite the fact that the Jacobins have called Jesus our world's first *sans-culotte,* we are to celebrate the glorious attributes of the canine instead of Christ's birthday on the twenty-fifth of December. But these are things that are impossible to explain to an eight-year-old child.

On October 21, however, Paschal's questions are impossible to avoid. The street criers are shouting that the Cult of Reason is now to replace Catholicism and that the first celebration will be held tonight in the Cathedral of Notre-Dame in praise of the Goddess of Reason.

"Who is the Goddess of Reason?" Paschal asks. "Is she real?"

My mother clenches her jaw. "No. She is blasphemy."

"Maman!" I exclaim. There are patrons in the Salon, and we are sitting at the *caissier*'s desk.

"I don't care!" she shouts.

"Yes. You do."

There are tears in her eyes. I leave the desk to buy a newspaper, and when I return, I read it to her in German. She must understand the seriousness of this. All deaths, marriages, and births are now to be registered under the civil registration law and not in the Church. And all saints and images of worship are to be taken down. Only statues of Citizen Jesus may remain. Synagogues have been closed down, and Jews who wear their *peyos* long must cut them off. From this day forward, all churches will be turned into Temples of Reason, and any person found harboring priests or rabbis will be killed.

My mother is silent, listening.

"What is it, *Grand-mère*? Is it very bad news?"

My mother takes Paschal's hand in hers. "Yes. May God help us," she whispers.

Chapter 54

February 17, 1793

The tocsin you hear today is not an alarm but an alert: it sounds the charge against our enemies.

—Georges Danton, revolutionary leader

He has heard that I am the angel of death, resurrecting those who have gone before us, so he has come to me. He looks exactly as I have sculpted him for our *National Convention* tableau, with a firm jaw and a chest so wide that Curtius had to use extra horsehair for his model. I should send him away. This is the man who, alongside Marat, called for the massacre of the Swiss Guards. Now is the time to exact my revenge.

"I have ridden nonstop for three days," he says. His clothes are filthy and worn. "*Please.* She is in the Madeleine Cemetery. They say you are there every night."

"For the dead," I reply harshly. "Not for the buried."

"I have unburied her! *Please,*" Danton begs. "She is in her coffin. I have opened the lid and she is perfectly preserved. She died while I was at the front." He cries into his hands, and although I should detest him, I am sorry for his loss. I think of my mother, torn apart by the deaths of Johann and Edmund. She would want me to turn Danton away. No, she would order it. But then I think of what Madame Élisabeth would do. "I will get my bag and shawl," I say.

I go upstairs, and Isabel asks if she should come with me. "Not this time."

"You are going alone?"

"With a man from the Convention."

She is wise enough not to ask who he is. My mother is in the next room.

I follow Danton through the streets and down the familiar path to the Madeleine Cemetery. The air is dank and smells of coming rain. I should have brought more than a shawl. A heavy white mist has settled over the trees, and only the burnished glow of Danton's lantern lights the way. We pass through the cemetery's iron gates, and the guard calls for us to stop. When he sees who I am, he tips his hat to me. I have become as familiar as the gravediggers in this place.

"We're here for Gabrielle Danton," I say.

The old man nods. "You know the way?"

"Yes," Danton replies.

I follow while Danton navigates a path between the markers. Although others are tossed into paupers' pits, Gabrielle has been granted her own place in the earth. I wonder if her death was punishment from God for the sins Danton committed against innocent men. Do blameless women die for their husbands' deeds? Is that how God works? Or is He merciful and forgiving, like our *sans-culotte* Jesus?

Danton stops before a gravestone bearing the name of Gabrielle Danton. A pair of shovels rest against a fresh mound of dirt, and next to the frightening hole in the earth is a wooden coffin. "Gabrielle," he whispers.

This is my moment for revenge. As he pries back the lid, I consider telling him that she is too far gone for a mask. But then I close my eyes briefly and think of his pain. He is weeping openly over her corpse. I know I should be afraid. After all, these are the scenes that nightmares are made of. But I have seen such death these past three months that nothing frightens me anymore.

I kneel over her coffin and look into the face of a beautiful woman the same age as I am. Her black hair covers her shoulders, and she has been dressed in a handsome taffeta gown. There is no sign of injury to her face and no way of telling that she is dead and not sleeping. "How long has she been gone?" I whisper.

He sobs. "Seven days."

I have never seen a body preserved like this. What would he have done if she had deteriorated completely?

"Can . . . can you model her?" he asks.

I look down at his wife. How strange to think that the birds above us will wake up tomorrow to blue skies and life but she will never open her eyes again. Even the fichu around her neck will outlast her. "Yes," I say quietly. "I can."

He holds the lantern while I work, and when I am finished, he asks how long it will be before he will have her back. It is not healthy, what he is doing. But I ask him, "A bust or an entire figure?"

"Her entire figure. With the same dark hair," he adds desperately.

I think of the models still left to do, including a replacement for General Dumouriez, whose defeat last month has resulted in his disgrace. "Two weeks." I stand, and he closes his eyes. "Danton," I say gently, "she has left this world."

"She has not left my world!" His voice echoes through the cemetery, and I take a step back. "I am sorry," he says at once. "I don't know . . . I can't control . . ."

"I have known loss," I tell him. "I understand."

He searches my face. He must know of the event I am referring to, and his voice is full of emotion when he replies, "I am sorry."

But we are all sorry when loss comes for us. The test of our character comes not in how many tears we shed but in how we act after those tears have dried.

Chapter 55

APRIL 7, 1793

In order to ensure public tranquillity, two hundred thousand heads must be cut off.

—JEAN-PAUL MARAT

TERROR. THIS IS WHAT DANTON HAS UNLEASHED IN THE WAKE of his wife's death. He is urging the National Convention to establish a committee to root out every enemy of the *patrie* and send them first to prison, then to the guillotine. He is like a man possessed, preaching about enemies wherever he goes, from the Jacobin Club to the floor of the Convention. This war against conspirators has given him a new reason to live, and he is not alone in his crusade. In one of his recent placards, Marat has calculated how many criminals can be guillotined in a single day. Even Robespierre has joined the call for a committee responsible for hunting down the enemies of equality.

On the sixth of April, the Convention takes Danton's advice, making him the first member of the Committee of Public Safety. Now he and eight other men are given the task of finding traitors by any means necessary, and only the *Chronique de Paris* is brave enough to write the truth. It begins by attacking Marat and Danton. Then, the author moves on to Robespierre.

> There are some who ask why there are so many women around Robespierre: at his house, in the galleries of the Jacobin Club, in the galleries of the Convention. It is because this Revolution of ours is a religion, and Robespierre is leading a sect therein. He is a priest at the head of his worshipers. He thunders against the rich and the great, and prides himself on how he lives on next to nothing. Then he talks of God and of Providence, creating his own disciples in the process. He calls himself the friend of the humble and the weak, yet happily receives the adoration of both women and the poor in spirit. He is a false priest and will never be other than a false priest.

I burn the paper in the fireplace. That evening, when the patrol comes to our house, they search our cabinets, our storeroom, the glass jars in our workshop. They scour our shelves for royalist books and make themselves comfortable in our salon, going through newspapers. When the men are finished, they congratulate us. "Not every house is filled with such dedicated patriots as yourselves."

We watch them leave, and I could cry with relief when they are gone. Not everyone is so fortunate. The news that comes to us every night through Curtius is terrifying. They have arrested a general who surrendered to the Prussians and sentenced him to death. When his young wife heard of this, she ran into the streets screaming, "Long live the king!" Tomorrow, they will both be executed in the Place de la Révolution.

"They are sending women who have just given birth to the guillotine," Curtius reveals. "Yesterday, a mother with an infant still at her breast was led to the scaffold. The executioner handed the child to an old man in the crowd, then bound the mother's hands and executed her." He lowers his head. "And everyone watched in silence."

We are all guilty. Every one of us. When Danton's Committee of Public Safety arrests fourteen girls discovered dancing at a Prussian ball in Verdun, not a single voice speaks out for them. Instead, the masses watch as the girls are led through the public square, their red chemises blowing in the warm spring breeze. Every day there is another story of a woman crying *"Vive le Roi!"* at her sentencing before the Revolutionary Tribunal. Wives are marching to the guillotine with their husbands, and daughters are going with their fathers and brothers. When the news comes that Madame Sainte-Amaranthe has been arrested for once gambling with royalists, I know that the world has gone mad. Where does it end? Who will risk death to tell the truth that the Committee of Public Safety is worse than any king who ever ruled in France?

"They have arrested her children as well," Curtius tells me. We both look across the room to the models of Madame Sainte-Amaranthe and her daughter, part of our *Parisian Beauties* tableau. I remember the morning when Émilie Sainte-Amaranthe came to sit for me. It was four years ago. The king's courtier came with the invitation for me to be Madame Élisabeth's tutor, and Robespierre advised me to turn it down. Émilie declared that to refuse would be insane.

Lucile once warned me that Robespierre never forgets an indignity or a slight. Has Robespierre remembered this and sentenced her entire family to death? "You don't think—"

He knows what I am about to say. "They still call him *The Incorruptible,*" he says wryly.

But that is only a name. A reputation he has built for himself.

Chapter 56

June 1, 1793—July 5, 1793

Clemency is also a revolutionary measure.

—Camille Desmoulins

No one can tell me why the Sainte-Amaranthe family has been arrested. Finally, when I pay a visit to Lucile, she closes the doors to her salon so that no one may hear us speak. "I would not appear too interested in their fate."

I study her face. "The day you gave birth," I say, "you said that Robespierre never forgets a slight."

She moves her hand through the air. "That was nearly a year ago."

"And has Robespierre changed? He sits on the Revolutionary Tribunal," I remind her. "He's as responsible for their fate as Danton and his Committee. Perhaps Camille—"

"No." She is firm in this. "He has other problems. We need more soldiers."

"From where? There are no young men left in the streets."

She puts a hand to her forehead. "I know. But they must be found somewhere."

I discover where they will be found the next morning. When my mother hands Curtius his morning coffee, he does not appear in any rush to finish. He drinks it slowly, allowing Paschal to sit on his knee and read his newspaper. When Isabel asks if Curtius will be needing the button on his military coat sewn, he tells her, "Rather sooner than later I'm afraid."

We all stop what we are doing. My mother puts her hand to her chest. "What does that mean?"

"I'm being sent on a mission," he says. "A trip to Mayence to report on the patriotism of General Custine. They want me to leave in seven days."

Paschal asks, "Will you be fighting?"

Curtius smiles. "I am too old for that."

"And you are too old for any mission," my mother says angrily. "Are they so desperate that they need old men?"

"It would seem that way."

"You will be careful," I worry. "You won't be mistaken for an actual soldier?"

He laughs. "I doubt there's any chance of that." He lifts Paschal from his lap and goes to my mother. "It will only be few months." He leans over and wraps his arms around her. But she is weeping. "I will return before Michaelmas," he promises.

"What Michaelmas?" she cries. "It's now the day of the cat, or the tree, or some pebble."

He holds her tightly. "It's only for a few months." But I know he is putting a cheerful face on a dangerous situation, and the night before he leaves, he takes me to his room and unlocks a metal chest. "These are all of our most important documents," he says. "If anything should happen to me—"

"You shouldn't talk like that."

"We don't know, Marie. Who would think that two of your brothers would be gone?"

Or that war would separate us from Wolfgang and Henri so that any correspondence would look like treason. It has been months since we have had a letter from them, and who knows how much longer it will be before they are able to send word.

"In here is the deed to the house." Curtius shows it to me. "Now it is fully paid. And this is my will, along with your inheritance." He puts away his papers. "Things are changing rapidly. Do not be surprised if they put the queen on trial."

"You can't go," I say desperately, and for the first time in many years, I see his resolution waiver. "What will we do without you?" I ask. "How will Maman survive?"

"She has Paschal and Isabel. And, above all, she has you."

"It's not the same."

His eyes fill with tears. "I know."

When our family gathers outside the Salon to see him off, the neighbors come to bid him farewell. There is the chandler, the grocer, a handful of actors who have remained on the Boulevard, and of course, there is Jacques. I remember the last time so many people gathered on this street to bid a carriage farewell. It was my first trip to Montreuil. Yachin had stood here, where I am standing now, and begged me for playing cards. But instead of bringing cards, I brought him death.

I go to the lamppost where the carriage driver is waiting and tear off Marat's most recent placard. It is a list of suspects he believes should be guillotined. I fold the paper and tuck it inside my sleeve.

"I wish we could walk across this city," Isabel admits, "and tear every one down. Last week, he wrote against the Polish Princesse Lubomirska, and someone posted it on this lamppost. They arrested her on suspicion of treason last night. It was in this morning's paper."

He is like God. He has the power of life and death. Princesse Lubomirska came from Poland in a golden *berline* to help fight for the cause of liberty. I keep the placard tucked in my sleeve, and the next morning I compare it to the list printed in the *Chronique.* Every name on Marat's placard is there. Wealthy, poor, women, men—they have all been arrested.

Chapter 37

July 1793

I am the anger, the just anger of the people, and that is why they listen to me and believe in me.

—Jean-Paul Marat

It is a different house without Curtius. Although the days are the same, the nights are quiet. Everything makes my mother nervous now. The ringing of the bells, the soldiers in the streets, Paschal's footsteps on the stairs when he is running. She is on constant vigil, waiting for another loved one to be snatched from her home. Only Curtius's letters from Mayence can calm her.

He writes weekly, telling us how it is on the fronts, of the cannon fire in the distance and the cries of men in the hospital tents. Though he has a sent a positive report of Custine to the Convention, both Marat and Robespierre are convinced that the general is secretly a royalist.

"We must remember," Marat writes on his insidious placards, "where the name Custine comes from. He was the *Comte de* Custine, an aristocrat no different from our tyrant king!"

As soon as I read these words, I know it is over for the general. He is summoned back to Paris, and because his children are here—hostages like the rest of us—he has no choice but to come. It is not enough that they arrest him. The Revolutionary Tribunal sentences his entire family to death: his son, his grandson, even his young daughter-in-law, whose only crime was to marry into a family that has displeased Marat.

When news of their sentencing reaches us on the Boulevard, Isabel comes to me in the workshop. "What does this mean for Curtius? He gave his word that Custine was a patriot."

"They will not turn against us. We are their angels of death, remember?" I know that my voice sounds bitter, but she understands the toll these masks have taken on me. On both of us. "And many years ago," I add, "we helped Marat. He came to our salons. When the king's men wanted to arrest him, we hid him for a week." It's been more than three years since the night we stood together on our balcony and watched the New Year fireworks. Johann and Edmund were alive, and in a small apartment in Saint-Martin, Yachin was celebrating with his family. "I believe he will keep his silence."

Indeed, he does, but not in any way I would have imagined. I am sitting with Isabel when Jacques-Louis David appears at the door of the Salon. He has not been here since he came with the news that the Swiss Guards had been massacred. That was nearly a year ago, and now my whole life is measured by this date. For every event I recall, I think, *Was that before or after Johann and Edmund were killed?* The Convention has their calendar, and I have mine.

Jacques-Louis must remember this as well. He approaches the *caissier*'s desk with hesitation. He is the Convention's favorite artist, the man commissioned to sculpt a Goddess of Reason for every Temple in Paris. But he is trembling. Either terrible events are unfolding or he is ill. "Marie," he says breathlessly, "you must come. You are wanted in the Rue des Cordelières."

"Why?"

He looks at Isabel. "I cannot say."

"And it's a matter of urgency?"

For such a slight man, he is sweating profusely. His hair is wet, and there are stains beneath his arms. "Of grave, *grave* emergency," he swears. I stand from the desk, and he adds quickly, "Bring your bag."

"With plaster?"

"And towels—everything."

"Let Maman know I've gone with Jacques-Louis," I tell Isabel. I gather my bag and follow him out the door and into the street. He is practically running. "What is this about?" I demand.

"A tragedy. An absolute tragedy!"

"Has someone died?"

"Yes!" he cries. He stops walking to look at me. In the harsh morning light, he looks all of his forty-five years. "They have murdered Marat. A *woman,* who bought a knife in the Palais, went to his apartment and asked to see him."

My heart is thundering in my chest. "He let her in?"

"She said she had the names of suspects who could be considered traitors to the *patrie.* So he invited her into his bathing room—"

"He was in the *bath*?"

"He spends much of his time there. For his skin."

"Yes." I remember the open sores.

"When she arrived, she gave him a list, and while he was reading . . ." He makes a stabbing motion with his hand. I know that Jacques-Louis is devastated, but I think of the bravery of this woman.

"And the girl?"

"Was apprehended at the door! She is still there. They are simply waiting for the National Guard."

We continue to hurry, and I ask him why this is a secret.

"We must discover her coconspirators before the news begins to spread."

"How do you know she didn't act alone?"

He gives me a look. "She is a woman. A *girl.*"

We arrive at Marat's apartment in the Rue des Cordelières, and Robespierre and Danton are already there. Robespierre appears the most distraught. He is pulling at his wig. "Jacques-Louis!" he cries. Then, "Marie! You have come to make the model?"

"Yes," I tell him, holding up my leather bag.

"He was assassinated. Killed for his belief in liberty and equality. They will come for me next. If they came for Marat, they must come for me."

I am startled by his use of the word *must.*

"You can't imagine the scene," Robespierre continues, gesturing toward the apartment behind us. "There is blood in the bath, across the walls, on the tiles. When the people hear of this, do you know what they will do? They will carry him through the streets like a martyr!" he exclaims, and I am sure I hear envy in his words. "Tomorrow, this will be in every paper," he adds. "For months, this is all we will hear about—"

Jacques-Louis interrupts him. "In this weather, the body will not last long . . ."

But Danton does not move. I think of asking him about Madame Sainte-Amaranthe, but with a murderess waiting upstairs, now is not the time. I follow Jacques-Louis into the hall of the apartment and am surprised to see a woman's touch in the furnishings.

"Does a woman live here?"

"Simonne Evrard," he says.

"He is married?" I hadn't known. What sort of woman would wish to bind her fortunes with Marat?

"He met her last year."

I imagine she is young. An idealistic and foolish child. We reach the stairs, and I can hear several men speaking above us. They are questioning a young woman, who is responding to them in a clear, calm voice. She does not sound like a killer.

Jacques-Louis studies me before we climb. "I know you are not a woman of weak constitution. But this death . . ." He chokes on his own words. "It is gruesome and unnatural."

And the deaths of the innocent men and women Marat sent to the guillotine are not? I say firmly, "I have brought a sachet." I take a small pouch of smelling salts from my bag. But whatever is awaiting me upstairs can never compare to the severed limbs and heads stacked in the charnel house of the Madeleine.

We climb fifteen steps to the second floor. A woman is sitting on a wooden stool, her hands tied tightly behind her back. Several men are standing above her, enjoying the view of her torn dress. Whatever happened here, there was a violent struggle. There is a bruise on her cheek, and I am struck by the even beauty of her features. I can see there is intelligence in her eyes.

"I know you," she says. "You are the sculptress Marie Grosholtz. You make masks of those who have died on the scaffold."

"Yes." That this should be my reputation in Paris—a vulture flapping around the carcasses of the guillotine's victims—makes me physically ill. I raise the smelling salts to my nose and inhale.

"When it's my turn," she says quietly, "I hope you will remember that *I* am the martyr, not him." She looks to the open door of the bathing room, where Marat's body lies in a tub of water and blood. The scene is less hideous than many I've witnessed. In fact, there is a calmness on his sharp, unpleasant features that was never there in life.

"What is your name?" I ask her.

"Charlotte Corday."

"How old are you?" With her tattered dress and disheveled hair, she appears to be sixteen or seventeen.

"Old enough to execute," Jacques-Louis replies. "A devil in women's garb."

But I think she is an avenging angel. She is as pale and serene as a Grecian statue, with her hands bound and her breasts exposed. I offer her my fichu. "For modesty's sake," I say swiftly to Jacques-Louis.

"Thank you," Charlotte whispers.

Jacques-Louis clenches his jaw, but I will not be threatened by him. Not when this young woman has shown such courage. "Are you ready?" he asks me.

The bathing room reeks of vinegar and blood. In the rising heat, the body is beginning to bloat and smell. He has been stabbed once in the chest, an obviously fatal blow, although it's doubtful that death would have come at once. He must have had time to shout to his wife, or perhaps to his servants, who came running to find the murderess with her knife. His head rests on his naked shoulder, and his arm is draped limply over the tub. He is still holding a quill, while the papers he was working on float amid the blood and water. I wonder how many lives will be saved because of what Charlotte Corday has done today.

I begin the process of making a plaster mask, and while I wait for it to dry on Marat's face, Jacques-Louis says, "The Convention will want a full figure. Bath and all."

"They want me to take his *bath*?"

"Or create a replica. It doesn't matter. Take the ink, the quill, everything." He covers his nose with his shirt and breathes deeply. "When the model is finished"—he comes up for air—"I will make a painting of it."

It will be a great deal of work. "I will have to sketch this first."

"Of course. I made my own sketches before."

"While he was dying?"

"Of course not!" Jacques-Louis flushes. "I came . . . for a visit." He means he came to deliver names. "When I arrived, he had already been murdered. His wife was screaming, and while she ran to find Robespierre, I stayed with the body. All of France will recognize his sacrifice when I am through. And the funeral . . ." Jacques-Louis is already imagining the grandness of the event. He has been behind every public funeral since this Revolution began. "We will honor him as he deserves."

It takes all my restraint not to rip the mask from Marat's face.

Outside, Robespierre is pacing so frantically that it's difficult to hear him. "We will find these conspirators if we have to search through every closet in Paris. No one will be above questioning. Not women, not children—"

"The cast is done," I tell him. "When the model is finished, where shall I send it?"

"To the Convention," he says, then he contradicts himself. "No—to the Revolutionary Tribunal. And we shall keep it as a reminder of our dangerous work."

Though I know the risk I am taking, I say, "Perhaps I should return to the Temple. If revolts are being plotted, it is possible the royal family will know of them."

He studies me through his green-tinged spectacles, and I realize that I have made a mistake. "I do not think that is a wise decision," he says slowly. "I believe the royal family has enough wax saints."

I CANNOT STOP thinking about Robespierre's words. Did the soldiers tell him? And if so, why? They had no reason to believe that the figure of Saint Denis was anything other than a warning. I recall Madame Royale's expression when I handed the wax miniature to her aunt. Did she report it to the guards, who informed Robespierre? But why would she do such a thing?

In the privacy of the workshop, I tell Isabel what happened. She puts aside her broom, and the color drains from her face. "It was a warning," she says.

"Yes, but who told him?"

"Obviously, the girl."

That is what I think as well.

"Marie, they will be watching you," Isabel warns. "First the model of Saint Denis, then your fichu." I have told her about Charlotte Corday. "They are going to think you are a conspirator!"

I am thinking of the young woman who murdered Marat. Of her strength and courage. "They plan to execute her today," I say. In the restaurants, her name will be on the back of every menu, among a list of others who have been sentenced to die. The crowds have been gathering since early this morning, and as soon as the bells chime noon, she will be brought to the scaffold.

"Have you been asked to model her?" Isabel asks.

"Yes." I think of her request that I remember her as the true martyr, and not Marat. What must it be like for Charlotte to know that I will be the last person to touch her face, her hair?

That evening, before we leave for the Madeleine Cemetery, I stand in the hall and look at myself in the mirror. As hard as I try, I cannot find the woman I saw in the glass of Henri's salon. That woman had been confident and single-minded, filled with lofty ideas about her place in the world. She was as deluded as men like Camille and Marat. Now I see where my talent has taken me. I am dressed almost entirely in black. Only the apron around my waist adds any color, and tonight, when I return from the charnel house, my mother will have to wash it again and again, rinsing the blood from the cotton and the dirt from the trim. I am thirty-two years old without a husband or children, and when I lie down tonight, it will be in a bed empty of warmth and love. Who will inherit everything that I have learned?

I go the the *cassier*'s desk and take out a quill and paper. I must write to him. Then at whatever the cost, I must find a ship that can take a letter to London—either through Belgium or Spain. Tears blur my vision, falling onto the paper and smearing the ink so that twice I have to begin again. The night I refused to leave with Henri will shape my life. Like my brothers' deaths, there will be *before love* and *after love.* I will never love a man like Henri again. But I do not write this. If I am to free him, I must tell him that there is someone else. Unless there is another man, he will wait. Seven years, ten years . . . Now his life in London may go on without me.

When Isabel finds me, I am sealing the letter. She looks at my face, then down at the name on the top of the envelope.

"I have freed him," I whisper.

She understands. Isabel never needs an explanation. She links her arm through mine and we walk silently to find the corpse of a young girl who was much braver than I. But we are not alone in the Madeleine Cemetery. When we reach the charnel house, a group of men are standing above the headless body of Charlotte Corday. They are dressed in black, and a bearded man is in the process of undressing her.

For a moment, I am paralyzed by fear. Then I realize what is happening. I have heard of men like this. "Isabel," I shout, "run and find the guards!"

"Wait!" the bearded man stands. "We are physicians."

Isabel pauses at the door.

"We have been sent here by Robespierre," he explains.

I back away. "I don't believe you."

The old man holds up a white-gloved hand. "We are here to inspect her virginity."

I step closer to Isabel.

"Robespierre has been elected to the Committee of Public Safety. It is now his job to investigate any enemy of the *patrie.* He believes that this woman may have had a lover, and if that is the case, this man may have helped her plan the assassination of Marat."

And these are the lengths he is willing to go to, to discover conspirators? I think again of Robespierre's words to me in the Rue des Cordelières and shiver. "We will wait outside."

Five minutes later, the men emerge, their faces solemn.

"Well?" Isabel whispers.

The bearded man turns to us, and I can see disappointment in the lines of his face. "She was a virgin."

Chapter 58

August—October 1793

Courage! I have shown it for years; think you I shall lose it at the moment when my sufferings are to end?

—Marie Antoinette

It is unthinkable. A queen, *our* queen, the Queen of France, has been separated from her family and moved to the Conciergerie prison to await a trial on the charge of treason. When the criers begin to shout the news, I turn to my mother in the doorway of our Salon. "Curtius warned me that this would happen," I whisper.

"This is the Committee of Public Safety's doing," she accuses. "They are the ones who have voted for this." Her lower lip begins to tremble. "I think of the monsters we have sheltered in here . . ."

"None of us could have known it would come to this."

"But Robespierre! He was so polite, so well-spoken. Curtius trusted him."

We are both silent. In a little more than a month, it will be Michaelmas. But every week, a letter comes to us from the front. There is another general they would like Curtius to investigate. Then another, and another. Each report he sends to the Committee is positive. Every man is a patriot, no man is an enemy. But how long before the Committee grows tired of innocence and begins to suspect him as well?

Throughout August and September, I hear news from the soldiers in the Madeleine Cemetery of what life is like for the queen. They have imprisoned her in the darkest, dampest cell, without any changes of clothes or a bath to keep herself clean. They say that she walks barefoot for want of shoes, and that the black gown she wears is so tattered that, as summer turns to fall, she will feel the change on her skin. "While she was strolling across Versailles in her fancy silk shoes," the guard outside the charnel house says with a laugh, "my wife was wearing rags. Let's see how she enjoys it."

But the silks and taffeta were expected of her. When she went barefoot in the tall grasses of her Hameau, every paper in France mocked her as a peasant. So what did they want? When she tried to economize, her own courtiers turned against her. Whom is a queen supposed to please? Her people? Her court?

On the twelfth of October the queen's trial begins. My mother does not come, but Isabel and I find seats the night before in the Salle de Spectacle, where the Convention now meets. We sit in the public galleries until morning, watching the gloomy space fill with spectators, lawyers, and eventually the members of the National Convention itself. Of course, it is all a grand farce. They will find her guilty, and nothing she can say or do will change that. The only surprise will be where they send her. Either back to Austria or to some convent in the Alps.

When the trial begins, a man announces, "Madame Capet," and the doors are thrown open for the woman who once held Europe in her thrall. Every spectator in the Salle de Spectacle gasps. An old woman appears in a simple white gown; her shoes are worn and her white hair is cropped carelessly at the neck. Yet for all her misfortune, she moves with the dignity and grace of a queen.

She sits and listens to their accusations in silence, even when they charge her with molesting the dauphin. "Still no reaction?" the prosecutor thunders from his podium. "Even when you are charged with corrupting your own son?"

There is a murmur in the galleries. Then, for the first time, she speaks.

"Because Nature refuses to answer such a charge brought against a mother. I appeal to all the mothers in here! Do you truly believe this?"

There are many in the crowds who are openly weeping, despite the danger of being seen to do so. Now that the prosecutor has had his wish and the queen has spoken, he hurries through the rest of his accusations without stopping to ask if she wants to reply.

The next day, the verdict is read. Guilty, on every charge.

There is a stunned silence in the Salle de Spectacle as the punishment is announced. In three days, on the Place de la Révolution, the queen shall meet her death as a traitor to the *patrie.* Isabel grips my hand, and there are women in the galleries who collapse in a faint.

When we return to the Boulevard du Temple, my mother and Paschal come running. They have already heard the verdict and want to know if it is true. "Have they really sentenced Madame Capet to death?" my mother asks.

"Yes," Isabel replies.

The three of them look to me, and I say, "I won't do it."

"You must," my mother cries. "If you refuse, they will know—"

"What?" I shout. "What will they pretend to know?"

But Isabel's voice is steady. "If you refuse, they will accuse you of treason. They have sent women to the guillotine for less."

"It is one head," my mother says.

"The *queen's* head!" I cry. I am trembling.

"What would Curtius want you to do?" Isabel asks.

He would want me to choose life over death, whatever the cost.

But I do not go to witness the miserable spectacle of the queen's last moments. When the time comes for Isabel to walk with me to the cemetery, I stop in the Salon and pull a hidden rosary from beneath the shirt of Robespierre. "The last place anyone would ever look," I tell her.

We pray together in the darkness of the Salon. Although it's possible that God has abandoned France, we ask forgiveness for what we are about to do, and for His protection in whatever lies ahead. Last, we pray for the queen's soul.

Chapter 59

NOVEMBER 6–8, 1793

She screamed, she begged mercy of the horrible crowd that stood around the scaffold.

—ÉLISABETH VIGÉE-LEBRUN, ROYAL PORTRAIT ARTIST

I LOOK AT THE SLIP OF PAPER THE SOLDIER HAS BROUGHT TO ME, and my hands begin to tremble. "This cannot be right."

But the young man is firm. "Those are the names. The cafés are printing them on their menus. Go early if you want a good view."

I wait for the young soldier to leave before I show Isabel the names of those who will be executed tomorrow. "Anyone who has ever been a royal or associated with one," I whisper. "The Duc d'Orléans, Madame du Barry, the Princesse of Monaco!"

"And anyone who has ever spoken out against Robespierre, *The Incorruptible.*" She points to the bottom: Brissot, Vergniaud, Lasource, Madame Roland . . . "I thought Madame du Barry escaped to England?"

"She returned to retrieve her jewels," I say. Death, for a handful of gold.

I go to the kitchen to show my mother the list. "So for all his posturing," she says, "calling himself Philippe Égalité, they have turned on the Duc d'Orléans as well."

Robespierre preached against despots, and now he has become one himself.

"We must go and show our support of this," my mother says quietly. "If they are willing to send their greatest supporter to the guillotine, they will send anyone." She has not seen anyone die on the scaffold since the terrible device was first unveiled. "We will go early," she adds, surprising me, "so that the members of the Convention see us." She looks into the hallway toward Isabel's room. Many of the spectators bring children, carrying them on their shoulders. "We will leave Paschal here and lock the doors."

The next morning, we are awake at dawn. A fine mist hangs over the streets, and carriages are navigating the slick cobblestones with care. My mother whistles for a cabriolet, and the driver guesses, "The Place de la Révolution?" We are no different from the thousands who will wait in the cold to see illustrious lives come to an end. I wonder how the Duc must be feeling, knowing this Revolution he helped to create will take his own life. There must be rich irony in this for some, but I find I can take no pleasure in it.

We are among the first to arrive in the square, so just as my mother had hoped, we find places next to the area reserved for the members of the National Convention. Robespierre, of course, will not be here. He never attends an execution. But Danton may come, and certainly Camille, who knew the Duc well. By eight o'clock we are already surrounded by people, and by the time the tumbrels arrive it is impossible to see the end of the masses. Unlike the king, common criminals are forced to ride in open carts, regardless of the weather or the abuse of the crowds. But today, no one is hurling stones. This is a different kind of execution. "Philippe Égalité" was a man of the people, and few seem sure of the charges against him. There was talk of treason. But isn't there always talk of that? And what of Madame du Barry, who must be fifty now, and far removed from her days as Louis XV's mistress?

The tumbrels roll with jerky movements over the cobblestones, and the prisoners are pitched forward each time the horses are forced to stop. Even from a distance I can recognize the Duc. He is the largest man in any of the carts. Like the others, he has been dressed in red. Is he thinking about his cousin, whose execution he voted for almost a year ago? Now, he will die by the same blade.

It is the prerogative of the Revolutionary Tribunal to decide on the order of deaths, and the prisoner they wish to punish most always goes last. Men must watch their wives and children die. Particularly hated traitors are forced to wait until the razor has lost its edge after so much work. It is Madame du Barry they are asking to go first. They call her name, and she stands in the tumbrel. Despite her age, she is still alluring, with piercing eyes and jutting cheekbones. They have chopped her hair carelessly at the chin, yet the cut only serves to emphasize the smallness of her neck and the delicacy of her features. A soldier reaches to grab her hand, and she pulls away

"Not yet!" she screams. But the executioner is waiting. Two men step forward to take her arms, and she struggles against them. "Why are you doing this?" she cries. "What have I done? Tell me, what have I done?"

They escort her to the scaffold, but she is too weak to make it up the steps.

"Get up!" one of the soldiers commands, but her legs have given out.

"Don't hurt me," she begs. "Please," she screams to the crowd, "don't let them hurt me!"

They drag her to her feet, and my mother buries her face in her hands.

"Please!" du Barry is screaming. It is heart-wrenching to see. "Just one more moment!" But the executioner forces her down on the plank. "Just one moment more. Just one last view of the sky!" The plank slides forward, and her head is trapped in the wooden lunette. "Don't let him do this to me!" she is screaming. "Somebody save me from this!"

But there is no one to save her. France's heroes are dead.

Sanson pulls the rope, and the blade comes down swiftly. He holds her head up for the crowd to see, but there is no clapping. Just a long, mortified silence. She is the first of the guillotine's victims to struggle.

While the others have gone like sheep, she wanted life, and she fought for it.

Someone shouts, "The Committee of Public Safety has gone too far!"

The cry is echoed across the square, and suddenly, there is hope for the Duc d'Orléans, who will certainly be last. But the next victim is brought to the scaffold, and no one moves. It is one thing to speak, another to act. The rope is pulled, and the young man dies. Then the next victim mounts the scaffold, and the next. When it is time for the Duc to die, he doesn't fight. Perhaps he is too afraid. He makes a feeble attempt to speak, but Sanson orders the drumroll and his words are drowned out. When he is gone, there are no cheers from the crowd. I can feel resentment building through the square. Where are the riches this government assured us? Nothing these men have promised has come to pass. There is anger and frustration as the people disperse.

"THEY HAVE SPOKEN out! Someone has finally spoken out!" The next morning, Isabel thrusts a newspaper at me. "They're calling for an end to this Reign of Terror."

I read the article—written by Camille and Danton!—and they've used those exact words. "But Danton established the Committee of Public Safety himself."

"And now that he's seen how it's being used by Robespierre, he wants it to end."

So it's Camille and Danton against Robespierre. I put down the paper. "We must be very careful these next few weeks."

Isabel frowns. "But they are going to do away with the Committee."

"We don't know that."

"Robespierre can't win. He has to see that the people are angry."

But for him, it's not about the people anymore.

Chapter 60

March—May 1794

My mother is hysterical. She finds me in the workshop, transforming the figure of the Duc d'Orléans into a different member of the National Convention. "Marie!" she shouts, and when she appears, she's not wearing her fichu or her cap. "Marie, they have arrested Danton and Camille!"

I stand from my bench. "How do you know?"

"I just came from the bakery." She is breathing heavily. "They were speaking about it in the lines. They have imprisoned them in the Palais du Luxembourg."

I untie and hang up my apron, then put on my fichu. "I am going to see Lucile," I tell her. "I'll be back before noon."

The streets are nearly empty. Who wants to venture out when it is obvious now that no one is safe? Not even Robespierre's oldest school friend, Camille. I cannot fathom how Robespierre could give the orders for his arrest; he stood as a witness for him at his wedding. My God, he is Horace's godfather! I reach Camille's apartment on the Place Odéon and bang on the door. When there is no response, I let myself in. Somewhere in the house, a woman is weeping. I follow the sound until I reach the salon.

Lucile Desmoulins is alone. For the thousands of followers her husband has had, in this moment of tribulation they have all abandoned her. She looks up to see who has come. "They have taken him,

Marie! Rob-Robespierre has signed the order!" She is beside herself, hardly able to breathe.

"Shh," I say, stroking her hair, the way Henri used to calm me. "Lucile, it is only an arrest. There will have to be a trial." I keep stroking her hair, willing her to be calm.

"You know these trials!" she cries. "There is something *wrong* with him," she says. "His own friend. His *only* friend!"

It's true. It was Camille he trusted, Camille he turned to, and now, like Judas, Robespierre has betrayed him.

"He was jealous. He saw this grand apartment, and he was consumed. He thinks Camille has betrayed his principles, that he's no longer a man of the people because he owns a stable. But *I* provided him with his horses. He wants equality for all even if that means we are all living in the dust. And he will get it, Marie. He will achieve equality if that means cutting off every perfumed head."

Including his own?

"He lives off charity. He prides himself on the fact that he owns nothing, wants for nothing." There are footsteps in the hall, and then seven soldiers appear in red and blue uniforms. This cannot be real, and I think of the passionate young girl who came to our salons hot for the cause of liberty. One of the men steps forward. "Lucile Desmoulins?"

She begins to shake. "Yes," she answers feebly.

"The Committee of Public Safety has ordered your arrest. Do you come willingly, or shall these men bind your hands?"

"I'm a mother!" she cries, looking from face to face. "Please, I'm a mother!"

"You should have thought of that before you betrayed your nation."

"Marie, take Horace and bring him to my parents." She looks around the room, and I don't know how to help her or what to do. "Please let me say good-bye to my son," she begs.

"Citizeness, our orders are for your arrest. You will come with us now or we will take you by force."

"Horace!" she screams as they lead her away. "Horace, I love you!"

The heavy doors of the apartment slam shut, and there is silence. The curtains rustle in the wind like a woman's skirts. I look around the chamber, at the tables and chairs and the handsome escritoire. Then I collapse onto the marble floor and weep. A child's cries startle me from my misery. I climb the stairs and find Lucile's little boy nestled in the blankets of a mahogany crib. He is crying, but I have no way of feeding him. He needs his mother. I take him from the only chamber he's ever known and carry him through the streets to his grandmother, Madame Duplessis. When she sees the precious cargo I am carrying, she understands and her world is crushed.

~

WHEN THE DEATH sentences are read, I am not there to hear them. But my mother and Isabel find me in the workshop, and I can read from the lines on their faces what has happened in the Salle de Spectacle.

"Even Lucile?" I whisper.

"Yes. When they asked for Camille's age," Isabel says somberly, "he told them, 'I am thirty-three, the same age as that *sans-culotte* Jesus, a critical age for every patriot.' Women were weeping."

"But no one stood up for him?"

"No. They were too afraid."

I look to my mother, who always seemed young and beautiful to me. But in the last two years she has aged. I remember how the queen appeared just before her death. It was an old woman they sent to the guillotine, not the happy, laughing young royal who would run through the fields of wildflowers in her Hameau. "When will it be?"

"Tomorrow. Marie," my mother begins, and I can hear in her voice that something has changed, "you must not go to the Madeleine Cemetery this time."

I blink back my tears. "Maman, I have no choice—"

"There is always a choice! Those men today who voted for Lucile's death, they made a decision to condemn an innocent woman."

"Because of Robespierre."

"They still had free will!"

Isabel is lost. She cannot understand our conversation in German.

"My mother believes I should not go to the Madeleine. She doesn't understand that if I refuse, I am signing our own death warrants."

"I understand," my mother says in French.

My cheeks are wet. I remember Charlotte Corday. In her last speech to the Tribunal, she told them, "I die so that a hundred thousand people may live." For as long as my family wanted life, I owed them my trips to the Madeleine Cemetery. But now my mother is firm. "And Isabel and Paschal?" I ask her.

"If they come for anyone, they will come for us."

So I refuse. I do not go to the Madeleine to search for the bodies of an innocent mother and her earnest husband. And on the tenth of May, when the Committee takes the life of Madame Élisabeth for being related to the king, I spend the morning in my room praying over my rosary. It is what the princesse would have wanted me to do.

That evening, there is a knock at our door. It is too early to be the patrols. Isabel answers while my mother and I hurry into our warmest clothes. We have laid out our sturdiest boots and best dresses, and we slip on two fichus and two pairs of gloves. Though it is May, there is no telling how long we may be gone. I can hear gruff voices approaching the stairs, and I whisper for my mother to hurry. "Another hat," I tell her.

When the men arrive, we are ready. I have spent a lifetime reading people's faces, and I need only one look at Robespierre's to know that he has come for our arrest. When animals have finished attacking their prey and there is nothing left to eat, they will attack each other. This is the real reason he has come.

"Citizeness Grosholtz," he says, as if he has not known me by the name of Marie for seven years. "Is it true that you have refused to cast the masks of the traitors who have recently been put to death?"

"Yes," I tell him.

He waits for more, but I offer him nothing. He turns abruptly to my mother. "And you?"

"We can no longer sleep at night," she says. "Death haunts our dreams."

"That is the price true patriots must pay."

"Then we are done paying."

He studies her for a moment, then snaps his fingers. "Arrest them." Four soldiers step forward. If they were expecting a fight, they will be disappointed. I look into Robespierre's eyes. There is only arrogance and self-righteousness there. No pity, not even the glimmer of recognition. Robespierre levels me with his gaze. "May Saint Denis watch over you."

~

WE ARE TAKEN to Les Carmes prison on the Rue de Vaugirard, and despite the warmth of the night and my layers of clothing, I am shivering. My mother holds my hand as we pass through the gates. Les Carmes once belonged to the Carmelite monks. Now it is the worst prison in Paris.

Inside the monastery we are inspected for weapons or anything of value. Our gloves are confiscated, and when the chief jailer sees my mother's rosary, he throws it to the floor and crushes it underfoot. "Do you speak French?" he shouts into her face.

"Yes."

"Then you can understand this. There is no God in Les Carmes. God died on the scaffold with the rest of the aristocrats." The soldiers around us laugh. "But there is money." He smiles. *"As-tu de la sonnette?"*

He is asking if we have brought enough livres-assignats to pay for our bedding. "Yes," I say at once, and indicate the guard who has taken my purse. "Inside."

The jailer holds out his hand. "Give it to me."

A black-haired guard passes him my small leather bag, and the jailer empties the contents onto a desk. He sorts through the paper, then looks up at me. "It's enough," he says grudgingly. Was he hoping we could not afford a bed, since straw is cheaper to provide? "Will there be more next week?"

I think of my instructions to Isabel. That she must find us wherever we are and leave money for our keep, but she is never to reveal her name to the guards. "Yes. Another fifty-six livres-assignats."

He studies me, and I meet his eyes. I am not a liar. There will be money. "Take them to the first floor," he says sharply. "There is space in the room with our lovely Rose."

The black-haired guard smiles. "Welcome to Les Carmes. Although I do not expect your stay to be long." He produces a key to the prison door, then turns the lock.

My stomach tightens, and I grip my mother's hand. A pair of guards walk behind us in case we decide to run. But where is there to go? The passages we are led into are dark and windowless. And the stench . . . When I cough, the guard says, "Get used to it. It's even better in the day." The halls are lined with buckets of human waste. Where do they empty them? And what do they do when the heat creeps in and the flies begin to gather?

Two years ago more than a hundred priests were massacred in these halls, and I now see that the walls are still stained with their blood. My mother crosses herself, and the guard behind us makes a warning noise. But what more can they do to us? We are in hell. The jailer was right. There is no God in Les Carmes.

We reach a cell, and the guard slides a key into the lock. There is the sound of voices on the other side, and as the door creaks open, the lantern light falls over a room filled with beds and burning candles. "New prisoners!" the guard shouts.

We are pushed inside, and the door swings shut behind us. I listen as the guard turns the key in the lock; then there is silence. My mother and I stare into the dimly lit chamber. There are twenty beds and at least fifteen women, all with the same short hairstyle, cut at the neck. One of these girls, dressed in a long chemise gown and tattered slippers, rises from her bed to greet us.

"Welcome to Les Carmes," she says kindly. "I'm Rose de Beauharnais."

"You and your husband came to my Salon many years ago," I say. She is so thin, and her face is so pale. "You both wanted portraits."

"*You* are Marie Grosholtz?"

"And this is my mother, Anna."

"This is Marie Grosholtz," Rose announces. "The wax modeler from the Boulevard du Temple." She directs us to a pair of empty beds. "Why are you here?"

My mother and I sit across from each other while the women gather around. They are all so young. How did they end up in Les Carmes? "I would not make the death masks of Lucile Desmoulins or Princesse Élisabeth. They were good friends to me, and I would not dishonor them."

Rose's eyes fill with tears. "And your mother?" she asks.

"Has the misfortune of being related to me."

The other women nod understandingly, and one of them puts her arm around Rose's shoulders. "Don't cry," she encourages. But tears are rolling down Rose's cheeks.

"She weeps whenever someone new is brought to our cell." The woman smiles. "I am Grace Elliott."

"The Duc d'Orléans's mistress," I say. All of Paris knows who she is.

"His *former* mistress," she adds quietly. "There were many other women after me, but we always remained friends."

"Is that why you are here?"

She laughs sadly. "Do any of us really know why we are here?" She looks around, and the women shake their heads. "We are much like your mother. We've been imprisoned because of those we're related to, or those we've slept with. Rose's husband was arrested two months ago, and they came for her next. They were both sent here."

"To Les Carmes?" I exclaim. "There are men here?"

Everyone laughs, and a blond woman steps forward. "My dear, you have come to the most exciting prison in Paris. Every morning the soldiers arrive with the carts and the jailer reads out the names of those bound for the guillotine. But each day you survive is another day of freedom."

I don't understand.

"Louise is talking about sexual escapades," Grace explains.

I study the blond woman's face in the candlelight. I have seen her before. "Louise Contat?" I ask. "The actress from the Comédie-Française?"

She makes a little bow. "I may be climbing the scaffold soon," she says, "but 'tis only a change of theaters." All the women snicker except Rose, who looks as though she may faint. "Tomorrow, we'll all get up and wait for the lists, and when that is over we'll go and find our men."

"Most of us have someone," Grace explains. "Even Rose, when she isn't crying."

My mother and I look to Rose, who says unabashedly, "My husband has found Delphine de Custine, and they are a far better match than we ever were. I have found Lazare Hoche. That is what Louise means by freedom. And if you become pregnant, there is a ten-month stay of execution."

A soft murmur fills the room. I think of Henri in London and the life we might have had. By now, he surely will have found someone else. My eyes fill with tears.

Rose instructs me to lie down and get some sleep. "Is there anyone you have left?" she asks.

"My husband," my mother says, though of course they are not married. "Plus my daughter-in-law and grandchild."

"I am sure they will visit."

"Is that allowed?" my mother asks.

"If they are willing to pay. My children used to come with Fortune."

I frown and Grace explains. "Her pug dog. But it's not allowed anymore. She should not tell you these things. Even if they come, it will be dangerous for them. Do not hope for it."

"And tomorrow?" I ask. "What will happen?"

"Whether or not your names are called, they will cut your hair.

Then, if you are not bound for the carts, you are free to do as you please. Once a week, they allow us a newspaper."

My entire life has revolved around news. When it's happening, where it's being made, whom it's being made by. But the news now will be here, in the corridors of Les Carmes. "How long have you been imprisoned?"

"Five months," Grace replies.

I am stunned. "And they have not called your name?"

"Sophie has been in here for seven."

"So there is hope," my mother whispers.

Grace gives her a smile that once won the hearts of men like the Duc d'Orléans and the Prince of Wales. "There is always hope."

Chapter 61

May 1794

The antechamber of the guillotine.

—Anonymous reference to Les Carmes

I cannot sleep. After the candles are blown out, I listen to the rats scurrying across the floors. Somewhere on the other side of the room, a woman is weeping softly. For all their brave faces, everyone is afraid. Tomorrow, the carts will come, and there is no telling whose beds will be empty by night. There are seventeen of us in this chamber. Will we all die at the same time? Or will they take us one by one?

When the sun rises, I look across at my mother and can see that she has not slept either. Because our beds are so close, I am able to reach out and take her hand. "Do you have regrets?" I whisper in German.

She closes her eyes, and I imagine that she is picturing Paschal. How he screamed when we were taken away and begged his mother to bring us back. *"Grand-mère!"* he cried. "*Tatie,* don't go!" I had planned for our arrest in a dozen different ways, but I had not planned for what we should do if the soldiers came and Paschal was still awake. My mother opens her eyes, and her voice is firm. "No," she says. "I have no regrets."

The barber arrives and, after locking the door behind him, announces that he is here to prepare Anna and Marie Grosholtz. He cuts our hair short for the guillotine. When the job is done, he asks if there is anyone we might like to leave it to.

"I left mine to my daughter," Rose says from her bed. "It will be her inheritance."

I do not want my nephew to remember me by my death, and I shake my head. The barber looks to my mother, who is just as vehement. The old man shrugs. He sweeps our long hair into a bag, and I wonder if it is destined to be used on a wax head someday. But I refuse to cry.

"When they first cut off my hair, I wept all day," Rose admits.

"It is only hair," I tell her. "It will grow back."

"If you have enough time! The carts are coming right now. It could be me, or you, or—"

"Stop that," Grace snaps, and I think Rose will die of fear before they take her to the guillotine.

"Twenty-one," Rose says. Her voice rises. "To die at twenty-one?"

"Or forty," Grace retorts. "Or fourteen. There is a boy in here who is thirteen years old. 'Kill them all, and God will know His own,'" she says. "That is their motto."

There is the sound of a key turning in the lock, and many of the women stand from their beds. Rose whispers, "It's time."

"The carts are here!" the jailer shouts before he leaves us to open the next door in the hall. Hundreds of prisoners fill the corridors, and we join the crowd as they make their way to a giant hall where the monks must have gathered to eat. My mother and I sit next to Rose and Grace. There are at least eight hundred people here. "How many names do they call each day?" I ask Rose.

"Three. Sometimes four."

"Then your chances of being called are only one out of two hundred," I tell her.

She stares at me with her wide, dark eyes.

"I spent a good amount of time counting money and balancing books," I say. I want to tell her, *At least you weren't arrested by Robespierre himself. He didn't stare at you and say that only Saint Denis could save your life now.* Then I think of Madame Royale living alone in the Tuileries Palace. I heard that, after Madame Élisabeth's death, they separated Marie-Thérèse from her brother, and that the soldiers were treating young Louis-Charles with particular cruelty. Whatever Madame Royale's deeds against me were, and only God truly knows them, I am willing to forgive her. Today, if my name is called, I will go with a clean heart.

I search the hall for familiar faces. There are just as many men as women, both old and young, *culottes* and *sans-culottes.* A young man seats himself next to me, and I am struck by how similar to Henri he appears. He catches me staring and asks, "You are new here?"

"Last night."

"I'm sorry," he says with genuine sympathy. "They do this on purpose," he reveals. "Gather everyone and make them wait. It's a sad spectacle," he adds critically.

The chief jailer appears with a list in his hands. Immediately, the entire room is silent. I can see the way he makes us wait, searching the hall and letting his gaze rest on particular prisoners, who immediately bury their heads in their hands. "Today's list," he says slowly, "has eight people."

"Eight?" Rose turns to me. "What are our chances now?"

"One in a hundred."

My mother makes the sign of the cross, and the chief jailer begins to read. He pauses after each name, searching for the victim so he may see the reaction. When he reaches the end of the list and we have not been called, I am suddenly elated. We have survived! Our first day in Les Carmes and we will live to see another.

But there are devastating cries across the room as loved ones are parted and must make their good-byes. At once, I feel terrible guilt for my joy. A woman is forcibly parted from her husband as she is begging him to look after their daughter. I cover my eyes with my hand, and the man next to me says gently, "Don't sit at the front tomorrow. When you sit in the back, there's almost nothing you can hear. It's better that way."

I lower my hand. "So then why are you up here?"

He smiles. "Because I saw you."

I know I'm blushing, and I realize I should introduce myself. But is it possible to court this way in a prison? "I am Marie Grosholtz," I reply.

He takes my hand and kisses it tenderly. "I am François Tussaud."

ONCE THE HALL is cleared of the condemned, the prisoners are given carafes of dirty water and bowls of soup.

"We can go outside," François suggests. "If we leave now, we might find a bench."

I look to my mother. "Go," she says. I follow François into a little herb garden where we are allowed to sit on the wooden benches. There are guards posted along the wall, grateful for the chance to stand in the sunshine rather than inside, among the latrine buckets and bloodied floors.

"So you were born in Strasbourg," François guesses. He must hear my accent.

"Yes, but I remember almost nothing of it," I say.

"Like Mâcon. That's where my people are from. But they moved to Lyon when I was four, and all I can remember are the water mills."

I think of Marie Antoinette's Hameau, with its pots of lilacs and clusters of hyacinths. The water mill was Madame Élisabeth's favorite place in Versailles. Is someone still feeding the sheep and milking the cows, or has the Convention abandoned the rustic sanctuary to the honeysuckle and ivy? "But Lyon must be much like Mâcon," I say, picturing the thriving city between Paris and Marseille. "The cities are close."

"Yes. It was. Of course, now there is almost nothing left of it."

I tell him about the Salon de Cire, and he tells me he was an engineer. "So we were both builders," he says. "Except now there's nothing to build in Lyon."

"Why? What happened?" I ask.

I can see that the memory pains him. "It was a massacre," he reveals. "The city refused to support the Committee of Public Safety and wanted a return to the Constitution of 'Ninety-one. It was civil war. The papers in Paris never reported it?"

"No." I am certain of this. "I would have heard."

"It was Robespierre's doing. When our citizens refused to support the committee, he instructed his generals to 'exterminate every monster in Lyon.' "

"He used those words?"

"Yes. And that's what it was. An extermination of two thousand people: women, children, even the old and feeble. Because my family were metalworkers, the men were chained together and executed on the Plaine des Brotteaux. I escaped because I was in a neighboring village. When I returned, I saw that the Convention's soldiers had razed every house and apartment to the ground. Any store or building that looked as if it belonged to the wealthy, they destroyed. But they kept the slums standing. The poor were allowed to remain in their shacks as the true patriots and victims of the aristocracy. Ten days later, Robespierre ordered a column to be erected over the site of the largest burned building. It read, LYON MADE WAR ON LIBERTY, SO LYON IS NO MORE."

My eyes are filled with tears. "I'm sorry," François says. "I should not have spoken of this to a lady. You will never have seen such blood—"

"I have seen it all, and more."

I tell him about my brothers in the Tuileries Palace and my task of visiting the charnel house each night, searching through the baskets of mutilated bodies for the heads wanted by the National Convention. "When Lucile Desmoulins was sent to the scaffold, I refused to go back to the Madeleine Cemetery."

"And that is why you are here?"

"And why they arrested my mother. My father doesn't know," I say. To explain what Curtius truly is to me would be too long, too complicated. "He is stationed on the Rhine. I can't imagine his horror when he returns to discover that we have been arrested." Or worse, that we have died and been buried, like Gabrielle Danton. I am weeping openly now.

I must look as sad and helpless as Rose.

~

IN THE MORNINGS, François sits with me and my mother in the back of the hall, and when the carts have rolled away, he leads us into the garden, pointing out the herbs and describing their uses. When my mother becomes sick from the water they serve, he brings her some peppermint. He tells us that after his family was murdered, he lived off the land for more than six months. "Eventually, the soldiers discovered me and I was sent here," he says. "They might have killed me right then, but a single soldier took pity. He was a school friend of mine."

At night, before we are locked in our cells, I spend time with François in his chamber. He shares a room with fifteen other men. Most of them are seated on their beds with female prisoners, playing cards made from paper and talking about the old days when anything could be bought in the Palais-Royal and the cafés were filled with coffee and bread. We are always thinking about food, and you can pick out the prisoners who have been here longest by the sharpness of their cheekbones and the looseness of their clothes. The Revolution has truly made us equals. Now we are all poor and hungry and ill-clothed.

It is stifling in these cells. We pretend not to smell the fetid latrine buckets collecting flies in the hall, but none of us can escape the rising heat. It has been two weeks since I have had a bath, and for many in here it has been much longer.

"I have something for you," François says one evening. He pulls a newspaper from under his pillow and puts a finger to his lips. "One of the guards gave it to me. I won it at cards."

"It's today's paper," I say, shocked.

"Did you think I would bet on old news?"

Chapter 62

June 15, 1794—July 1794

[I] cut off my hair myself; it is the only remembrance I can leave my children. Now I am ready to die.

—Princesse de Monaco, prisoner in Les Carmes

Ten days later, François bursts into my cell before the guards can lock it for the night. The other women are in various states of undress, but none of them bother to cover themselves. The men have seen it all at Les Carmes. What is there to hide?

"I have the *Chronique de Paris*!" he exclaims. He comes to my bed, and the women quickly gather around us. He watches my face as I read the first article. "They have guillotined Madame Sainte-Amaranthe," I whisper, "along with her children, Émilie and Louis."

There are cries of horror, and Rose nearly collapses. Her skin is clammy, and her hands are shaking. "I knew Madame Sainte-Amaranthe," she says.

"She was a well-known royalist," Grace whispers. "I played cards in her salon last year, and she still had a portrait of the king above her mantel."

The women shake their heads. So foolish, to risk your life like that. "I modeled Émilie five years ago," I say. "She would be nineteen now and her brother sixteen."

"Every day the list is getting longer. First four, then eight, now it's ten per day. What is that, Marie?" Rose asks. "What are our chances?"

"One in eighty." I should never have told her about odds. I should have left my calculations behind with the Salon de Cire.

"There is a second article," François points out, "you may want to read. The Committee of Public Safety has passed the Law of 22 Prairial."

I skim the contents. "Those who stand before the Revolutionary Tribunal," I say, "are no longer permitted to have anyone speak in their defense. And all citizens who are found guilty are to be sentenced to immediate death."

"*Immediate?*" Rose grips my arm. "But that doesn't mean us. We have already been sentenced. That will only apply to those who come after."

Grace looks over my shoulder and reads aloud, "Every citizen is empowered to seize conspirators and counterrevolutionaries, and to bring them before the Revolutionary Tribunal. It is the duty of every patriot to denounce all traitors to our *patrie* as soon as they know of them." She continues, "For slandering patriotism, for inciting rebellion with dangerous words, for corrupting the purity of the Revolution, and for spreading false news."

"It is the second Inquisition," François says.

He is right. The next morning as we assemble in the hall, several hundred new prisoners are brought into the room. There is no space at the back, so we are forced to sit with Grace and Rose and listen as the names are called. First five, then ten, then fifteen in total.

"The blood will pool so thick beneath the guillotine that it will take an ocean of water to wash it clean," Grace predicts.

And every day it is like this. More prisoners, more victims, until in the middle of July there are forty women sharing our cell. The mood in the hall every morning becomes frantic. Grace believes there will be another prison massacre, like the one that resulted in the Princesse de Lamballe's slaughter. She tells us how the revolutionaries placed the beautiful princesse's head on a pike and shoved it through the window of her cabriolet. "It was only because I was Scottish that they did not murder me right there."

Of course, that is no protection now.

To escape, I spend much of my time in the gardens. In the mornings, François walks with me, and in the evenings, I go with my mother and Grace. But as July's heat intensifies, no one feels like moving. "What is the point?" Rose asks. "It is cooler in the cells than it is out there." When I ask her about the smell of festering waste, she replies, "At least there is nothing to remind us in here of the world we will never rejoin outside."

So I go alone to the garden in the middle of the day and am not surprised to see an empty bench. It's directly in the sun, but why should I care about my complexion? Will the executioner's job be any different if I am dark or pale? My mother and I have been here now for two and half months, but there is no one I recognize in the garden. New prisoners arrive every day, replacing the ones who are sent away in carts. But someone thinks he recognizes me.

"Marie?"

The voice is immediately familiar. I turn, and as I shade my eyes with my hands, my vision blurs. It's impossible. I rise from the bench. No . . . I am dreaming.

"Marie," Edmund says, "it's me."

I grab the back of the bench in case my legs give out, then look around the garden for help. *Is this real? Do the others see him as I do?* But when my brother steps closer, I know that it is him. He is dressed as a common *sans-culotte,* with a loose white shirt and dirty brown pants. His hair is longer than I have ever seen it, even when we were children, and instead of being tied back with a band, it hangs around his shoulders. I am caught between the desire to beat him and the impulse to embrace him.

"Marie, I am a coward," he whispers. "I escaped," he says in German. "I fled the Tuileries after Johann was killed."

I back away from him.

"You have to understand—"

"That you left Maman in agony? That you let us believe you died in the worst possible way?" The other prisoners are staring, but I do not care. He reaches out to touch me, but I slap his hand away. "You betrayed us!" I cry. "Where have you been? Did you ever think of Maman's suffering?" I ask. "Did you ever wonder what happened to Wolfgang and Abrielle and Michael?"

"Please, sit," he begs. He is a different man. Tired, beaten, full of regret. "They died."

"No, they are living in London—with Henri!"

Now it is his turn to be shocked.

"You were prepared to let Maman believe she had lost three sons."

"I was a coward, Marie. Why would Maman want to see a coward?"

"Because you are her *child.*" I am weeping, and the guards are watching us. They probably believe this is some lovers' spat. "So while we were marking your grave," I confirm, "you were hiding in Paris?"

"For a week. I knew if I came to the Boulevard they would find me. But I was arrested on the eighth day. I gave them a different name, and they took me to La Force."

"And you didn't think to send word?"

"They were going to kill me. Why would I make Maman suffer twice?"

In the heat of the day, it is difficult to think. I put my hand to my head.

"I was imprisoned at La Force until last week," he says.

"*Two* years?"

"Twenty-two months. They think I am the son of a farmer. It's the only reason they haven't executed me."

I stare at him in the harsh light of the sun. His face is pale, and his broad chest, which once filled out his Swiss Guardsman's uniform, is no longer well muscled and defined. "I assumed you were among the first to die."

He flinches. "It was a massacre. I am not proud of what I did."

"What does it matter?" I ask sharply. "Johann is dead because he remained."

We watch each other, and a lifetime of bitterness hangs between us.

"I am sorry, Marie. There were many things I could not appreciate before I was imprisoned. Family, love . . ."

My throat closes. Perhaps we were more alike than I believed. "Henri asked me to go with him and I refused."

My brother nods. "We were married to our ambition."

It hurts to hear this from him. But he is right.

"How long have you been here?" he asks.

"Two and a half months. Curtius is at the Rhine, and Maman was arrested with me."

"She is here?"

"You must not go and see her! She lost you once. She cannot lose you again. What if your name is called tomorrow?" I ask. "Or the next day? Or the next?"

Though I can see how this pains him, he understands. "Of course. I will make sure she never sees me." It is difficult to reconcile this Edmund with the Edmund I knew. He must guess at what I am thinking, because he adds, "Two years can change everything."

We embrace, and I feel the thinness of his body through his shirt. They have starved him in La Force. "Perhaps we can meet again here tomorrow," he offers.

"No. Maman comes and walks with me sometimes. Once after breakfast, once at noon, and another time at sunset."

"I will be careful," he promises. "In case you ever look for me, I am Émilien Drouais."

He squeezes my hand, and despite the many betrayals and heartaches between us, he is still my brother. "I hope we will meet again on the outside," I say. "If not, I will see you in heaven."

I TELL NO one about my meeting with Edmund, but I search for him every morning in the hall, praying that they will never call Émilien Drouais. He is the one I think about as the list grows longer each day. Eventually, the guards are forced to keep order while the chief jailer reads. Throughout Les Carmes they are blaming this escalation on the Law of 22 Prairial.

On the twenty-third of July, when the chief jailer reads the name "Alexandre de Beauharnais," Grace grabs Rose's arm and I implore her to sit down. It is all we can do to stop her from flinging herself at the guards. When her husband crosses the hall to embrace her farewell, she faints. She is not conscious to watch as his lover begs the guards for one more moment. They warn his mistress to keep back or join him in the cart.

François takes my hand. "Keep strong," he whispers. "We have seen worse than this."

But I am so tired . . . "I just want to lie down and never wake up," I tell him.

"Don't say that. We will get out of here, Marie."

"Yes, in a cart or a coffin."

He can see that I am giving up. When the sun sets, he sleeps on the floor beside my bed, telling me stories about the famous silk manufacturers of Lyon and what it was like to grow up in a merchant city. The guards have stopped locking the doors at night. What is the point when there are so many prisoners that the beds spill out from the cells into the hall? I have no idea if Isabel still brings fifty-six livres-assignats for the jailer each week, and it no longer matters, really. Straw, no straw. A bed, no bed . . .

On the twenty-sixth of July, forty-three names are called. At this rate, we will all be dead by September. That evening, I do not take supper with the rest of the prisoners. I remain in my cell, and François joins me on my bed. We sit facing each other, trying not to breathe too deeply of the rancid air. "If we are ever released from this prison," he says, "I would like to marry you."

I think at once of Henri. Almost certainly he will have found a wife by now. They will be living together in an apartment in London. Or perhaps, if she is wealthy, they will have bought a house, even started a family. "I had thought to go to London," I say.

He stares at me. "We are at war with England! It could be another twenty years before any Frenchman is allowed to cross the Channel."

I close my eyes. *Why didn't I take my chance when I had it?*

"Marie, I want you to be my wife. Tell me you will marry me."

"It's likely we'll meet our deaths tomorrow."

"Then we can live our last day together in hope."

I search his face and see that he is earnest. He is a handsome man, with a good education and a tender heart. From the moment we met here in Les Carmes, he made it his mission to watch over me. I cannot undo what's been done. If I am ever set free, it will be to live my life in the confines of Paris. "Yes," I tell him, and he kisses me. For a moment, I am back in Henri's embrace, smelling his hair, caressing his skin, and brushing my lips against his.

Chapter 63

July 28, 1794

Welcome, day of delivery [July 27]
You have come to purify a bloody land.

—Hymn to July 27

"He has been arrested!" someone is shouting. "Robespierre has been arrested!"

We scramble from our beds into the hall, where a guard is standing at the top of the stairs with the keys of the prison clenched in his hand. "Follow me!" he cries.

The sound of a thousand prisoners hurrying up the stairs echoes above our cell. It is just after dawn, but everyone is awake. There is laughing and crying. We can hear men cheering from the great room. We follow the other prisoners up the steps into the hall, and inside it is chaos. Soldiers from outside the prison have arrived with kindling for the fireplace, and they are burning the chief jailer's records, paper by paper. François finds the guard who has been so generous as to lose at most games of poker and asks him what's happening.

"They arrested Robespierre last night," the guard says. "The National Convention has charged him with being a tyrant."

The irony of this is not lost of any of us.

"When he realized they were coming for him," the guard adds, "he attempted to shoot himself." He smiles. "All he succeeded in doing was shattering his jaw. They are taking him to the Place de la Révolution. They are to guillotine him this morning along with all of his accomplices."

As the news spreads, there are shouts of relief and tears of joy. But at noon, when word comes that Robespierre is dead, there is a startled silence.

It is real. The Terror is over.

A soldier stands at the front of the hall and announces that we are all free. Throughout the room, men and women are crying. I embrace my mother, and we weep into each other's arms. I think of all the people we shall live to see again. Curtius, Paschal, Isabel . . . Edmund.

Next to me, François caresses my cheek. His eyes are red and his hands are trembling. "Madame Tussaud, will you escort me to freedom?" He takes me by the arm, and I am filled with the most immense gratitude I have ever known.

God, it seems, exists even in Les Carmes.

Epilogue

England

August 11, 1802

As the ship sails into port, Joseph rushes to the rails, begging to be picked up so he can see the shore. At four years old, my son wants to run, and touch, and explore. Everything is an endless adventure for him. I lift him onto my hip and ask what he can see on the docks.

"Happy people," he says.

I smile. Yes. There is one man, in particular, who will be happy to see us. I search the crowd for his face, and he is standing beside my brother and his wife. After ten years, it is as if nothing has changed. He wears his hair loose around his shoulders, and there are still smile lines around his eyes. From the cut of his coat, I can see that he is doing well for himself. Then, for a moment, I panic.

What if he is disappointed in what he sees? I am not a young woman anymore. In the eight years since Robespierre's fall, I have been married and given my husband two sons: Joseph, and Francis, who is two. They have not been easy years. After the end of the Terror, whatever money I earned, François gambled or drank away. We have been poor, then wealthy, then poor again, and now my fortune has changed with rise of a Corsican general named Napoléon Bonaparte. He has taken for his wife a young woman I once knew as Rose de Beauharnais, renaming her Joséphine and promising to someday crown her Empress over all of France. Together they have rebuilt what was once torn down, and though I did not think I would live to see peace between England and France, Napoléon has signed a treaty. It has allowed me passage to the man I have yearned after now for ten years.

Much has been given up for this voyage. I have left my mother behind with my second son, since she is too old to travel and Francis is too young. It is my hope that François will take care of them. The models I did not bring on this ship, I left with him. But my guess is that it will be Maman and Isabel who will run the Salon de Cire in my absence. Under the constant threat of death, François was one man, but in the aftermath of war, he became another. Still, he has given me two beautiful gifts, and for that I will always be thankful. I look at my son and ask if he has ever seen such tall, white cliffs.

As the ship is being secured at the dock, I catch my reflection in a small window. I would like to believe that I am not much different than the thirty-one-year-old woman Henri left in Paris. On the inside, however, a great deal has changed. I take Joseph's hand, and we step together onto the plank. At the bottom, just as he promised he would be, Henri is waiting.

Whatever happens for me here in England, I shall not betray my heart again.

After the Revolution

Marie Grosholtz

After Marie arrived in England in 1802 with her elder son, Joseph, she never looked back. Henri was there waiting for her, as were several other émigrés who had fled the Revolution. Together, they took their shows throughout England, traveling from city to city for the next thirty-three years. In 1822, Marie, Henri, and Joseph boarded a ship bound for Ireland, where they hoped to tour. The captain of the *Earl Moira,* however, was inebriated, and the ship went down off the coast of Liverpool. Of the more than one hundred passengers on board, only half survived, including Marie and her party. In the disaster, however, all of Marie's wax figures were lost.

After the shipwreck, Marie set about re-creating each of her models, basing them on her exceptional memory and a box of miniatures she'd been able to salvage. When word reached France that she was not one of those who had drowned, her younger son was overjoyed. He left his father in Paris to join his mother's traveling exhibition. Meanwhile, François Tussaud was delighted to hear of Marie's rescue for another reason. It meant that he could continue to harangue her for money.

Marie's marriage to François Tussaud in October 1795 had been one of her greatest errors in judgment in a life that would span almost nine decades. An inveterate gambler with an aversion to work, François Tussaud saw her as his meal ticket to an easy life. Their short union resulted in three children: a daughter, who died in infancy, and two sons. In what is an extraordinary document for the time, Marie's marriage contract stipulated that she would retain all of the possessions with which she entered the marriage. This turned out to be a very wise decision. Within five years, it was clear that the marriage would never be a partnership. Whatever money Marie made, her husband gambled away, and for a woman obsessed with financial security, this must have been devastating.

Within months of Napoléon signing the Treaty of Amiens (1802), Marie had begun preparing for her trip to England. She knew that her husband would never consent to her taking both children, which meant she was forced to leave Francis behind. She hoped to send for him as soon as she had the funds, but life on the road was incredibly difficult and made more so by François's frequent letters demanding more money. Finally, in 1804, Marie wrote to her husband, "My enterprise has become more important to me than returning to you. Adieu, adieu, we must each go our own way." She never communicated with him again.

At eighty-one, Marie created her final figure, a self-portrait that can still be seen in many of her wax museums around the world. In 1850, just eight years later, she died in her sleep in London. She lived long enough to see the rise and fall of Napoléon, the return of the monarchy in France, the crowning of Queen Victoria in England, and the commemoration in stone of the Swiss Guards' massacre. This monument can be seen in Lucerne, Switzerland, dedicated to the nearly eight hundred Swiss Guardsmen who were killed in 1792. Carved from sandstone, the sculpture shows a dying lion impaled by a spear and resting on a pair of shields, one of which bears the symbol of the French monarchy. Mark Twain called the Lion Monument the "saddest and most moving piece of rock in the world."

PHILIPPE CURTIUS

After Robespierre's fall, Curtius was sent home from his prolonged mission along the Rhine. Having been for so long responsible for reporting on the patriotism of various revolutionary generals, he returned severely ill and emotionally exhausted. Less than a month later, on September 26, 1794, he passed away. Curtius left Marie all of his possessions, including mirrors, candelabra, and the *caissier*'s desk where his protégée had learned to manage money.

ANNA GROSHOLTZ

With Curtius gone and Marie in England, Anna Grosholtz dedicated the rest of her life to raising her grandson Francis Tussaud and watching over the Salon de Cire. After her death, Francis joined his mother in England.

FRANÇOIS TUSSAUD

In 1802, when Marie left for England with her elder son, Joseph, François remained in Paris, ostensibly to take care of their two-year-old son and run the Salon de Cire. All the money and property Marie had left in his care, however, was swiftly lost to his gambling. Hearing of his wife's success in England, François began sending letters asking for financial support, until finally she cut off all communication. However, at seventy-two years old, François decided that it was time to renew their correspondence. After four decades of silence, he wrote to remind Marie that she was still legally his wife and that he would like to be given power of attorney. Predictably, Marie rejected this request. François's demands for money continued until his death, in 1848.

THE DAUPHIN, LOUIS-CHARLES

After the Reign of Terror came to an end, the world seemed to forget about the nine-year-old dauphin, Louis-Charles. Horribly abused by his captors both mentally and physically, he was forced to live in a tiny cell surrounded by rats and covered in his own excrement. Now Louis XVII of France, he had been imprisoned in solitary confinement from the time he was eight years old, and no one seemed interested in rescuing him from his torment. On June 8, 1795, Louis-Charles died at just ten years old. Numerous impostors later claimed to be him, but DNA testing performed in 2000 proved that Louis-Charles did, in fact, die in the Temple.

MADAME ROYALE, MARIE-THÉRÈSE

Marie-Thérèse was the only member of her immediate family to survive the Revolution. After being separated from her brother, she was imprisoned by herself in the Temple until 1795, when the new French government agreed to her release the day before her seventeenth birthday. Sent to Austria to live with the family of Holy Roman Emperor Francis II, Marie-Thérèse was persuaded to marry her cousin Louis-Antoine, the Comte d'Artois's son. The marriage was a very unhappy one, and it is unlikely it was ever consummated.

In 1824, the Comte d'Artois became King Charles X of France, and Marie-Thérèse became Madame la Dauphine, next in line for the throne along with her husband. After a three-day Revolution in 1830, Charles X was forced to abdicate. Marie-Thérèse then became Queen of France and her husband became King Louis XIX. Their reign lasted for only twenty minutes, however. Recalling the Revolution that had taken his aunt's life only thirty-seven years before, Louis-Antoine abdicated on the spot. Marie-Thérèse lived the remainder of her years in exile. She died in Austria in 1851 at seventy-two years old.

Rose Bertin

In 1795, Rose returned to France, where she discovered that new fashions had emerged from the dirt and grime of the Revolution. Gone were the days of liberty caps and tricolor cockades. In their places were rich silk pantaloons, pashmina shawls, and transparent dresses modeled after those of Greek and Roman goddesses. Rose continued to dress the wealthy women of Paris, and her customers included Empress Joséphine, formerly known as Rose de Beauharnais. In 1813, at sixty-six years old, Rose passed away in her house in Paris.

Marquis de Lafayette

Perhaps no man was more devastated by the failure of the French Revolution than the Marquis de Lafayette. Having been instrumental in the American victory over the English, he truly believed that, after the storming of the Bastille, the French were on the threshold of democracy. A key to the Bastille that he sent to George Washington can still be seen on tours of Mount Vernon in Virginia. It was accompanied by a note that read, "[Here is] the main key of that fortress of despotism. It is a tribute which I owe as a son to my adoptive father, as an aide-de-camp to my General, as a Missionary of liberty to its Patriarch."

But Lafayette's role as a "missionary of liberty" was short-lived. After being declared a traitor to France, he fled to the Dutch Republic, where he was arrested by the Austrians and imprisoned at the citadel of Wesel. His wife petitioned Emperor Francis II to live with her husband in prison, and this is where she died in 1797. Several months later, Napoléon Bonaparte negotiated Lafayette's release.

For the rest of his life, Lafayette remained active in politics. In 1824, he returned to the United States to tour the country whose liberty he helped secure. He visited George Washington's tomb at Mount Vernon, and his reunion with Thomas Jefferson that same year deeply affected those who saw it. Jefferson's grandson recalled that the two shuffling old men "threw themselves with tears into each other's arms—of the 300 or 400 persons present not a sound escaped except an occasional suppress sob, there was not a dry eye in the crowd." The men had not seen each other for thirty-five years. Another witness to this emotional reunion was Lafayette's own son, George Washington. Ten years later, Lafayette died in France. He was buried at the Cimetière de Picpus under soil from Bunker Hill.

JACQUES CHARLES

Rather than flee the Terror, Jacques Charles remained in Paris, where he continued his scientific experiments. In 1793, he was elected to the Académie des Sciences and became a professor of physics at the Conservatoire des Arts et Métiers. He died in 1823 at seventy-six years old and is credited with the law of volumes now called Charles's Law.

JOSEPH AND FRANCIS TUSSAUD

Fifteen years before her death, Marie and her sons moved their traveling exhibition into a permanent location on Baker Street in London. From here, the small family worked to promote and improve what would eventually become the world's most famous wax museum, Madame Tussauds. In addition to curiosities such as the shirt the French king Henry IV was wearing when he was murdered, Marie and her sons purchased King George IV's coronation robes, adding authenticity to what would already have been a very realistic exhibit. After their mother's death, Joseph and Francis Tussaud continued working at her trade. In 1884, when rent became too high at Baker Street, Marie's grandson moved the exhibition to its current location, on Marylebone Road. Today, Madame Tussauds has expanded across the globe, with museums in Berlin, Los Angeles, and Shanghai, among other locations.

Historical Note

It is hard to relate just how turbulent and bloody the years of the French Revolution really were. The fall of the monarchy and the subsequent rise of a far worse, far deadlier tyranny make for what can be a challenging read, simply because so many innocent people perished in the name of liberty, equality, and fraternity. Although estimates differ, up to forty thousand people may have met their end by guillotine. And contrary to popular belief, more than eighty percent of those victims were commoners.

What began as an earnest desire for freedom ended in a bloodbath that would eventually claim the lives of up to half a million citizens all across France. The highest casualities came during the war in the Vendée, where entire villages were wiped out in what some have considered the first modern genocide. The National Convention approved of this slaughter, and their captain, Charles-Philippe Ronsin, suggested deporting the unruly Vendéans and replacing them with patriots who knew what it meant to believe in "liberty." Soon, the Convention began looking into ways of achieving mass extermination. Gassing was considered by General Rossignol, while General Cordellier dispatched enemies of the *patrie* with swords rather than guns (to save on powder). Women and children were massacred en masse, and arrests were made for offenses such as spitting on a liberty tree or wearing clothes deemed "too fancy."

Yet Madame Tussaud did not let the horrors of the Terror define her. Marie's life before the Revolution was filled with the richness and variety of being a show-woman on the Boulevard du Temple as well as a tutor to the king's sister. Few women from this period are remembered as having straddled both worlds and lived to tell the tale. And just as fascinating as Marie's time at court was her time in England, when she transformed herself into the famous wax artist Madame Tussaud. While much of her memoirs is fabricated (including what should be obvious facts, such as her place of birth), we are fortunate to know a great deal about Marie's life. Her fixation with money and the fact that she was one of the only women in her time to draw up a prenuptial agreement speak volumes about the woman behind the wax masks. Marie was Curtius's daughter through and through, if not literally (and there is some debate on that), then at the very least in spirit. In a critique written by Monsieur de Bersaucourt, Curtius was described as a man willing to take advantage of any situation. Bersaucourt wrote:

> He is wily, this German! He changes all the time according to the wind, the situation, the government, the people in power. He removes "the King at Dinner," and replaces it with figures of the deputies of the Gironde. He is successively Feuillant, Girondin, Jacobin, Maratiste, Hebertiste, Robespierriste, Thermidorien. He goes with what is in fashion, Curtius. He is a follower of the on-going government, whatever that may be, both supporting and applauding their success. One does not have a strong opinion if one is Curtius, the "Vanquisher of the Bastille."

The same critique may be made of Marie, whose opinion of the Revolution is never made clear. When Curtius died, he bequeathed to his niece nearly all of his possessions. Yet what she chose to take with her to England is telling. She left behind a sword commemorating her uncle's participation in the storming of the Bastille, his Bastille rock (with its certificate of authenticity), and the wax bust of him in his National Guardsman's uniform, which now resides in the Carnavalet

Museum in Paris. Perhaps this was the politic thing to do when sailing for the land of King George III. Or perhaps her true sympathies lay with the royalists. While we may never know, one of the greatest joys in being a writer of historical fiction is the ability to include little gems from history within the novel.

The chamber pot, for instance, with Benjamin Franklin's face on the bottom, really was a gift from King Louis to one of the women at court. And a planisphere clock that could mark the phases of Jupiter's moon was first built in 1745 and can be seen today in California's J. Paul Getty Museum. It may come as a surprise that France at this time was rife with competing newspapers, from the *Gazette de France,* established in 1631, to Marat's short-lived *L'Ami du Peuple.* Journalists wielded as much power as—if not more power than—members of the various revolutionary governments.

But perhaps the most intriguing bit of history I came across was the importance of cafés in the Revolution. The choice of café indicated a person's politics to the world. From the time they were first established in Paris, in 1669, coffeehouses were places to meet, drink, play chess or draughts, and talk over politics. The Café le Procope served luminaries such as Danton, Marat, Robespierre, and Napoléon. And it was at the Café de Foy that the course of Camille Desmoulins's life was changed forever. According to the French historian Jules Michelet (1798–1874), just before the Revolution,

> Paris became one vast café. Conversation in France was at its zenith. There were less eloquence and rhetoric than in '89. With the exception of Rousseau, there was no orator to cite. The intangible flow of wit was as spontaneous as possible. For this sparkling outburst there is no doubt that honor should be ascribed in part to the auspicious Revolution of the times, to the great event which created new customs, and even modified human temperament—the advent of coffee. Its effect was immeasurable. . . . The reign of coffee is that of temperance. Coffee, the beverage of sobriety, a

> powerful mental stimulant, which, unlike spirituous liquors, increases clearness and lucidity; coffee, which suppresses the vague, heavy fantasies of the imagination, which from the perception of reality brings forth the sparkle and sunlight of truth.

And as the Revolution began, the English traveler Arthur Young (1741–1820) had this to say:

> The coffee houses present yet more singular and astounding spectacles; they are not only crowded within, but other expectant crowds are at the doors and windows, listening *à gorge déployée* to certain orators who from chairs or tables harangue their little audiences; the eagerness with which they are heard, and the thunder of applause they receive for every sentiment of more than common hardiness or violence against the government, cannot easily be imagined.

In a time when politics were changing as rapidly as fashion, Marie Grosholtz was there to chronicle it all. The Salon de Cire became almost as important a news source as the dozens of papers being printed daily across France. And her uncanny talent for memorizing facial features and replicating them later, first in clay, then in wax, made her exhibition one of the most popular in Paris. Of course, it helped that her uncle knew all of the important men of the time—including Voltaire, Rousseau, Robespierre, Marat, Desmoulins, and the Duc d'Orléans—and invited them to his salon.

Yet Marie's family was in the precarious position of straddling two worlds. Despite her past as a tutor to Madame Élisabeth in Montreuil, she was given the task of making death masks on behalf of the National Convention. Philip Astley, a neighbor on the Boulevard du Temple whose circus was so famous that it earned a mention in Jane Austen's *Emma,* recalled the terrible scene when the mob brought Marie the heads of de Launay and de Flesselles:

> Curtius was not at the Salon de Cire when the mob rampaged up the hill to 20 boulevard du Temple, bearing on pikes the heads of M. de Launay and M. de Flesselles. Delighted with their bloody trophies they demanded that Marie take casts of the heads to commemorate the actions of the day, which she did reluctantly, insisting on working outside on the pavement, for she refused to let the mob into the Salon.

Many of the most shocking scenes in the novel are based on contemporary accounts. The inspection of Charlotte Corday's corpse to determine whether or not she was a virgin really took place, as did Danton's desperate act of digging up his wife to make a final mask of her face. The last moments of Madame du Barry were recorded by those who witnessed her execution. Her desperate pleas so rattled the crowd—used to seeing people march to their deaths in dignified silence—that the executioner feared there would be a revolt. After her execution, the jewels for which she had unwisely returned to France were sold in London at Christie's auction house in 1795. They fetched £8,791.

It is tempting to imagine how different the course of events might have been had the royal family succeeded in their escape. But from the beginning it was a doomed plan. As Lafayette remarked, the queen seemed "more concerned about looking beautiful in the face of danger than about staving it off," and for months before her flight, she planned the kind of wardrobe she would take. She placed lavish orders with Rose Bertin and, in the process, made one of her servants suspicious. If that was not enough, her husband was a man of great ambivalence. In 1791 the Marquise de Bombelles wrote in what are known as the Vaudreuil Papers, "The feebleness of our sovereign puts me in a rage . . . you cannot imagine how he is despised . . . or what his nearest relatives say of him." The opportunity for escape had presented itself many times, but always he was uncertain. Looking back on the early events of the Revolution, Napoléon believed that if King Louis XVI had only "mounted his horse, victory would have" been his. But the king was a man of thought, not of action. When he finally decided it was time to flee, he left behind a note condemning the Revolution and ensuring his own demise should he be captured. The resulting fiasco when he was apprehended in Varennes began the quick and steady march to anarchy.

In the years after the royal family's failed escape, France experienced rapid changes in government, beginning with the establishment of the National Convention. A new calendar was declared, along with a new method of counting the years. And while Jesus was regarded as an upstanding citizen and a fine example of a *sans-culotte,* the practice of any religion was abolished. In their fanaticism to spread liberty and equality, the revolutionaries created a tyranny. Thomas Jefferson watched these events unfold from the other side of the Atlantic, and he reflected on the prospects of democracy surviving beyond a single generation. "I predict future happiness for Americans," he wrote, "if they can prevent the government from wasting the labors of the people under the pretense of taking care of them." It was this pretense that led to the establishment of the Revolutionary Tribunal and later the Committee of Public Safety. And yet, after all the bloodshed in the name of freedom, it was Napoléon Bonaparte who came to power next, declaring himself Emperor of all of France. More than fifty years of monarchy followed his reign, including the eighteen-year kingship (1830–1848) of Louis-Philippe I, son of the Duc d'Orléans.

Yet while I tried to convey these events as best I could, there were details I changed to better serve the story. The dates of Madame du Barry's execution, of Lucile Desmoulins's and Princesse Lubomirska's arrests, of Robespierre's whereabouts when the book begins, and the publication of Jeanne de Valois's scandalous memoirs were all altered slightly. Similarly, Camille's journal, *Les Révolutions de France,* began in November 1789 (not July), and the members of the Jacobin Club—so named because of where they chose to meet—were not actually called Jacobins until 1791.

As for the guillotine, it was initially called *le Louison* after Dr. Antoine Louis, who designed its prototype. In 1789, however, it was Dr.

Joseph-Ignace Guillotin who stood before the Assembly and suggested that any criminal sentenced to die would do so painlessly if this new machine were used. Although personally against the death penalty, Dr. Guillotin wanted to see an end to messy executions by ax or breaking on the wheel. After he remarked, "Now, with my machine, I cut off your head in the twinkling of an eye and you never feel it," Guillotin's name became associated with what is arguably the world's most infamous device. Mortified by this connection, Dr. Guillotin's family petitioned the government to change the guillotine's name. When their petition was refused, they changed their family name instead. It is a common misconception that the guillotine ceased to be used once the Revolution was over. It actually remained an official method of execution in France until September 10, 1977, when the last guillotining took place.

Other changes were made in the book as well. What we would consider science, for example, was actually deemed philosophy, and scientists were called philosophers. There is also no evidence that Madame Royale ever informed Robespierre about Marie's royalist sympathies, although her character in the novel is true to contemporary accounts of her personality. As for the men who were given the task of fighting the Revolutionary Wars, Luckner was not made a general until after Lafayette's flight to Liège, and there is no evidence that one of Marie's brothers became a captain in the National Guard. In fact, the fates of all three brothers remain unknown, although Marie claimed in her memoirs that all of them perished during the tragic massacre of the Swiss Guards. Last, because this period of French history is so turbulent, filled with frequent changes in government, some of the major influences on revolutionary politics had to be skipped, such as the presence of the Girondists and the establishment of the Paris Commune.

Yet however complicated and chaotic these politics may seem, Marie Grosholtz followed them all in her exhibition on the Boulevard du Temple. Even after Marie gathered her wax models and left for England, the Boulevard continued to play an important role in history. Only forty-four years after the Reign of Terror, it was on this street that the chemist Louis Daguerre took the first known photograph of a human being. In the picture, you can see the individual cobbles in the road and the tree-lined streets where Marie once walked. Although the photograph appears completely devoid of people, they are simply too blurry to see, because the exposure time was over ten minutes. If you look carefully, however, in the bottom left you will see a single man, his coattails and tricorn hat just visible. Although we will never know his name, his place in history is assured simply because he was standing still long enough for the image to develop. And if you look very closely, you can just make out why he was standing in one place: his boots were being polished. Chance placed him in the frame, alone in a street full of ghosts.

Sometimes, it is not the kings and queens who make for the most fascinating history but the shadowy souls who happen to be in the right place at the right time. While Marie certainly would not have considered herself lucky to have lived through such a devastating period, history is fortunate that she remained still for long enough to record the events that raged on around her.

Photograph by Louis Daguerre

THE BOULEVARD DU TEMPLE, 1838

Glossary

À la mode de Provence: dyed, then perfumed with flowers such as orange blossom or jasmine.

Ancien régime: "the former regime," meaning the political system that existed for hundreds of years before the Revolution, dominated by the monarchy, clergy, and aristocracy.

Aristocrat: a member of the Second Estate, or nobility.

Armée Révolutionnaire: This force of *sans-culottes* and Jacobins was unleashed on the countryside to spread revolution and to direct the dwindling food supply to Paris and other towns.

Assignat: a bond secured by the value of seized church property. After April 1790 assignats functioned as paper money but were soon almost completely devalued as the Constituent Assembly issued vast amounts of assignats to finance the deficits.

Bailliage: an administrative unit, roughly equivalent to a county, overseen by a king's *bailli* (bailiff).

Baiser: formally, to kiss; colloquially, to have sex with.

Berline: a four-wheeled luxury coach.

Cabriolet: a horse-drawn carriage with two wheels and a single horse, often used as a vehicle for hire.

Cachot: an underground cell, dungeon.

Cahiers de doléances: lists of grievances drawn up in early 1789 by regional bodies representing all three estates (clergy, nobility, and commoners).

The proposals for reform were put before the Estates-General and the king.

Caissier: a cashier.

Caliper: a device for measuring small distances with accuracy.

Champ-de-Mars: Paris's principal military parade grounds, on the left bank of the Seine (similar in purpose and name to Rome's Campus Martius). This was the site of the Fête de la Fédération on the anniversary of the fall of the Bastille, as well as the massacre of July 17, 1791.

Chemise: a woman's undergarment, often made of linen. It was designed to look like a short dress with elbow-length sleeves.

Chemise gown: Also known as the *chemise à la reine,* this dress was made popular by Marie Antoinette. It was made of a light, flowing fabric (linen or white muslin), which did not require a corset, prompting the public to accuse the queen of appearing in her chemise, or undergarments. While all fashionable young women adopted the style, the queen was criticized mercilessly for wearing these gowns. The portrait of her by Élisabeth Vigée-Lebrun dressed in this attire created such an outcry that it had to be removed from the Royal Salon.

Coach-and-eight: a large, typically royal, coach pulled by eight horses.

Cockade: a colored ribbon, worn as a badgelike ornament.

Cocotte: a whore.

Committee of Public Safety: the twelve-member group (chaired by Robespierre during the Terror) that, between 1793 and 1795, wielded executive power.

Commode: a small cabinet or chest of drawers.

Coquine: a naughty, mischievous woman.

Cordeliers: an ultraradical club founded by Danton, Marat, Hébert, and Ronsin that had a populist appeal among both sexes.

Corvée: a tax paid in manual labor to the crown during the *ancien régime.* Peasants were typically required to work a number of days per year on roads and in other public service.

Cravat: a neckband often trimmed with ruffles or lace.

Culottes: knee breeches.

Dauphin: the heir to the throne of France.

Deputy: an elected or nominated member of a government or committee.

Eaux de propreté: lotions used for personal cleanliness.

Émigrés: the tens of thousand of mostly aristocratic exiles who left France after the fall of the monarchy. Many plotted a counterrevolution and their eventual return.

Estates: the three orders of society: clergy, nobility, and commoners.

Estates-General: an assembly summoned in 1789 to advise the king at Versailles on issues of finance and politics. It comprised roughly one-half commoners and one-fourth each clergy and nobility.

Fauteuil: a chair with arms.

Fête: a grand celebration or party.

Fichu: a kerchief worn in front of a lady's bodice.

Firedogs: metal instruments designed to hold wood inside a fireplace.

Gaul: the Roman provinces corresponding to the modern countries of Belgium, France, and Switzerland.

Grand Couvert: an antechamber in the queen's apartment.

Heder: a Jewish children's school, often in the home of the rabbi.

Holy Roman Emperor: the official title of the man who was King of Hungary, Archduke of Austria, and Grand Duke of Tuscany.

Hôtel de Ville: city hall.

Jacobin Club: a revolutionary group that met in a former Jacobin (Dominican) monastery on the Rue Saint-Honoré. The Club became a focus of increasing radicalism, and chapters spread throughout France. Widely seen as the incubator of the Terror, the Paris chapter was closed by the National Convention in 1794.

Laiterie: a dairy.

Legislative Assembly: the political body that succeeded the National Assembly in 1791 and ended with the declaration of the French Republic a year later.

Lettres de cachet: Hated symbols of the monarchy, these were sealed instructions directly from the king that had the power to, among much cloc, imprison without trial. Voltaire was famously incarcerated in the Bastille by one of these documents.

Libelles: satirical pamphlets noted for their biting political attacks.

Libellistes: writers and publishers of *libelles.*

Livre: a unit of currency (divided into twenty sous) originally valued at one pound of silver.

Maquereau: a pimp.

Marchande: a merchant.

Ménage: a household unit.

Muff: a fashion accessory usually made of fur and used as a hand warmer.

Muscadins: anti-Jacobin street touts, often armed with metal clubs and known for their foppish dress.

National Convention: After the fall of the monarchy in 1792, this seven-hundred-member body was elected to write a Constitution.

National Guard: citizens' militias that spontaneously arose to defend cities from the outbursts of street crime and mob violence during the Revolution.

Orangerie: similar to a greenhouse, a building where orange trees and other fruits could be grown.

Panniers: hoops intended to extend the sides of a skirt while leaving both the front and the back flat. The hips were widened dramatically to display the fine embroidery or painting on a dress.

Patrie: country, fatherland.

Peyos: sidelocks worn by Orthodox Jews.

Robe à la française: a satin dress with a tight-fitting bodice and a voluminous, hooped skirt.

Salle: a room.

Sans-culottes: the trouser-wearing commoners, who preferred this simpler dress style to the knee breeches of the upper classes.

Santons: "little saints" or clay nativity scenes that came to replace the larger but banned church displays in revolutionary France.

Sou: a coin valued at one-twentieth of a livre.

Tableau: an arranged scene.

Tabouret: a padded stool.

Taille: a direct tax by the crown, levied on land owned by commoners.

Third Estate: the common people, as opposed to the clergy (First Estate) and the nobility (Second Estate).

Tocsin: an alarm bell.

Tuileries: a palace and garden complex that housed Louis XVI and Marie Antoinette after their removal from Versailles. The Tuileries, or tile works, were later used by both the National Convention and Napoléon. The site is now a garden, adjacent to the Louvre museum.

Tumbrel: a two-wheeled cart used to carry condemned prisoners to the guillotine.

"Vive le roi!": a toast and rallying cry for royalists meaning "Long live the king!"

Acknowledgments

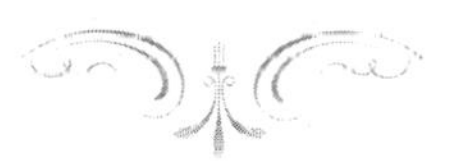

As always, my deepest and most heartfelt thanks go to my family. I could not imagine life as a writer without the support of my infinitely generous husband, Matthew Carter, who knows more about the publishing industry than any husband should ever have to. I am also thankful to my father, who passed on his love and passion for history, and to my mother for her constant and unwavering support. To my brothers, Robert Moran and Robert Small, thank you for your unflagging encouragement. And to the many friends who have supported me behind the scenes, I hope to repay you in kind someday. Long before I was ever published, my friends and family considered me a writer, and this is one of the greatest gifts an author can receive: belief and encouragement.

I have also been incredibly fortunate in my relationship with Crown, a division of Random House filled with some of the most dedicated and wonderful people in the publishing industry. I owe an enormous debt of gratitude to my copy editor, Susan Brown; to my production editor, Cindy Berman; and to both Patty Berg and Jay Sones in marketing, Dyana Messina in publicity, Jennifer O'Connor in the art department, and Kira Peikoff. Crown's sales team has seen to it that my novels have been distributed far and wide, and I am deeply appreciative of their support. And to Laura Crisp, who was the driving force behind Target's pick of *Nefertiti* as one of their Book Club selections, I cannot thank you enough.

Of course, my biggest thanks of all goes to Heather Lazare, my editor extraordinaire. An editor's job extends *far* beyond the process of editing, yet Heather wears multiple hats with ease, making every day an absolute pleasure to work with her.

To Giulliana Benavides, Jessica Bracamontes, Sarah Crosthwaite, Chantelle Doss, and Ashley Turner, tremendous thanks for helping me sort through all of my research on Versailles and the French Revolution. And none of that research would have been possible without the incredible scholars who have written about the eighteenth century. Of the many books I used as resources, there are some that stand out as having been indispensable. Kate Berridge's wonderful biography entitled *Madame Tussaud: A Life in Wax* comes to mind, as does Caroline Weber's *Queen of Fashion: What Marie Antoinette Wore to the Revolution*, Antonia Fraser's *Marie Antoinette: The Journey*, Elisabeth de Feydeau's *A Scented Palace: The Secret History of Marie Antoinette's Perfumer*, and Simon Schama's *Citizens: A Chronicle of the French Revolution.*

I am enormously grateful to Kathy, Dusty, and Ashley Rhodes, who allowed me to write this novel in their historic home in Southern California. And I owe a similar debt of gratitude to the many wonderful bloggers who have written about my books—the blogging community is very dear to my heart!

Last, I would like to thank my fantastic agent, Dan Lazar, whose guidance and advice have been invaluable to me. I have never known anyone who works so passionately at what they do. And to Maja Nikolic and Angharad Kowal, who have helped bring this novel to readers around the world, I am exceptionally grateful.

3/11 B+T